ATTICUS

ABELIA SUMPTER

Note from the Author

Atticus is a new adult historical fantasy romance and is not suitable for those under 18 years of age. Please see abeliasumpter.com for a full list of content warnings.

CHAPTER I

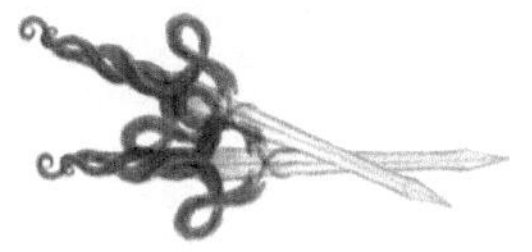

REPUBLIC OF VENICE - 1402

I was only twelve when I came to the conclusion that I could never be a god. For if I were a god, the beings I deemed wicked would find hell to be a mercy.

I run through the grassy yard of my family's estate, sprinting at full speed in a wild chase to reclaim my wooden horse. "Juni, give it back!" My black waves curl up further from the humidity.

"Only if you can catch me!" My sister yells over her shoulder. She may only be ten, but she's as mischievous as boys my age. Maybe more so.

I grumble and persist in my quest to regain my wooden horse. Father brought it back for me on one of his many travels. It's one of my most prized possessions and Juni knows it, so anytime I won't play with her, it's her only leverage.

I run past my mother, who is preparing soup for tonight's dinner over a small outdoor fire. A wooden fence post surrounds this part of our home, overlooking the nearby forest.

"Juni, I'm serious!" I catch up to her, grabbing the back of her worn-out dress, yanking her back.

She laughs and screams at the same time. I wrestle her to the ground, prying my toy from her small fingers.

"Don't touch my things." I frown down at her.

"Then play with me, Atty!" Her laugh from the impromptu game fades when she realizes I have no intention of carrying out her request.

I stand, brushing damp dirt off my pants. My father says I'm becoming a man, despite me being only twelve. And men don't have time to play silly games with their sisters. I should be studying my books on astronomy and core magic so I can do...whatever it is my father does. I've asked my mother a million times what he's up to on his trips. Her reply always stays the same.

Work.

Eventually, I stopped asking the question.

I head toward the house, gripping the toy tightly in my fingers in case my sister gets any ideas. Juni flies to her feet and rushes behind me, pounding her fists into my back. "You act like I'm some slimy worm under your boot! I hate you, Atticus!"

"No, you don't." I glower.

"Atticus Desimir de Oderzo!" My mother's voice pierces through the yard.

Juni stops her assault on my back, and we both turn to face our mother.

Mother stands with her arms crossed. Her wooden ladle stirs the colorful soup behind her using levitation, one of the three tenets of core magic. A medley of vegetables and herbs stains her apron. Though we have many servants, my mother sent them away this morning after word arrived that Father would be home today. She insisted on cooking tonight's dinner herself. My mother loves to cook for Father anytime he returns from one of his long, endless trips.

My mother places her fists on her hips. "Junipera wants to spend time with you, and I expect you to get along with her."

"But Mother—"

"One day, you'll look back and regret all the times you could have spent with her. Life passes quickly. Heavens, I haven't seen either of your uncles in over five years! Every day, I think about how much I miss them. Now they have their own lives and families and live halfway across the country."

Juni is beaming at my side, her hands clasped behind her back, her smile wider than her face. A small breeze brushes against her pin-straight chestnut hair. I don't hate her, but playtime feels so primitive and childish. Maybe I'd spend more time with her if she enjoyed the things I did, like mastering chess or studying botany. But no, all she can think about are games of hide-and-seek and tug-o-war.

My mother approaches me and pinches my cheek. "Don't be in a rush to grow up so fast, Atty. You'll have plenty of time to mold yourself into being the man your father is." She smooths my curls off my forehead. "I have an idea. You and Juni can run to Madame Bronson's shop to fetch me some parsley."

"But..." I bite my tongue. I want to argue, but there's no point with my mother. The adults in our town call her the goddess of wisdom. Most people are enamored with her and constantly remind me of how lucky I am to have her as a parent.

If anything, I can buy some mum bomb seeds while I'm there with the coins I've saved up. A boy my age should have some means of self-defense besides his own fists.

"Fine," I say.

Mother smiles and digs a few coins out of her apron. "Good. And don't be too long. Your father will be home within the hour."

Juni holds my hand as we stroll through the village to Madame Bronson's Apothecary.

When we enter the shop, a song crow perched at a counter caws a bitter tune three times, extending its golden wings as it sings. The aroma of lavender overpowers the other dried herbs hanging from the ceiling.

Most herbalists either sell enchanted herbs for spells or for consumption, but not Madame Bronson. She's known for selling both and even enhancing or transforming the power of magical herbs by using edible ones.

Juni immediately veers off to a display of fabric dolls. Madame Bronson has them stuffed with herbs soaked in charmed potions and sells them to treat various things in children and infants like colic and impulse control.

When I discovered that a year ago, I burned mine in the fireplace. Shortly afterward, my mother informed me that mine was filled with bergamot leaves and nothing more.

Madame Bronson whips around the corner from the back of the shop with a wide and curious smile. "What brings Leandro and Marguerite's children here at this hour?"

Juni jumps and lands with her arms and legs outstretched as if she's a star. "Parsley!"

I roll my eyes.

Madame Bronson is a large woman who dresses better than most nobles, with her colorful, finely tailored dresses. Not one mole, scar, or blemish stains her dark skin. And nobody has ever seen her without her signature wide-brimmed hat.

"Parsley, you say?" Madame Bronson approaches a shelf filled with large bottles of ground herbs. She hovers her hand above them, then plucks one bottle into her too-long fingers.

"I also need mum bomb seeds," I say, a neutral expression on my face. Though I'm not allowed to wield magic until I'm thirteen, I can still use herbs. All humans can use magic, but many choose not to use it beyond household chores. I think those who don't use it are fools. Who wouldn't want such power? Especially when it's your birthright.

Madame Bronson raises an eyebrow. "And what would you be needing that for?"

"I...uh." I swallow. "It's for my studies."

She doesn't take her eyes off me as she scoops parsley out of the glass container into a smaller bottle, then wraps it in sackcloth. "I don't sell such herbs to...children." As she says the last word, she tightly pulls string around the sackcloth to secure it.

I'm not a child. But adults like her and my mother will never understand. If I didn't fear the lashing that would come from stealing, I'd swipe some while her back is turned.

"But I can offer you spike cotton seeds. All they do is pop, but maybe it would assist you in your...studies...as you say."

Madame Bronson hands me the parsley and spike cotton and I give her the coins. I pull Juni away from the herbal toy display. She shrugs my hand off her arm as we near the door.

"You two stay out of trouble now!" Madame Bronson sing-songs across the shop as the door shuts behind us.

The evening fog grows thicker as we walk through the village toward the estate. Juni holds my hand with her cold one.

"Atty, why did you ask Madame Bronson for mum bomb seeds? Mother and Father wouldn't be pleased if they found out."

"It's not a big deal. Forget you heard me say it."

"Tell me, or I'll tattle."

"You wouldn't."

She smiles.

"You're lying, Juni."

"No, I'm not! I'll tell Mother about the mum bomb seeds and the other herbs you have hidden under your bed!"

I throw my hand with the parsley up in the air in defeat. It was stupid for me to share my secret herb collection with her. Now she leaves me with no choice. "I wanted to protect myself. And...and there's a girl I want to impress using them."

Juni's smile grows. "It's Aurora, isn't it?"

"Shut up."

She giggles and pokes my abdomen, which only reminds me of how little muscle I have compared to Father. Father is strong and mighty. Maybe even invincible.

"Well, well, if it isn't Atticus and Juni Desimir."

Juni and I both freeze. Her little hand tightens against mine.

Jervany Bova and three of his friends block our path. They're all at least three years older than me. And our fathers aren't exactly friendly with one another, though I've never been told why. Because of that, Jervany has made it his personal mission to make my life *unpleasant*.

I take a step back. "We don't want any trouble. We're expected back soon for my father's arrival."

Jervany sneers. "Then, by all means, continue your journey home." He extends his hand, jokingly stepping aside.

Juni, oblivious to Jervany's sarcasm, attempts to keep going, but I tug her back.

Jervany chuckles and takes a step toward us.

"I'm warning you," I grit through clenched teeth.

Jervany sprints and crashes into me, wrapping his arms around my torso. My hand releases from Juni's as my body slams into the ground, the package of parsley falling from my grasp. I grunt in pain.

"Atticus!" Juni screams.

Jervany socks me in the gut, knocking the wind out of me, reminding me of how much stronger he is. Of how incapable I am of defending myself, let alone my sister.

I wheeze out, desperate to catch my breath.

"Desimirs will never be as strong as Bovas. You and your pathetic father would do well to know that." He spits in my face.

Jervany rises and prances toward my sister, leaning down to her height. "Do you want to play a game, Juni?"

She shakes her head at him and chews at her fingernails. I need to get up. If I don't, they'll hurt her.

"If you lay even one finger on her—" I take in a shaky breath, my lungs still heaving for air. "I'll kill you."

Jervany sticks his pointer one inch from Juni's shoulder. She squints her eyes shut, as if his finger holds the touch of King Midas.

Jervany's friends laugh behind him, imitating her nervous body language.

"Stupid little Desimirs," Jervany says. "Always so much bark, but never any more bite than a few childish words. Don't worry, this will all be over soon, and we'll send you back to your mother to help you lick your wounds."

Jervany pokes Juni's shoulder, laughing at me as he does.

My anger bubbles over. I reach into my side satchel and pull out the spike cotton seeds. There's no way this will work, but what other options do I have? With their attention focused on Juni, I pour five of the seeds into my palm and hide them in my fist. With weakened legs, I force myself to stand as I cradle my abdomen.

"I'll throw mum bomb seeds at you! Madame Bronson herself just sold them to me."

Jervany folds his arms and immediately starts laughing. "Really, Atticus? Madame Bronson won't even sell them to me, and I'm much older than you."

I force a smirk. "She and I have an understanding. And unlike you, she trusts me."

"Ha! As if the woman would ever trust you."

I raise my hand above my head.

The four buffoons take a step back as I conjure up the most sinister smile I can muster. It isn't often people fear me, if ever. It's a feeling I rather like.

"Juni, move!" I yell.

She jumps out of the way just as I hurl the spike cotton seeds at them. The seeds crack at their feet, letting off smoke in their wake.

I smile as the three of them yell out in a panic. With them distracted, I seize Juni's hand and grab the parsley from the ground. We sprint as fast as we can. Any second now, they'll learn I was bluffing about the mum bomb seeds.

"Next time I see you, Desimir, I'm beating the shit out of you!" Jervany yells after us.

I don't let his words stop us from running.

By the time we're in front of the estate, our lungs are on the brink of collapse. We don't stop to catch our breath until we cross the threshold of the gate.

"Keep this our secret, Juni, got it?"

She nods in agreement.

Father doesn't need any trouble on his first night back. I worry about messing up when he's around. There's always this inkling of worry within me that misbehaving will scare him off. That he'll find his trips more desirable than being with us. If that is the case, I want to stay the well-behaved boy mother raised me to be.

When Juni and I enter the house, Mother and Father are speaking in hushed conversation near the fireplace. Mother looks worried.

At the sight of Father, both our faces light up.

"Father!" Juni shrieks and runs into his strong arms.

"My little June bug!" My father picks Juni up and spins her around.

As a man, I keep the urge to rush forward to a minimum. "I'm glad you're home, Father."

He sets Juni down and smiles at me. "Atticus, my boy." He opens his arms, inviting me in.

I fake hesitancy before darting up to him and firmly wrapping my arms around his thick torso. "I missed you."

"And I you, son." He steps back, staring down at me. "It seems my protégé has grown since I last saw him."

I straighten my posture to add even more height to myself. "I have. One whole inch. Tell him, Mother."

Mother laughs while she spoons soup into wooden bowls. "Yes, he has. Just about every day, he asks me to measure him."

"That's my Atticus for you." Father chuckles, firmly patting my back. "Let's eat and add even more meat to those bones." He lightly nudges my bicep with his elbow.

I will eat two whole bowls of soup just to show him I'm willing to do anything to become as strong as him. Then maybe, one day, he'll tell me what it is he does in secret. Father may think I'm not able-bodied enough to handle the truth. That I'm too young. But one day, I'll prove myself to him.

CHAPTER 2

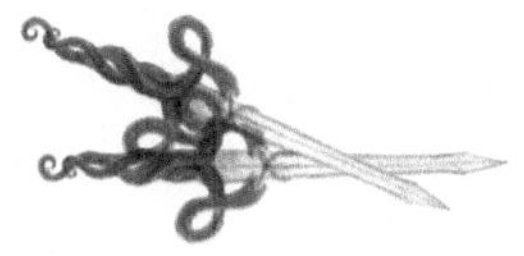

When I sip the last spoonful of soup, I feel as though I may vomit. There's a glimmer of regret looming over me from stuffing myself like a pig. I slump back in my chair, arms hanging by my sides.

"You must be growing," my mother remarks. She reaches over and dabs soup remnants off the side of my lips.

My father laughs at the sight of me inebriated on soup. "There's no need to show off, Atticus."

Father had the same amount of food as me, and he shows no signs of tumbling over the way I am. I have to increase the capacity of my stomach so I can eat as much as he can. Then the food will go straight to my muscles.

I had once spent every morning lifting bricks behind my house, and by the end of the month, I had nothing to show for it. I asked my father why, and he laughed. Then he told me to eat more.

"Any room for dessert, Atticus?" Father asks. "Your mother tells me she made chocolate cake."

If it was a sin to hate the idea of eating Mother's famous chocolate cake, I just committed it. My eyes widen.

"Do not worry, Atticus, you can have it tomorrow," Father says.

"But I can do it!" I say, lowering the tone of my voice slightly. "I can eat it now with all of you."

"And I don't particularly want to clean vomit off the floor. You've had enough for one night." He winks at me, giving me permission to skip dessert.

I relax my shoulders and rest my forearms on the table. "Where did your travels take you this time?"

Father leans back in his chair. "So many places. Too many. Milan, Verona. I wish I had more time while I was there to see all the sights."

A deep sadness comes over me. All I heard was, *I wish I had more time away from all of you.* I know that's not what he means. I know he loves us. He's not cold and cruel like Jervany's father, but it still hurts.

Juni stands on the chair and spreads her arms. "Presents?"

"Junipera, sit down," my mother says.

My father has that slick grin painted across his face. "I'm so glad you asked my June bug!"

He leaves the table for a minute and goes into the foyer before returning with two ornate gifts wrapped in silky cloth.

When Father sets one in front of Juni, she unravels the cloth like a wild animal.

He sets mine down on the table, but he keeps his grip on the present. "Wear this and cherish it."

His eyes are serious. All I can do is nod. Father removes his hand and sits back next to Juni.

"A bracelet! Father, thank you!" Juni throws her arms around him.

"It's not just any bracelet. Try it on!" Father helps Juni secure it around her tiny wrist.

"Now think of a color." His arm rests on the top of her chair.

Juni squints her eyes shut. Seconds later, beautiful bubbles of pink appear around her head. She beams at the sight of them, popping two with her fingers. Then she closes her eyes again and more bubbles appear, this time the shade of blueberries.

Father sticks out his pointer finger close to one of the pink bubbles and directs it to collide with a blue one, making a beautiful blend of purple.

"How lovely, Leandro." Mother rests her chin on the backs of her hands.

"Atticus, open yours now," Father says.

I unbind the strings from around the silk wrappings. The box is etched with three serpents. I open the lid, and inside sits a silver necklace with a pendant in the shape of a cobra. It's a bit terrifying with the mouth opened and fangs on full display, but I keep my fears at bay in front of my father.

"Thank you," I tell him and secure it around my neck.

"When you turn thirteen, I'll finally get to teach you the three tenets of core magic. And of course, how to safely use more advanced herbal magic. Because of that, you'll need protection charms when you're in combat. This necklace works only once before it shatters, so use it wisely. If you're ever in danger, pull back the tail of the cobra and spin it once."

It is something I never want to resort to. If I do, the necklace will crumble, and I'll lose this present forever. Though the best gift father could ever give me is that of magic.

For that reason, my birthday can't come soon enough. I'll finally get to learn core magic, as well as my family birthright—Desimir magic. Some find it overtly dark, as it's used to break minds as opposed to bodies. And then there's the controlling of shadows, which some call demonic. It's why I assume Jervany and his father hate my family so much. At least, it's the only thing that makes sense.

Later in the evening, a servant arrives to help my mother clear away dinner. Tomorrow, the rest of our servants will be back. Many of them have been around most of my life. They're like family to me.

While the servant works, the four of us gather around the fireplace while my father tells us more about his two-month trip around Italy. Like always, his stories are filled with heroic tales of magic and humor. One story, about his companion who accidentally let his horse drink from a barrel of mead, has all of us deep in laughter.

Every once in a while, he stumbles over his words. Like he realized he was about to say too much. I'm not completely naïve. Father's work meddles in dangerous territory. There are nights when he's away that I've caught Mother weeping by the fireplace. Sometimes when he comes home from his trips, he has a fresh wound or scar.

Perhaps when I'm thirteen and I can wield magic, he'll tell me his secrets.

The four of us laughed around the fire together for hours until much too late. My mother's words, not mine. Eventually, Juni sank into slumber in my father's embrace, so he carried her to her room for the night. Father was kind and let me stay up even later with him.

The two of us play chess together at the table as we sip warm tea.

Father moves his queen's bishop near the center of the board. "Remember what I say every time we play chess?"

I smile. "That the moves parallel our lives. That one unwise choice, no matter how insignificant, can destroy empires." I move my pawn up. Maybe I can capture his bishop.

"Certainly." Father raises an eyebrow at my choice to move my pawn. "Though you're already forgetting my other rule."

I lean on my forearms. "What?"

"The goal of chess isn't to capture pieces."

And then I see it. The way I left everything wide open.

Father checkmates me. "The goal is to checkmate. Short-term goals can blind us to long-term ambition. You must look at life this way too. Don't waste your time on trivial things. Not unless they lead to greatness. And above all, make wise choices."

I groan at the loss. Not that I've ever won against him before.

Father chuckles. "You'll beat me one of these days, I know it. Keep practicing."

He puts the board away and sends me to my room for the night. I stare up at the ceiling, my eyes heavy with the sandman's curse. If I didn't have to sleep, I'd have more time to study and grow strong. One day, I'll not only beat him in chess but also in sparring. Though, my father always emphasizes the importance of rest and how it's the key to staying in shape.

Thoughts and fantasies eventually turn into dreams. Dreams where I'm as old as my father, traveling the world and fighting the monsters that inhabit it. Once, when he was still in the army, he fought two rabid wolves with nothing but his bare hands after a dark lord temporarily stripped his magic with an herb.

I flinch awake at the sound of heavy boots running just outside my room. Mother has a small bladder, but never enough to run like that. She must have had too many glasses of water before bed.

I close my eyes once again, trying to lull myself back into the sweet dreams.

Then a blood-curdling scream rips through the estate, sharp and shrill enough to shoot me straight to my feet.

It's Mother.

I throw my robe on and rush to my door. When I throw the door open, a dark-haired man stares down at me, as if he was just seconds away from barging into my room.

I'm completely frozen. He appears human, but I know from the embossed symbols across his neck that he is not.

An immortal—a being gifted with incomprehensible magic since birth and nearly unconquerable in combat. There is nothing known to humanity that can kill immortals, and human magic does almost nothing against them. Immortals like this one have strayed from their kind. They don't fight for countries or armies, but for people. Rich, corrupt people who have enough coin to hire them.

They're stronger and taller, with sharp jaws and white lace-like tattoos along the smooth, youthful skin of their necks that swirl into the symbol of infinity.

Before I can slam the door in his face, he grabs my upper arm. "Not so fast, young one. You're coming with us."

"I don't understand... What's going on?" I try to wrestle my arm out of his burly hand.

He yanks me out of the room, grabbing my hair to keep me contained. I yell for my father, scratching the man's wrists. Anything to get away from him, but it's as if I'm a twig amid a hurricane.

"Juni!" I yell out.

Where is my sister? Is she all right? Maybe she's still fast asleep in bed. I shouldn't have shouted for her.

The immortal drags me to our estate's drawing room. I cower at the sight of Mother and Father on their knees, hands raised in defeat.

There are six men in the room in total. Four of them are immortals. Two of them are human.

And one of those humans is Jervany's father. I told Jervany today that my father was arriving home. *Oh no!* This is all my fault.

"Father!" I hold back tears. None of this makes sense. "What do these men want from us?"

"Quiet, Atticus," my father says through gritted teeth. "I will resolve this in a minute."

The dark-haired immortal grips my hair tighter with such force I fear he may render me bald.

The other human has an arrogant, superior air to his gait as he approaches my father. He's dressed like high nobility in his black doublet and royal-blue shoulder cape. It's far beyond what most in our village could afford.

The nobleman speaks. "We warned you what would happen if you mettled in the affairs of the pope."

"The antipope, Sir Raveen," my father says, correcting him.

Sir Raveen's face grows harsh. I twitch as the man takes his cane and whacks my father clean across the face. If I weren't immobilized by this immortal, I'd rush forward to the fire and throw burning coals at him.

"Alexander is the rightful heir to the artifact. Besides, he should have been named pope all along."

"The artifact isn't a blood right. It's not inherited. You know very well that the United Magic Council chooses the eight holders."

"A rule that should be done away with. But, Leandro, you weren't careful when you were in Milan. An informant watched you sneak into the cardinal's home the eve before he was poisoned."

"Anti-cardinal." My father corrects him again.

This time, Sir Raveen, the nobleman, grabs my father's throat and squeezes. My father chokes, but doesn't fight back. There's no point in resisting when there are immortals around.

Sir Raveen releases him and brushes his hands off on his noble attire as if my father is nothing but filth. "You probably already suspect what needs to be done. An eye for an eye, as they say. Alano will oblige you." He looks to the immortal with the short, brown beard.

"Do whatever you'd like to me," my father says, with gasping breaths. "Just don't harm my family."

"Leandro, your wife knows far too much to be left alive."

My mother's face fills with tears.

"Him first, Alano," Sir Raveen says.

No, not my father. They can't kill him. Father is strong, he can fight back. He may not be able to kill the immortals, but he's powerful enough to stop them, or at least distract them and escape.

My father watches the immortal with a predatory gaze. When the bearded immortal nears, father jumps to his feet and throws mum bombs and spike cotton seeds to the ground. Immediately, the entire room fills with explosive smoke. Sir Raveen yells to the immortals and Jervany's dad to find my father.

"Atticus, run!" Father shouts through the fog.

I knew Father had something up his sleeve! He would never submit so easily to these wicked men. I fight against the dark-haired immortal who still has a tight hold on me.

My fear reignites as the color purple fills the room—an immortal using his magic to suck the smoke into his palm.

When my eyes readjust, I freeze. Alano's sword is lodged through my father's chest. Blood drips down his back and off the tip of the blade.

I feel as though I may faint as I watch his body thump to the ground.

This isn't real. He's faking it. Mother says he knows all sorts of spells to conjure illusions. Any minute now, he'll reappear and thrust a dagger through the heart of Sir Raveen. Then we'll escape the immortals. All four of us!

My mother shrieks and falls onto her hands, sobbing and shaking. *Don't cry, Mother. He'll be back soon; just wait and see.*

The enemies are silent for a minute while my mother cries her heart out. She's weeping like this is the end. Like he's really—gone.

He's gone.

No. He's alive. *Be patient, Atticus.*

Father's blood soaks into the rug. Illusion spells don't interact with the environment. Perhaps he's using fake blood from Madame Bronson's shop to trick the men.

When the moment of realization hits me, it's as if someone stuck needles beneath my fingernails all at once.

I can't move.

I'm paralyzed.

"Austrie, her next," Sir Raveen says.

"No! You bastards!" I scream out. "If you touch her, I'll—I'll—"

The immortal with the silver hair, Austrie, scoffs with a smile as he walks up behind her. "You'll what? Kill me? I'd like to see you try, little one."

My mother tries to conjure up a spell within her hands, but the immortal is faster. His dagger slices across her throat, her blood spilling to the ground.

The body of my mother, my sweet innocent mother who would never so much as step on an ant, lies cold and lifeless on the bloodied rug.

And I'm sure to follow.

I don't care if I die anymore. I don't care if I'm wiped off the face of this horrific planet. Without them—there's nothing.

With the immortal's hand loosened, I break free from his hold, rushing forward at Sir Raveen. If I can't kill him, I'll at least take an eyeball with me, even if I have to use nothing but my short fingernails.

The bearded and silver-haired immortals grab hold of my arms and kick me to my knees. They hold me there while the dark-haired immortal buries his fist into my gut. I heave, tasting blood in the back of my throat.

I fold to the ground. Still, I force out words, even though my lungs beg me not to. "Is that the best you got?"

The dark-haired immortal smiles, kicking me once more in the abdomen. I cry out and grunt at the impact.

Off to the side, the fourth immortal with golden hair stands, watching the assault. His face stays completely neutral.

"Atty?" a small voice squeaks at the doorway.

Blood drips down the sides of my mouth while I struggle for air. The immortal eases off me. Everyone's attention now focused on my sister.

No, Juni. Go far away from here and never stop running until the sun rises.

The bearded immortal walks toward her, taking her small hand in his, and guides her deeper into the room. Then Jervany's father shuts the door.

Juni's just a girl. A child.

At the sight of our parents, Juni trembles, her eyes filling with tears. "Mother. Father."

I force myself to stand, using a nearby chair for support. I need to get to her.

"Konstantin, we'll spare the girl," Sir Raveen says to the dark-haired one. The immortal who dragged me from my bedroom. The one who kicked me when I was already down.

I breathe a sigh of relief at hearing they'll spare Juni. But it isn't enough to stop the impending sense of doom for my own life. I need to stay alive to take care of her and protect her. We both need to get out of here, and fast.

Atticus, in combat, check your emotions at the door. A true man never lets the heat of the moment get the better of him. Patience and mental fortitude are winning checkmates in a battle. My father's words.

With tears and snot covering her face, Juni curls her small fist. "I hate all of you! They should hang you for what you've done!" She runs up to the dark-haired immortal, pounding her fists on his large hip.

"Back away, child. That's enough," he warns.

No, she needs to stop! If she doesn't then—

She beats him even harder.

"I said, that's enough!" The dark-haired one grabs her by the neck and throws her small body across the room.

I reach out. "Juni!"

Then I hear it. The crunching of bones as her spine cracks against the hard wall.

Immediately, she falls to the ground, completely still.

Ignoring the horrendous pain in my abdomen, I crawl across the room. "Juni?"

The immortals and humans launch into an argument behind me.

"What the hell, Konstantin!"

"She wouldn't stop. What else did you want me to do, Austrie?"

I hover my shaky hand over her mouth. *No breath.* The eyes that stare back at me are void of life.

I smooth her tear-stained hair off her face. "Wake up."

She doesn't respond.

"Juni, say something. You can hear me; I know you can. I swear to you, if you say just one simple word, I'll play with you every day! We'll play all your favorite games for the rest of our lives. We won't become like our uncles and Mother. We can even build houses right next to each other when we're adults!"

But she doesn't move. The golden-haired immortal, the quiet one, bends down next to her with me. He peels one of his gloves off and feels for her pulse.

"I'm so sorry," the immortal whispers.

I wrap Juni in my arms and stare down at her delicate porcelain face. "You're not dead!" Tears soak my skin, but I couldn't care less. "One day, you told me—you *promised* me—you would grow up and become an acrobat! Don't give up! Open your eyes!"

Nothing.

I set her head in my lap, then my arms go limp.

The quiet, golden-haired immortal gently takes her away from me and into his arms, setting her on the rug near my parents and covering her with a blanket.

"Kill the boy," Sir Raveen says. "Who knows how much he knows about all this? His father could have been training him this entire time as his successor, regardless of the law."

Something breaks in me, a darkness entering like I've never felt before. The feeling supersedes any grim fairy tale or scary story the older girl at the lake used to tell Juni and me. It exceeds any nightmare.

If I die, they'll never pay for their sins. There will be no one alive to make sure of it. Even if I don't want to be alive, they must *suffer* for what they've done. Slowly. Tortuously. In a way so unbearable, they'd beg for death over the misery I would put them through.

"We'll do whatever you wish, master," the bearded one says.

Sir Raveen nudges my father's corpse with his foot. "Make the boy's death quick."

Footsteps creep up behind me, as well as the unsheathing of a sword.

When I look up at the golden-haired immortal who stands in front of me, he signals at his collarbone, as if he's directing me to do something.

Use the necklace, he mouths.

Is he—helping me?

I don't have another second to think. I grab my necklace and pull back the cobra tail, spinning it once.

CHAPTER 3

I mmediately, a field of blue energy booms around me, covering my body from head to toe. The necklace shatters, the metal pieces falling onto the wooden floor like glass.

"What is this!" Jervany's father yells.

"Some kind of protection charm, sir," Austrie, the silver-haired immortal, answers.

I spin within the protective bubble just in time to see Sir Raveen kick my father's uninhabited body in his anger. "Get the boy out of there and slice his throat!"

"You know as well as anyone else those charms can work for months at a time," the dark-haired immortal says. My sister's killer. Konstantin. His name, I will never forget. Him, I want to kill more than the rest.

The nobleman tightens his fist with such force, his old, wrinkly knuckles turn white.

The golden-haired immortal steps forward, hands laced behind his back. "I'll keep watch over him until the charm wears off. No matter where he goes, I'll follow."

The noble glares at the immortal, then at me. "Very well." He huffs. "Stay here until the charm wears off. Then burn him alive."

I swallow at the vileness in his words. The way he spits them like venom.

"Understood, sir."

Sir Raveen takes one last glare at me before exiting out the doorway. The rest of the murderers funnel out behind him.

The room grows quiet, only the crackling of the fireplace filling in the gaps of silence. It's just me, the immortal, and three lifeless bodies.

So this is my life now? Being followed around by this human-like creature until this protection charm bursts and I'm burned alive?

I don't know what to do. Should I run? This immortal saved my life but then volunteered to kill me. I shouldn't trust him.

I scoot away from him, still sniffling, trying my best not to look toward Juni's covered body, nor my parents' bloodied ones.

He rakes a hand through his ruffled golden hair. "I'm not going to hurt you."

I say nothing.

The immortal sighs. "Would you like to go into the library while I clean up here? I'll walk you to it."

I shake my head. There's no way I'd go anywhere with him. He's probably trying to trick me. But something about him makes me want to take a deep breath and fall into a sense of safety. But that feeling doesn't run deep enough for me to trust him.

He looks around the room, scanning the bodies, then my huddled-up position on the floor. "Please, you need to leave this room. For your own good."

I stay completely still for a second, contemplating. Once I leave this room, I know I'll never see my family again. Yet I don't want to look at them like this.

"Suit yourself." He immediately walks over to my father's body and searches his clothes.

What is he doing? I spring forward, my fists curled. "Don't touch him!"

The immortal pulls a small key from inside my father's shirt with such confidence, one may have thought he knew it was there all along.

He walks past me and up the stairs.

"Get back here!" I run after the immortal, but because of the protection charm, I cannot touch him.

He ignores me as he enters my father's study, walking up to a bare wall.

"What are you doing? This isn't your house!"

The immortal fits the key between a crevice inside the wall that I once thought to be a simple crack. When he spins it, a section of the wall pops out like a tray. He pulls a singular piece of paper from it.

How did he know it was here? It's as if he knows my home inside and out.

As if he knows it better than me.

"What is that? How did you—"

"Why don't you take a seat, Atticus?"

I don't move from my spot in the middle of the room.

He folds his arms. "My name is Lorenzo. But please, call me Vec." Vec appears to be in his thirties, but he's likely centuries old. His dark doublet is decorated in hems of golden embroidery. Golden-blonde hair frames his wrinkle-free face and sharp jaw, his immortal status making him the pinnacle of beauty any human man would envy. His muscular stature is on the leaner side compared to most immortals, though still more defined than the majority of human men.

"And you're going to kill me?" I blurt out with malice.

He shakes his head. "Lucky for you, I'm on your father's payroll. And the sole executor of his will if something were to happen to him."

A double agent? If it's true, father must have known that something like this may happen one day. It also explains why Vec was only pretending to work for Sir Raveen. But he also stood idly by while they slaughtered my family. "Why should I believe you?"

"Let's go to the library for now. You need time to process."

I'm hesitant but concede. After all, he knew where to find my father's key. He knew secrets of my father's office even I wasn't aware of.

I follow him through the house, the metallic scent of my family's blood still strong throughout the halls, making me queasy.

Once we're in the library, Vec doesn't make an effort to keep speaking to me. He sweeps an arm around his head, using immortal magic to light every candle in the room.

I curl up on the ground, far across the room next to a stack of books, holding back tears that beg to fall.

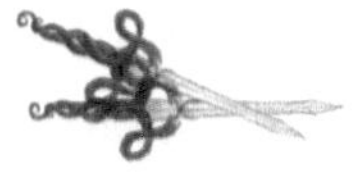

Vec doesn't speak for the next few hours, but the last thing I want to do is sleep. He just sits in my father's old chair, his arms resting on his thighs, seemingly lost in thought.

I sit up, wrapping my arms around my legs. "Who were you to my father?"

"There's no need to cower," Vec says. "Come closer."

I stay put. I'm willing to hear him out. In fact, I need to. But I won't go near him. Not until I get more answers.

Vec huffs. "I am responsible for your care. Essentially, I'm your god-father."

"My godfather?" I almost scoff. "As if I want an immortal for a guardian." I wipe cold sweat from my forehead. "Why did they kill Father?"

Vec sits back in the chair, crossing his legs. "Your father was a dangerous man, and his line of work created a great deal of enemies. He was a killer, an assassin, and his latest target created more waves than he intended."

An assassin? I always thought him a warrior, but not a killer. "But why? Who was he meant to kill?"

"He worked for the Bilancia Syndicate, as I do."

"I don't understand."

Vec rubs at his temples. "Once your father graduated university, he was scouted by the Bilancia Syndicate, a subset of the United Magic Council. Eventually the top priority shifted to stopping the antipope from causing a civil war in pursuit of Italy's artifact. In the right hands, countries can use it as leverage to keep other countries from invading. But in the wrong hands, it could destroy entire continents, if not the world."

I know the pope temporarily inherits one of the eight artifacts during his lifetime, but I never knew of its vast power. I even know about the antipope Sir Raveen mentioned, Alexander V. He wasn't chosen as pope, so he proclaimed himself to be so. Father talked about him often.

I connect the dots. "So Father's job was to protect Italy's artifact? And he killed to do so?" The thought of Father assassinating people makes me shudder.

Vec nods. "For the most part. Though we often take on other kill-for-hire jobs to keep the operation running. As it is a dangerous profession, the humans put the immortals in their wills as assurance that their families stay protected."

My heart weighs Vec's last sentence. I take it all in. Father being an assassin and hiding it from me. In his protection of the artifact, he lost his life. Mother and Juni's lives. I almost want to be angry at him, but I cannot. I know in protecting Italy, he was protecting us.

Vec stands and walks over to me. I don't move away. He crouches in front of me. I keep my gaze locked on him, refusing to look weak.

"Your father was the Savant, the highest title of honor in the entire Syndicate. It's typically a title passed on to family when possible. He believed you were strong enough to one day replace him, and I'm the one meant to train you in his absence."

Father thought I was strong? Strong enough to be as feared a killer as he was? It's bittersweet. He'll never be able to put me through training himself. He'll never see who I become. "I don't want an immortal training me."

"Who better to train you than I? Humans trained by immortals tend to be stronger. Grittier. Because we can't die, we push harder than any human trainer ever could. It creates molded, strong killers. Though I don't blame you for being wary of immortals."

"No shit."

"Language."

"Don't treat me like you're—you're not my father and you never will be!"

"Fine. Then we'll be friends. There? Happy?"

I don't answer.

"Go pack your bags. We have a long journey ahead of us."

"I'm not leaving my family like this. They need a proper burial."

"And I'll ensure they have it."

"I need to go after those men. My father has plenty of rare herbs stashed away that I can use to sneak up and explode them into ribbons." I want to kill the immortals more than I want air. Same goes for Sir Raveen and Jervany's father. They must *pay* for what they've done.

"Atticus, you don't understand, do you? You'll try, and you'll perish, just as countless others have done before you. Immortals cannot die. In fact, pain often makes us stronger. Someone once strapped me to a table and tortured me until all my organs were thrown onto the floor. Within minutes, my body called them back and repaired me. The regeneration strengthened my muscles so greatly, I was able to break free and murder my captors in the same way they had just afflicted me."

My mouth gapes open.

He scratches the back of his head. "Perhaps that was too detailed for a child."

"I'm not a child."

"Well, you're certainly no man either, at least not yet. With time and training, you will be. I will make you into the man your father once was. I will form you into the one who can defeat the antipope's immortals."

CHAPTER 4

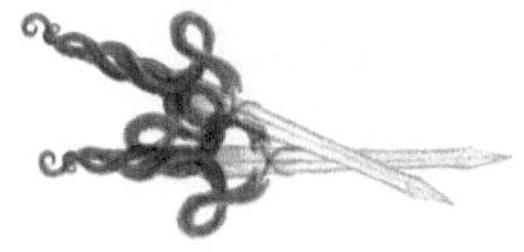

Vec and I ride our horses for days on end. I didn't expect my training to start the second day after we started our travels, but he's spent hours lecturing on herbology and magic.

Then he starts quizzing me.

I want to push back, but anytime he isn't speaking, thoughts of my family consume me. Every night when we stop to camp, tears soak through the spare tunic I use as a pillow.

Juni invades my mind more than Father or Mother. She didn't deserve what happened, even more so than our parents. After the second night of camping, I learn to replace my painful thoughts with those of vengeance. Anytime she and her bubbly smile pop into my mind, I replace it with fantasies of breaking Sir Raveen's bones in half and sawing him open from the inside out.

The journey is long. We travel through many cities and villages, like Vicenza and Verona, stopping only at night.

I ask Vec dozens of questions about immortals, their magic, and the rumors that surround their origins. Of course, I know they are a higher form of being, their magic mysterious and powerful. Some say they are children of the gods. Vec denies this but won't admit their true beginnings. All he tells me is that they look like humans because his ancestors chose to.

A while back, in a nearby village, a teenager spread a rumor of the immortals originating from an execution gone wrong in 1500 BC. The boy claimed that a man falsely accused of murder was tortured to death with dark magic and leeches. But the leeches were of a magical variety and absorbed the dark magic to protect the poor man, and in doing so, turned him into the first immortal. Since the leeches protected him, he shared them with others in his village, turning as many of them into immortals as he could until the leeches died.

The rumor traveled so far across Europe, women everywhere were using leeches to keep their youth. Such loggerheads. Don't they know leeches only work to treat illness?

Most immortals consider themselves "observers of humankind." It's why their race has never attempted to take over the Earth. But some, like Vec and Konstantin, deviated from their lifestyle and became killers of men for men, as if it brought them some sort of fulfillment. For some of them, life became mundane, and they needed more purpose, no matter how dark. The problem is, the more time an immortal spends with humans, the more they become like one. In more bad ways than good.

We arrive at a manor house in Brescia. It's extravagant and easily ten times the size of my house.

My old house, I mean.

Vec helps me off my horse and shoves my belongings into my chest. "There are only a few hours until nightfall. After we eat dinner, I'll give you time to rest and explore, if you so wish. Then in the morning, we train."

I shrug, looking down at the ground, pushing dirt around with the tip of my shoe.

Vec lifts my chin up. "Stand up straight. And stop showing weakness. It looks horrible on you."

With my chest puffed out, I grit my teeth and stand up as straight as I can. "I'm not weak! I'm a Desimir, and I'm as strong as my father!"

"Better. Now let's get inside."

Servants lead our horses to the stables as Vec guides me into his manor.

I gawk at the foyer and the marble staircase that branches out in two directions up to the second story. A chandelier made of antlers hangs from the ceiling.

"You live here alone?" I ask.

"It's just me and my servants, though I'm rarely ever home. The Syndicate has kept me rather busy. But now that you're here, you are my sole mission."

Vec leads me up to the third story of his house and whips the wooden door open to a room with a large circular bed and a crackling fireplace. The comforter is a deep red with enough pillows to fill half the mattress. I remain standing at the threshold.

"Don't be shy," Vec says.

I walk up to the bed and set my belongings on it. Not one bone in my body wants to accept that living in this estate with Vec as my mentor is now the reality of my life.

Vec stokes the fire. "Wash up and meet me downstairs for dinner." He leaves, closing the door behind him.

I immediately sink to my knees, my arms limp by my sides. After being with Vec for days on end, with barely enough privacy to urinate in peace, I had no choice but to suppress my grief, and now I'm exhausted.

When I am able, I head downstairs. The extravagant dining room is decorated with lavish paintings and venetian crown molding. Vec doesn't speak much while we eat dinner together as servants wait on us. He reads a book as he delicately pierces a piece of chicken with his fork, bringing it to his mouth. The way he eats is insufferably proper. Why do immortals bother eating, anyway? Starving won't kill them, or even waste away their muscles.

After dinner, I head upstairs and plop right into bed, my arms outspread. Immediately, I see Juni's face. I scrunch my eyes shut, trying to wish away the memories of her tiny form breaking against the wall. The way she squeaked.

I place my hands behind my head and start doing sit-ups. Training with Vec tomorrow is too far away. I need to get stronger now. And once I'm capable, I will hunt down every one of them. I'll rip their skin apart with my bare hands, and one day, I will rid the world of all immortals. I don't care if it's impossible.

Somehow, I'll find a way.

Every day, I train from the moment I awaken until the moment I fall asleep. Vec starts every morning drinking tea while he watches me jog around his estate for an hour. Then I lift and throw large stones till mid-morning. After, we eat breakfast together, then head back outside for two hours of combat training.

After the fiftieth day, Vec stops taking it easy on me. I go to bed with aching muscles and fields of bruises. If I complain, he makes me bathe in conjured ice he summons with immortal magic. He said there's no time to stop and mutter during a proper fight, and he won't tolerate it during practice.

I don't hate Vec though. At night, we laugh over dinner together. He often permits me to sip wine with him during the evening.

In the late afternoons, he teaches me English. Vec knows over fifty languages as opposed to my two—French and Italian.

When I finally turn thirteen, he teaches me how to wield all three tenets of core magic—levitation, air manipulation, and illusions. Though I'll have no need for illusions once I'm taught Desimir magic.

Every human, since the dawn of time, is born with core magic abilities. Where things branch off are family bloodlines. Eighty percent of families have no blood magic and cannot perform more than core magic.

Desimirs are known for a magic most believe is wicked from the core. We can invade a person's thoughts, break them from the inside out, control shadows. And with herbs, the possibilities for our magic are endless. Unfortunately, it only works on those with weaker minds. Or those who allow it to happen, which is rare.

My mother's bloodline, the Boisclairs, gives me the inherited ability of short-term invisibility. I can only perform it for up to five seconds, but it's quite useful in confusing an enemy during combat.

Using magical herbology is where the real fun happens. People will have different herbs woven into clothing, jewelry, and hair pieces to increase their abilities. Some herb's powers last an eternity. Others fade after a few uses. The herb lurdow causes an explosive gust of wind that can collapse a house. But when combined with coriander, it can relieve chest pain.

One day, Vec brings out my father's will and shows me the portion on Desimir magic. Father never got to teach it to me before he died. Vec helps me train with my family's magic, even though he cannot wield it. Every session, he becomes more uneasy by its dark nature.

Weeks turn to months, and months to years. I'm fifteen now. A man, even more than I was three years ago. Still, Vec says I'm just a boy even though he makes no effort to hide the noises that come from his bedroom on weekends when the local tavern ladies stop by.

Father and Mother never told me what sex was. And neither did Vec—technically. I found out ever so graciously one midnight when I went downstairs to pour myself water and walked in on him buried inside some woman.

We never spoke of it again.

Months before my sixteenth birthday, Vec and I sit in his study and sip ale out of silver mugs.

"I think you're ready for these." He hands me a large box from where he sits opposite me near the fireplace.

"You didn't need to get me anything."

"This is more of a curse than a gift."

I raise an eyebrow and open the lid. Two black daggers sit inside. Their handles are gold, made of two metal snakes coiling and twisting around one another. "You never let me train with knives."

Vec raises his cup and throws one leg over his chair's armrest. "And now you're ready."

I run my callused fingers over the smooth metal. It's time. Not only will Vec advance me in my training, but he'll start sending me on missions. Small ones at first—like spying or pickpocketing nobles. But eventually, he'll have me carrying out assassinations and executions. I'll become the Savant. The feared title my father once held within the Syndicate. And when that time comes, I'll be making a few of my own stops.

"Get that look out of your eye, Atticus."

"What look?" I smile, running a hand through my curly raven hair.

"The one where you look at cutlery and imagine carving out the hearts of certain individuals. You will not kill without my blessing. I am your guardian, after all."

"No, we're friends. And you just happen to be my mentor too."

"Not when it comes to assassinations."

I bite my tongue. All I can do is promise Vec that I'll never actively seek out my family's killers until the time is right. But if I run into them organically—I can't promise him anything.

I shut the box and set it off to the side. As much as I hate to admit it, Vec is usually right about these things. I think of the way Vec and I have grown close over the years, and how he's spent every minute of his life dedicated to training me. He doesn't take any time for himself. Anytime I ask him when he'll visit the immortal homeland, he brushes me off with a tangent on how he has all the time in the world—literally.

"I don't think I've ever asked," I say. "What were your parents like?"

He takes a sip of his ale. "They *are* a pain in my ass."

"Right." *Even Vec still has parents.* "Doesn't life get boring after a while? Being alive for so long sounds rather dull."

Vec gives me one of his looks. "That's just something mortals say to make themselves feel better."

Ouch.

CHAPTER 5

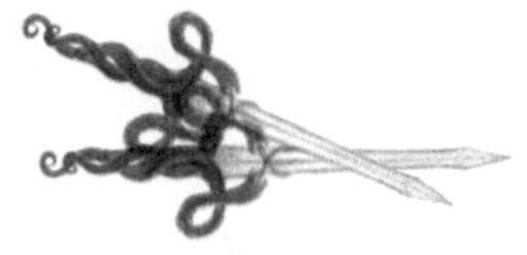

YEAR 1410

"Run!" a man shrieks from down the hallway. "It's the Savant!"

"He's going to kill us all!" a panicked voice yells.

"Fuck!" screams another.

I stride down the long hallway of the extravagant mansion, the golden hilts of my daggers in each of my hands. This residence is more like a castle, with its own set of guards and territorial flags, all just for show. Perhaps if my target still had immortals as companions, he wouldn't be in this situation.

Over the last five years, Vec has sent me on three-hundred and thirty missions and assassinations. I've dreamt of this day for ages. And it's only the first of many days I crave. Days where my blade will carve out immortals' hearts.

I pierce my Desimir magic into the sage and an enchanted hallucino-genic herb beneath my coat, causing thick, red smoke to emit from my feet and throughout the halls.

A sadistic energy surges through my veins at the guard's screams from the sudden lack of visibility. Servants scramble through the house in fear of me. As long as they stay out of my way, I won't touch them. Two male servants already learned their lesson on what happens when someone interferes with my work. *Someone really should clean up that mess soon. Vec will burst a blood vessel when he learns I got blood on my doublet.*

I run up the stairs just as a door slams shut and bolts from the inside. *How annoying.* I sheath my daggers.

Unlocking things isn't a tenant of core magic that all humans hold. If it were, there would be no point in locks. I wear a silver ring that has zeledian melted into it, which compliments my magic and allows me to open any door or safe I please. Zeledian is rare, and I had to do unspeakable things to gain access to it.

I'm sure the loggerhead on the other side of this door thinks he's outsmarted me right now. He still thinks I'm the weak twelve-year-old boy who could do nothing but scream when he ordered the immortals to take my parents' lives.

Energy rushes through me as I imagine what I'm about to do. The pleasure I will feel from ending Sir Raveen's life in the most inhumane way I can conjure up.

But it's been eight years since that day. Eight years of fantasizing about the way I'd carry out Sir Raveen's death, and now, it will all come to fruition.

Sir Raveen and Jervany's father were the two humans there that dreadful day. Just last month, luck rewarded me greatly when I finally found the location of Jervany's father. When I can't fall asleep at night, I think about the way Jervany's father screamed as I tortured him straight into his grave.

I press my hand to the door and close my eyes, directing my energy into the zeledian ring. I can see the bolt in my mind's eye. When I tighten my free hand, I hear it slide open.

Sir Raveen yells as I kick the door in with my boot. He tumbles backward as I enter the room, his arm outstretched, trying to scoot away from me. His fear is palpable, familiar; his face reminding me of the way I felt when I once feared for my life.

A smile spreads across my face as I look down at him. Watching him lose control of his bladder feels better than I'd ever imagined.

"P—please," Sir Raveen begs. "What do you want? Money? Power? I can give it all to you, Savant!"

I lean my head back and laugh. Oh, he really doesn't remember, does he? I suppose I look drastically different from the last time he saw me, and eight years of time and training does a lot to a man's body. The lanky, pathetic, weak boy he once knew is no more. That boy could have found an ounce of compassion in his heart. But now my muscles are corded in the way I once thought to be a childish fantasy. I can take on small armies all by myself. People seek my services as if I were an immortal.

I bend down in front of him, trying my best to avoid scrunching my nose at the stench of urine. I extend my hand out to him. "Atticus Desimir. It's nice to see you again, *old friend.*"

Sir Raveen's eyes widen. He doesn't take my hand. "D—Desimir?" His shoulders shake. "Please, I'm sorry. It was at the direction of the antipope that I had to do such a thing to your family. I'm a pawn, just as you were!"

I roll my eyes. Really? He's just an innocent victim in this? Why didn't he say so sooner? My gods, I must spare his life! Heavens, what a mistake I've made.

As I stand, I cackle. Then I raise my hand and flick two of my fingers up and manipulate the energy in the room to slam the door shut and bolt it.

"No—no!" Sir Raveen is practically whimpering. So distasteful for a man his age. There's only one activity I like to hear a man whimper during, and I'd never do it with the likes of him.

I slide my daggers out of their sheaths.

"I will give you everything I own! And I'll betroth you to my granddaughter. She's about your age! You'll have enough riches to last you multiple lifetimes!"

My chest tightens. He has a granddaughter and still had the heart to kill a child? I wish he was immortal like the others on my kill list so I could make his punishment last decades.

His lips stutter, realizing how his words backfired.

"Wrong move, sir." I slice a dagger across his face.

Sir Raveen screams bloody murder, holding his wound.

For the next two hours, I draw out his killing, slowly and mercilessly, mutilating his body while he can do nothing but scream, piss, shit, and blackout. I make no effort to keep my clothing clean as blood splatters out of him from every open cut of skin.

I don't stop the torture until he's lost enough blood to never regain consciousness again.

I use one of Sir Raveen's own daggers to deal the final blow through his eye socket and into his brain.

Once the air is free from blood splatter, I take a deep breath that only adds to the euphoria racing through me.

It's done. Both humans are finally dead. I sit back on my legs from where I kneel as ecstasy pulsates through my muscles.

Now only the immortals remain. Killing Sir Raveen isn't nearly as sweet as the way I'll feel when they're finally dead. Sir Raveen may have ordered my family's deaths that day, but the immortals carried it out.

They are the ones who truly haunt my dreams.

When I arrive back at the estate, Vec stands in the foyer, his arms crossed. I'm not even three strides inside before he starts his usual post-mission interrogation.

"Is it done?" Vec asks.

I unsheathe my bloodied knives for him to see and cock my head before handing them off to the maid for washing. Blood still streaks my face, and I'm thankful my clothes are dark enough to hide the blood-stains from his view. He hates when I ruin my clothes.

"Very good, Atticus. You've done well." Vec leans against the railing of the stairs. "The maids drew a bath in your room. And per your request, there are courtesans upstairs awaiting your arrival." He walks up to me and sniffs. "You smell like piss."

"Not mine."

"And the blood splatter on your neck? How did it get all the way up there?"

I grin.

"You're maniacal." He shakes his head. "Your father assassinated with poise and grace. He respected bodies, even when they were the most vicious criminals in all the land. But you—your enemies might as well be lambs for the slaughter."

I climb the first few steps up the marble stairs. "Because they are."

I trudge up to my room and through the hallways lined with candlelit sconces and paintings locked within gold frames. Some of the paintings are of Vec's own creation.

My relationship with Vec has always been unconventional. It's one where he is just as much a guardian as he is a friend in the way only an immortal can be. But even after I entered adulthood, he still nags me constantly about my bad habits and for the unorthodox use of my family's magic.

It's no secret that he hates Desimir magic and the methods I use in assassinations. But I get the job done, so he turns a blind eye.

When I enter my room, I instantly harden at the sight of two naked courtesans lounging on my bed, feeding each other grapes off a vine. They smile and giggle when they see me. After a long day of killing, I need this. I deserve this.

Besides, I don't just take. I give. And I'm sure lying with me is a fine break from all the middle-aged, wrinkly nobles they're normally bedded by. And unlike those raisins of men, I don't let the festivities stop until *everyone* is satisfied.

The women scoot off the bed and prance over to me. I extend my arms to give them access as they help me out of my clothes. The blood puts neither of them off. These two have a long history with me. They're more than used to the blood that precedes our time together.

I was eighteen when I lost my virginity. And it's not that I didn't want to or wasn't allowed. In fact, I never thought much of it. And with constant training and Vec's strict schedules, there was never any time.

My first time was unconventional, as everything in my life tends to be. I had walked into what I thought was a pub after a long day of killing, and a beautiful young woman mistook me for a party guest. She clasped my hand in hers and pulled me into a back room where pure debauchery was occurring. People were bent over tables and pressed up against walls. Men and women alike pleasured one another. Something beautiful snapped within me. The next thing I knew, multiple sets of lips were on my skin and around my cock. They tied ropes around my wrists and ankles as they did exquisite things to me in ways I never thought possible.

And a strange thing happened that night. My mind went quiet in a way not even alcohol could replicate. From that moment on, I was hooked.

Once I'm undressed, the girls follow me into the wooden tub and our night of fun ensues. They help wash my hair and scrub the dried blood off my back that had soaked through my clothing.

One beauty moves her lips to my neck while the other kisses me, her mouth tasting of delectable fruit. Everything becomes a mess of lips and tongues, causing me to groan. So many of my nights are like this now. Vec moved his bedroom to the opposite end of the estate just to get a peaceful night's rest away from the noises. As if he's any quieter.

A hand grips my length beneath the water, working me steady and slow. My head dips back from the pleasure shooting through me. This girl knows my cock better than anyone else I've bedded. She pumps me in just the right way. Knows when to switch the speed. Even when to pass her thumb over the tip.

I stop her before I come, moving the three of us to the bed once we dry off.

My use of courtesans isn't the only way I get off. Sometimes, I go to the local pubs and find a man or woman to distract me. It normally starts with me giving them a look, making them feel like they're the only person in this world I've ever given any sexual interest to. Then things normally get heated in an alleyway or a local inn. Vec tells me I should be more careful. But I can't seem to stop.

Because if I'm not drinking, killing, or fucking, my mind falls into the depths of hell. A hell where my family's soulless faces stare at me, begging to be avenged. Then I tumble deeper into the abyss to a reality where immortals are impossible to kill. A reality where carrying out my revenge is nothing but a childish fantasy.

I banish the thoughts from my head, pounding into one courtesan and unleashing the darkest depths of my soul into her body. From behind, I grip her hair with one hand and clamp my fingers around her hip with the other. She's screaming. Begging. Just how I like them.

I smirk at the other courtesan who's sitting up near the bed frame. Her eyes turn to glass when I mouth the words, *you're next.*

She bites her bottom lip, but I can tell she's nervous. I'll take it easy on her, but I can't help but tease her. After killing Sir Raveen, I have enough energy to last me late into the morning. For tonight, I'll spare these girls and take the leftovers of my enthusiasm to the pub tomorrow night. It's only fair. If I did everything I wanted to this evening, they may be too exhausted to service their less *energetic* clients.

After I've had my way with both of them, and I've received my release, the girls fall asleep, holding me in their arms between them.

CHAPTER 6

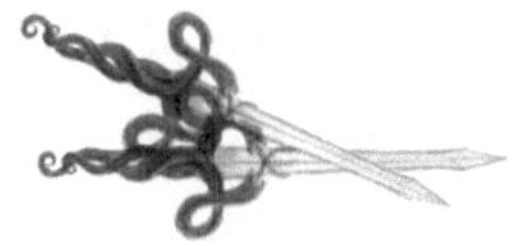

V ec delivers news to me the next day that Sir Baldassare Cossa of the Bilancia Syndicate assassinated the antipope, Alexander V, last night. For years, Cossa has been infiltrating their ranks, then finally poisoned the antipope during a nightcap, ending his faux reign once and for all.

Which means my father's life mission is complete. Any threat of the antipope's efforts to steal the artifact is now gone. It was he who directed Sir Raveen to kill my family. Alexander should have been heavier in my mind over the years. After all, it's his fault my family was ripped away from me. But it wasn't he who dealt the killing blows to Father, Mother, and Juni. And though he became an afterthought, I'm glad he's dead.

I wonder if my father watches me from the stars. If he does, I'm sure he's smiling.

I spend the day in the village visiting herbal shops, asking around to get my hands on more rare, forbidden herbs, just like zeledian.

As the sun sets, I enter the local pub. It's fuller than normal for a weekday. When I sit at the worn-down bar, the bartender slides over ale before I can even ask. Smart man.

Some time passes before a short brunette woman walks in. A four-strand braid lies over her shoulder. Her dress is modest, yet hugs her in all the right places. Her features are delicate. Gorgeous. Not to mention, she's the only woman here, if you don't count the scantily clad prostitutes scoping out the bar from the second floor.

She sits at the bar two stools away from me and orders mead. Already, many men are gawking behind her. I scoff. Do they have no class?

Once she's served, I scoot close to her before any of the other men can claim her. When I do, I immediately hear grumbles. Most of them are also regulars, so they know once I set my sights on someone, they're mine.

"I haven't seen you around here." I lean onto my forearms.

"Well, it's been a rough evening."

"Care to elaborate?"

She takes a few giant gulps of her drink and sets it down firmly. "Nope."

"Then tell me, how is a fair girl like you not afraid of being in a pub all alone with this lot? Are you not scared?"

She shrugs. "Finding a place to drown my sorrows overrides any fear I have of them. Or of you."

"Well, it seems we're one and the same, dearest."

That makes her smile.

I gently place my fingers on her wrist, circling my thumb over her skin ever so slightly. With her confidence, I expect her to whip my hand away, curse at me, then call me a pervert.

But she doesn't. In fact, a slight blush coats the skin near her cheekbones.

My, my, dear stranger. Are we here for the same reasons? Is mead only an appetizer for your true intentions here tonight? Shall we drown our sorrows together with our bodies pressed against one another and my teeth nibbling your flesh?

I lean close to her until my lips are mere centimeters from her ear. "Follow me to the alley."

She nods slowly. I take her hand and lead her out the back entrance of the pub. Before she can stutter, or ruin the moment with nervous words, I press my mouth to hers. She whimpers as I grab her hips and push her into the wall. My tongue sinks into her mouth, the little sounds she makes driving me wild.

I adjust her skirts and pick her lower half up. She instinctively wraps her legs around me. As I roll my hips between her thighs, she moans.

The back door to the pub swings open and a man stumbles out. I pay him no mind, and whatever-her-name-is doesn't let his sudden intrusion stop our fun.

I watch him in the corner of my eye while I kiss along the girl's jaw.

He walks in the opposite direction, muttering. "Do humans not have the decency anymore to purchase a room at the inn? Or have they reduced themselves to farm animals?"

The man is speaking as if he's not one of us. Not—human.

I drop the girl to her feet, taking a few steps back.

"What's wrong?" She folds her arms from the chill in the air.

Compared to most men, his stature is substantial. His thick black hair lies in a state of disarray from his inebriation.

My heart shudders when I see the white symbol of infinity etched into his neck. The symbol of immortals.

It can't be one of them. I'm hallucinating. And not all immortals are automatically evil. I need to be sure.

"Konstantin?"

He spins around with an annoyed scowl on his face. "What do you want, swine?"

It's him. The one who slammed my sisters into a wall like she was a toy. Shattered her body like glass. I can't stop shaking. Not from fear, but pure anger.

The glimmer of a thought pops into my mind. One where Juni is grown up and smiling, living a happy life with a family of her own. But that isn't the case. She's gone—and because of *him*.

Blinded by rage, I sprint at him from behind, pulling a dagger from my belt. Then I'm on him, piercing the blade into his neck.

The girl shrieks and falls to the ground.

Blue blood with a shimmer of silver drips from his neck. Konstantin doesn't yell out in pain, or even react in self-defense. He rolls his eyes, as if the dagger in his neck is nothing but a pinprick. I step away from him and grab my other dagger.

"This is for my family, you fucker."

Konstantin studies my face, smiling in realization. "Ah, Atticus Desimir. Seems you're still the foolish boy I remember from all those years ago. Figured I may run into you one of these days. How's Vec?" He chuckles. "I've had my fair share of betrayals over the last few centuries, but even I did not know he was working for the Syndicate. Once I learned that, I knew you'd be at my throat in no time."

My hand shakes as I hold the knife out toward him. I haven't felt nervous like this since—since...

The world is caving in around me. I'm twelve again. Helpless. Weak. No match for an immortal, not even with Vec's advanced training.

Konstantin walks toward me, a cocky prance in his step. "You should know better than anyone that your efforts to end my life are futile."

"It doesn't mean I won't try." My words emerge like a shaky whisper.

Before I can attack him again, Konstantin lunges forward and socks me in the gut. I fall back against the wall. My dagger clatters as it hits the stony floor. I sink to the ground, groaning in pain. The girl isn't in the alleyway anymore. Ran for her life, no doubt.

The immortal kneels in front of me and picks up my dagger. He runs a finger over the blade, then looks at me. "I think I should teach you a valuable lesson today, Desimir. Perhaps after this day, you'll finally abandon your quest to seek us out."

I won't arrive in the afterlife without avenging my family. "No. Never."

He takes my blade and presses it into his own forehead. "You see, Atticus, you need a simple lesson in science." He slides the blade down his face, through his eyebrow and doesn't stop until he's just past his cheekbone. Blue blood follows in its wake, dripping down his sharp jaw and defined throat.

And now he'll do the same to me.

He can't do this. I won't let him! I'm strong. Mighty.

Before I can propel him away from me, he sits on the back of my hands with his kneecaps to prevent me from casting magic. Then he takes my blade and places the tip into my forehead, slowly dragging it down my face. He draws out the pain as I howl.

I'm weak. I'm weak.

His motions are controlled as he makes a thin, deep line down my skin, creating a replica of his.

I refuse to beg him to stop. But I cannot contain my body's natural reaction of crying out from the agony. My hands go numb under his body weight.

The pain is worse than anything I've ever experienced, almost as if he's using a dark form of magic to amplify the misery of scarring my face.

The blade clatters to the ground. I'm shaking. All he does is watch me. I turn my head, refusing to look at him.

I'm pathetic. I'm a child.

I can't even protect myself, just like I couldn't protect Juni.

"Look at me." Konstantin grabs my jaw and forces my gaze. The wound he inflicted on himself has already healed. He doesn't have to say anything to make his point.

The sight of him is blurry. My breaths are shallow.

This scar will last until I die. No herb can heal scars that are this deep.

Konstantin steps back. "This was a mercy, Atticus. Next time you try to lunge at me, I'll be sending you to Hades." He leaves the alleyway.

I grab a handkerchief from my pocket and press it into my face.

Pathetic.

Weak.

I've lost everything. Even the ability to tolerate my reflection. I stagger to my feet, feeling more boy than man.

A complete and utter failure.

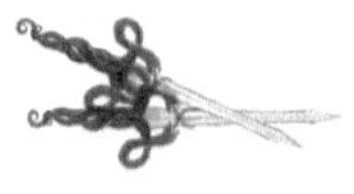

I stumble into the foyer of Vec's estate, still cradling my wound with the handkerchief. Once Vec sees this, he'll scold me. He'll think I sought the immortals on my volition.

Inside the greenhouse, I pick dolinian leaves off one plant and calendula off another. I place them in a mortar at the workstation, only a single candle to light my work. The bleeding has stopped, so I set down the handkerchief as I crush the herbs together with a pestle.

I should have walked away. I should have held the fury of my blade for a decade more until I knew I could kill him. Konstantin's guard will be up now more than ever, my chances of revenge slipping through my fingers.

The greenhouse door flies open and Vec storms in. I turn my head away from him, using the shadows to cover the evidence of my weakness.

Vec's fists are on his hips. His breaths are short and angry. "Tell me why a maid just reported to me that you arrived home with blood dripping down your face!"

"I had an accident," I say. "Go back to sleep."

Vec charges forward and grabs my wrist, forcing it from my face. I keep my head turned away, but it's too late. I know he's seen it.

He throws my wrist down. "Have I not told you to keep a low profile? What is this from, huh?" Vec signals to my face. "A bar fight gone wrong?"

I shouldn't say it, but I do. "I ran into Konstantin. Couldn't control myself." My eyes fill with hot liquid. It's been eight years since I've cried and I refuse to reduce myself to a blubbering child in front of Vec.

To my surprise, Vec's eyes soften. His one rule is that I don't kill without his permission. Even though I wasn't successful, I disobeyed him. And against an immortal of all people.

"So he knows what you look like now?"

I nod.

Vec grips his hair and then throws his arms out. "Shit, Atticus. You're fucked. We're fucked. It will be impossible to send you on missions now for the Syndicate!"

"I don't regret it."

"That's a given," he says sarcastically as he motions at my scar.

I take a deep breath and go back to crushing the herbs. They'll reduce the scarring minimally and prevent infection. But I'm forever marked. "Something must be done about Konstantin, Austrie, and Alano. You know I've never applied their crimes to your entire kind, but we cannot allow immortals to go on without the prospect of death. Now that my father's affairs are complete, I will travel the world if it means killing them."

"Atticus, no immortal has ever died since the dawn of earth unless by their own volition."

"That will change. It must."

Vec has that stupid look of pity on his face. The one where he's looking at me more like a sympathetic mentor than my friend.

"Stop that," I say.

"I want to help you. But all the options I can think of are ludicrous."

I raise an eyebrow. "Try me."

He leans against the table. "Just know it's not a solution. In fact, it may be the biggest waste of time in human history."

A solution? "What is it?"

"I know of a spring. One created by the immortals to preserve the bodies of their human lovers. When immortals fall in love with humans, they only spend five to ten years a century with them. For the other decades, the human sleeps submerged in the spring water, encased inside a coffin-like contraption. It's the only way for an immortal to spend centuries with their human.

"If you sleep in the spring, I can scout the world for you looking for solutions. I can do it for centuries if I must. Perhaps time is the only thing you need. One day, a solution may come along. And then you'll have your revenge."

I stop and stare at the floor, my mouth agape. Sleep in a coffin like some vampire? And Vec will be so lonely while I'm away. Not to mention, I may never have a chance to visit my uncles and cousins. It's been almost a decade since I've seen them. Why introduce myself when I'll never see them again?

Am I willing to stop time in search of a solution?

The answer comes quickly. "Yes."

"Yes?"

I must come to grips that every mortal I know in this time may be dead by time I wake up. But it's a sacrifice I'm willing to make. Finally, I will be one step closer to vengeance. *Hold on Juni. Mother. Father.* I'll throw the immortals into the depths of hell, even if I'm dragged down with them.

"Put me to sleep, Vec."

CHAPTER 7

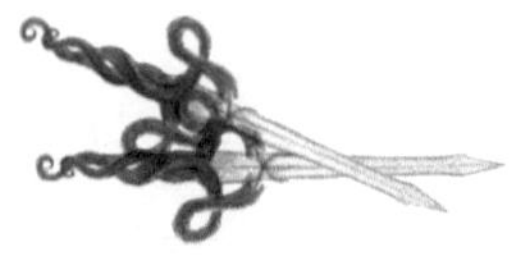

Three days later, Vec travels to his immortal homeland of Eltheriah. And two months after, he returns with a wagon full of water barrels from the Spring of Perpetuity as well as a coffin made of black obsidian.

As the servants carefully carry the barrels to the cellar, Vec leads me to his study.

He shuts the door behind us, locking it. "Are you sure you want to do this, Atticus?"

I stand by the fireplace, leaning my body weight against the mantle. "I was having second thoughts. But then I dreamt of Juni on the night she died. The dream was so vivid, it was as if I relived it. Once I woke, I knew I'd never been more sure of anything in my life."

"The water will cover your nose and mouth."

I nearly fall over. "You didn't mention that before."

"I didn't think of it. Having second thoughts now?"

I'm already feeling claustrophobic. And I'll have to breathe in water like a pitiful fish. I stand up straighter. "No. It doesn't change my mind."

"Right." Vec walks up to me, anxiety painted across his face.

"What?" I fold my arms.

Vec embraces me. Tightly. Too tight.

I grunt. "Settle down, old man. I won't be gone forever."

Vec's been alive for centuries. I never thought he'd get so sentimental at my temporary departure.

He releases me and places a hand on my shoulder. "I never thought I'd find such a friend in the likes of your kind, yet here I am."

"You're going to make me gag."

We laugh for some time before his face grows serious again. "Are you ready?"

I nod. "Let's do it."

We take our time walking to the cellar as I bury any apprehension. Any weakness. This is not something anyone can talk me out of, not even myself. If I don't do this, I'll spend the rest of my life in agony, wishing I could have done more.

Under Vec's direction, the servants fill up the stone casket halfway while the maids help me strip down to nothing. I cannot bring anything inside the tank with me, other than flesh and blood.

"Lie down and we'll fill the rest of the tank. Once the water is covering your face, breathe it in as fast as you can. It will be uncomfortable for a minute, but once your lungs fill, you'll fall asleep," Vec explains.

Yes, that fun little detail Vec failed to mention earlier. I'll essentially be drowning myself. I climb into the tank, the cold air of the cellar prickling against my skin. Once I'm on my back, the water partially covers my ears.

Vec stands next to the tank, looming over me. "I'll wake you as soon as I find a solution. If more than a millennium passes, I'll wake you."

I scoff. "If I wake up in a thousand years, I'll know I truly failed."

Vec signals to the servants. A group of them drag the final water barrel over to the tank with me. I clench my fists, more nervous about the prospect of breathing in water than anything else.

"Goodnight, Atticus."

"Don't have too much fun while I'm gone."

The servants pour the rest of the water into the tank. Within seconds, my nose and mouth are submerged.

A few seconds pass of breath holding until I finally pinch my thigh and force myself to suck in the water. It burns, but I don't stop breathing it in until my lungs are on fire. Soon the stinging turns to peace. My eyes grow heavy, and if I didn't know any better, I'd say that I'm dying.

No dreams take over, only a pleasant tranquility.

CHAPTER 8

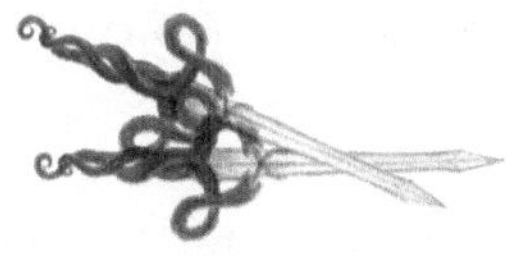

Water muffles the sound of a nagging voice. I'd prefer to sleep longer.

"Atticus, wake up."

I ignore the voice, slipping back into ethereal bliss.

"It's time."

I'm jolted awake by a pain shooting through my body. Everything hurts. My joints ache. My lungs burn. And it takes all my might to open my eyes.

My vision focuses and concrete stares back at me. Am I on the floor?

Then I gag, a coughing fit taking over as the water tries to expel itself. I can't breathe.

A hand is on my chest now, injecting immortal magic through my chest into my lungs, drying up the rest of the water.

Vec stares down at me and throws a blanket over my crotch.

"How long did I sleep?" I breathe out. It feels like it was only hours ago that Vec and the servants poured spring water over my body. Though the water has dissipated, a weight sits deep in my lungs. "And what the hell are you wearing?"

Vec's clothes look absolutely ridiculous. As does the tall hat on his head. He straightens his collar. "It's called a suit. And if we can get to the point, you'll be wearing one soon too."

Like I'd ever wear something so vile looking. "What year is it?"

Vec hesitates, pursing his lips. "It's 1890. Atticus, you slept four hundred and eighty years."

My hands go numb. It's been almost five centuries? Everyone I knew in the 1400s is dead? Servants. Maids. Courtesans. My uncles and cousins. A part of me hoped Vec would find a solution quicker than decades or centuries. That I'd only be asleep for a few short years.

Calm down, Atticus. There's no time for regrets. "Explains why you look so strange."

Vec removes his hat. "That's the Atticus I remember." His hairstyle is different too. His golden hair used to be longer and unruly, but now it's slicked back with an oily sheen.

I stand, wrapping the blanket around my lower half. There's a strange source of light on the ceiling. It's like a candle wrapped in glass. I stare at it so long it induces a headache, as if I just stared directly at the sun.

"It's called a light bulb," Vec says.

A light bulb? "Is it made from magic?"

"No. From science."

"How do they put a little fire all the way in there? And how does it stay lit while hanging upside down?"

Vec runs a hand down his face. "Once I update you on everything else, I'll give you lessons on the workings of this time period."

Right. Vec waking me means he learned how to kill immortals. There's no time to get distracted by the silly little details of a time centuries after my birth.

The cellar looks different from what I remember, the charm of Italy gone. "Did you redesign the estate?"

"No. We're not in the Republic of Venice anymore. In fact, it fell almost a century ago at the hands of France. I moved the tank here to London shortly before it dissolved."

My home is gone? Father never liked the powers that ruled, but it was still my home.

Vec waves me toward him. "Come on now. There's no time to waste. I have almost five centuries to catch you up on."

I follow Vec up the stairs. His new—estate—is quite small. In fact, it's not an estate at all. Apparently, it's called a townhouse. When I pass a maid in the hallway, she keeps her eyes forward, careful not to stare at my half naked body. I do a double take at her outfit—a long-sleeved black dress with an equally long white apron and a pleated white hat.

Her outfit is hideous, even compared to Vec's *suit*. Especially the horrid puffy sleeve shaped like mutton.

While Vec leads me to his new study on the third floor, I take in the walls, the furniture, the ceilings. It's all so—practical.

His office is similar to the one in Brescia—everything in the same place, from the wooden desk to the ornate furniture. In the corner, there's a large piece of silver, amplifying the clearest reflection of myself I've ever seen. I've seen my reflection before in glass and water, but nothing like this.

"It's called a mirror. And before you ask again, no, it's not magic." Vec hands me a stack of clothing. "Put these on."

I stare at the suit and new-age undergarments. "I'd rather not."

Vec rolls his eyes. "Just for now. I haven't seen you clothed in centuries."

I chuckle. "Whatever you say, but I'm seeing a seamstress later."

"You're going to have to blend in if you want to last in this time period."

I ignore the sight of my scar in the reflection of the mirror as I get dressed. Vec teaches me the name of each piece as I put them on. I want to tell him not to bother, because I'll immediately forget them when I find an alternative outfit more suited to my needs. But he'll likely slap me if I say that.

"Things have changed drastically since you slept, Atticus. Magic isn't like how it once was. Magic-wielding humans aren't either. The core and generational magic you and I both know is drastically different now. Time has bred magic out of most of the population. Only half can wield it now, and they're known as venitors and venitrixes."

"Magic is disappearing?" I can't believe this. Growing up, magic was a part of everyday life, from cooking to cleaning. Even the games we'd play.

Vec steps forward with the tie and secures it around my collar. A tie that I plan to burn later when I acquire my own wardrobe. "Technology is replacing magic rapidly. Those who are born with magic go through training from birth into adulthood. And those who want to actually use their magic to change the world go to university. Because of that, venitors are stronger and more skilled than your generation.

"Fifty years ago, I learned that someone killed one of the immortals, Alano, but none of my kind could figure out how it happened. It turns out a fellow by the name of Ezekiel Blythesea had killed him using his family magic. Society banished the Blythesea family because of Ezekiel's actions. That family is the only holder of necromantic magic. You see, the only way to kill an immortal is with the use of another unkillable being, in this case, the undead. Though they're more like demons."

I can't believe this. Alano is dead? I should be happy. Ecstatic even. But I would have preferred that I killed him with my own two hands.

Konstantin and Austrie remain. I'll seek restitution in the vile nature of the torture I'll inflict on them both.

Especially Konstantin.

"But how can I learn Blythesea magic without being part of their bloodline?"

"You'll have to convince a member to transfer their magic to you. Family magic in this age is inherited through tradition, not blood. Another product of magic changing over the centuries."

"How difficult is it to get the Blythesea family to hand over their magic?"

"Difficult?" Vec laughs with sarcasm. "It's near impossible considering they changed their last name. And the family treats their dealings more like a clan. Anyone who teaches Blythesea magic outside the family bloodline is burned alive. At least that's how it was a hundred years ago. With times changing, I suspect they banish the perpetrator now, which is why I woke you. With less stringent punishments on Blythesea descendants, your ability to exploit one to teach you is drastically improved."

I don't grovel at the threat of burning. He should have woken me fifty years ago. My sins deserve a worse punishment than that. "What is their new last name?"

"Ashworth. Though that's a closely guarded secret I tortured out of a decedent thirty years ago."

"And where do I play a part in all this?"

Vec holds a finger up, using magic to levitate a stack of papers off his desk and into my hands. The lettering is so neat and precise, I almost forget to read the words out loud. "Roche University... An application?"

"Yes. I've pulled some strings and enrolled you in the second year of their program. The first quarter starts in a week."

I throw the papers down on the desk. "Surely I can just torture the information out of the loggerhead."

"That *loggerhead* is not to be meddled with. Unknown to his classmates, Dominic Ashworth is dangerous, or at least, his power is. I've been trailing him for four years. He has a darkness lodged within him he doesn't let many people see. If he chose to steward his magic further, Dominic could have the skills necessary to wield dark magic as if it's core magic. Sort of like a certain someone I know."

Dominic. What a handsome name. "Desimir magic isn't dark magic."

"It's disgusting. May as well be."

I should be offended, but all I can do is grin. "You have a point."

In order to find Sir Raveen's whereabouts, I once broke into one of his former guard's minds to torture the information out of him. Deep in his thoughts, I threw him off cliffs, projected images of goblins and ghouls, and mimicked the sensation of tar oozing through his nose, ears, and mouth. It was wickedly wonderful. I'll never forget how good it felt making him squirm into revealing his former master's location. Of course I had to kill him after. Couldn't have him reporting back to Sir Raveen.

"The next few days will be intensive. I'll need to teach you this decade's terminology and manners. For instance, *loggerhead* isn't exactly a known insult in this time period."

"The first thing I'd like you to teach me is what swear words to use."

Vec ignores me. "You must learn how new-age magic differs from the magic you learned growing up. You won't be able to use herbs or Desimir magic in class. I'm not even sure your blood allows you to learn new-age venitor magic, but we'll find a workaround."

If I'm not able to wield this age's core magic, that could pose a problem in classes. Maybe Vec's being too optimistic about that part, but I have my ways.

"I've already met with your headmaster. He thinks I'm your uncle."

I scoff. "Likely story. You're only ten years my senior in body." Immortals stop aging at thirty.

"I use immortal magic to disguise my appearance and appear older. We'll spend the next few days with tutoring, then I'll help you move into the dormitories."

"I won't live here with you?"

"You need to get close to Dominic. I know little about him besides who his father is. And if you'll miss me that much, you can visit on weekends."

I roll my eyes. "Oh yes, Vec, I'll be sure to crawl back to you with teary eyes every Friday and suckle at your teat."

"Knock it off."

I snicker. So that's it then? I move into Roche University and live my life as a student to stalk my prey? How annoying. But after centuries of sleep, I'm looking forward to stretching my legs and working my magic to get exactly what I want.

What's in your head, Dominic? What makes you tick? I look forward to meeting you. Sinking my claws into your fears, vulnerabilities, and desires.

Breaking you before you even realize what I've done.

Vec spends the next few days doing exactly what he promised—boring me out of my mind.

He teaches me about modern inventions, table manners, cycling, current events, slang, euphemisms, fashion trends, how to handle electricity safely—then a quick side lesson on how to combine electricity with magic to electrocute a man to death.

My English is more-than fluent, so I have no issues pronouncing newer words. He even takes me to a restaurant to practice my new lingo with the waiter, though the lesson ended abruptly after I tried a newer liquor called tequila.

One morning I ask Vec for coinage so I can visit a few shops to which he corrects me and tells me to call currency *pounds*.

Compared to the tranquility of Venice, London is a suffocating and crowded abomination. Friendliness is a foreign idea, the people bustling by stop only to do business, eyes searching nothing but signage and the road beneath them. Horse-drawn carriages fill the streets, unapologetic to the walking populace.

I enter the seamstress shop and tell the young woman behind the counter what clothing I require. She scratches her head at my very specific and unusual requests.

Days later, I enter the shop once again, a bell jingling on the door to mark my arrival.

I try on the newly made clothing. The large dark overcoat ends near my mid-calves, silver fabric lining the hems. Copper buttons secure pieces of leather to keep the overcoat pinned together in the front. Beneath the overcoat, I wear a jacket resembling a black gambeson.

Once it's all on, I stand on a large block while the seamstress makes last-minute adjustments. She blushes while she works. Once the finishing touches are complete, the seamstress packs two boxes full of dress shirts and trousers that I also ordered, as well as a pair of boots. When she hands them to me in the middle of the shop, I promptly set them down, then flick my fingers up to lock the shop door, staring at her deviously as I do.

I grip her hips as she lets me guide her into the dressing room, a soft glow lining her cheeks. I push her into the wall and kiss along her neck, working her body until she's screaming. I spend the next hour taking four-hundred and eighty years of celibacy out on her beautiful porcelain body.

After my *romp* with the seamstress, I stop in an accessory shop. The old clerk tries to direct my attention to the hats, but I'm more fascinated by the rows of spectacles. Partially the circular, tinted ones. When I try them on, I sigh in relief. They block the stinging burn of light bulbs.

We haggle over them, even though I have more than enough pounds to pay premium from the allowance Vec allotted me.

I leave that shop with my new tinted glasses, eager to hear Vec's opinion on my take of this new era's fashion.

CHAPTER 9

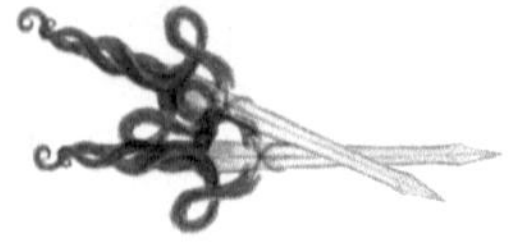

"**Y**ou look like a numskull." Vec sighs from across the dining room table.

"It's a lot better than the suits you force upon me."

"The outfit is passable, though I'd be lying if I said I didn't notice the stark medieval influence. You're lucky you chose a talented seamstress."

Oh, she was talented indeed.

I shake my head in dismissal, piercing my fork into the best-tasting chicken I've ever had. Spices in this era are easier to come by, so everything tastes like the gods themselves brought it down on a silver platter.

"The servants are spending the evening moving your belongings to the dormitories."

"What belongings? I own nothing besides a few changes of clothes and two daggers."

"You know what I mean. Just before I woke you, I bought all the items you'll require for your time at Roche. Nightclothes, school supplies. And an entire trunk of attire you refuse to wear."

I straighten my tinted frames. "What will I be doing every day?"

"I'll give you your official schedule tomorrow. But all your classes are for second years—crystal tinctures, tenets of modern core magic, secondary magic, and stone enhancing, to name a few."

"I thought you said core magic was a thing of the past."

"No, I said it differed from the four core magic abilities you're familiar with. Your magic is now referred to as atavistic magic. Venitors can still levitate and move objects and control gusts of air for combat, but conjuring illusions is a thing of the past. Modern magic has six tenets as opposed to the three that atavistic magic had."

Great. They probably believe the ability to conjure illusions is an ailment bestowed by the devil himself. "And their core tenets are?"

"Air manipulation, levitation, reflection, transmutation, regeneration, and enchantment. Don't ask, I don't have all night. Most venitors don't even have a basic grasp of all of them at graduation. You'll learn."

"And if I can't because of my blood?"

"You're Atticus Desimir. You always find a way."

Vec and I sit across the desk from Roche's headmaster, Ernest Montgomery. Before we left his townhouse, Vec disguised his youthful features into that of a middle-aged man. Even his signature blonde hair has streaks of gray. But age looks good on him.

Headmaster Montgomery and Vec talk like old friends with a long history, a wise investment on Vec's part and mine. He spent painstaking hours preparing for my awakening. Now, he's simply dotting his i's and crossing his t's to get me into the most prestigious university in London as a second year, which is apparently even more rare.

"Tell me about your first-year studies at Belworth University, Mr. Desimir." The headmaster folds his hands together. At forty years old, he is clean shaven with chestnut hair, free from even the smallest touch of gray.

I straighten my posture and recite what Vec and I rehearsed. "I excelled in all my courses in the Americas. West Virginia, to be precise." I motion to the card in front of him with near-perfect marks. "After the first year, my mother passed away, and I wanted to be closer to family, so Uncle Vec took me in." My gloved fists tighten around the wooden armrests at the mention of my mother. The story may be a farce, but her absence in my life is very real. Painful and suffocating. "Although I thought I would have to sacrifice my education for it, as no university would take a venitor student in during their second year."

"And that's where we come in." Headmaster Montgomery rests his hands behind his head, leaning back in his chair. "Your uncle has been a friend of mine for five years now. And after he did me a favor a few years back, this is the least I can do to repay him."

"Thank you again for this, Ernest," Vec says with a half-smile. "I'll never forget your generosity and understanding."

"There's no need to thank me." The headmaster stands and we follow suit. "You're free to start classes. If you have any issues with your studies, Mr. Desimir, feel free to stop by." The headmaster winks at me in a way that sends an uncomfortable shiver down my spine.

"Of—of course," I answer.

Vec shakes his hand. "And don't be shy, let's get drinks sometime. I'm sure you have lots to catch me up on since the wedding."

The headmaster chuckles. "Yes, indeed."

"Good. We'll be off now." Vec turns around and heads toward the door. "Come, Atticus."

I shake the headmaster's hand with haste and stride behind Vec until I catch up to him down the next hallway. High ceilings and detailed wooden architecture fill the halls of Roche University. We pass sculptures of legendary venitors and memorial paintings.

Roche's green-gold emblem hangs along one of the walls, the symbol of the ouroboros in the center. Their motto is printed on a plaque directly below:

Praestantia magica. Disciplina usque ad mortem.

Excellence in magic. Discipline until death.

"The headmaster is a little strange, if you ask me," I say. "Did you see the way he winked at me?"

"There's something you must know about Headmaster Montgomery," Vec says. "Though I've kept him close over the years for your benefit, I find him insufferable. And quite the pervert. Stay away from him."

"Isn't he married?"

"That man is only concerned about two things—his cock and anything he can stick it in. He's had more dalliances in his brief marriage than paramours I've had in the past half-century."

Vec and I enter one of the men's dormitory buildings on the far side of campus. It's five stories tall and must fit at least a thousand students. As we ascend the spiral stairwell to the third floor, many students have their doors open, and are rearranging their desks or dusting the grime of summer away.

When we arrive in front of the room, Vec places his hands on my shoulders. "Report to me at least every two weeks. Visit on the weekends if you can. If you don't visit, then send a telegram. And if I learn anything worthwhile, I'll contact you. Are you ready to see your room?"

"You're awfully dramatic."

"I'll take that as a yes." Vec whips open the door.

A guy sitting on one of the two beds quickly stands, hiding a book under his pillow.

Vec narrows his eyebrows. "Are we interrupting something?"

"No, sir." The guy stands straighter with his hands behind his back. "Just catching up on some reading for the semester. I'm Arlo de Vries. We'll be roommates."

Vec never told me anything about a roommate. If he had, I would have hired a hit on this boy long before the semester started. Or taken him out myself.

Arlo wears brown suspenders over a white shirt. His blonde hair is pulled back into a tiny ponytail against the nape of his neck. He's about a head shorter than me. Thinner too.

I glare at Vec out of the corner of my eye, but he ignores me.

"I'm Atticus Desimir. And this is Vec."

"Address me properly, boy," Vec snaps.

I'm taken aback by Vec's sudden change in personality. His false persona of guardian is really starting to piss me off.

"Sorry. *Uncle* Vec." I grit the words out with a clenched jaw and a sarcastic half-smile.

Vec shakes Arlo's hand. "I hope my nephew treats you well this school year. If he acts up, you let me know.

Arlo's mouth gapes. "I'm sure that won't be necessary—"

I fold my arms. "I'm twenty years old, Uncle Vec."

"Don't be disrespectful. What would my late sister think of your insolence?"

I don't flatter Vec's ego with an apology this time. "Arlo, I'm eager to get to know you better. Perhaps we can study together throughout the school year?"

Arlo smiles and nods.

Vec places his hands on both our shoulders. "Look, only a few minutes and you're already the best of friends. If you need nothing else, I'll be on my way."

I sit down on my new bed. "I'm fine. Goodbye, Uncle Vec."

Vec waves to the two of us. "Good day."

Once he's gone, I lean back on my hands and stare at Arlo. He seems nervous.

I smile deviously. "What were you reading?"

Arlo goes pale. "I—I said I was studying."

As if I believe that for a second. I stand, rushing to his bed. He yells at me to stop, to which I catch his head under my armpit and hold him there.

"I'll report you!" He wrestles against my grip, but I'm taller. Stronger.

When I grab the little booklet, he sounds as if he's going to cry.

I laugh as I open it, flipping through the pages. "Oh, how scandalous."

The booklet is filled with pages of promiscuous drawings of lewd women in compromising positions. As I flip deeper through the pages, the drawings slowly become more fixated on bondage. My arm relaxes slightly as I become mesmerized and entranced.

"Did you draw these?" I flip to another page of a woman pleasuring herself as a man watches. Arlo doesn't strike me as the dominant type, but I suppose anyone can be anybody.

Arlo escapes my loose hold and snatches the book from me. "Please don't tell anyone. It's a hobby of mine."

I ruffle his hair. "Arlo, I think we'll get along nicely. Do you take requests?"

"No!"

Pity. I have a few escapades he may enjoy adding to his little collection. "I'll keep your secret, as long as you pay no mind to what happens in my bed. If you're keen on it, I'll even let you watch."

Arlo frowns. "You're vile."

"Is that a yes?"

Arlo scratches the back of his head. "Just don't bring any girls back past midnight."

I extend my hand to him. "Deal."

Begrudgingly, he takes my gloved hand and shakes it.

Arlo offers to take me on a tour of the campus around dinner time. We eat in the dining hall together and he explains the workings of the university. Students use levitation magic to carry their plates to their tables. When the kitchen door opens, chefs multi-task with levitation magic. The food is heavenly, making me lick my plate clean.

Besides classrooms, Roche also has fighting arenas for dueling practice. Already, students are out practicing and use the different tenets of core magic to toss each other around. It's riveting, but when a guy uses a magic I don't recognize, my legs stiffen a bit. It will be a challenge to disguise my lack of new-age magic during classes. But I'll manage. I always do.

"There are plenty of parties to attend during the week, but they get a little rowdy," Arlo says as we walk back to our dorm room.

I adjust my tinted glasses. "Do I look like the prudish type to you?"

He sighs. "No."

Arlo hates having me as a roommate, just as much as I loathe sharing a room with him. But our perspectives are alike when it comes to sex—women are enchanting creatures. Masterpieces that deserve to be tended to and sculpted.

When we turn in for the night. Arlo seems bothered that I don't sleep with any clothes. It's preferable to wearing a ghostly costume to sleep as he does.

As I doze off, I think of Dominic. What does he look like? Are his eyes a dark shade of green like mine, or something brighter? Or what does it feel like to hold such forbidden magic and the weight of its secrecy?

I chuckle to myself. *I suppose I'll find out soon enough.*

CHAPTER 10

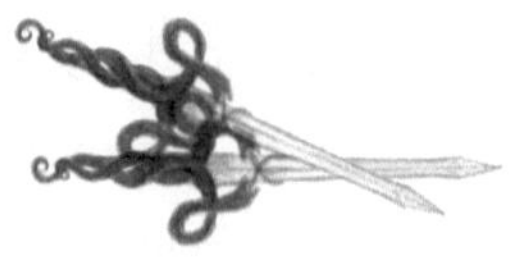

DOMINIC

Last night I dreamt of a train. A massive thing, with an endless number of boxcars. It moved with more speed than I thought possible, careening down the tracks with no sign of stopping. I had tried to escape, but in the end, it derailed and I awoke in a cold sweat.

I don't often dream, but when I do, it's always the same nightmare. Sometimes there are too many boxcars. Sometimes too few. Some dreams have people. Most do not. On occasion, I even survive the crash, waiting in agony for rescue to arrive. It never does.

What's always the same is that there is a train, and I always die.

Memories of the dream followed me through the dormitory halls that morning, to the dining hall, and into the secondary magic classroom. I was the first to arrive. Now I sit alone, as I watch Professor Felicity Doyle at the front of the classroom, arranging different gemstones on the display table in front of her desk. Stones that can enhance our core magic and help us gain abilities we don't naturally carry.

Oliver enters the classroom and plops down into the seat next to me. "No way. Is Dominic Ashworth—early to class?" Last I saw my roommate, he was sound asleep, unbothered by any outbursts from my early morning nightmare. Today, like every day, he wears a collar tall enough to cover both sides of his neck. It's not the most fashionable, but I know why he does it.

"I couldn't sleep." I know from experience not to waste time attempting to. I cut my losses and walked around campus until the sun rose.

"That explains why you were already gone when I woke." Oliver pulls his notebook and fountain pen out of his briefcase. He's always been the responsible one. The one siding with authority and scoring perfect marks. The one who makes me listen to the voice of reason, even when I don't want to.

I'm skilled at magic and score decent marks. Decent enough to make my father happy. But I know more about alternative forms of magic than other students. Abilities they can only dream of possessing. Magic that's forbidden by society—but useful when wielded by the correct hand. Without having Oliver around to keep my wild ideas in check, I might have already delved too deep and regretted the outcome. Not that he knows about my family's magic.

More students funnel in. Eventually the clock tower bell gongs across campus, and Professor Doyle takes her place in the front of the room. She whips her fingers out, manipulating the air to shut the doors.

"Welcome, students. I hope your summer and holidays were wonderful." Professor Doyle is younger than most professors; only a decade older than me. Most of the men in university gawk at her, despite her obvious attempts to hide her beauty with oversized glasses and a tight blonde bun. "Let's take attendance, shall we?"

While Professor Doyle goes down the list of names, I tune out as I stare across the room at the girl in the second row of the round classroom—Haylow Solace. Every time I look at her, even accidentally, I go weak in the knees.

The doors of the classroom fly open so suddenly, they almost hit the wall.

I spin around, my mouth gaping at the sight.

A man dressed like darkness enters, stepping down the stairs of the tiered classroom like he owns the place. The air of his black overcoat is like a symphony of dark notes, only amplifying the chilling obsidian of his curly hair. Metal bits are sewn into the leather of his gloves. And is he wearing tinted glasses—indoors?

"I'm sorry, am I late?" the guy asks, his gaze locked on Professor Doyle.

"I'm afraid so, Mr.—"

"Desimir. My name is Atticus Desimir." He smiles.

I don't remember Atticus from first year. He must've not made much of a name for himself. Most likely, he has low marks and has kept to himself within the program. His father is probably someone important. He'll have a rude awakening when he realizes Roche won't put up with pompous arrogance for long.

Professor Doyle's smile draws into a curt line. At least the professor thinks as I do. "Ah. Well, Mr. Desimir, since it's the first day, I won't mark you tardy. Please, take a seat."

Atticus slides into a seat next to Arlo de Vries. Arlo's thin frame looks even smaller sitting next to him.

I watch him—Atticus—as he leans back in his seat, crossing his legs while Professor Doyle finishes up attendance. There's this permanent smirk on his face that tells me all I need to know about the kind of guy he is. Girls whisper and giggle as they stare at him.

My body tenses as his eyes lock onto Haylow. Even though she can't see him from where he sits behind her, he tilts his head as if he just placed a mark on her.

Now I definitely don't like him.

After Professor Doyle finishes taking attendance, she holds up a stone. "Let's begin. Can anyone tell me what orange sapphire does when combined with air manipulation?"

A small woman in the first row raises her hand and speaks before she's even called on. "I know! It allows the user to create a gust of smoke!"

"Correct, Edith."

Oliver takes vigorous notes as the professor explains sapphire and the uses of each color. It's a refresher lesson for the first day of class. I let my mind wander, and seemingly against my will, my gaze falls to Atticus. He sits aloof, paying no more attention than I am.

He doesn't seem like the kind of guy who has any aspirations to go to university, let alone excel enough in his youth to make it into a university as prestigious as Roche. It seems all he wants is girls by the way he scans the room, undressing everyone with his eyes.

Even Professor Doyle.

Every time he looks back at Haylow, my body tightens. Just because I haven't locked her down yet doesn't mean I don't plan to. And if this new guy gets in the way of that—

"Dominic, would you care to demonstrate?" Professor Doyle asks.

I snap out of my trance. "I'm sorry?"

"After excelling in last term's year-end exam, I thought I'd allow you to show the class just how effective blue amethyst can be in a combat situation. Of course, you'll need a partner to assist." She scans the audience.

Atticus stands and straightens his coat. "Allow me to assist."

"Splendid!" Professor Doyle waves him to the front.

Great. Just dandy. I can't wait to duel with this pompous asshole. But if I must, I'll show him what I'm made of. Guys like him need to be reminded that Roche isn't prestigious for nothing. Maybe it will slap that devious smile right off his face.

Atticus and I make our way to the front of the classroom and stand facing each other from several feet away.

She places a walnut-size piece of blue amethyst in each of our hands. "Now remember, most stones must be touching your skin for you to extract their magic. Hold on to them tightly."

Atticus slips one of his gloves off. He bounces the stone in his bare hand, feeling its weight. I simply let the stone's energy seep into my skin, letting it flow free. All stones are unique, but blue amethyst is deceptive like water. Grasp too tight within your mind, and the power flees.

"On the count of three, you may both cast your energy into your stones and perform the attack."

I bite my inner lip, suppressing a smile. I can already tell Atticus is in over his head. His stance is wrong, too stiff. His grip on the stone is vice-like.

"Ready? One, two—three!"

I cast my energy into the stone as I push my right hand out toward Atticus.

Before the stone's powers come to fruition, an image of a rabid wolf pops into my head, scratching at my face. It's so real it feels as though I'm actually staring one right in the teeth.

I lose control of the stone. Atticus thrusts out his hand, casting the stone's energy into me. A shriek of blue noise knocks me back, slamming me into a stack of books on the floor.

When I regain my senses, the entire class is on their feet. Professor Doyle runs over and helps me up, but I wave her off and stand on my own. *What just happened?* I was fine and in control. Then some strange image popped into my head and made me lose my wits? I know I barely slept last night, but was some sleep-deprived, intrusive daydream really enough to knock me off my game?

Professor Doyle turns back to Atticus. "Excellent work, Atticus, though it may be best to hold back its power in a classroom. Nonetheless, I'm impressed."

Atticus stares at me, his infuriating smirk beginning to rise. "Sorry about that." He extends his hand in apology, and I brush him off, walking shamefully back to my seat.

As I pass by Haylow, she giggles with the girl next to her. Is she laughing at my failure? Or gawking over Atticus? My feet shuffle fast until I slump into my chair. How much worse can this day get?

For the remainder of class, I ignore all the notes Oliver passes to me. It takes all my energy not to glare at Atticus.

Professor Doyle dismisses class early for our first day.

Oliver stands and starts packing up his things. "Should I even tell you what I'm thinking?"

"He caught me off guard, is all. If I duel him again, I'll win," I say.

Oliver gives me a sympathetic smile. Two girls walk up to Atticus, their faces lined with blushes. I roll my eyes. But Atticus doesn't give them any attention.

Instead, he's staring at me.

"What is that guy's problem?" I ask Oliver.

Oliver looks over his shoulder. "Perhaps he's ready to give you that rematch you just spoke of."

Atticus strides past the girls, heading in our direction.

"My gods, he's coming this way." I pack my things up quicker.

"He seems friendly enough. Just give him a chance, Dominic."

Before I can buckle my briefcase and rush out, Atticus is in front of Oliver and me.

He places a palm on my desk, resting his body weight on the surface. "That was quite the duel."

"I'm good with blue amethyst. You just caught me at a bad moment."

"Oh, did I now?"

Oliver extends a hand to Atticus. "I'm Oliver Edevane."

Atticus shakes his hand. "Atticus Desimir. Nice to meet you."

"You made quite the first impression on the class." Oliver chuckles. "I've heard rumors that a new second year was joining our class. How did you manage that?"

"I have my ways."

So he broke Roche's long-standing tradition not to admit new students after the first year? How deep in nepotism is this guy?

"There's a party at Haylow's home tonight to celebrate the new year. You should come," Oliver says.

My eyes widen. "But Oliver—" How could he invite Atticus? Isn't it obvious that I don't want to be anywhere near him?

"Is there a problem?" Atticus's dark green eyes stare at me through the tinted frames.

I look to Oliver. "I...I just think maybe you should ask Haylow for permission before inviting people to her home. That's all."

"What are you talking about? It's an open invitation to all students. You know this, Dominic." Oliver chuckles, patting my back. Then he turns back to Atticus. "Well, will you join us?"

Atticus smiles. "I would be delighted."

"Smashing. Can't wait to see you there. I'll be off now." Oliver grabs his things and hurries away.

"Wait!" I attempt to reach for Oliver, but he's beyond my grasp and gone from the classroom before I can say another word.

I stand there with Atticus, scratching the back of my neck, avoiding his eyes. Behind him, three girls wait to speak with him.

I fold my arms. "You have an audience."

Atticus looks over his shoulder. "I suppose I do. I'll see you tonight then?"

"Yes." I hold back the disdain in my voice.

If Haylow wasn't hosting this party, I would be a no show.

CHAPTER II

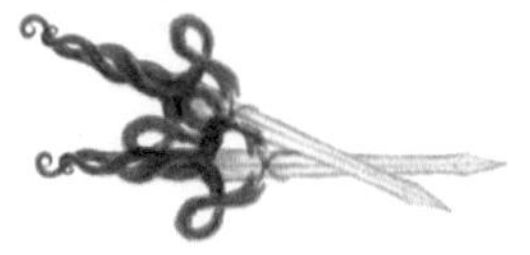

ATTICUS

I sit on the edge of my bed in the dorm, flipping through my textbook on stone magic.

Oh, Dominic, did you really expect me to feed into your ego? Let you win? Perhaps I should have let you. But you need to know straight away that I'm stronger than you. That at any moment I could overpower you. It's only fair that I balance the scales right from the get-go. With the Blythesea magic you secretly hold, I really am no match for you. But you already knew that, didn't you?

I was lucky that stone magic is almost identical to herbal magic. Nobody from my time knew that stones could be used in this way. Here we were adorning them in jewelry, unaware of their hidden magical properties. It appears stones must be touching the skin for them to work. With herbal magic, all I had to do was have it somewhere on my person.

Though I had to use Desimir magic to beat Dominic, I knew he had me from the start. If I hadn't distracted him, he may have thought I was weak. It's good to know I can use stone magic. It's one less thing to worry about.

Arlo sits at his desk, doodling.

"Are you coming to the party tonight?" I ask him.

"I'm not much of a party guy." He doesn't look up from his drawing.

I walk over to his desk and stare at the lewd act of pleasure he's drawing. Arlo may not look like the type who knows how to please a woman, but his drawings say otherwise. If a lady overlooked his short and scrawny nature and gave him a chance, I'm sure he'd be the most sought out man on campus. He sure seems to know what a woman likes.

What they *actually* like.

"I'll leave you to your—hobbies—then." I grab my coat and leave the dorms for my night of fun.

As I walk to the edge of campus, I ignore the stares from venitor and venitrix students. Maybe Vec was right about my attire, but I'd rather garner a few curious looks than wear the ridiculous outfits they have on.

I find the townhouse address on a cobblestone street a tram ride away. Such an interesting contraption. It doesn't even need horses to move.

The party is at the residence of Haylow Solace. From what I hear, this is only one of the many homes her wealthy father owns, and this is one of their smaller properties. Still, it's large for a home in the city.

When I enter, Roche students are everywhere—couches, chairs, the stairwell, leaning against walls in conversation. Many of them have crystal glasses in their hands filled with various liquids. A quartet is playing in the corner of the sitting room.

The home is similar in design to Vec's. I push through the crowds of students until I'm in the dining room. Empty glasses and bottles of wine and liquor fill the table.

I read the labels on the bottles, then decant a beverage called bourbon into a glass goblet.

"Woah!" Oliver comes up behind me with a glass of white wine in his hand. "Maybe just sip that. Why are you using a red wine glass?"

"I don't know." I take a sniff of the drink and my eyes water. "Does it need a specific vessel to get the job done?"

Oliver laughs. "I suppose you're right. Come. Dominic and I have seats over on a couch."

I follow Oliver into the next room. Dominic sits on a couch, his hand raking once through his auburn hair. When he sees me, his brown eyes turn to ice. Whether or not Dominic knows it, darkness suits him, enhancing his already handsome features.

I beat Oliver to the couch and take a seat directly in the middle and extend my arms over the back, still holding my glass in one hand. Oliver takes the spot on my right.

Dominic moves to the edge of the couch, avoiding my arm like the plague. "Are you enjoying yourself?" he asks sarcastically.

"Very much." I smile at his unsubtle annoyance. Here I am, sitting next to the man who will make everything I've dreamed about for years a reality. But that reality will only happen if I can get close to him. Slowly, but surely, he needs to trust me.

I nudge Dominic's arm, signaling him to take a drink from his glass. Dominic rolls his eyes, but concedes, taking a larger-than-expected gulp of hard liquor.

I wait until his eyes grow glassy with inebriation. "Tell me about yourself, Dominic. What's your story?"

His eyes move rapidly, as if he's holding back the slurry of his family's secrets and misfortunes. How taxing it must be to choose his words wisely in every conversation. After all, one wrong move would expose his prominent, scandalous family name.

"There's not much to know. I come from the Ashworth family. My father made his fortune in the iron industry. I also have a sister and a brother."

"What do your siblings do?" I lift the glass to my mouth, taking a swallow of the burning bourbon. Perhaps Oliver was right. I poured too much, even with my tolerance.

"My sister graduated from Charlington recently with her degree in venitor magic. She's engaged. My brother—"

Oliver reaches across me and places a hand on Dominic's forearm. "You don't have to speak of him if you don't want to."

Dominic's brother is a hard topic for him? Are they enemies? Did he pass away?

"No—it's all right." Dominic takes a deep breath, the alcohol controlling his next words. "My brother, Archer, was in a train derailment two years ago. He survived, but his brain no longer works. He's been in a stasis ward ever since. Regenerative stone magic keeps his body alive."

His brother's mind no longer works? "And there's no magic that can help?"

"No." Righteous anger paints Dominic's face. "But ever since it happened, I've been looking for a way to bring him back. As long as his body stays alive, I can still save him. There must be a solution. And I'll do nearly anything to find it."

Anything?

There it is.

My way in.

Vec likely knows a way to awaken Dominic's brother. If Dominic will do *anything* to save his brother, I can mold him. Extort him. If Juni were in the same situation, I'd do virtually anything to help her. Dominic and I are one and the same, and I know better than anyone what it's like to lose a sibling.

At the passing thought of Juni, reminders of her face bleed into my mind. I take a large swig of my drink.

"I'm so sorry to hear that." I lean forward and rest my forearms on my lap, giving Dominic his space.

Dominic nods.

The host, Haylow Solace, enters the room with a glass of wine in hand. Dominic immediately straightens his tie and smooths back his hair.

Oh, does Dominic have a crush? Though she's the girl I had my eye on earlier in class, I'll make sure not to fuck her. Dominic may forgive me for humiliating him in front of our peers, but screwing his girl would be unforgivable.

Haylow looks around the room and then heads back to the kitchen.

Dominic stands. "Excuse me. I want to thank our host." He follows after her.

Dominic, you dog.

Oliver stands up, stretching his arms. "I'm going to get some fresh air. It's dreadfully hot in here."

"Take all the time you need," I say.

I inspect the hoard of students in casual conversation around me. Most of them come from extreme wealth. But there is a peer or two who look out of place. Their outfits just barely meet the standard to be accepted by Roche's society. Or they have a few more stray hairs than their noble peers.

A girl sits down in the empty spot to my right. She has a feisty appearance and her dark locks flow like raven wings. "Atticus, right?"

"That's me."

"Need company?" She scoots closer to me, her rosy face glazed over with lust.

I lace my hand around her waist, pulling her closer. "Company? From a gorgeous girl like you? Always."

We're about to have a grand old time.

CHAPTER 12

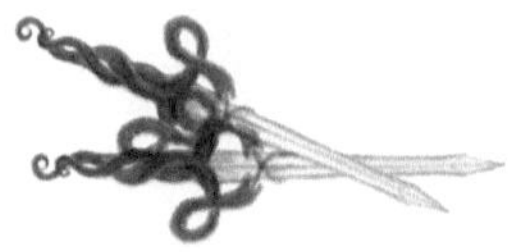

DOMINIC

*Y*ou *can do this, Dominic, just speak to her.*

I stand at the threshold of the kitchen, watching Haylow converse with a servant. Even in her stress, she's beautiful, her dark hair pinned up into an elegant updo. A gray dress lines her perfect form, the gown likely from one of the finest seamstresses in London. She's everything I dream about. Everything I breathe.

A maid walks away, and Haylow pinches the bridge of her nose.

I approach her from the side. "Miss Solace?"

"Oh, hello, Dominic. I'm so glad you could make it." She smiles, but it's not enough to conceal her concern.

"Is everything all right? Is there anything I can assist with?"

Her eyes brighten, making my heart pound faster. "Well, there are more guests than I anticipated, and I'm running low on glasses. On the second floor, there's a cabinet with more. I just haven't found time to grab them yet. And to make matters worse, someone broke a vase in the back room, and I still have to clean that up, as the maids are too busy. It seems I keep having to put fires out."

"I could grab them for you." I stand taller. "And I could clean up the vase."

She smiles widely. "Would you really? You're a lifesaver!"

"I'm happy to do it. This is your party; you should enjoy it." I swallow. "And I've been meaning to ask, maybe after class sometime—"

One of her friends walks in. "Haylow, more guests have arrived."

Haylow turns back to me. "Dominic, would you excuse me? I'd like to go greet them."

The light inside me flickers out. "Yes, of course."

My shoulders slump as I make my way to the back room. I curse under my breath as I clean up bits of the broken vase with my levitation magic. It takes longer than expected to find all the shards strewn across the marble floor and in the crevices, even with magic.

I'm still grumbling under my breath as I walk up the stairwell. It was just my luck to be interrupted by her insufferable friend when I had finally found the confidence to make my move. I sigh.

There are three years of classes left. I'll have another chance.

I'm not sure which room holds the cabinet. Haylow's primary residence is at her mansion on the other side of London, so her family isn't here. All these rooms should be safe to enter.

I turn the handle of the first door and push it open.

Bloody hell!

Bound at the wrists to the bedpost, a woman moans and writhes, her back arched as Atticus slams inside her.

"You can take it," Atticus grunts out. Even in his nakedness, he's still wearing those damn glasses.

I close my eyes. "I'm so sorry!" *Does he have no decency?* I open one eye enough to see him smirking at me.

"Oh, do you need something, Dominic?" Atticus slows his thrusting, but he doesn't stop, not an ounce of shame in his expression.

"No! Yes! Glasses from the cabinet." Which is in this room, to my horror. Why am I still in here? "I'll be outside."

He calls after me to just go ahead and grab what I need, but I refuse and slam the door. Then I slump down against the wall.

I knew it. Atticus is a madman.

I cover my ears to block out the noises, but it isn't enough. Grunts and moans still seep out of the room, along with the vile things he says to her.

And to think I opened up to him about my brother. He didn't deserve to hear about Archer, but I didn't want him to think I was fragile. He's already humiliated me enough.

A few minutes later, the door opens. The girl leaves the room first, fully dressed. Atticus is still shirtless and leans against the door frame. He's stronger than most men my age, corded in muscle, as if he works in hard labor. "Sorry you had to see that. Can't blame a man for wanting to have a little fun, right?"

I scoff and rise to my feet. "That girl is from a respectable family."

"With the mouth on her? I'm sure it's all just a ruse."

He doesn't budge from blocking the door frame, so I slide past him, my wrist accidentally brushing his abdomen. He watches me while I fit as many glasses between my fingers as possible.

Once I have enough, I barrel past him to leave. "Goodnight, Atticus."

"What? You're leaving?"

I refuse to look at him. "This night has been more than enough." Then I descend the stairs without another word.

After I deliver the glasses to the dining room, I leave without saying goodbye to Oliver or Haylow.

And especially not Atticus.

"How has he been?" I ask.

The nurse readjusts my brother's position to prevent bedsores. "Stable. Enough to live up to seventy more years as long as the regeneration stone stays strong." She gives me a sympathetic smile.

With a dash of pity.

Every time I visit Archer, I ask her or the physician the same set of questions.

Any updates? Is the magic holding?

Is there any hope he'll wake up?

She leaves me alone with my brother. To think he'll be able to start practicing magic if he wakes up by his sixteenth birthday, the legal age to wield magic in London. He'll start at a respectable boarding school, and I'm sure he'll be at the top of his class.

Swirls of blue and green magic circle his head and chest, the regeneration powered by a large red beryl gemstone on his bedside table. A beaded line wraps around his upper arm, connecting him to the beryl. The stone is the size of a coconut and large enough to last a lifetime. It cost my father our holiday home to afford it. But nobody cared about trips or leisure once the accident happened. We still don't.

I hold on to Archer's limp hand, squeezing tightly. "Can you hear me?"

He gives me nothing but silent breathing.

"I started my second year of university this week. You'd love the classes. I know you would." I turn my head away for just a second, my throat choking up. "One day, you'll attend Roche, and I'll be at your graduation. You'll become one of the most skilled and powerful venitors in all of Europe."

Still nothing. It's been like this for the last two years. Me speaking. He pretending to listen. This last summer, I visited venitors and venitrixes around the continent, searching for solutions. All I found were some half-baked theories and con artists.

My father didn't know I was searching for treatments for Archer on my trip. He thought I was receiving tutoring from high-ranked venitors.

The two of us have very differing views. At one point, he brought up the notion of letting Archer pass away. I completely lost it, shattering a newly purchased vase against the wall. It made my mother cry.

We never spoke of it again, but it's an argument always lingering in the background at luncheons and holiday seasons. I can tell everyone is on edge when Father and I are together, just waiting for one of us to say a wrong word.

I place a kiss on Archer's forehead, readjust his pillow, then head toward the stasis ward's courtyard to travel back to Roche.

Archer, I'll find a way to wake you up, no matter how far into the depths of Hades I must reach.

CHAPTER 13

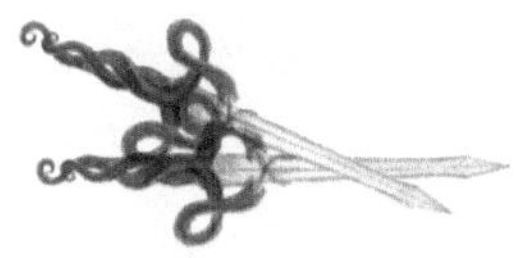

ATTICUS

I kick my feet up on the couch in Vec's study. "How many more weeks of this do I have?"

Vec dips his brush in blue paint. "You've been at Roche less than a week. Don't complain." He paints a picture of a swan from memory using every color of the rainbow. It's a hobby he picked up in the late 1400s while I was asleep. He's been painting ever since. Decades ago, he even created an alias to sell them at high prices and grow his estate. He's a prodigy around London.

"I wasn't complaining," I say.

"I've been alive a long time, Atticus. I know when someone is using a sentence to complain."

"There are just so many classes."

"Uh huh."

"And I keep having to use illusions from atavistic magic to appear as though I'm doing the same type of magic as them."

"You what!" He puts down his paint supplies and turns to me, folding his arms.

"I know you said never to use illusion core magic, but I had no choice. They're pulling water from fruit to use in combat."

"Atticus, someone may notice your magic is different."

"Would you rather I failed?"

Vec clenches his jaw. "No. But I'd prefer you find a discreet tutor to see if you're able to wield this magic without resorting to the old methods." He sighs. "As long as you didn't use Desimir magic, I'll forgive this one."

Perhaps I'll keep that one a secret from Vec.

Vec turns back to working on his painting. "How have things been with Dominic?"

"I'm positive he hates me, but he'll come around."

Vec groans. "What did you do now?"

"Nothing! Well, not nothing. I humiliated him in front of the class. And then just when I thought he may forgive me, and after he opened up to me about his brother, he walked in on me—letting off a little steam with a pretty lady."

"You're hopeless." Vec sighs. "What's this thing about his brother?"

"His mind no longer works. They're keeping his body alive with stones. Dominic said he'd do *anything* to wake him up. *Anything,* Vec. And as an immortal, I figured you may know a thing or two about healing this ailment."

Vec works on painting the outstretched wings of the swan. "Hmm... There are ways to bring a brain back to life. But it's difficult. It will take a lot of effort on your part, and probably his, as it requires the blood of an immediate relative."

"Go on." This is brilliant. If Vec knows a way to revive Dominic's brother, I'll be slitting immortal throats in no time.

"It requires a combination of blood, herbs, stones, and, of course, an immense source of magical energy."

"Like a powerful user? Or an immortal?"

Vec scratches his temple. "More like—an artifact."

My face drops. Vec should have just said from the beginning that it was impossible. "There are only eight of them in the world."

"Yes there are, but lucky for you, all of them are in the possession of world leaders, including the prime minister here in London."

The artifact is the exact thing that got my father killed. They give every country who is part of the United Magic Council an artifact to keep their countries safe from each other. The artifact can destroy entire nations. Most are kept behind lock and key, even from their owners, due to their whispering temptations. Some say they're evil at their core. Only one has ever been used, and that was before I was born. It was just supposed to be a contained test, but it went horribly wrong. The test destroyed three island nations and set off a massive hurricane, causing even more destruction. But it also has other mysterious abilities not known to most. Though I'm sure the immortals have been around long enough to know exactly what they do.

"Atticus, I understand if you want nothing to do with the artifact."

"I can handle it." My words are sharp. If helping Dominic will allow me to take his magic, I'll steal the very thing my father dedicated his life to protect.

"Stealing it won't be easy. You must do it with the utmost discretion, and no one must know it was ever gone. When you're done with it, you must put it back. If the prime minister learns someone stole it, it could start wars between nations."

I pretend as if I have paper and a fountain pen in my hands, writing his words carefully. "Don't keep the artifact and commit world domination. Duly noted."

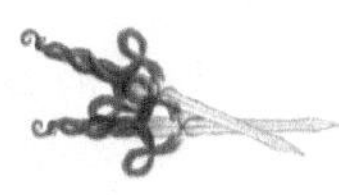

I'm supposed to be headed to Dominic's dorm room, but let's just say I got a little—distracted.

My tongue explores the mouth of the guy I have pressed against the closet wall, my gloved fingers tangling through his hair. A girl is sandwiched between us, undoing my faux gambeson and shirt, nibbling along my chest. The two are courting one another.

We all got to talking after class about the nature of their intimacy and how they were looking for a little more *excitement*. I was happy to oblige, barely able to keep my hands off either of them as we laughed and walked through the halls to find some privacy.

I suck on his neck, making him groan, his chest vibrating against mine. But it's been some time since I've given his girl some attention, so I break the kiss and lean down to capture her lips.

I move to her neck, leaving my mark there, just like the one I left on her lover. This closet is small, holding janitorial supplies. Perhaps I should have chosen a better spot.

Just as I undo the top few buttons of her blouse, the closet door flies open, the hallway light flooding in.

We're fucked.

The girl gasps and quickly refastens the buttons. The guy runs a hand down his face. I grit my teeth while I fix my clothes.

Professor Felicity Doyle stands there, completely speechless. Times may have changed since I've been asleep, but not enough for this not to be grounds for expulsion from Roche. I must think quickly.

"I—I can't believe this. I must report all three of you to the headmaster!" Professor Doyle places a hand against her forehead. To my surprise, there's a slight blush rising along her cheeks. She bites down on her lower lip, but her teeth quickly retreat as I notice. *Interesting.*

That evidence alone is all I need to get out of this. I'll start by taking the fall. "Professor, it's not their fault. We were trying a strange enchantment spell, and it all went wrong. I'm the one who cast it incorrectly."

She frowns. "I know of no such spell."

"It's a rare enchantment. Though somehow I managed to cast it on all three of us. How we ended up like this is beyond me, but thanks to your entry, the distraction broke the trance. Let's go to your office, and I'll show you where I found it. But please, do not blame..." Dammit, what were their names? "Do not blame my peers for my horrible idea."

Professor Doyle holds her temples, looking completely unconvinced. "If you can prove it, which you can't, then we'll forget this situation ever happened."

"Of course, professor." As I exit the closet, the couple gives me nods of gratitude.

I follow Professor Doyle to her office. The closet was supposed to be a safe, fun place for a midday rendezvous. Shame she had to ruin it, but little does she know, I always have the last laugh.

As she shuts the office door, I take a seat on the opposite side of her desk while she searches her shelves for the textbooks. "If you're lying to me, you could be suspended or even expelled."

There's no way I'll be able to prove it to her. I've barely even cracked open my textbook. Cooking up an explanation to cover my lie will be near impossible in a world where I don't know the magic.

But if there's one thing I do know, it's women.

"Tell me, professor, why aren't you married yet?"

She gives me an uncomfortable stare. "That's improper for a student to ask."

I know her type. And when I figure someone out, I practically own them. Everything from her mind to her body is a game of chess, and I'm going straight for a checkmate. "You're a beautiful woman, you know?"

"Mr. Desimir. That is highly inappropriate."

I stand from my seat and pace toward her. "Oh? Paying someone a genuine compliment is inappropriate, is it? Do you consider it lewd to make truthful observations as well?"

She turns around to face me, her back inches from touching the bookshelf. Her mouth opens to say something.

"Don't play coy, Felicity. Do you really think I haven't noticed the way you look at me while you preach your lectures? Or the way hues of red crept down your neck and chest when you saw the three of us tangled together in that closet? The way your breath hitched."

Her eyes dart in a panic. "Mr. Desimir—"

I place a gloved finger against her lips and shush her. "You spend week after week attracting men who don't deserve you. If you would stop trying to hide this face—" I reach behind her head, unclasping her clip, letting her blonde hair tumble down her back. Then I remove her large glasses. "—you wouldn't be able to stop the line of suitors. Now tell me...why do you hide?"

"I—I don't know." Professor Doyle stares up at me, her chest rising and falling deeply. Her cheeks grow rosier every second. Felicity can't be older than twenty-nine, maybe thirty. She still holds the beauty of youth.

This will be fun.

I lightly wrap my gloved hand around the front of her neck and lean into her, pressing her into the shelf. My lips are inches from hers. "Since the moment you first saw me, I became your forbidden fruit."

My mouth captures hers, working her lips gently. She doesn't push me away. By now, she must realize I'm a total liar, but she's already gone far enough for me to blackmail her. Besides, she wants this just as much as I do.

My hands explore her body, moving from her abdomen up to her breasts. She finally submits, wrapping her arms around my neck, deepening the kiss. My lips become more ravenous; my desire still pent up from earlier.

I push up the long skirt of her dress and hoist her up so her legs circle my waist. My lips stayed glued to hers as I move us to her desk, pushing her papers aside, and laying her on her back.

"Mr. Desimir—"

I shush her. "Let my tongue do the talking."

I undress both of us and splay her out on the table for me. My mouth works her clit, drawing out her pleasure with tantalizing detail. When I bring her to her first release, she looks up at me as if she's never experienced the *little death* before. And I have no doubt that was her first one.

I move to her chair, having her straddle me. She moans as she lowers herself onto my cock. She's so tight I can't help but groan.

"Good girl, Felicity." I hold her hips, enhancing her movements. "You're doing so well, don't stop."

My head dips back. Little sounds leave her throat when I reach down, playing with her bundle of nerves with deep and calculated movements.

It doesn't take long for her to cry out my name. And my name on her lips sends me over the edge, my hips bucking up into her as I come hard.

As my orgasm fades, I bite along her collarbone, whispering tall tales into her goosebumped skin.

She slumps in my arms. I hold her limp, yet tranquil, body for a few minutes as we sit there in silence. She must have regrets. I have none, but I need to keep her complacent and leave her wanting more.

I trace the details of her face. "Such loveliness. You're an angel, Felicity." I make sure to use her first name to make her feel young again.

"T—thank you." Her eyes soften. *Good.* She climbs off my lap and picks up the remnants of her clothing.

Professor Doyle faces away from me while we both get dressed, as if I didn't just see her completely naked.

"You're free to go." She stares at the corner. "Let's just forget this ever happened."

I step forward and kiss her cheek. Her face turns a soft rose.

The entire walk back to my dorm, I can't help but smile. In the end, the need for love and acceptance will always be humanity's greatest pawn.

And I believe that, my dear...

Is checkmate.

I knock at Dominic's door with deceptive words in tow. All last night, I rehearsed my words carefully. It's not like I can say to Dominic, *I know how to awaken your brother; now let's get to work. Also, in exchange, would you mind handing over your Blythesea magic? Don't ask me how I know.*

That would be a horrible idea. He may kill me right then and there.

Oliver answers the door. His light brown hair is messy, as if he's just woken from a midday nap. "Atticus, it's nice to see you" He keeps the door half-closed and looks over his shoulder. He mouths something behind the door to another party in the room.

"May I speak to Dominic?" I can't see Dominic with the way Oliver's blocking the door, but I know he's here, even though he's doing a horrible job of hiding it.

"He's uh—" Oliver looks across the room one more time and narrows his eyebrows, mouthing the word "now" at Dominic. "Yes, just give him a minute, and I'll send him out."

Oliver shuts the door. They immediately start arguing, the walls thin enough for me to overhear a few keywords like "promiscuous" and "asshole."

The door swings open, and Dominic stands there dressed in a long-sleeved cotton shirt tucked into trousers. The two uppermost buttons are unfastened. Dominic is rather dashing, isn't he?

"Can I help you?" His words are sharp, almost menacing.

I stare at the revealing sliver of his bare chest, and my body nearly reacts. Did I not get all my steam out with Professor Doyle? How annoying. I'll have to take care of myself once more when I arrive back to my room. Hopefully, Arlo isn't back at the dorm. But even if he is, he can just shut his eyes and block his ears like I instructed him to do yesterday.

"I'm here to apologize. I'm sorry I didn't lock the door," I say.

Dominic scoffs. "You really think that's the only reason?" He tries to slam the door in my face.

I catch the edge with my palm and pry it back open. "Dominic, let me make it up to you. Come out with me tonight. I found a lovely place on Roshinere Street. Let me treat you to a few drinks. I'd prefer not to start this school year off poorly."

Dominic's clenched jaw softens. His eyes move in contemplation. He has a keen sense of discernment; I can feel it. Deep down, he knows something is off about me. But right now, he can't see past the wicked display he walked in on at Haylow's party.

"Fine," he says.

Yes, *finally*. "I'm so glad. Meet me tonight at Rosette's Palace at seven o'clock."

Little do you know, Dominic, you have taken one step closer to becoming ensnared in my clutches.

CHAPTER 14

DOMINIC

I take a step back from the doors of the lewd establishment. Atticus never told me we were meeting at a gentlemen's club. Why did I let him convince me to meet up tonight? This is the most idiotic thing I've done. And for all of it, I blame Oliver.

Men step past me and into the establishment. I breathe in, gathering my wits, and follow behind them. The room is filled with men drinking and laughing, scantily clad women, and the smoke of cigars.

I know not all gentlemen's clubs are bad... No, who am I kidding? They're all sleazy. It doesn't matter how much leather, premium liquor, and mahogany you put into a gentlemen's club; it remains a place for men to commit pure debauchery.

It's a higher end club, and only someone with great wealth can afford a place like this. Which means Atticus may be better off than I thought. I wonder what his family does.

"Dominic, over here!"

Over in one of the corners, Atticus waves me down from where he sits on a leather chair, a drink in one hand, and a girl's waist in the other. She's wearing so little, she may as well be naked. There's a small table next to him and an empty chair, unfortunately, for me.

"I didn't realize you frequented such clubs, Atticus." I take a seat across from him. If the police caught wind of this club, they would shut it down for solicitation. That is, if the commissioner wasn't across the room this very second with his tongue down a girl's throat. What a horrible world we live in.

A waitress struts over to us. "Can I get you anything?"

"No." I keep my voice flat.

"Oh, Dominic, don't be boring. I'm paying. Tell the pretty woman your order unless you want me to order double of something you don't want."

I narrow my eyes at him, then turn to the waitress. "I'll have a—"

I'm interrupted by the noises of the scantily clad girl moaning while she kisses Atticus.

"I—" I keep my eyes straight on the waitress. "Just bring me the strongest, darkest liquor you have."

The waitress leaves. I turn to Atticus, doing my best to dissociate from watching the girl's lips on his neck and his gloved hands gripping and caressing her thighs.

"Do you mind, Atticus?"

Atticus breaks away from the girl's lips and chuckles. "Oh, you'd like some company too?" He looks around the room, then waves over another girl, who rushes over quicker than the curse words I'm ready to deliver. "I'm sorry. I should have had her ready to go before you got here. Silly me."

The girl plops down on my lap wearing less than undergarments.

"Atticus—" One glance at her cleavage, and I'm already hard.

I've seen women naked before, and I've had my fair share of rendezvous, but I keep them quiet. And I certainly don't engage in public orgies as Atticus surely does.

I want to rush out of here; leave, smack Oliver, and never see Atticus again. But right now, this girl's body is the only thing covering the evidence of my arousal. If I leave now, I'll be a laughingstock. And the last thing I want is to be humiliated in front of Atticus again.

She places her hands on my chest and moves them down my torso. I suck in a sharp breath. "Atticus, don't you think we should converse? I'm not sure I want—this." I look at the woman straddling me. "No offense, dear."

Atticus sighs. "If that's what you wish." He shoos the woman off his lap, and the one on mine follows. The second she's off, I quickly cross my legs.

"May I ask…" I make sure the waitress and girls are out of earshot. "How did you get into Roche with your—clear and very vehement issues?"

"Ha, you insult me." He takes the biggest gulp of hard liquor I've ever witnessed from a man. "Sex is something we men need. Something we crave. There are two types of men, Dominic. The ones who embrace lust and fuck to their heart's content, and the ones who pretend they don't. Oh, and the ones who want to, but are too coy to approach a woman. So three, I apologize."

I'm too stunned to speak. The waitress delivers a glass of cognac to me and I take a sip. Atticus Desimir is the type of man to live life on the edge. The type of man who you read about in the papers who died under obscure circumstances with a smile on his face.

"I've been thinking about the story you told me about your brother. I'm fascinated by his condition, and I started doing some digging," Atticus says.

He went straight from raving about sex to discussing my brother's ailments. This man needs a shrink. "And?"

"What if I told you I could wake him up?"

A slicing heat of anger shoots up within me. I slam my fist down on the table, both our glasses rattling. "My brother is none of your concern! Don't you understand how cruel it is to bring up false notions of cures in front of someone who's clearly grieving?"

He's still and quiet. Others in the club peer in our direction, but I don't care. If there were no witnesses, I'd wring Atticus's neck.

Atticus reaches into his pocket and grabs a paper from his coat that looks like someone ripped it out of a textbook. A large corner of the page is gone. He slides it across the table to me.

I snatch it from him. Painted sketches of some sort of recipe fill the pages. I mumble under my breath, "a relative's blood, dolinian, calendula, olivine, and the artifact. Where did you find this? Some fiction book?"

Atticus shakes his head. "Where I got it is none of your concern. Just know it's real. Haven't you ever wondered what other powers the artifact contains? Did you ever consider that it could save your brother?"

I shouldn't believe Atticus. But this page is so detailed. So specific. It's hard not to feel a sliver of hope rise in me. "A piece of the page is missing."

"Yes. There's one more element needed for the treatment to work, but I ripped it off in case this paper ever got into the wrong hands. It's nothing important. I'll tell you what it is when the time is right."

It makes me uncomfortable that he's hiding part of the treatment. But something about that makes this feel all that more believable.

No, Dominic, you're being stupid. Atticus Desimir is a scandalous prick who can't possibly have a caring bone in his body. "Stealing the artifact from the prime minister is no easy feat. What's in it for you?"

Atticus smiles and leans an arm onto the small table. "Just one simple thing. When it's time to activate the treatment, I'll show you the ripped off piece of the paper. You'll hand over the element to me with no questions asked, and I will be the one to integrate it into the cure."

"What is it? Some stone?"

"It's nothing you won't mind giving over once your brother's life is within your grasp."

I consider his words, still not liking what I'm hearing. What he's asking isn't just difficult, but impossible. "All that aside, we don't have access to the artifact. The prime minister isn't going to hand a pair of schoolboys the most powerful object on the planet just for asking, and you can't seriously be suggesting we break into the manor and steal it?"

"That's exactly what I'm suggesting."

"You're mad."

"Nothing great has ever been accomplished by sane men, Dominic."

I grip my glass. Atticus and I could go to prison if we're caught. Actually, they'll execute us since the government holds venitors to a higher standard.

But the alternative is to leave Archer asleep for the rest of his life. Deep down, I know this is the only true course.

I extend my hand to him. "We have a deal."

His lips curl, and he shakes my hand back. "It will be a pleasure working with you, Dominic." He waves to the waitress. "Bring us another round of drinks! We need to celebrate."

"We have classes tomorrow. Shouldn't we take it easy?"

"Nonsense. Live a little!"

The waitress brings over a tray of various glasses of liquors. Atticus pounds down drinks while I sip mine. He asks me more questions about my life. I try to tell him the positive things, outside of my brother's condition, like my father's iron empire, and the wonderful family holidays we used to take once a year.

Every time I try to ask him a question about his family, he tenses up and takes another drink, then completely changes the topic. Perhaps he's not as submersed in nepotism as I'd thought.

Eventually, Atticus slumps in his chair, half asleep. I'm pretty drunk myself, but I push up from my seat and stumble over to him.

"Atticus, let's get back to the dorms."

"No—"

I tug at his collar, but he refuses to move. Great, now I'll have to drag him back to Roche. I bend over and throw his arm over my shoulder, hoisting him off the chair. Thankfully, he finally stands and doesn't concede to throwing all of his dead weight onto me.

I drag him out of the bar. His glasses pinch into my skin from where he rests his head on my neck.

"You're one of the best friends I've ever had." Atticus slurs his words. "I love you."

"Yah, yah," I grumble as we walk down the sidewalk. I need to find a buggy, or this walk could take all night.

Finally, a buggy passes by. I wave the driver down and practically shove Atticus inside. It takes all my effort to adjust him in the seat. Once I'm seated, his head falls onto my shoulder. I don't push him away, but if he gags, I'm shoving him off.

London is quiet this time of night. We pass the glittering street lights and drunks stumbling back to their residences.

Atticus mumbles as we ride back to campus. "Please forgive me—I tried my hardest—I was weak."

What's this about? If it's about him deciding to get blackout drunk, I think he should apologize to himself when he wakes up with a pounding headache.

His voice cracks. "Juni—I'm sorry."

Juni? Of course. Even the high and mighty man he is must have had his heart broken by a girl once in his life. Explains why he's always at the bottom of a bottle.

Once we get to campus, I haul him across the grounds and up to Arlo's dorm room. Arlo doesn't look surprised when he opens the door and helps me throw Atticus down on his bed. We turn him on his side so he doesn't choke to death in his sleep.

I remove his glasses and place them on his bedside table. Like this, with no facial coverings, and no maddening permanent smirk, he doesn't seem all that menacing. He could be a respectable man if he would stop all the charades.

I run my finger along the scar that starts on his forehead. It's long healed, but quite deep. This is the first time I've noticed it, likely because he wears it with so much confidence. As if it's part of him. But with his defenses down and his face softened, I can only imagine what he went through to get it. Perhaps his father did it to him, and that's why he refuses to speak about his family.

I thank Arlo and head back to my dorm room. Atticus may be a thorn in my side, but I can't deny that he's strong and cunning. If anyone can help me find a treatment for my brother, it's him.

Archer, I'll awaken you soon.

CHAPTER 15

ATTICUS

Arlo shakes my shoulder. "Atticus, get up. You'll be late for class."

My head is pounding. I squint as I probe my bedside table with my hand. The room is already too bright without my glasses on a normal day. With this hangover, it feels like I'm looking straight at the sun.

I sit up and place the dark spectacles over my eyes. "I'll meet you there." At least I'm already dressed.

Arlo grabs his briefcase. "Suit yourself."

When he leaves, I pour myself a glass of water from the pitcher in the corner of my room, remembering bits and pieces of yesterday's events.

Vec put his artistry to work, dredging up the recipe to show Dominic the treatment. Little did Dominic know he was staring at every ingredient needed. The part of the paper I tore off was none other than Blythesea magic.

I suppose I could have just lied to Dominic. Perhaps made up some farce where I admitted I was from the past and could heal his brother by combining my Desimir blood with Blythesea magic. But I'm not completely heartless. I know better than anyone what it's like to lose a—

My muscles tense up at the thought of Juni. I replace thoughts of her with thoughts of Konstantin and Austrie. I focus on the beautiful images I conjure up of binding them to wooden stakes and melting them over and over before finally ending their existence.

The fall sun is warm against my face as I walk to class with my books tucked under my arm. If I wasn't plagued by constant thoughts of revenge, would I enjoy life as a venitor student? What would my future even look like? A family? A career?

When I enter the core magic classroom, students murmur amongst themselves. I slump in the seat next to Arlo. The topic for today's lesson is written on the chalkboard.

Enchantment.

I groan and rest my forehead on my fist.

Great. A tenet of core magic that I have seemingly no ability to wield. On days I visit Vec, he lets me practice enchantments on him and his servants, but it appears I cannot use that ability with my old blood.

No worries, there are other tricks up my sleeve.

Dominic and Oliver sit in the second row together. He looks just as hungover as me, even though I know he didn't drink nearly as much.

The professor of core magic, Felix Abbot, takes his place in front of the classroom. He's ancient and should be well into retirement. I suppose some people just don't know when to quit.

"I'd like everyone to pair up and practice a command enchantment. Of course, you'll have to let down your mental barriers to allow your partner to place it on you. I'd be disappointed if any of you could be so easily enchanted," Professor Abbot explains.

"In a real-life situation, you must weaken your opponent's mental state, and find creative ways to increase their fear and confidence levels. So, in other words, the better you do in combat, the more likely your enemy's barriers will fall, and then you can command them to do whatever you wish. Which is why you must always be the most skilled venitor or venitrix in the room."

Such interesting core magic. It's a shame I can't use it. Though it has some subtle similarities to Desimir magic, so, of course, it intrigues me.

Students arise from their desks and prepare themselves to practice on each other. Arlo and I follow, standing in the middle row of desks, facing each other.

The others begin, and I study their movements carefully. It seems like they're using a hand motion where they use three fingers to circle in a clockwise direction. Good, I can replicate that.

Arlo looks nervous, as he should. It's nice having him wrapped around my finger.

"Who should go first?" Arlo asks.

"Hmm. Let me have the first swing." Best to get it over with.

"Uh—all right." Arlo takes a deep breath and closes his eyes, letting down his mental barriers, whatever that means.

I take a step back and start my simulated performance. All I have to do is make Arlo, and everyone in the room, believe I commanded him to do something against his will. Piece of cake.

I move my fingers in a circle. "Arlo, there's something I want you to do for me."

"Yes?" He doesn't look entranced at all. In fact, he appears confused.

Desimir magic trickles around me. Then I summon a shadow unknown to those around us. With my mental commands, it crawls across the floor and climbs up Arlo's body, seeping into the skin around his neck.

I smile. My talons are in, and I can feel every crevice of his mind. I have dominion over him and everything he is. "I want you to scream for me."

I jerk my little finger back, injecting vivid images of ghosts lunging at him. They drip with blood from every orifice of their body.

Arlo's eyes shoot open. He screams, lurching back, nearly falling to the floor. His breaths are heavy and he hasn't blinked once.

Perhaps I was a bit too cruel. Desimir magic tends to leave a mark.

Everyone stares in our direction.

Professor Abbot clears his throat. "Mr. Desimir, when using command enchantments on other students, please be respectful."

I give a half-salute to the professor. "Yes, sir. Sorry, sir"

At least my faking of command enchantments proved fruitful. I'm safe for now as long as Arlo believes his own mind conjured those images.

Arlo grabs the chair next to him.

I take hold of his arm and help him to his feet. "Sorry about that, Arlo."

He brushes off his suit. "No matter. It's my turn now." Something snaps behind his eyes. His cheek indents from where he's biting the inside of his mouth.

Oh dear, I think I've angered him.

I don't know how to raise or lower my mental barrier. Desimir magic works on weak-minded individuals and against those who have a propensity for fragility, which isn't something that can be changed in the span of a few seconds.

Arlo moves his fingers to cast the enchantment.

"Arlo, how do I—" My entire body goes tense. I can't move a muscle, and I fear Arlo is up to no good. I fall onto my knees. Oh, he'll get his revenge on me. I can feel it, and I don't like it.

Losing control of my movements turns my amusement of Arlo into something terrifying. I like to stay in control, even in the bedroom. This is deplorable. Humiliating. And he hasn't even commanded me yet.

Excitement fills Arlo's eyes, and a bit of fear, because he knows I won't let this go unpunished once class is over.

"Atticus, I want you to repeat after me, Arlo de Vries is better than me. He's more handsome in every way. And of course, he's stronger."

I pinch my lips together, but it only lasts for a second. "Arlo de Vries is better than me in every way. More handsome and strong—" I do everything to resist, but even biting my tongue doesn't work. I don't want to say that. *Nobody is stronger than me. I'm not weak.* "And stronger than me."

The enchantment releases and I gasp, even though I wasn't holding my breath. My headache from my hangover worsens from trying to resist the enchantment.

Arlo smiles like an idiot, and a few others around the room are laughing.

Including Dominic.

I pretend like it doesn't faze me, even though part of me feels like it tumbled down a hill and back into that home in Oderzo. That home where I really was weak and could do nothing about it. I rise to my feet and pat Arlo on the shoulder. "Well played, my friend. Well played."

Arlo flinches at my touch. I smile. Oh, he knows I won't let this go. I'm sure he'll avoid our dorm the rest of the day, but he'll have to come back eventually, and when he does, he better be prepared to defend himself. Or who knows, maybe I'll draw it out and make him flinch for weeks.

Such a strange friendship, the two of us have. Perhaps this is what it's like to have a brother. He sure is fun to pick on.

Sure enough, Arlo is nowhere to be seen later on in our dorm. Perhaps he's making sleeping arrangements for the night at a local inn, which would also be in my favor. I wouldn't have to deal with him trying to tune out my activities with partners, even though I know he uses such events as inspiration for his drawings.

I'll play the long con with Arlo. Pretend to forget, maybe for weeks, and when he least expects it, he's finished.

There's a knock on my door. When I open it, I'm surprised to see Dominic on the other side. I thought I'd have to pursue him for our next interaction, even with promises of a treatment for Archer. "Funny seeing you here."

Dominic folds his arms. "We're working together now, or did you forget?"

I smile. "I'd never forget."

Dominic walks past me and takes a seat on Arlo's bed. I follow suit, sitting on my bed across from him.

"So—where do we start?" Dominic fiddles his thumbs together. He's so ready. So eager. When Archer is on his mind, he loses any sense of reason and discernment. Exactly where I need him to be.

"Like anyone who is deciding to commit a treasonous act—we plan. Do research. Build alliances from the outside in."

Dominic raises an eyebrow. "You speak as though you have experience in this field. Don't forget, we're still schoolboys."

I can't very well tell him about my time in the Bilancia Syndicate. Or how I took assassination jobs on the side, can I? Everything in this time is so regulated and restricted. They probably don't even assassinate each other anymore and likely just throw the perpetrator in jail like civilized folk.

"I am capable enough to get something like this done, thank you very much."

"Then where do we begin?"

I hand him a handbill. "This party. We need to get close to people. And with your father's connections, I don't see any reason this should be an issue for you."

He takes it from me. "The Tulip Ball? This weekend? You're absolutely mad. RSVPs must have been due six months ago!"

The prime minister will be at the Tulip Ball, as will parts of his staff. Dominic and I need to befriend one or more of them. That will be our entry into the prime minister's home.

"But your father knows diplomats? Correct?"

Dominic nods. "Yes...but I don't think he'll help me." He hands me back the paper.

Interesting. "Why?"

"We've been distant ever since my brother's accident. There's been disagreements about keeping my brother alive. He thinks we should let him pass. But I would never do such a thing, not when Archer has a chance of waking."

Oh Dominic, if there's one thing that drives you absolutely mad, it's this brother of yours. No doubt about it. If I hadn't shared in a similar type of misery as you, I may find you cruel for forcing your brother to sleep indefinitely. He could be in pain. But Archer's pain is a small price to pay for a second chance at life.

"That feeling you feel right now, hold on to that, Dominic. That anger you have toward your father for even having the type of heart to let your brother die—use it to your advantage. When you speak to him, bury that anger, and remember the benefits of getting us into that ball. If that's the only driving force for you to get this done, then take it. Nurture it. You'll see that anger can bring a man a very long way."

Dominic grips the edge of Arlo's mattress, lost in thought, contemplating my words.

Perhaps I was too forward.

He looks up with dark electricity in his eyes. "Tomorrow I will go see him at his office. Despite that, I can't make any promises."

I take in a silent breath of relief. "Do what you must. Just know that your brother's life may depend on it." I'm learning the ingredients of Dominic's heart. What ignites his passion. Then stirring it all into a cauldron for my benefit. It's cruel.

But so is what the immortals did to my family.

CHAPTER 16

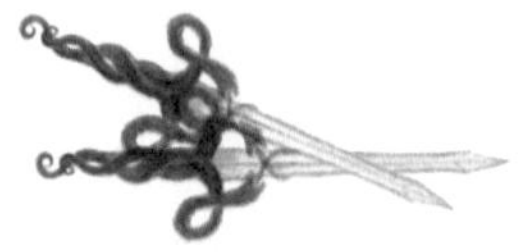

DOMINIC

Atticus's words from yesterday stick in my mind all throughout the stagecoach ride to my parent's house.

The last time I met with my father, we barely spoke to each other besides basic formalities. My mother was a mess the entire time, even though she didn't say a single word about it. If she had her way, she'd cast enchantment magic on both of us and command us to talk like we used to.

I knock at the door of my father's study.

"Come in," he says.

My fist grips the doorknob. The sharp wave pattern of the knob always leaves an imprint on my palm for a few minutes. Sometimes I make a game of it, aiming to finish our conversation for as long as the imprint lasts. I gather my wits and enter the room.

Father's primary study is bigger than some people's homes. He's intimidating to most, but I can see through the harsh exterior of his curled mustache and furrowed brows. He's the father that would stay up late to speak with us and give us well-thought-out gifts, even amid running his company eighty hours a week.

He's not a terrible father. Just not one I always agree with.

"Good morning, Dominic." He doesn't look up from his desk as he writes in a ledger. "I wasn't expecting you."

"Is it wrong for a son to visit his father?"

"Considering you haven't initiated a meeting with me over the past two years, I have my reservations."

I run my finger down the wall of books until I find the one I'm looking for. I tip back the lever disguised as a faux book. It triggers a mechanism, and a drawer pops out a few shelves over.

He puts his pen down. "What are you doing?"

"Just reminiscing," I say.

I walk to the shelf and pick up the old book. *The History of Blythesea Magic.* Even though the existence of our magic is no secret, the fact that we own a copy is damning in itself. You can find this book in the library. It's my father's possession of it that is the scandal.

If anyone knew we were Blytheseas, high society would banish us, and they'd see us as lower than demons. Yet, also fear us more than one.

Our family name once carried weight. We were employed by the crown itself to fight venitors of great power. But now, it's all been taken away.

In 1840, when my grandfather was in his thirties, and living in Scotland, he had a scuffle with a man while he was drunk. They fought with their fists. In my grandfather's inebriation and anger, he released the full extent of Blythesea magic, allowing the dead to devour his enemy. Not only did he kill the man, but almost everyone within a one-kilometer radius. There were a few lucky ones who survived, but with critical injuries. My grandfather barely survived his own magic, as the dead that accompany the magic wanted to take from him too. Once the authorities found him, he was arrested and executed. My grandmother fled with my father to London, changed their last name to Ashworth, and buried the scandal as far as it could go.

If anyone learned we were Blytheseas, my father's company would collapse. Nobody would want to work with him anymore. Even decades after the accident, people still fear our name. We're one of the few families that still pass family magic down through generations, except it's not through our blood like in the medieval times, but through tradition and teaching. My father transferred a duplication of the magic to me when I turned sixteen, as I am his heir.

The scary part is anyone can wield Blythesea magic if taught. All it takes is a quick transfer from a willing holder. It's another reason we now go by Ashworth. Who knows what lengths criminals would go to in order to torture the magic out of us?

I sift through the pages of our history, even turning back to the 1500s. It's strange that I have distant relatives who also know this magic who are spread throughout the world. And all of them had to abandon their societies and start over with new last names. All because of my grandfather.

My father throws down his fountain pen and sighs. "Dominic, please, just put that back and sit."

I secure the book back in the hidden shelf, then take a seat across the desk from him. He's not a stern man. Before Archer's accident, I would have fought anyone who spoke an ill word against my father. But now, it's like we don't even know one another.

"How are your studies?" he asks.

"They're going well. I'm receiving excellent marks." No matter how I position myself in the chair, I can't seem to ease the discomfort of my nerves.

"And you're utilizing your spare time well?" I know he's referring to practicing my magic. He gets on me every time I go too long without training. Every time I practice, it leaves nightmares in its wake. Ones that seem too real. Ones that bring Archer's pain to life and place me on that train, experiencing every fear and torment he did. But if I don't practice and meditate, the magic will attempt to take over and tempt me. Sometimes having this feels like a curse.

"I'll admit I took some time off, but I practiced recently." I swallow. "I visited Archer last weekend." The words leave me before I can stop them.

My father's muscles get tense, as do mine.

"It's kind of you to visit your brother."

My anger boils. He speaks of his own son as if he's just a friend of mine. "What about you? When was the last time you visited him?" I grip the armrest harder.

"Please, Dominic, let's not do this again." Father pinches the bridge of his nose.

I've barely been in here five minutes, and I'm already causing division. Atticus's words pierce through my head before I continue to rip into my father, reminding me I'm not here to fight. I'm here to get something. And if I can hold my tongue, perhaps I can prove to my father he was wrong about Archer's survival.

"I apologize, Father." I bury my boiling fury, setting our differences aside. "Truly, I am visiting to catch up and mend our bond. I want to speak like old times."

Father contemplates my words before nodding. "You're my son, and I want nothing more than to be cordial." Though his eyes droop, he forces a smile.

I also force a grin. "As do I."

"Then tell me, besides school and magic, what have you been up to?"

I must convince him to get invitations for Atticus and me to the Tulip Ball. That is why I'm here. The *only* reason I'm here. "I met a girl."

My father's face lights up. In the last two years, I've only seen a genuine smile from him maybe three or four times. "How splendid! Your mother and I met at university, you know?"

"I know." I'll never forget the story of how they met. They were both in their third year and paired up together for a group project. My father was practicing transmutation magic and accidentally turned her beloved hat, given to her by her late aunt, into a toad. She cursed at him and stormed out of the room. But just a day later, he spent half his earnings on a new hat for her, and since she knew his pauper financial situation, she instantly forgave him. The rest is history. "I might court her."

"Courting? Well, that's significant!"

I scratch the back of my neck. Haylow barely knows I exist. This is quite the lie. "She spoke of her dream of going to the Tulip Ball, but I think it's impossible at this point."

"Oh! If I would have known earlier, I would have requested an invitation." My father rubs his chin. "Perhaps there's still a chance, or some cancellations. What's the girl's name?"

"She asked me not to say anything public yet, even to my family." There's no way I can tell my father that I'm actually planning on taking Atticus Desimir. "I hope that's all right?"

He nods. "Yes, I understand."

"Thank you, Father. For everything. This would mean the world to her. And to me." The words are bittersweet. This is the first positive interaction I've had with him since Archer died, and it's all based on lies.

Father and I speak for an hour longer. The conversation goes well, but there is this game of tug o' war playing behind the scenes of every word. A game in which neither of us is willing to broach the subject of Archer and risk descending into despair.

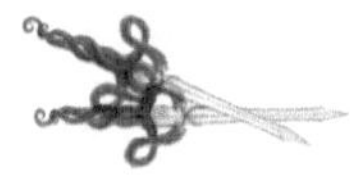

When I receive the invitation a day before the ball, I breathe a quiet sigh of relief. And it includes the plus one. Perfect.

I was growing nervous that my father wouldn't be able to pull it off. Or he'd be too busy with work and completely forget about me. But he never was one to forget when it came to the three of us kids. Even with his busy schedule, he always did his best to make life magical.

If only the train derailment didn't shatter everything for us.

I rush to Atticus's dorm room with the invitation. Before I even knock, Arlo steps outside the room and quickly shuts the door behind him. Then I hear it. The pants and moans leaking through the wall.

I tilt my head. "Arlo?" He didn't leave *before* Atticus began his romp with whom knows who? "I'll take it Atticus is predisposed?"

Arlo doesn't make eye contact with me. He places his hands on his hips and nods his head, a sketch book tucked under his arms. "Uh—quite."

"Do you normally stick around when he—uh. You shouldn't have to put up with this."

"It's... complicated. We have an arrangement." He immediately widens his eyes and presses the book tighter into his side.

A piercing, pleasured scream rings out from whichever girl Atticus has laced within his web.

"Well, if you'd like a different arrangement, perhaps you should let the dean know." I don't have time to wait for how many rounds Atticus has planned for his current conquest. With a huff, I bend over and slide the thick invitation under the door.

The squeaking bed comes to a halt. I hear Atticus's faint voice say, "Darling, I'm afraid you have to leave. I have a meeting."

A minute later, the door flies open. The girl glares at me, and intentionally knocks her shoulder into mine as she burrows past.

Arlo goes back into the room to grab his briefcase, then hurries away too.

I'm left in the dorm room with a shirtless Atticus. He holds the invitation between two fingers up in the air and smiles. "I see you found favor with your father."

"Don't you think you should be careful with the girls around campus? You'll create a name for yourself."

"Yes, do educate me, Dominic. What do you think they'll call me?"

I shrug. I'm thinking *libertine*. He's probably thinking *sex god*. "Regardless, don't you want to be married one day? You're going to scare away a good, proper wife."

He goes stone-faced. "No. Not even a little."

I suppose he doesn't seem like the husband type. A lot of venitors avoid marriage depending on what sect of work they are looking for after graduation. There's a lot of death involved with the more government roles, but not with me. When I graduate, I'm going to start a stone magic business and find ways to further increase their power.

He places a hand on my shoulder. "One thing you need to know about me is that I wasn't put on this earth to love or nurture anyone or anything."

I brush his hand off me. "I'm sure that's not true."

Everyone is capable of love and being loved. I think of Haylow and how beautiful she'd look in a white wedding dress, walking down the aisle to meet me. How I wish my words to my father were true. That I really was courting her. Instead, I'm stuck taking Atticus Desimir to the Tulip Ball.

"So, what's the plan for tomorrow?" I ask.

"Plan?" Atticus laughs. "The only plan for tomorrow is to get inhumanely drunk at the ball and befriend as many of the prime minister's staff as possible."

"But...shouldn't we–"

"We have invitations. There's no need to be sneaky." Atticus throws a loose dress shirt over his shoulders. "These ventures are best left unplanned. Trust me."

CHAPTER 17

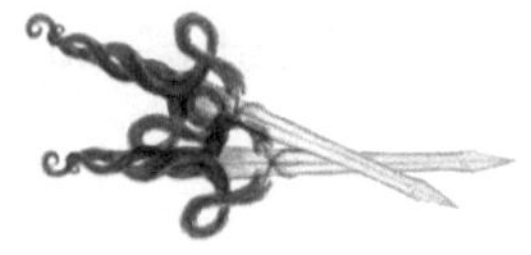

ATTICUS

Vec forces me to wear something more formal to the Tulip Ball. I reluctantly agree, under the stipulation that I have the final say.

The tailcoats the men wear in this age are tight and make them look like seals. I straighten the shirt collar beneath my sculpted frock coat that ends just past my knees. Gold detailing swirls along the dark fabric of the coat's hems. It's the only part of my getup that isn't black.

Vec rolls his eyes when I exit the guest bedroom. "Boots, Atticus? Really?"

I kick my heel out, showing one off. "They're dress boots."

"You're going to stick out like a sore thumb." Vec steps forward and uses his spit to smooth down one of my black curls. "Don't speak to anyone other than staff. If you're seen as suspicious by anyone higher up, it could cause problems."

"I won't."

"And don't fuck anyone."

"Can't promise that."

Vec slaps the back of my head. "It's too risky at an event of that caliber."

"Ouch! And fine! I won't!" I rub my skull. "Lighten up a little."

Vec grumbles. "I'll be leaving for my art tour tonight. So if you need to get in later, use this." He hands me a key. "Just don't touch anything."

"I'm surprised you haven't given me one already."

"Can you blame me?"

No. No, I cannot.

"There's a buggy outside. Now get going before you're late. You'll worry Dominic," Vec says. "And good luck."

"Won't need it." I step outside and head toward the buggy.

It takes off toward O'Stanley Castle, located in west London in the countryside. Perhaps Dominic and I should have ridden together. The buggy ride is going to take quite some time.

The prime minister has his own personal staff of maids, servants, assistants, and lower politicians. The politicians are of no use to me. I'm more interested in the help. The ones who clean his home, transport him, and overhear the conversations he wishes to remain secret.

As we near the red brick mansion, there's a line of buggies traveling down the long cobblestone path with us.

The home is magnificent. Even more beautiful than Vec described. *Oh Dominic, what a grand night the two of us will have! I only wish we could stay friends once I'm finished with you.*

A valet opens the buggy door for me. The bustling energy of the Tulip Ball leaks out from the open doors. There's the chattering of politicians and socialites. A small orchestra plays elegant music.

I position myself at the top of the steps, leaning against one of the many tall pillars as I patiently wait for Dominic to arrive. An older woman gives me an annoyed glare, as if she's appalled by my casual posture. I'm tempted to stick my tongue out at her.

Dominic's buggy pulls up. He steps out onto the cobblestone, dressed to the nines in a black tailcoat and bow tie. His auburn hair compliments the dark ensemble. Normally I find tailcoats horrid, but when Dominic wears them, he looks rather—dashing. He carries himself like he's been to his fair share of social events. His formal body language with the valet has already put me to shame.

Dominic notices me and smiles. He walks up the stairs in my direction.

I pull at my collar to cool myself down.

"So, what now?" Dominic asks.

I smile. "No hello? Or I'm happy to see you?"

"It's good to see you, Atticus. Now what first?" Dominic's determination is quite annoying when we have an entire ball to enjoy.

"First, we'll scope out the party. Perhaps see what's in store and learn which staff the prime minister brought along. Then we'll charm them and find out everything we can."

"Seems simple enough. But won't it be strange to speak to his help and not other guests?"

I shake my head. "Not at all, unless you're planning on caring what these hags think of you. A servant will be flattered that a noble is taking an interest in them. Use it to your advantage."

"Unlike you, Atticus, I have plans for my future. And you're forgetting that some of the more powerful venitors in the country are attending tonight. I'm planning on making such powerful venitors into clients once I graduate."

"Oh? Tell me more."

His voice grows nervous. "I—I want to find a way to increase the power and duration of stones. It would be a business venture of sorts."

Dominic wants to increase the power of magical stones? I'm not familiar enough with stone magic to even understand the demand. All I know is that they are more stable than herbs. More boring too. I doubt there's a stone that can turn skin into ash without the use of fire in the same way parsley and hemshade do when combined.

"Perhaps you'll allow me to join as a business partner one of these days." I nudge his shoulder.

"Not a chance in hell."

Dominic and I near the entrance and hand the attendant our invitations. It's strange attending the event together as bachelors, when most men here have a lovely lady on their arm.

The party resembles heaven, and the ballroom is unlike anything I've ever seen. It has every symbol of luxury—a chandelier, wainscoting, and decorative tile. Even though my father was higher in society, I've never attended a ball like this.

Walls of ivory are detailed with golden trim and the pillars are twisted like vines. There's a second-story balcony surrounding the entire room where socialites laugh and drink together. Others are on the floor dancing. Greenery hangs from the balconies, brought in just for tonight before the leaves wilt.

In the center of it all hangs a blinding crystal chandelier, concocted by the devil Thomas Edison himself. I'm thankful I didn't allow Vec to convince me to leave my tinted spectacles at home. Even with them, I feel a headache coming on.

A male servant approaches us with a carefully balanced tray of champagne flutes. I gladly take two, to which the servant gives me an annoyed glare.

Dominic takes one flute out of my hand and sets it on a nearby table. "Do you have no class?"

"It's my compliment to this ball's beautiful amenities." At that, I stare at the other *beautiful amenities* gliding throughout the room. Their floor-length gowns of various colors flow around the ballroom as men spin them in dances. If only they weren't donning those revolting bulbous sleeves; I'll never get used to those.

I scan the room for any signs of which man may be Cecil Graystone; the prime minister of the United Kingdom.

"Any idea where the man of the hour is?" I ask.

Dominic shakes his head. "I don't know what he looks like."

"Then let's split up," I say. "We'll both ask around and see where that leads us. Meet me back here if there are any issues."

"Got it."

We branch off from each other, but even as I parry through the chattering groups of people, I keep Dominic in the corner of my eye. Not because I don't trust him, but there's this glimmer of confidence in him tonight that makes me curious.

As I round the ballroom, I watch Dominic as he approaches a regal, middle-aged couple. Within minutes, he's smiling and laughing with them. Then he shakes the man's hand as if he'd just completed a business transaction.

Dominic turns to me from across the room and points to a bearded, bald man standing by a large pot of flowers, conversing with other equally important people.

Lord Graystone, do you think you can hide from me? Whether you like it or not, the artifact is as good as mine.

Just off to his side stands a blonde girl. She's around my age and positively stunning.

Is she his secretary? A servant of his? I'm eager to find out.

I move around the ballroom until I come up behind her. The longer I stay out of the prime minister's sight, the better.

Now's a great time to make all my dance lessons with Vec worth it. With all the times I stumbled during practice, Vec's maids have more than enough bruises on their feet to last a lifetime.

I stand next to the young woman and lean down to speak. "Would you like to dance?"

She jumps and places a hand on her chest. "Heavens, you scared me."

"I apologize. I did not intend to startle you. You must be busy with your political duties."

She laughs. "You think I work for the prime minister?"

I frown. "Sorry if I misinterpreted." *Dammit*, now I have to dance with someone who can't even get me closer to the artifact. This will delay Dominic and me immensely.

"I'm his daughter. Cadence Graystone." A silver jeweled band lines her head like a crown.

Daughter? My eyes light up. Now that I can work with. I do as Vec taught me and take her hand, covered by an elbow-length white glove. "Atticus Desimir." With a bow, I place a kiss on the back of her hand.

"Pleasure to meet you." She studies me under calculating eyes, the curve of her lips betraying the thoughts beneath. "And yes, I will dance with you, as long as you promise not to squish my toes. I've had one too many experiences of men flattening my feet at balls."

"Wouldn't dream of it." Perhaps I shouldn't promise that.

I guide Cadence to the ballroom floor just as the orchestra starts the grand march. All the couples walk down the center of the ballroom, then we split apart in tandem after the leader does. My eyes search for Dominic before rejoining Cadence.

Gallopade dancing begins and I finally have a chance to work my charm. Since Cadence is the prime minister's daughter, perhaps I have an even better chance with her than with a maid. But I'll have to play things carefully. She's not someone I can just fuck and get what I want. If I fail, her father could have me executed.

"Are you a venitrix?" I ask her.

Before she can answer, the dance calls for us to break apart and gallop away, before returning to each other. "Yes? What a strange question. All politicians must have magical blood to be in office."

"Oh, yes, you're right. How clumsy of me. I must have had too much wine." That could have been a disastrous slip up, but I doubt her first thought is that I'm five-hundred years old. I spin her.

"You can never have enough wine," Cadence says.

"My kind of girl." I bring her back into my chest, my hand melded into her slim waist.

All the dancers face the middle of the room. The women skip to the middle, then quickly skip back. Then the men. It's an absolutely mind-numbing dance, like we're all part of some insane ritual. But at least it will benefit me in the end.

"Where are you from?" Cadence asks.

"Oderzo."

"In Italy? I wouldn't have guessed. Your accent is so native. I see you had an excellent tutor. What are you doing in London?"

I'm manipulating Dominic Ashworth into handing over his precious Blythesea magic so I can kill the men who murdered my family. And now I'm manipulating you, Miss Graystone.

"I attend Roche University."

"A venitor then. Though I could have guessed that by your attire alone." Cadence stares at me with twinkles in her eyes. Her glimmer tells me all I need to know about her heart. She's the type to get attached quickly, which makes her all the more bendable.

"My attire?"

Cadence laughs. "Some venitors like to dress like they're *different* from everyone else. Like it gives them power."

Oh, so she thinks my outfit is arrogant? Well, at least I don't look like a seal like the rest of the men here, but I won't say that. While I take the lead in dancing, Cadence leads the conversation. She tells me a thing or two about where she attended primary school and some of her interests. Apparently, being prime minister means her father has less attention for a beautiful daughter. I do my best to remember it all.

The dance winds to a close, and I see the prime minister standing off to the side. He looks bored, as if he's ready to turn in for the night. I need to act quickly.

Before Cadence can slip away, I bow gracefully, taking her hand in mine and planting a kiss once more on the back of her hand. "My dear, Cadence. It would be a shame for this to be our only interaction. I'd like to see you again after tonight if you'd allow it."

A light blush coats her cheeks. "I'd like that. But Father doesn't like guests at the manor, and we've only just met."

"I understand. Meet me on Wednesday. Two o'clock. Loughty Park. We'll have a picnic."

"That sounds wonderful...but...I'm not someone who can just leave the house without security or a chaperone."

Of course, daddy has her all locked away where men like me can't hurt her. As he should.

"What about using an enchantment to disguise your appearance?"

She looks unsure, but the rest of her body language screams desire.

I lean forward and place a delicate kiss on her cheek. "I'll be waiting. Even if you decide not to show."

Cadence nods. "I'll do everything I can to be there."

I'm counting on it. If she doesn't show, this entire night will have been a massive waste of time. When I look across the ballroom floor, Dominic waves me down.

I nod at him. "Goodbye, dearest."

She laces her gloved fingers together. "Goodbye, Mr. Desimir."

Dominic stands by a table of delicious hors d'oeuvres as I walk over to him. We venture toward the back door. Upon opening it, a splendid garden and intricate labyrinth greet us.

"Any luck?" Dominic adjusts his tie as we walk along the outside of the labyrinth. I study the two rings on his right hand. One is a simple golden band. The other is a silver ring with a stone in the center. Has he always worn those?

"Yes. I have a romantic outing with the prime minister's daughter on Wednesday."

Dominic's eyebrows draw together. "You were supposed to befriend a servant, not his family! This is too dangerous."

"Nonsense. It will only be a matter of time before she invites me over. And when that happens, I'll be able to search her home for the location of the artifact. And once we are finished with it, I'll return it without anyone suspecting a thing."

"Atticus—"

"Just trust me. Have I ever steered you wrong?"

Dominic mutters something under his breath. As we turn the corner of the hedges, a man nearly collides with us.

"So sorry, sir," Dominic bows his head.

I bow my head too. But when I look back up, I nearly piss myself. My facial scar burns at the sight of the man, and I'm completely frozen.

I had planned on finding him eventually—but now—

"No matter. Accidents do happen." Konstantin smooths out his attire, magic hiding his immortal tattoo.

Then his eyes catch mine, and I'm pinned to my spot. His smile may appear friendly to Dominic, but I know better.

Konstantin's true thoughts are laced deep behind his eyes. "It's been a while, Mr. Desimir."

The child in me is screaming to kill him. I have my knives under my coat. And one in my boot. But the man in me, and the scar seared into my face, reminds me I'm no match for him.

"Yes—yes it has, Konstantin." No matter how much I beg my muscles to relax, they stay stiff. I hope Dominic doesn't hear the shake in my words.

Four-hundred and eighty years later, and he still recognizes me. I keep my posture as straight as I can, even as my breaths grow shallower. If I get emotional in front of Dominic, it could blow everything.

And just like that, the chess game of words begins.

CHAPTER 18

DOMINIC

Something is wrong with Atticus. I may not consider him a close friend, but his entire demeanor changed when this man whipped around the corner.

The man is taller than most men I've met in my lifetime, and his build is strong. His stature is more similar to a gladiator than a man from the upper class. So much so, I'm surprised I never saw him in the ballroom. His black hair is slicked back.

"How's Vec?" Konstantin asks.

The vein in Atticus's neck throbs. "My uncle is fine."

"Ah. I always found it so honorable that he took you in after your family's tragic—demise. My condolences."

Atticus can't stop wetting his lips. "And my condolences for Alano. How unfortunate. It must make you think of your own mortality from time to time."

Konstantin tilts his head. "Alano made mistakes, and he paid for it. Nothing so horrible will ever happen again."

Atticus curls his fists. I cannot decode the hidden meanings behind both men's words. All I know is that this may get ugly quick.

"You must have had a nice long *sleep* to maintain this physique since last I saw you." Konstantin scans Atticus's body. "I take it your business in London is purely personal?"

"Very." Atticus's signature smile is nowhere to be found. Only the cold darkness pooling beneath his eyes.

I'm overwhelmed by what I'm hearing, even without the ability to decode their words and glares. Even more so, I'm shocked to learn Atticus's family is dead. Whatever emotion he's feeling right now scares me. I'll lie. Anything not to watch this play out. I place a hand on Atticus's shoulder. "I'm sorry to interrupt, but our buggy is arriving shortly. It was nice meeting you." I shake Konstantin's hand.

"You too, Mr. Ashworth." Does Konstantin know me? Then again, it's not too strange given my father's notoriety.

Atticus takes a step back at the mention of my name on Konstantin's tongue.

I grab Atticus's forearm to force him away from the man. I don't know what all that was about, though I know they are certainly not friends. But Atticus didn't just seem angry at Konstantin. He seemed scared.

And I've never seen Atticus scared.

Atticus and I take the same buggy back to town. He doesn't speak to me the entire way, even when I bring up questions about Cadence and his plans for her.

I count the streetlights out the window all the way back to Roche. Once we exit the buggy, Atticus tries to dart away.

"Atticus. Wait a second!" I chase after him toward the mathematics building. "Where are you going?"

He stops, his back still turned.

"I don't know what happened, but I'm sorry about your family. And for whatever that man said to propel you into this state," I say.

Atticus spins slowly in my direction, death in his eyes. I retreat as he strides toward me. My back hits the wall of the building and he slams his palms on either side of my body, boxing me in.

He's so close his angered breaths brush across my face. "Don't ever—*ever*—bring up my family in front of me—got it?"

I nod, staring into his eyes through his tinted spectacles.

"Glad we're on the same page." Atticus pushes off the wall. Instead of going back to his dorm, he heads toward the city.

To a bar, no doubt.

Atticus isn't at any classes on Monday. He even missed a quiz in stones class.

On Tuesday, Oliver and I pair up in tinctures class for an experiment. We get to work liquefying an amber gemstone and turning it into an elixir. Unlike some stones, it isn't edible. Instead, the tincture is poured down the left forearm during combat to increase its fighting ability, giving the user the ability to spit fire.

At another workstation, Haylow and Arlo practice another form of tincture brewing called soaking. Harlow places a piece of chalcedony into a jar, then Arlo follows by pouring alcohol over the top.

If we weren't venitors, it would take an entire year to soak a gemstone. But using a variation of regeneration magic allows Haylow and Arlo to place their hands on the jar and have it brewed within minutes.

Oliver scrubs a piece of amber in a small bowl of water. "You really haven't seen Atticus since the party?"

"No. He just waltzed toward the city, never to be seen again." I take the stone from Oliver and use a rotary to smooth the amber out.

I haven't told Oliver about what Atticus and I are up to. If I did, it may ruin everything. Oliver is the motherly type, always being the voice of reason and forcing me to weigh the risks and benefits. He supports me in my journey to wake Archer, but not some theories I've presented to him over the last two years.

"Have you asked Arlo?" Oliver asks.

"No."

"Why not?"

"Because Atticus can take care of himself. When the time is right, he'll be back." I say it as if I know exactly who Atticus is and what moves he makes. He's still a mystery to me, but something tells me he just needs time to himself.

As class goes on, I can't stop thinking about him. Oliver's words nip at me, making me more concerned than before.

Class ends, and much to Oliver's delight, I approach Arlo's station.

Arlo stuffs his tincture tools into his case. "If this is about Atticus, I haven't seen him either."

I give Oliver an *I-told-you-so* look.

"Do you have any idea where he may be?" Oliver asks.

Arlo stops to think for a moment. "He may be at his Uncle Vec's home."

Vec. Konstantin mentioned him during the strange interaction at the Tulip Ball. He must have taken Atticus in after his family passed.

"Do you know where Vec lives?" I ask.

Arlo rubs his neck. "His uncle gave me his address the second time we met. But I don't know that I'm allowed to give it out—"

"Please. We're worried about him," Oliver interjects.

With a sigh, Arlo digs out a scrap of paper and writes out the address. "Fine, but you didn't hear it from me. Atticus's uncle was very firm with me when he told me to only stop by for near-death emergencies. In fact, he almost implied that he only wanted me to stop by if Atticus was actually dead. Must be a private man."

My lips draw into a thin line. It seems Atticus's family is as strange as he is. And if I wasn't so concerned about waking Archer, I'd feel the temptation to dig into his past. But there's no time. I need to find Atticus and obtain the artifact once and for all. He has an outing with the prime minister's daughter tomorrow, and I'm going to ensure he shows up to it.

Oliver and I take a buggy to Vec's townhouse. Is it strange that a part of me is worried about Atticus? Or even a bit sad? I disliked him greatly after our first interaction. But knowing he has no immediate family etches a softness for him into my heart.

The buggy arrives at the townhouse. Or perhaps I should call it a mansion. It's enormous with a white brick exterior, French-style balconies, and draped greenery. What does Vec do for a living? If he was a mogul, surely my father would know him?

"Do you think we'll get Arlo in trouble?" I ask Oliver as I step out of the buggy.

Oliver follows behind me. "We'll just say that we heard he lived here from a fellow student who followed him home one weekend. A love-struck girl."

"I suppose that's viable."

Oliver and I stand on the doorstep and use the golden knocker.

A maid answers, her eyes widening when she sees our faces. "And you are?"

I remove my hat and place it against my chest. "Dominic Ashworth. I'm here to see Atticus."

The maid looks behind her, then back at me. "He's not well at the moment, and his uncle is away. So I don't know…" All her words tell me is that the master of the house isn't here, and in turn, we may act without restriction.

"Please. We need to know if he's all right. For the sake of his studies," Oliver interjects.

"Atticus told me to stop by whenever needed," I lie.

"He's never had friends over before." She raises an eyebrow. "Right now, I don't even know if he's decent for guests. Hasn't been for the last few days."

I can't leave here without checking on him. And, so help me, he'll be at that outing tomorrow. I sense by the energy in the air, and her position as a maid, that this girl isn't a venitrix.

It's horrible for me to do this, but I must. Before she can say another word, I push my finger forward and tap her head, hitting her with a paralytic enchantment.

Oliver rushes forward and catches her limp body. "Dominic!"

"I had no choice." I step past them into the home.

Oliver shuts the front door and places the maid's unconscious body in a corner. He follows me up the stairs. "You know I don't approve of using magic for such things."

"Oh, I've heard, Mother."

Paintings cover the walls, a signature of a *V* in the corner of all of them. So, Atticus's uncle is an artist? His art is erratic. Unique. I understand why he's so wealthy. My mother would love to own even one of these.

We explore each floor and every room we can. The only reason I'm comfortable doing this is because Vec is out of the house. I'll need to perform an amnesia enchantment on the maid before we leave.

Finally, Oliver and I approach a large door. The hallway smells of a sweet aroma lined with hard liquor.

"I really don't want to go in there." Oliver shakes his head. "What if he's dead?"

"He's not dead." Of that much, I'm certain. I turn the knob and throw the door open. The room stinks of bourbon. Bottles of empty liquor line the floor.

Atticus lies on the bed, dead asleep, only a thin sheet covering his decency.

"That's it, I'm out. I'll keep a lookout down the hall." Oliver leaves me to deal with this mess.

I sigh and step into the room. One thing is for certain—Atticus's wellbeing isn't even close to being recovered. But I don't care. He's going to get dressed, come back to school, and together we're going to get the artifact.

"Atticus." I shield my eyes with my hat in case he moves and exposes himself. I shake his shoulder. "Get up."

Atticus groans.

"You have an important date tomorrow. Now make yourself decent and get up!"

Before I can peek over the hat to see his expression, an arm locks around my neck and yanks me down. I fall onto the bed, ensconced in Atticus's arms.

"Atticus, let me go!" I struggle against him.

He doesn't let up. Even with closed eyes, he holds me near. A shiver runs down my body when he exhales against my neck. I've never been this close to another man in my entire life. As he holds me, my body rejects his closeness. Yet, the warmth of his skin is inviting. I quickly push the foreign thoughts out.

The dark scent of bourbon tumbles off his breath and into my nose. Then he snores.

"For the love of—" I press a hand against his hard chest. "Oliver!"

Oliver's voice leaks in from the hallway. "I'm not coming in!"

"Get over yourself and help me!"

Oliver grunts and stomps into the room. "Why are you in bed with him?"

"I'd like to know the same thing. Hurry, my hands are too subdued to use magic. Use a command enchantment."

Atticus's eyes shoot open, and he flies into a sitting position. He sits at the edge of his bed, the sheet still covering his manhood. "You'll do no such thing."

W—what? Was he pretending?

I rush off the bed and stand next to Oliver.

"My head's killing me." Atticus groans, squinting his eyes and pressing his palms against his temples.

"What's gotten into you?" I ask.

"I needed a break, that's all."

Oliver steps forward. "You can't just disappear whenever you'd like. There's school—responsibilities!"

"I'm sure the administration will understand. Don't get your head in a tizzy."

"Well, are you coming back?" I fold my arms.

"I'll come back when I'm good and ready."

This won't do. He has an outing with the prime minister's daughter. An outing I will surely not let him forget. He can't just promise me the world and then take it away.

"Please, Atticus. Come back to school," I say. "Whatever happened will blow over in your mind, I'm sure of it."

"And if I don't?"

"I can't imagine your uncle will be pleased."

Atticus's face goes still, as if he forgot the ramifications that ditching school would have once his uncle finds out. "Speaking of Vec, he will be very upset that you two are here." Atticus slides off the bed and lets the blanket slide off him as he walks to his wardrobe, his entire backside exposed.

Oliver and I look at each other to keep our eyes off Atticus's nakedness. Even in Atticus's lewd display, I'm relieved he's all right.

I can't say too much in front of Oliver. He has no idea of what Atticus and I are up to, and if he did, he'd reprimand me, I'm sure of it. On top of that, if Oliver knew I was a Blythesea, I don't know if he'd ever look at me the same again.

Though, I believe he'd forgive me in time. He has his own demons and I have mine. It's why we get along so splendidly.

"Your maid opened the door for us," Oliver says.

Atticus slips on undergarments and a pair of pants. "Maggie? No, she'd never disobey Vec's orders."

"Fine. I used an enchantment on her. And before I leave, I need to use an amnesia enchantment. But what else was I supposed to do? Another missed day and the professors may go to the police."

Atticus pauses as he buttons up his dress shirt. "I didn't consider that." He looks lost in deep thought.

Oliver chimes in. "You're going to need to come up with a good excuse. Roche is very strict. Even one missed day can jeopardize your time in the venitor program."

Atticus smirks. "I assure you, they'll give me no trouble for the missed days."

I have no idea what he's insinuating, but how he manages to stay enrolled at Roche is his problem. "If we leave shortly, you can still make it to mathematics. There's a buggy just outside."

Atticus takes a swig of bourbon from the bottle on his bedside table, then presses it into Oliver's chest as he walks by us. Oliver gives me a look of annoyance, which makes me feel somewhat good. He was so pressed on making me get along with Atticus, and now it seems he's just as annoyed with him as I am.

The three of us stand in front of the unconscious maid near the front door.

I turn to Atticus. "Well, what are you waiting for? It's your maid. Complete the enchantment, or your uncle will lose his marbles."

Atticus stares at her, rubbing the back of his neck. "Shouldn't the one who created the mess be the one to fix it?"

An amnesia enchantment is so easy against humans without magic. This shouldn't even be a discussion. Unless... "Don't tell me you haven't mastered a simple amnesia enchantment yet?"

Atticus scoffs. "That's preposterous." He heads toward the door. "I'll be waiting for you two outside."

Oliver chuckles as Atticus slams the door. "And here I was thinking Atticus Desimir knew everything."

I kneel in front of the sleeping maid and place my fingers against her forehead in the shape of an upside-down triangle. "Now, now, you and I have our own weaknesses within magic." I complete the spell, but also ensure the paralytic enchantment from earlier won't wear off until we're long down the road.

"Yes, Dominic, our weaknesses involve secondary magic, and more advanced core magic, like transmutation. Not an amnesia enchantment. That's elementary."

"In all honesty, he's probably just being stubborn. You're forgetting, they accepted him into Roche University. And as a second year. He's probably stronger than us all."

"Maybe you're right."

Regardless, Oliver and I have one last laugh, then cram into the buggy with Atticus.

CHAPTER 19

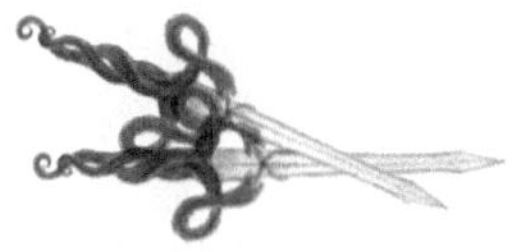

ATTICUS

My eyes grow heavy as I listen to the old bird croak out her soulless mathematics lecture. The math Roche teaches is more chemistry than sums. For instance, if you use levitation and air manipulation with blue amethyst and orange sapphire, you get screeching smoke and your enemy indisposed. It's all set up in this strange formula, then you have to cross multiply some random numbers some crazed mathematician added to confuse us all.

Is it useful? Perhaps to the venitors who can actually wield it, but not to me. Though if these modern-era venitors get it wrong, it can lead to horrific consequences. Herbal and atavistic magic is a lot less predictable. Perhaps that's why it's been outlawed throughout the world. But who has the time to sit down and write an equation into the dirt in the middle of combat? It's all about memorizing the outcomes, if you ask me.

Still, if I want to make it at Roche, I'm going to have to excel at the equations, at least till the end of the year. Once Dominic hands over his magic, I'll have no use for this place. But Vec didn't prepare me for how demanding this university would be, even for the short time I'll be enrolled.

Professor Palmer passes out a pop quiz. I nearly groan out loud.

Any minute I'm not plotting out plans for Cadence and Dominic, I spend hunched over my dorm room desk deep within textbooks. I've even assigned Arlo to shake me awake every time I doze off at my desk. Though every time he does so, I panic and sock him in the gut. Of course I don't mean to, and Arlo swears every time he's done helping me. But he always comes back around.

Though for the last few days, studying was the least of my worries.

All I can think about is Konstantin.

When I saw him, it took everything within me not to tear him limb from limb. I remembered every fantasy, every ill will, every pain, as if it had happened yesterday. Juni's face haunted me for days on end.

Even now, I can barely keep it together. But I didn't want to show weakness in front of Dominic and Oliver.

Especially Dominic.

I thought I was hallucinating when I heard his voice in my room. I even dragged him into bed with me, just to see if he was real. And once he was near, I couldn't seem to let him go.

His presence reminded me of our mission. That if I gave up now, I'd never avenge Juni and my parents. That giving up would be the real failure.

I would have held him longer under the guise of sleepwalking if he hadn't threatened to cast an enchantment. After Arlo performed one on me, I vowed never to feel that weak ever again.

As class nears the end, Headmaster Montgomery slips into the room. Students mumble and whisper. This is a rare occurrence. We usually only see him at required assemblies.

Montgomery speaks in hushed conversation with Professor Palmer. Then they both look at me.

"Mr. Desimir, could you see me in my office?" Headmaster Montgomery asks.

Shit.

Everyone stares straight at me, even Dominic and Oliver. Best-case scenario, he'll ask me about my attendance. Worst case, Professor Doyle ratted me out.

I stand and follow Montgomery out of the classroom, nodding at Oliver and Dominic on my way out. As we tread down the long winding halls, he stays silent, causing me even more uncertainty.

Once we're both inside his large office, he shuts the door with a thud. "Please, have a seat."

I obey, sitting on the other side of his desk. He takes a seat across from me. Montgomery folds his hands and stares straight through my glasses, waiting for me to speak.

I'll go for the best-case scenario. "I apologize for my attendance the past few days. My uncle gave me his horrible flu while I was visiting him. Such helplessness overtook me, I could barely walk. Please accept my apologies for not sending word sooner."

He looks stunned. "I wasn't aware you were absent, but if that's the case, I'll assist you in meeting with your professors to make up your classwork."

Professor Doyle must have snitched on me then. When I get my hands on her—

"You're actually here because I tried to request your academic records for Belworth University in West Virginia, but it shocked me to learn that such a college doesn't even exist."

Oh fuck. Leave it to Vec not to cover all his bases. But I can't blame him. He's quite literally made me the focus of his life for centuries. Even if the university was real, he wouldn't have been able to request my records, regardless.

I force a smile of confidence as I concoct my next lie. "I should have said so sooner. Belworth University closed halfway through its summer term after I left. There was a horrible fire." I'm glad Vec chose the Americas to place our false university. It makes it more complicated for Montgomery to corroborate my story.

"A fire?" Montgomery doesn't look like he believes me for a second.

"Precisely."

The headmaster stands from his desk and circles behind me as he paces in thought. Though he's probably doing it to make me nervous. I stay locked in my seat. I'll do anything to stay enrolled here. Anything except letting Montgomery believe he has control over me.

I have only one trick up my sleeve.

"Tell me, headmaster, what do you do to keep yourself so youthful at your age? You must only be in your thirties at best." *Hardly. He doesn't look a day under forty. Good thing he is handsome. Please don't let his looks be an enchantment.*

"Genetics. Don't flatter me."

"When my uncle gets back from his trip, we'll have this straightened out right away."

"Of all the times for him to be out of town." The headmaster's hands rest on my shoulder from behind. His hand lingers there for one moment too long before he lets up and continues his pacing.

"Pity, isn't it?" I smile.

"There is another matter we need to discuss. Sunday's room checks."

Room checks? We're university students. What business does the administration have sifting through our belongings? Good thing I keep anything too compromising back at Vec's home.

Headmaster Montgomery stops at his desk and opens the top drawer. He takes out a set of heavy iron manacles and tosses them onto his desk. They land with a thud. "Let's see you explain this one. Your roommate certainly had no words."

Well, fuck again. "There is a perfectly good explanation for that." I don't like this. The way he thinks he has superiority over me.

"Go on."

"Let me demonstrate *exactly* what I use them for."

It will be delightful to give the man a taste of his own medicine.

After I turned my *disciplinary meeting* with the headmaster into his own, I left his office knowing I'd never be called into his office again on behavioral or attendance issues. Nor the status of my faux university in the Americas.

When I tell Oliver of my romantic outing with Cadence, he's kind enough to prepare a picnic for her and me. God knows I'm certainly no good at meetings with women performed for the sole purpose of romance. And Cadence doesn't seem to be the type to hand her innocence over to me. Perhaps it's why I'm intrigued by her.

Under no circumstances can I sleep with this woman. She's off limits. Bedding her could mean jeopardizing everything now that she knows my face.

At the park, I choose a place guarded by a large tree, so we're not burned alive in the town square for being alone without a chaperone. I set out the tan picnic blanket, then the rest of the elements from Oliver's basket. He was ecstatic to help me when I told him I was wooing a lady.

I admire the display—a vase filled with white flowers, bread on a wooden cutting board, grapes, crystal glasses, and a decanter filled with juice. There's also a pie in a silver tin. Oliver really outdid himself. He deserves a girl like Cadence more than I.

Five minutes late, Cadence arrives in a tulle gown and hat, carrying her own basketful of goodies. I stand as she approaches.

"Mr. Desimir, I hope I didn't keep you waiting."

"Not at all." I lean over and kiss her on the cheek. "You look lovely." And I mean that. Her dress complements every curve of her body, even beneath the fabric. I wish with every bone in my body that I could spread her pretty legs right now.

She kneels down on the picnic blanket. "It's always such a chore to sneak out."

I settle beside her. "You sneak out often?"

She takes a grape off the stem. "If I didn't, I'd practically be a prisoner. Is it horrible to wish that my father doesn't get reelected?"

"Not at all. If someone tried to keep me locked up like that, I might go absolutely insane." I take a big gulp of juice.

Cadence laughs. "Once I'm married, hopefully my husband won't keep me on such a tight leash."

I almost choke on my drink. How could I forget? Nobody goes out with a woman all alone for the sole purpose of cordial company. Not in this time period or my own. It's a ring or nothing. *Well, Cadence, you won't be getting any nuptials out of me, not even if your father holds me at gunpoint.*

She places her hand on mine. "Tell me about yourself, Atticus."

Perhaps I should have rehearsed my backstory more. I'm not prepared for the toll memories of my past take on my body. But as long as I imagine this fake mother of mine from the Americas instead of my actual mother, I can prevent myself from falling. "I was going to school in West Virginia."

"The Americas?"

"Yes. My mother passed away after my first year, leaving me with no immediate family. After a long grieving process, I packed my bags and sailed back to Europe to live with my uncle. He worked his magic and helped me get into Roche, since I excelled as a student in America. The rest is history, I suppose."

"I'm sorry about your mother. You had no siblings? What about your father?"

If I let her pry too much, things may get ugly quickly. And my headache, which still hasn't left, will grow even worse. "How about you tell me more about you? What was it like when your father became prime minister?"

She throws her hands up. "Horrible. I preferred his time as secretary of state, but of course a young woman like me has no voice in his life. I begged my mother to convince him not to run, and she simply scoffed at me."

"I'm sorry, Cadence. Perhaps one day you'll make your own way in life."

"I'm nineteen. All he does is scold me for being unwed. I don't like any of the men he's introduced me to. I should get to decide for myself who I want to marry."

I need to get her mind off marriage. There is a hidden meaning in her eyes beyond the words she speaks. She rejects all the men her father brings home, but is perfectly fine being alone with me? She's of marrying age and—*Oh, no, what have I gotten myself into?*

Unless I want to be the prime minister's son-in-law with one too many children running around under my feet, I need to change the topic *now.*

"What about the Eight Elect? Him being on the United Magic Council is a bonus, isn't it?"

"I don't care about any of that. My father won't let me go to university until I'm married, so all my magic is still that of a novice." Cadence points her finger at her basket and uses levitation to remove the fabric covering, bringing a pastry to her hand.

I clear my throat. "And—you want to go to university?"

"Of course! I want to foster my magic, so that one day, I don't need any man to fend for me."

All I can hear are the words, *Marry me now. Wed me. Let me chain you to my heart, and then I can go to university.* Well, not today. Not ever. Cadence is pretty, and I'd love to know the way her voice and body respond to my touch. But marriage? I may as well kiss my entire revenge plan goodbye.

But if marrying Cadence meant avenging Juni, would I?

The key is to make her think I may be willing to, without ever actually saying the words. Unfortunately, I'll have to play with her heart, which will inevitably create another enemy. And I've learned the hard way, countless times, that a scorned woman can be nearly as terrifying as a murderous immortal. "Cadence, I wish terribly that one day you'll get your freedom."

"Thank you."

"And perhaps, one day, there will be a way I can help you obtain that."

Cadence sets her pastry down on the blanket, her expression hopeful. "You mean—"

I scoot close to her and take her delicate chin in my gloved hand, tilting her head up. "I want you to have everything you want in life. You deserve it."

Cadence is silent. Then her eyes dip to my lips for a fleeting second. After one more glance to make sure no one is in sight, I press my lips to hers. If anyone were to see, they'd force me to marry her, and like I said, that will never happen. The last thing I want is to ruin her reputation. I'm not a villain.

She melts into it. Like I suspected, Cadence is the rebellious type. Just the way I like it. I'm probably not her first kiss. And I most certainly won't be her last if I have the final word.

I move the basket out of the way and press her body back into the blanket. It takes everything in me not to rip her dress off or push her skirts out of the way. I explore her curves over her clothes. She groans when I tease her mouth with my tongue, but never take the plunge. If I did, I don't know that I'd be able to stop.

Finally, I pull away and stare down at her, breathless. "When can I see you again?"

With glassy eyes filled with innocence, she swallows. "Soon, hopefully. I'll send you a telegraph."

Note to self—learn what a telegraph is.

I push off of her. "I'm looking forward to it, my sweet."

She blushes at the pet name. We end up talking for another hour. Or rather, she talks and I pretend to listen as I side-eye the nearby clock tower. Though I remember bits and pieces. Particularly the parts where she mentions her father.

Eventually, Cadence leaves with her basket. She even gives me a few pastries to take back to campus. Arlo will love them.

I rehash my plan on the walk back to the dorms. If I'm going to parasitize my way into the prime minister's life, and eventually his residence, I'll need a way of unlocking whatever vessel houses the artifact.

In my textbooks, I've seen no mention of a stone that unlocks any lock, which is probably why herbal magic is banned.

I need to find zeledian root, as my ring from centuries ago is now obsolete. It's the only herb that can unlock. Though, I don't know if society grows magical herbs anymore.

Perhaps Vec will know.

CHAPTER 20

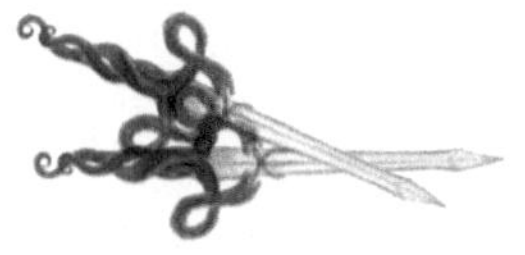

ATTICUS

Vec arrives home with three of the servants. I stand in the foyer as he waltzes in with his suitcases in both hands.

"How were your travels?" I fiddle my fingers behind my back.

Vec looks at me and sighs. "Please explain why the house reeks of bourbon?"

Right. I haven't told him anything yet. Not about my bender, nor of my interaction with Konstantin. "Maybe you should sit down."

Vec drops his suitcases near the door. "Dammit, Atticus. Who raised you?"

"You, mostly."

He grumbles. "Well, I did a damn bad job of it. Come."

I follow him to his study, and he locks the door, wary of the servants overhearing.

Vec's servants know little about me or my past. And unlike the servants back in Brescia, they're completely ignorant of Vec's immortality status. Immortals are thought of as myths in this time period after their kind went silent in the 1600s.

There came a day when humans wholeheartedly feared them after an immortal attempted to take over the world in 1599. No longer could they relax in the company of mortals. When they walked openly in the streets, people avoided them, disappearing into shops or back into their homes.

And though immortals are never in any imminent danger with their invincible bodies, they retreated from society and were long forgotten.

Since the only way an immortal can die is by their own will, some even chose willingly to pass onto the next life. So if he's found out, it could upset the modern venitor system.

Immortals have magic that humans cannot wield. Children in this time period are told cautionary tales about them and the rumored stories of their so-called evil spells. Well, I'd like to tell everyone that immortals are a lot better at nagging than dark magic.

Vec pours himself a glass of water from the pitcher. "What happened?"

"At the ball—I bumped into Konstantin."

Vec nearly chokes on his drink. "I see you left that encounter without any permanent scarring this time."

"I've learned some self-control," I say between gritted teeth. "You didn't tell me he was in London."

"He *wasn't*," Vec says. "Last I checked."

"And how long ago was that?"

He goes still. "A few decades." Typical immortal. Time passing feels so different for them. It's why Konstantin could remember me like he scarred my face yesterday.

"And he knows who Dominic is. Though Dom didn't seem to recognize him. Konstantin must know we're planning something."

"You're giving the boy nicknames now?"

I hadn't even realized I'd done it. Is that the first time? "Never mind that. If Konstantin knows Dominic is a Blythesea, he may be after him too."

"Well, his grandfather did kill Alano. But if he knew Dominic as a Blythesea, the Konstantin I know would have killed every Ashworth family member by now. And since they invited Konstantin to the Tulip Ball, it's more than likely that he is simply part of high society."

Maybe Vec is right. But it doesn't change the fact that I'm rattled. What if I'm at an event with Cadence and I learn Konstantin is there? It could cause a pointless massacre if I'm unable to take control of my emotions. One where I stab him relentlessly, only for him to heal seconds later while every man, woman, and child scream in fear. "Can you find out more about his whereabouts?"

"I'll hire a private investigator. In the meantime, you must focus on Dominic. Where are you in the process?"

I explain to Vec about my date with Cadence and her relation to the prime minister. Of course, Vec is just as upset as Dominic that I chose an immediate family member to become my prey. But once they see the big picture, they'll thank me. Everything will go as planned as long as I don't end up married to Cadence Graystone.

Which brings me to my next topic with Vec. "Once I get into the prime minister's home, the artifact will likely be under lock and key. I'm going to need zeledian."

"Atticus, there are very few reasons that Britain uses the death penalty in this age. Murder, piracy, treason—and wielding herbal magic. It's the only way they were able to make herbs an archaic form of magic. They see it as powerful and unstable."

I scoff. "Clearly, nobody in this age has ever given it a go."

"In 1671, a man used lurdow improperly and destroyed a fleet of docked ships. Stone magic was making a debut during that time, so the government started phasing out herbs in textbooks, and banned them altogether in 1701. And as their use stopped, the population's blood weakened. Even when magical herbs are found in the wild, less than a percent of the population can actually wield their properties. Though, if you ask me, the higher powers suppressed them out of their own selfish fears."

Back home, you could be killed for something as little as petty theft. The prospect of execution for the simple use of an herb means nothing to me. "So—where can I find zeledian?"

Vec sighs and unlocks a drawer on his desk, then pulls out a small booklet. "Here, take this."

I take the booklet and flip through the pages full of various lists. It's incredibly incriminating—black market dealers, nobles whose blood is still strong enough to wield herbal magic, even lists of banned stones and where to get them. "You've done your homework."

"Well, I have a lot more time on my hands than most."

"How much would zeledian root set me back on the black market?" Trying to find zeledian root, even back in the middle ages, was next to impossible. Most wouldn't accept currency for it, but incriminating favors.

"No, no. Just like back then, this isn't the kind of thing you can simply buy. You'll need to steal it from the underground vaults of nobles."

"You're not making this easy on me, are you?"

Vec smiles. "Start here." He points to a name and address of a noble named Hugo Bates. "But don't get caught. He's a psychopath."

"Just my type."

I'll need Dominic's help if I'm to infiltrate Mr. Bates's vault. Two venitors are better than one.

All throughout secondary magic class, Felicity keeps staring at me during her lecture. I haven't touched her since that day in her office. Even though she insisted she wanted to pretend like nothing ever happened, women get a certain way. She wants me to notice her. Some classes I give her little winks and smirks when nobody is paying attention, relishing the ways she tries to hide her blushes.

But I'm not looking at her today, I'm looking at Dominic. Should I tell him I'm able to wield herbal magic? If I want him to help me, I'm going to have to come up with something.

When class ends, he darts out of the classroom before I can catch up to him. I scurry down the hallway until I am behind him. Then I grab his arm and pull him into an empty classroom.

He stumbles into the room. "Heavens, Atticus. You could have just called after me."

"What fun would that be?"

Dominic rolls his eyes. "How did your outing with Cadence go?"

"Oh splendid, besides the fact that she's already mentioned marriage a concerning number of times."

"So it went well?"

I walk over to the chalkboard and doodle. "If that's your definition of well, then yes."

His hands are on his hips. "What now?"

"Once we get our chance to steal the artifact, we need to ensure we're able to unlock whatever is housing it." The chalk screeches against the board as I draw a circle.

"So you'll need a key? Or a lock picking kit?"

"Something of the sorts. I know where to get something that can unlock anything."

"And what would that be?"

I will not tell him. I can't. Even now, I still don't know if I can trust him. He could be scared senseless and run to the authorities, regardless of his brother. "Just trust me."

Dominic strides up to me and snatches the chalk from my grasp. "No more secrets. We're in this together or not at all. I'm tired of you hiding things from me."

I lean against the board. "It's dark. Maybe illegal. The more ignorant you stay, the better."

"I know darkness. More than you know."

I have no doubt about that, Dominic. "Are you sure you want to know? If you don't, you can feign innocence if we're caught."

Dominic places a hand on my shoulder. "Tell me."

I hesitate. Vec wouldn't like this. But I need Dominic and his immortal-destroying magic if I'm going to pull this off. And if Hugo Bates catches us, Dominic's magic is my insurance that I'll make it out alive. "It involves herbal magic. I can wield it, and there's a certain noble who holds such an herb in a vault of his. We'll need it to make this work." I scan the room for places to hide Dominic's body when he inevitably starts running for the authorities.

Dominic takes a step back. Perhaps I could con his father for magic instead.

"It makes no difference to me," he says.

My jaw softens. Then I smile. I should have known Dominic would be willing to go to great, even execution-worthy, lengths to save his brother. "You aren't going to report me?"

"Not at all. Just don't tell Oliver. He may not be so kind."

"May I ask why?"

Dominic folds his arms. "His family is like you and can still wield herbal magic. Years ago, when Oliver was only an infant, his mother tried using herbal magic to calm him down. She had no formal training, as no one does anymore. It didn't work, and she ended up breaking her mind. One day, she couldn't take it and almost killed him. She scarred his neck and chest with a dull kitchen knife before taking her own life. If his father hadn't gotten home early from work, he'd be dead. He may not remember it, but his body is still scarred. It's why he always wears high collars and scarves."

We'll have to be careful around him. He seems nice, even kind enough to throw Dominic right into my lap. But he's also one to hold fast to laws and traditions. It could cause trouble in the long run.

"When do we act?" Dominic asks.

"Tonight."

"Tonight! Don't you want to plan this out?"

"No. The vault is underground. There's not enough planning in the world to help us, and it will only delay our efforts." And it would prolong the amount of time I have to spend with Cadence.

"Fine. I'll meet you in front of the mathematics building after supper."

CHAPTER 21

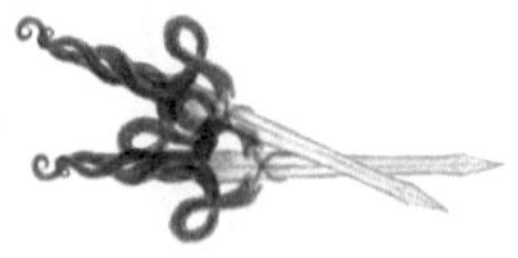

DOMINIC

Atticus is late.

To be fair, we never agreed on an exact time, but I figured he would eat at six o'clock, and we'd meet around seven. Even though I didn't see him in the dining hall, it's an enormous room, making it easy to miss someone.

After thirty minutes of waiting, I almost give up. But as if on cue, he struts around the corner, replacing his gloves and adjusting his tinted spectacles as he walks.

I fold my arms. "Late dinner?"

"No. I ate at six."

I throw my arms out. "Then what took you so bloody long? Do you really eat that slow?"

"No. I got—sidetracked."

I suck in a breath. "If you tell me you're late because you were bedding some girl, I'll place an enchantment spell on you and make you eat dirt."

He tilts his head. "No, I did not rendezvous with some girl."

We're both silent for a minute.

"It was a man."

I raise my hands, pretending like I'm about to make good on my promise, but he catches both my wrists.

"Dominic, please, I am only joking!"

I rip my wrists out of his hands, not believing his lies for a second. "Like hell you are!"

Atticus strides off toward the city without a backward glance. It's like he knows I'll just go along with whatever he does. I finally follow, grumbling under my breath all the way to the nearest buggy.

I climb into the buggy after him, wrestling the door shut. "Have you ever considered that you have a problem?"

He flicks his hand out. "What problem? I have no problem. Is your issue that I'm too strong? Too smart? Too handsome? If you consider those problems, Dom, perhaps you're the one with the issue."

He's in complete and utter denial.

"I'm talking about your very clear and pressing addictions."

"Addiction to what? Success?"

I'll get nowhere with him unless I'm direct. "Sex, alcohol." And some deep-seated anger issues, if you ask me. I'm careful not to bring up Konstantin or his family. Who knows what will happen if I dredge that up again.

"Sex is wonderful for the body. I read it in a book somewhere. And alcohol? Men our age are supposed to drink and be merry. Lynch me for having a little fun."

I audibly sigh and mentally raise a white flag. He's his uncle's problem now. I just wish he'd be prompt for things. One of these days, his issues will get him in trouble, and quite possibly, me.

The buggy pulls up a block away from a large mansion. We pay the driver handsomely and meander down the sidewalk toward the home.

Once we're near the front lawn, we hide in the shadows near the front gate.

"Who is this guy, anyway?"

"Hugo Bates. He's a crime lord. If you get caught, slit your throat." Atticus hands me a dagger.

"Excuse me?"

"No time to explain. Let's go."

"Wait—Atticus!" He never said anything about this man being involved in crime. But what did I suspect? This mansion is housing illegal magical herbs. Maybe I thought I'd get lucky and the owner would be some old man who inherited them.

I'm a fool.

It's almost pitch dark, and I can barely see where I'm going, the only source of light leaking from the windows of the mansion and into the yard. I grab onto the back of Atticus's overcoat so I don't get lost.

Atticus finds a compromised part of the gate hidden by overgrown vines. We slip past it. I almost trip as I shimmy through. We creep across the yard, which is slightly more visible.

"Where is the vault?" I whisper.

Atticus scans the yard and places his hand on the ground. He closes his eyes, as if sensing something. "This way."

Did he just use magic? And if so, what kind?

We crouch as he guides us to a large oak tree in the center of the lawn.

"What now?" I ask. We're in a very exposed part of the yard. If anyone looks outside, they may see us.

"It's inside this tree," Atticus says.

"That's preposterous."

"There must be a lever or something." Atticus searches around the tree, tearing off pieces of bark.

My whisper turns harsh. "We should have planned more!"

Atticus pulls down a stumpy branch, and it clicks. An enchantment charm disappears off the trunk, revealing a hollowed-out section hiding a stairwell.

"You were saying?" Atticus folds his arms.

I'm left without words. He really found it. "Don't rub it in. After you."

Atticus lightly elbows me in the side and leads the way down the narrow stairs.

"Is the underground connected to the mansion?" I keep my hand on the stone wall for support.

"Most likely."

"How did you know the entrance was here? What magic were you using?"

"It's a secret."

"I thought we weren't keeping secrets anymore."

"That was your wish, not mine. I never agreed to it."

As we near the bottom, Atticus peeks around the corner. He turns around and presses a finger to his lips.

I nod and keep my mouth shut.

Then I hear the sounds of laughter and conversations. Guards. Goons. Whatever they are. This vault is no joke. Something about hearing them makes this feel even more real. I want to chicken out, but my love for Archer overpowers it all.

I nearly gasp when Atticus laces his hand with mine and pulls me in a sprint across the hall behind a large crate. We both bend down behind it on the dirt floor. Atticus doesn't let go of my hand, as if I'm on a leash now.

I peer over the corner of the crate to get a better look at the large underground. It's nearly the size of a warehouse. I'm shocked something like this hides beneath a city like London. Thousands of dried herbs hang from the ceiling. Fresh herbs grow in beds, separated by type. Because they're all of magical varieties, I don't recognize any of them. Their scent looming in the air is pleasant, but vastly unfamiliar. More similar to cologne than a flower.

Atticus looks in the opposite direction and yanks me to another crate when a patrolling goon almost walks by. He's scouting out the location as if he has veteran experience in it. Practical stealth isn't taught with basic venitor magic at Roche unless your focus is to one day join the Venitor Brigade. But it seems Atticus is already a professional.

How will he know which herb is the zeledian? It's not as though herbology is taught in schools anymore. I've seen sketches of herbs like hemshade and dolinian, both light blue, but never zeledian.

As the goons face away, Atticus releases my hand and darts out from behind the crate and runs in a crouched fashion between two herb beds. Of all the times for him to run off without me. I run in a crouch, my legs burning.

Atticus grabs different types of herbs and stuffs them—roots, dirt, and all—into his large pockets. He finds a clump of silver-pink herbs with green stems, then lies down on his stomach behind them. I rush over and follow suit.

"Is this it? The zeledian?" I whisper.

"Yes."

"These herbs don't need sunlight to grow?"

"No. Most only need water."

I reach for it, but he slaps my hand. "It's poisonous when touched with bare skin." Atticus grabs as much as he can fit in his gloved hand and tucks it into a pocket under his coat.

"What are the other herbs for, then?" I motion to his dirt-and-herb-stuffed pockets.

"Recompense." Atticus looks over the herbs for a second too long. "Shit."

"Intruders!" a man yells.

My nerves fire up. Ten men run between the herbal beds in our direction.

I shake Atticus's forearm. "Dammit, what now?"

His eyes dart. "Fight." Atticus jumps to his feet and casts air manipulation at the men, knocking them onto their backsides.

I stand up and press my back against his, covering all our sides visually. We're surrounded. How many goons does one crime lord need?

Truth be told, I've never been in real-life combat before. Sure, I've dueled other students and dummies. But nothing like this.

A man runs at me. I bring my hands close to my chest and move my fingers as if I'm plucking a harp. My transmutation spell hits him, turning him into a statue. I only have minutes before he transforms back.

There's only two of us and ten of them. And no matter how strong Atticus is, he'll never be able to take them by himself.

"Fight dirty, Dominic. Transmutation is too kind for the likes of them."

"I don't want to kill them!"

"They'll have no qualms killing you."

I swallow. He's right, but I don't want him to be.

Atticus runs forward and pulls a knife from his boot. I fall back in shock as he plunges a dagger up into the man's ribs. Blood drips down Atticus's gloves and wrists.

The worst part of it—he smiles and laughs as he removes the blade, letting the man bleed out. I don't have another second to process as a man levitates me off the ground. I act fast before he can fling me into a wall. I push my hands out and use a reflection spell, nulling his magic for a few seconds. A grunt escapes me as I slam to the ground.

A short man enters the vault. His top hat is taller than his head, and his frame significant, given his height. "It's been too long since anyone ventured as far as stealing from me directly. I missed the thrill of it, you know. I hope you know how much I'm going to enjoy this. I'll teach you boys a lesson you'll never forget."

My body goes cold. This is the man Atticus told me about. How I'd be better off slitting my throat if he caught us.

"Do your worst," Atticus sneers.

Mr. Bates smiles, almost with pity. "Oh, I will. You have no idea how much I'm going to enjoy this, do you? But first..."

He snaps his fingers, and two men gang up on Atticus, one grabbing him from behind, the other using air manipulation to knock the wind out of him.

Atticus heaves. "Is that the best you got?"

Mr. Bates pulls out a gun. *Shit, shit, shit.* He points it at me, and I lunge, the bullet catching the bricks instead of my leg.

A goon catches me in another levitation, then uses air manipulation to push me to my knees. He knocks me onto my chest, subduing my hands with his.

I force my head up and stare at Atticus. Blood drips down his mouth.

Mr. Bates uses some herb to cast an enchantment on Atticus.

Atticus's eyes and mouth clamp shut with an invisible force, muffled yells barely escaping. The binding spell dampens his senses.

He is blind to the world, and deaf to my screams.

We're doomed.

Mr. Bates walks closer to me now, grinning wide with pleasure. He pulls a knife from his belt, long and curved. For carving. "You don't understand, do you, runts? Down here, I'm the headmaster, and I'm going to relish every slice as I slowly feed you to my dogs."

How could any human be so cruel?

There's only one option left for us, and the choice almost makes me gag. I've never called them in the open like this. Never against other men. I was told never to let another witness the Blythesea power, but what choice do I have? Is death a preferable option? Maybe for me, but not for Atticus. Thankfully, he remains bound and blinded by the enchantment, and will not see what I will unleash here.

Mr. Bates closes the distance, his hand gripping my collar.

I empty my mind of all emotion. It's the first tenant of Blythesea magic. To have any negative emotion, like anger or resentment while you're summoning the dead, gives them far too much power.

The cobblestone at my feet morphs and twists, as the dead begin to swirl up from the ground. A hand grasps Mr. Bates's leg, and his skin flushes pale. No words escape his lips, even though I can feel his terror. I feel it every day, knowing what lurks beneath the surface.

Already the thoughts invade my mind like a disease, voices yelling out for me.

"*Kill, kill, kill,*" they beg. The dead rise all around us now, grasping hold of all the goons, threatening to pull them under. "*Kill, kill, kill.*"

How sweet the words of the dead, and how tempting their offer. I do not wish to kill them. But they've seen my power and cannot live to tell about it. The realization makes me nauseous.

Then I see the dead closing around Atticus. He still thrashes against his invisible bindings, completely unaware of what's happening around him. I'm too much of a novice to control the dead with such precision. They'll kill everyone in the room or none at all. My thoughts unravel, the tranquil peace I'd built up shattering at once.

Pale, bony hands grasp at my own legs now, but I do not cower. The faces of the living already show their terror enough for all of us. I force away the final temptations of death and utter a single command, banishing the dead back into the earth, where they belong.

Just like that, the room returns to normal. All the goons are frozen in terror, kneeling upon the stone. Mr. Bates is the first to break free from his trance, rising on shaky knees with fury in his eyes. I'm far too exhausted to retaliate, my body weak and my mind even weaker now that the remnants of my magic have left my system.

But before Mr. Bates makes it even another step, his body halts, frozen in place.

The enchantment that bound Atticus breaks.

"A critical error, Mr. Bates, letting your attention slip from me," Atticus says, reaching for the herbs in his belt. With an unnerving smile, he stomps one foot on the ground, tendrils of purple cracking the dirt floor and crawling toward the other men.

No courage remains for any of them to even run. Cracks form beneath them, and Atticus holds his palms out, tilting his head toward the ceiling. A deep, wicked laugh escapes his lips. Something darker lies beneath his magic, the herbs merely amplifying it.

In one last ploy to stop the attack, Mr. Bates lunges toward Atticus. Vines burst forth from the dirt, encased in shadow, and lace around Mr. Bates's ankles, dragging him into the dirt. He's choking and gagging on the soil as Atticus buries him alive.

I cower, trying not to watch as the others are pulled beneath the surface. Purple electric beams shoot through the vines, electrocuting more of the men.

Soon, all the men are dead.

Atticus remains in a complete trance. He can't stop chuckling while the power radiates from him. I shudder. All the men have perished. He needs to stop before he loses all control.

I crawl on my belly across the dirt, afraid he'll see me as a foe.

But Atticus is still lost within his trance. And though I'm relieved that he never saw my magic, it may not matter in a second. He whispers tales of death to the sky, his laughing more of a cackle. The dirt vines rush toward the pillars now. He's going to kill us both.

I grab his ankle from where I lie on the ground beneath him. "Atticus, stop!"

He's laughing with his eyes closed. He can't even hear me.

The vines seem to know that I'm safe, though I still fear Atticus will turn on me. I take a deep breath and hop to my feet. Then I swipe the herbs from his left hand.

The vine collapses and spreads into dust. Atticus takes a step back and looks around.

"Shit." Atticus stares at his handiwork. The blood. The shallow graves of buried bodies.

I take his wrist, pulling him out of his stupor. "There's no time. We have to go!"

We sprint to the exit, hearing a new cluster of yells and shouts in the distance. As long as they don't see our faces, we'll get out of here unscathed. Mostly.

I can't stop replaying the events in my head as we run. Atticus's mysterious powers. The way he used herbal magic. It's all too much to process.

Once we're a block away from the mansion, we hide behind a shed at a nearby home. Atticus slumps down against the wall, grabbing his torso.

"Are you hurt?" I ask.

"I'll be fine."

I nudge him. "Let me see it."

"Just give me a minute."

I sigh. He could have internal bleeding with how they beat him. I kneel next to Atticus and start undoing his coat.

He grabs my wrist.

"Atticus, just let me look. You know very well that you can't use regeneration magic on yourself."

He keeps his face hardened but releases my wrist and places his hands by his sides. I undo the belt-like clasps, and then the jacket underneath. I should probably let him unbutton his own shirt, but he seems half out of it.

I undo the buttons until his chest is bare. As suspected, bruising has formed over his ribs. His breath hitches when I pass my fingers over the wounds.

"You could have died if you kept this hidden." Inspecting his chest brings my face an uncomfortable distance from his. The darkness of the night masks my uneasy expression.

"I've survived this long, haven't I?"

"Twenty years of life isn't long."

He tilts his head, his expression—confusing.

I place my palms on both sides of his ribs. There's more bruising than skin in some parts. This won't be fun for him. Regeneration magic brings with it a certain degree of pain.

"This is going to hurt. Squeeze my arm," I instruct. "It will make things go faster."

"Believe me, Dominic, I can handle a little pain."

I bite my inner lip to cause myself some pain to allow the regeneration magic to build. The magic seeps through my hands and into his skin.

Atticus chuckles. "This is nothing. Just a little warmth."

"Right."

"Holy fuck—" Atticus's head slams back into the shed. He covers his mouth to avoid screaming out. Even the high and mighty Atticus can't handle regeneration pain, I see.

"I told you to squeeze my arm," I say. "I need both my hands. If you cause me some pain, it will make things easier on you."

A bead of sweat runs down Atticus's forehead. "You need more pain to ease mine?" He gasps as another wave of pain takes over him. "Why didn't you just say so?"

He whips his head forward. I try to pull away, but the regeneration spell already has me stuck like glue to his skin until it's complete. Atticus yanks away my jacket and shirt collar, then bites down into my shoulder.

"Dammit." I grit my teeth. He's not easy on me either. "Could you have thought of anything else? You're going to puncture an artery."

But I can feel it working. The regeneration speeds up from the bite. When I move my hands a little lower to his abdomen, another excruciating wave spikes through him. He sucks in a breath, and in turn, my skin.

My face heats when his tongue passes over the bite for a split second. It was probably an accident. And my face is only reddening because I'm embarrassed by his error.

I bite back groans of pain from Atticus chewing on my shoulder until the regeneration completes. I shove him off and grab my shoulder.

Saliva instantly coats my fingers. "I swear if you left a mark—"

Atticus buttons his shirt. "Oh, I most certainly did." He grins. "Has anyone told you that you taste delicious?"

I scoff and rise to my feet, adjusting my shirt. Is he flirting with me? He never has before. But with both of us readjusting our clothing like this, I almost feel like one of his conquests. And I'm reminded that Atticus doesn't only prefer women.

I shake off the thoughts and help Atticus to his feet. Then I hesitate, a fresh surge of fear passing through me. All the men who saw me use my magic are dead, but my paranoia builds.

"Atticus," I say, "Did you...see anything down there?"

"I couldn't see a damn thing until the spell was broken," Atticus says. "Why do you ask?"

"Only curious," I say, wincing slightly. "We should get back in case more men are hunting for us."

"That's a given."

It takes an entire mile of walking to find a buggy to take us back to campus.

When I get back to my dorm room, Oliver is fast asleep. I remove my shirt and inspect my shoulder in the mirror.

Atticus marked me. I should be angry, but I find myself tracing over the hickey instead. He was only sucking in his breaths because of the pain, but I hated the way my body reacted to it. It's been months since I've touched a woman; that's probably why. All because I was crossing my fingers for Haylow to notice me, and I didn't want her to overhear anything if I bedded a woman. But now I have no choice.

Tomorrow, I'll go to one of the many parties hosted by Roche University students and get all of this out of my system. As much as I judge Atticus for his incredulous amount of fornication, a man still has needs.

My sleep becomes erratic, dancing on the line between dreams and reality.

There's a hand running down my bare chest, but I know it isn't real, so I let it continue down. My breathing runs unsteady as lips consume mine, a tongue tasting of mint exploring my mouth. A hand teases just under my beltline.

When a clothed pelvis presses in between my legs, I groan.

The mouth smiles against my lips. "You see, I knew you'd like that."

My eyes stay glued shut. "Atticus!"

I push him off me and lurch back, but the dream fades away, leaving me all alone in my empty dorm room, sweat dripping down my neck. Thank goodness Oliver has left for the day.

I rush to the basin and splash my face with cold water. *It was just a dream. Your body is just confused because you've been deprived too long. That's all.*

With Oliver gone, I should release some steam. I deadbolt the door and lie down in my bed.

Once my bare length is in my hand, I close my eyes and let images of Haylow Solace overtake me. I'm filled with relief when the conjured fantasies of her bare body edge me closer. How her breasts would feel against my palms. The way she'd moan and blush as my hands would explore her body.

Finally my release explodes, but as it does, another image plagues me. A mental picture of my hands running down Atticus's chest yesterday.

I shake my head and try to focus back on Haylow as I ride out the tail end of my release. Pleasuring myself isn't enough to get these thoughts out of my mind. I need a good, real-life woman to detox me, and fast.

CHAPTER 22

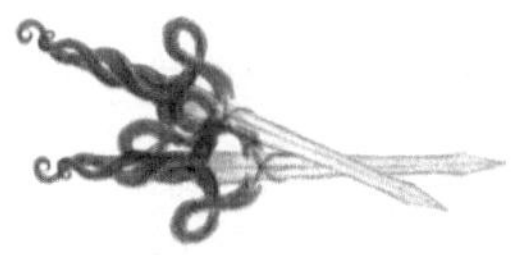

ATTICUS

When I awaken, it's late in the morning. My stomach growls. I sit up, expecting a shock of pain to shoot through my ribs, but I feel nothing.

Arlo sits on his bed with his legs folded, studying his textbook for our next stones exam.

I can still taste Dominic's skin on my tongue. The regeneration magic was so agonizing, I could hardly handle it, so I had no qualms causing Dominic a little pain to ease mine. Besides, I ran my tongue a time or two over the wound just to soothe the bite.

Regeneration magic wasn't present in humans during the atavistic age, and only immortals could wield it. It's a nasty thing, almost as painful as the time Konstantin carved my face with his knife.

Arlo doesn't look up from his textbook. "You were out late."

I rub my eyes. "It was a Friday night, of course I was."

"You woke me up when you came in." I know why he's not looking at me. I never got back at him for his charade during core magic class.

Upon his first arrival back at our dorm after he humiliated me, I acted as if I had forgotten the incident entirely. His shoulders had relaxed when I didn't bring it up, and now he falsely believes it slipped my mind altogether. But I know he fears pissing me off too much.

It's been fun watching him pretend like he's not scared of what I'll do. Playing the long con is incredibly satisfying.

I head to my trunk and pull out a pair of dark trousers, slipping them on. "Arlo, do you remember the other day when—"

"No." He interrupts me and whips his head up. "I don't remember anything."

I clear my throat, sneaking my rook toward his king. "When I brought a girl home past midnight. I wanted to apologize for breaking our agreement."

His voice shakes slightly. "Oh. It's fine. Bring them up till one in the morning if you'd like." He rubs a page of his textbook between his fingers.

I bite the inside of my lip to suppress a smile. "Why are you nervous?"

"I'm not!"

I stride in his direction. Arlo immediately backs up on his bed against the wall, his textbook falling off his lap and onto the mattress.

I crawl onto his bed and kneel in front of him. "If you're not nervous, then what's this?" I place the pad of my thumb against his forehead, wiping a bead of sweat away. He practically whimpers in fear because this isn't the first time I've punished him. Or the last.

"Please—Atticus. I'm sorry."

I can't help but smile. Even in a situation as innocent as this, hearing someone beg brings me great satisfaction. "You humiliated me greatly in core magic class."

"I know. Please. Don't—"

"An eye for an eye."

"No! Atticus please!" His voice trembles.

I grab his neck and push him down onto his bed. He tries to get away, but I'm faster, straddling his abdomen between my legs.

I pin his wrists down with my kneecaps, staring down at him. "Ready?"

"Please!"

I wet my pointer finger and shove it in his ear.

Arlo tries to get my finger off by scrunching his shoulder up high. "Atticus, stop!"

Honestly, I don't think most people would get so worked up over a prank like this, but Arlo certainly hates it. Enough that he's practically sobbing.

Jervany used to do something similar to me back when I was a child. I'll never forget the look in his eyes as I cut his father apart.

"Are we having fun yet, Arlo?" I pull my finger out and wet my middle finger.

"Stop. You already got me back!"

"Just to remind you." I stick my finger in his other ear.

He yelps out. "That's it! I'm changing roommates!"

"That's the fifth time you've threatened that this quarter. And the dean will tell you the same thing. Nobody wants to switch, so you're stuck with me." I push off him and head to my closet to get dressed for the day.

Arlo grabs his briefcase and rushes out of the room, slamming the door behind him.

He'll come around. They always do.

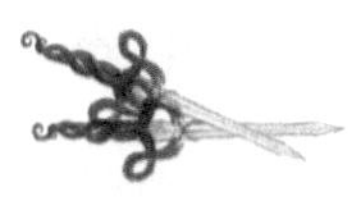

I spend the next hour reluctantly studying for the core magic exam this week. It's aggravating that I must do this at all, as if I didn't spend nearly eight straight years training in atavistic magic with Vec. But he reminds me I have hardly any knowledge of venitor magic in this new age.

If I would have studied before my visit to Mr. Bates's vault, maybe I would have known regeneration magic hurts like a bitch.

After my head finally explodes from studying, I venture into the school's courtyard toward the dining hall. It's almost noon and I have yet to eat a single thing.

A familiar face sits at the fountain, writing in a diary imprinted with vines, her brown hair pinned perfectly into an intricate bun at the nape of her neck.

Haylow Solace.

A strange emotion passes through me when I see her. Not lust or attraction. Something more negative. Whatever it is, it makes me think of Dominic.

I should walk straight past her, not sparing another glance. But instead, I find myself striding toward her. This is idiotic. There's no need to introduce myself, yet I can't make myself stop.

Haylow shuts her diary as I near, her expression completely neutral.

"I don't think we've been properly introduced." I kiss the back of her hand. "Atticus Desimir."

Haylow laughs. "I most definitely know who you are, Atticus. We're in most of the same classes, and you attended my party. How could I not?"

"I suppose you're right. The party was lovely, by the way."

"You mean the party where you practically destroyed one of the rooms?"

"I thought we cleaned up quite nicely."

Unlike most women, Haylow's body language isn't so open with me. She's not blushing as I stand over her. Nor is she picking at her nails or adjusting her hair. She raises an eyebrow and collects her things off the side of the fountain, stuffing them into her bag; annoyance in every aspect of her body language. "You left restraints around the bedpost and the sheets in tatters."

I scratch the back of my neck. "I apologize."

Once her belongings are together, she stands and laces her hands in front of her. "I'm going to tell you something everyone else is too lust-stricken to say: I don't trust you."

Well, this isn't good. "Just because I enjoy frequent bedroom activities doesn't mean I'm not worth trusting."

"I'm not talking about that. There's something off about you. The way you perform magic, even the way you dress. I've always learned to trust my intuition, and you are a wolf in this henhouse."

I tilt my head and ignore Vec's *I-told-you-so* voice snickering in my head. "Well, your fears are based in madness. Good day, Miss Solace."

She huffs as I turn away. I refuse to look back in her direction.

Who does she think she is? Not trusting me? If anyone is the weird one, it's her.

I pick at my food in the dining hall. My muscles tense every time Haylow's suspicious expression pops into my head. No matter how much I try to banish thoughts of her, my worries of being found out increase tenfold.

Students around me whisper of a party, so I focus my attention on that. It's at the Blake residence in the countryside. And apparently everybody is going to be there, which means Dominic and Oliver will probably attend too.

At that prospect alone, I must attend. How delicious it will be to see him again so soon.

When I arrive at the Blake's mansion, I'm pleasantly surprised by the decorations of the house party. Stringed light bulbs cover the hedges. The chill in the air is tolerable enough for the majority of the party to remain outdoors. Some students are laughing around the gardens or conversing around small tables. Others funnel indoors to escape the night air.

There's a full-service bar outside staffed with a bartender, unlike Haylow's chaotic party, which had a bunch of crystal glasses strewn about a dining room table like a madhouse.

I order a whiskey, then lean against a nearby wall, scoping out the party. Perhaps one day, after I endlessly torture Konstantin and Austrie, I'll settle down in a home like this. Just Vec, me, and the servants. Maybe he can put me to sleep another hundred years. I'd like to see what the 1990s will offer.

I lower my glass as Dominic and Oliver arrive. I wave at them, but they don't see me over the clusters of people. They head indoors. I release a sigh and go in through the rear entrance to hunt them down.

The inside is just as gorgeous as the outside, with high ceilings and a spiraling staircase. It screams luxury with mahogany walls, grandfather clocks, and mirrors encased in detailed, golden frames.

I'm already too late. Dominic is by the fireplace speaking to none other than Haylow Solace. I don't want to go anywhere near her. She'll pick me apart, and in front of Dom, no less. Near the grand piano, Oliver speaks to one of our classmates. He turns his gaze in my direction, immediately smiling when he sees me.

"Atticus!" Oliver spreads his hands. "I see you've wasted no time." He points to my drink.

I take a sip. "Would you like me to grab you one?"

"I'll grab one later." He looks over to where Dominic is shamelessly blushing while speaking to Solace. "It seems Dominic's already had some luck tonight."

I bite the inside of my cheek. "I don't see what kind of luck he could have with a girl like her."

"What? You don't like Miss Solace?"

"I'm sure she's lovely. Just not my type."

"I didn't realize you had a type."

"Well, I do. And she's not it." Nobody who speaks to me the way Haylow did could ever be someone I'd take any interest in. And the way she's monopolizing Dominic's time right now? Doesn't she know it's not appropriate to be alone with a man? I suppress my fury and take a gulp of whiskey.

After what feels like hours, Haylow excuses herself from Dominic. When she turns, we lock eyes. She glares.

Is that a challenge? So be it.

I wait till she's out of the room before I rush to Dominic, completely ignoring Oliver's tangent on his mishap with topaz when he was studying yesterday.

"Funny bumping into you here." My words are too fast. Too erratic.

He looks uncomfortable with my presence. "Oh, hello, Atticus."

"Is everything all right?"

"Yes." He looks around the room as if he's searching for someone. I follow his gaze to a girl sipping water in the corner. His eyes grow hungry.

So that's what he's after tonight? I should reprimand him for all the judgment he's shown me for my charades. But at least she's not Haylow.

Then something rages in me. I want him to enjoy the party with me, not this random girl. He and I are friends. He shouldn't be dallying away with women when Oliver and I are here. "Would you like to grab drinks? The bar is just outside."

He doesn't look at me, still eyeing the girl. "Please excuse me."

I grit my teeth. I want to yell after him, but what good would it do? My anger only increases as I ignore his incessant flirting with the girl and walk back to Oliver. He's still deep in his tangent about topaz with the bugger from earlier.

I interrupt. "So Dominic's bedding women tonight?"

Oliver snickers. "You're one to talk."

"I've never seen him interested in fucking until now. I've always seen him as the traditional type."

"On the way here, he told me it's been months. He's a man with needs, just like the rest of us."

My throat bobs. "Can't he just rub one out?"

Oliver chuckles. "You know it's not the same. This is a real human woman we're talking about."

I suppress my grumbling. My heart drops when Dominic takes the girl's hand and leads her up the staircase.

I need more whiskey.

CHAPTER 23

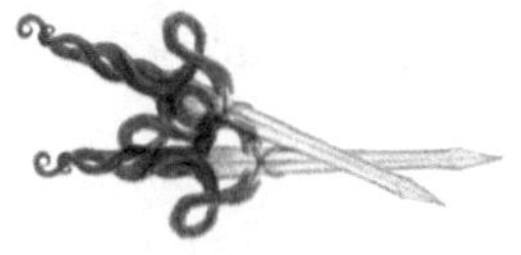

DOMINIC

I guide Priscilla up the stairs into an empty guest room. High society holds virtue and chastity on a pedestal—or rather, the illusion of it.

"Is this room all right?" I ask her. The room is fit with a queen-size bed, tapestries, and a lit fireplace.

Priscilla nods. "It's a lovely room. Finley's family sure knows how to decorate."

I lock the door behind us. My nerves fire along with a bit of excitement.

Priscilla stands in front of me on the center rug, her eyes sparkling. I run my thumb across her chin.

She lets out an adorable moan when our lips press together. Priscilla isn't the type of woman I want to marry. But she and I agree on what this is. We both need someone to draw our minds away from other pressing issues.

My lips work her neck, my fingers fumbling with her dress. She assists with the many clasps and strings.

I want her naked now. But strangely, I'm not getting hard as quickly as I expected.

Once I have her bare, I stare upon her body. Her small waist, perfect breasts. To my relief, I finally grow hard. Priscilla undoes my trousers. I slip them off, then unbutton my dress shirt. She pulls it down my arms and kisses along my pecs and collarbone. I want to be inside her.

I run my hands down her goosebumped spine as she kisses me. I grip her hips and back her onto the bed.

Our bodies meld together as I kiss her softly. She moans out as I thrust into her. The warmth of her core shoots pleasure through me. Yes. This is what I needed. I don't understand why I was getting so worked up earlier. I like women. In fact, I love them. A bite on my shoulder doesn't change that.

Priscilla takes the lead and rolls us, pushing me onto my back. I groan as she rides my cock. My toes stiffen as my climax nears. All my focus and sanity will return once I come.

She's dripping as the end nears. My neck arches back and Priscilla closes her eyes as she moans out my name, her walls tightening around my cock.

As my orgasm is about to crest, there's a distant laughter from the party that pierces through the room. It's a few men laughing, but only one chuckle sticks out to me.

Atticus's.

Suddenly, he's in my head, lips on my neck, teasing and taunting me for thinking about him while I'm fucking another. No matter how much I try to think of Priscilla's breasts or her soft curves, my body tenses and I release with a mighty fury.

No. This is worse than anything I could have imagined. But it was just a coincidence, right? I came because I was about to. It was just a strange turn of events that I heard his voice at the same time as my release. I'm being ridiculous.

Priscilla slows down as our orgasms fade and I go soft. She rolls off me and lies to my side.

I rest my wrist against my forehead as I stare up at the ceiling.

Her fingers run down my arm. "Was it good for you?"

I bite my bottom lip. "Yes."

Yes, it was.

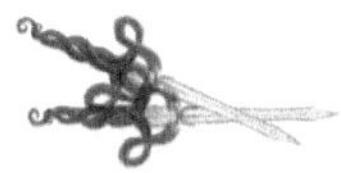

When I descend the staircase, nobody at the party pays me any mind, yet it feels like everyone is staring. It's like if I break my neutral expression, all the partygoers will know exactly where my mind went while I was upstairs.

How I came to the sound of Atticus's voice.

Never in my life have I ever thought of being with a man. At least, I don't think I have.

I can't accept this. It was just the intrusiveness of hearing him laugh, as I was already on the brink of climaxing. If it wasn't for the thin walls of this mansion, the entire debacle would already be behind me. I need a drink and quick.

Once I'm outside, I self-induce tunnel vision all the way to the bar. As the bartender pours my vodka, I rub my temples. This was supposed to be a fun night out for Oliver and me. I didn't even know Atticus was going to be here, and now look at me. I feel like a fool.

A hand lands on my shoulder. I jump and spin around, my heart dropping when I see his face.

"Finally. I thought you were going to be up there all night." Atticus has a drunken smile upon his face.

Butterflies gnaw at my chest. I wish he would just leave. If I could banish him out of my life and still save my brother, I would. But at the moment, I have no choice but to tolerate his presence. I turn my head, refusing to look at him.

"You seem upset. Was it not a good time?" Atticus asks.

I narrow my eyes. "Priscilla is more than equipped at pleasing a man."

"Then why the long face? I sure hope it's not because I killed a bunch of men in front of you. You're welcome for saving your life by the way."

Every word from his mouth fills me with fury. I barely process my own actions as I slam my glass down. "Because you won't leave me alone! Just because we're associates doesn't mean we need to spend every waking minute together!"

A pang of hurt swirls across Atticus's face. "We're friends."

"Acquaintances, at best."

Atticus adjusts his glasses and rakes a hand through his raven hair. "Fine. I'll leave you alone. We don't need to speak until I get closer to Cadence."

This is too much. I went too far. He didn't deserve any of that. I'm lashing out at him for reasons I can never tell him. "Wait... Atticus."

He swipes my drink off the bar and disappears into the house.

Dammit. I was too harsh. What if he doesn't want to help me find the artifact anymore? I should have kept my mouth shut! I take a deep breath and order another drink, hoping this will all be a distant nightmare in the morning.

I peer across the yard and another set of eyes is locked on me. Haylow signals me over. Is she really waving at me? I force a smile at her, wishing it were real. Usually it is. But after fighting with Atticus, my energy is shot.

I need to talk to her. I must. She and I already spoke once tonight. Perhaps she's finally warming up to me. And if anyone can get my mind off Atticus's tantrum, it's Haylow.

I take the plunge and shimmy past groups of students. Haylow Solace is my dream girl. When I think of my future, her face is always in it. If she became my wife, I'd be a very lucky man. She carries so much poise and confidence and isn't caught up in societal expectations, yet still possesses so much elegance.

"You again." I chuckle as I sit down across from her at one of the outdoor tables.

Lights hang above us, adding a glow to Haylow's skin. "I saw you were having a rough time with your friend there. Thought you may need some cheering up."

"Atticus just has his moments, is all."

She adjusts her lace glove. "You really don't see through him, do you?"

I raise an eyebrow. "What do you mean?"

"There's something strange about him. Don't you think?" Haylow tilts her head.

Yes, there is definitely something off about Atticus. But considering I've watched him kill ten men with execution-worthy magic, I'll let his other secrets slide. "You don't think him handsome like the other girls?" If Haylow preferred Atticus over me, I may crumble.

Her face scrunches up in disgust. If I didn't know better, almost hatred.

Oh, thank the gods.

"He's arrogant, I hate the way he dresses, and he's completely out of touch with the times!"

Should I propose to her now? No, I'm getting ahead of myself. Finally, someone agrees with me and doesn't see Atticus like some campus king. "I'll admit, his outfits are quite vintage."

"I completely agree." Haylow opens her mouth to say more but holds back. I suppose it's not ladylike for an honorable woman to gossip, but I like when she does it. Already my mood has improved, but I don't want to force her words.

I change topics and ask Haylow about her hobbies. Her interests. Apparently, she loves to knit and write. Sometimes she likes to fish on the weekends with her father and uncle.

I simply listen. And normally, I'd absorb her every word like a salivating dog.

But no matter how hard I concentrate on her, the gnawing feeling doesn't relent, and the back of my mind is consumed with thoughts of Atticus.

CHAPTER 24

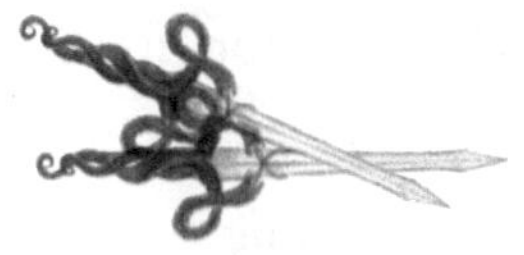

ATTICUS

Priscilla screams into the palm of my hand as I thrust into her inside the small closet. Her nails dig into my back with almost enough force to draw blood.

This is fucked. Seducing the girl my friend just bedded and taking her for myself, just to spite him. She isn't Dominic's and the only way to solidify that is to make her mine, too. In fact, I'll do this to every girl he gets the ingenious idea to sleep with when I'm around. I'll seduce them. Fuck them. Anything to get this feeling out of my system.

Once we release, we're both panting messes. Priscilla's eyes are glassy and exhausted, as if she's never been fucked like this. Tomorrow, when she wakes up sore and unable to move, I'll be the one on her mind, not Dominic. She has no need to ruminate on him, and he's not hers to think about.

After we dress in silence, I travel to Vec's home instead of the dorms. The last thing I want is to bump into Dominic.

When I enter the townhouse, Vec lounges in his sitting room, his legs crossed, drinking tea, and reading the paper. I didn't expect him to be up so late. Even immortals have to sleep.

He lowers the paper onto his lap. "You look like shit."

I slump into a chair and lean my head back. "Let's just say not all parties are a good time."

"You look like you could sober up. Tea?"

"No."

"Suit yourself." He sets his teacup on an end table. "How's Dominic?"

I seethe at the mention of his name. "Good. He's thrilled when he's not around me. Thank you for asking!"

Vec frowns. "I hope you're not getting too close to him."

"Dominic and I aren't close. He's made it clear he wants nothing to do with me unless it involves saving his brother."

"And why should you care?" Vec scoffs and shakes his head.

"Because—" I refuse to say it. Even to myself. Something has changed in me. The way I feel about Dominic—I don't like it. "I thought I finally had a friend besides just you. For years, I've done nothing but train, kill, and fuck, with never any time for normal friendships. But I guess it felt nice to feel needed." It rolls off my tongue so neatly, I almost believe it. But there is some truth to my words.

Vec opens his mouth to say something, but stops, covering an impending smile with the tips of his fingers. "I'm sorry, Atticus. Once this is all over, you'll be able to settle down. I want that for you. I wouldn't have spent centuries hunting Konstantin and Austrie down if I didn't."

"Thank you." I pinch the bridge of my nose. I hate being sappy with Vec, but the alcohol is burning away my defenses.

The quicker Dominic and I can get the artifact, the quicker these feelings will vanish.

I hope.

Dominic doesn't look in my direction at all throughout classes on Monday. I try to distract myself by sketching random shapes in my notebook, but it does almost nothing to dull the ache. The drawings become darker and more erratic as the class drags on, enough for Arlo to look concerned and scooch his chair a few inches away.

Yesterday, Cadence sent a telegram telling me to meet her at a tea shop later today. If I can progress with her, and report my success to Dominic, maybe he'll come around. We'll be friends again and whatever nonsense is plaguing his mind will vanish.

Class ends and I gather my belongings. I have a few hours before I meet with her. Maybe I'll just sleep the time away. I exit the classroom, keeping my eyes locked forward so I don't catch a glimpse of Dominic.

"Atticus, wait!" Oliver calls after me.

What does he want now? I stop, sigh, then spin around in his direction. "Oliver, it's nice to see you."

Oliver wears a gray scarf today, though even with it, scars peek out. It really wasn't until Dominic pointed it out that I realized how badly his mother wounded him. The scarves and high collars barely hide it.

"Why aren't you and Dominic speaking?" he asks.

Oliver noticed? "Wish I could say. He blew up at me at Finley's party, and we haven't spoken since."

I still don't know what Dominic's deal was. It all started after he healed me with regeneration magic, but he seemed fine on the way home. Perhaps using regeneration magic has side effects. Irritability being one, if you ask me.

"He'll come around. Trust me. Ever since his brother passed, he gets in spats for no reason at all." Oliver places a hand on my shoulder. "In the meantime, I could use a dueling partner today to practice for the skills exam. If you have time, of course."

Typically, I never duel outside of classroom time with other students. But Oliver is Dominic's closest friend, so it would be wise to keep him close. "Yes. I have time."

"Excellent!"

The two of us journey through the mahogany halls and stairs of Roche University to the dueling circle near the training fields. One girl has a tutor helping her perfect air manipulation by throwing gusts of wind against large bags of sand.

I'll have to play this carefully with Oliver. Especially if he wants to practice enchantments. Desimir and atavistic magic can mimic certain enchantments when used correctly. But if he wants me to perform other types, I'll have to come up with a convoluted lie.

"Can I practice non-harmful spells on you?" Oliver asks.

It's better than enchantments. "Go for it, but you better not use transmutation on me. I'd like to stay human if at all possible."

"As you wish." Oliver starts by levitating me off the ground. At one point he raises me so high, I worry for my safety. At any second, he could lose control and drop me. But he never does. As always, Oliver emulates control of everything he does.

He lowers me to the ground. "Throw air manipulation at me. I want to practice reflection."

"Gladly." I conjure up a gust of air, flinging it at him, and he reflects it up toward the sky with impeccable skill. The second time, I increase the intensity of the blow. It slides his feet back, but he reflects it in time.

Then he grabs turquoise from his pocket and turns my air manipulation into a flurry of dust above his head.

"Oliver?" He's not planning on hitting me with that—is he?

He flings one hand back, ready to hurl the dust in my direction. I don't have reflection magic. In my day, we just dodged it. But in the small arena we're in, I have nowhere to leap to avoid it.

Oliver laughs. "I'll finally be able to say I beat Atticus Desimir in a duel."

He thinks I'll let him beat *me* just because we're practicing? I have no choice but to use herbal magic. And lucky for me, I keep it on me at all times, ever since I stole some of my favorites from Mr. Bates's home. God rest his soul.

If Oliver becomes suspicious, I'll think of something to tell him. Or convince him I used an enchantment to manipulate his memories. I direct my energy into the toad's bark in my inner pockets and stomp my foot onto the ground. Ink words of an ancient language form in a circle around him.

Before Oliver can chuck the dust cloud at me, I direct the remainder of the energy into the vial of rosemary under my coat, activating the circle. Oliver's eyes bug out and his mouth gapes as he loses his ability to breathe. He loses control of the dust and grabs at his throat.

The toad's bark causes a chamber of airlessness and the rosemary complements it, nulling his magic. My goal all along. Though it's a shame that I have to asphyxiate him to get to that point.

Oliver reaches a hand out, begging me to stop. And once I'm sure I've won, I release the herbal magic. He coughs and gags on his hands and knees, barely able to catch his breath.

I walk forward. "Good practice. Perhaps you'll beat me next time. Though, in the future, warn me of your intentions first before you ask me to duel."

Oliver sees the remnants of the black words in the dirt and touches them, his hand shaking. "You—" He heaves, then stares up at me with darkness behind his eyes. "How did you get your hands on toad's bark?"

Shit. Double shit. He knows I used herbs? *Relax, you can talk your way out of it.* "It's a stone, combined with an enchantment. I learned it in a fourth-year textbook."

"No stone asphyxiates! Nothing with stone magic is this dark!"

I should have known better than to use herbs in front of Oliver. Damn me, letting childish pride get in the way. Now I'm completely exposed.

"This is dangerous, Atticus. They'll execute you if you're caught!" Oliver pushes to his feet. "My mother played with fire. It's how I ended up mauled." He pulls his collar down, showing me the gruesome scars that run down his neck and disappear under his shirt.

"Fine. I suppose there's no point in lying." I pull the two vials from my coat. "Toad's bark and rosemary, as you suspected."

"I knew you had your quirks. But not this. *Never* this. Does Dominic know?" Oliver stays four arm's lengths away from me, as if I'm some kind of criminal.

I stuff the vials back in my pockets. "He is very aware. And approves. After all, I'm helping him save his precious little brother."

Oliver tightens his fists. I've never seen him burn with anger before. It's almost scary. "I'm more hurt that Dominic has hidden the depths of his pain from me. I knew he'd get himself into some kind of trouble one of these days with his quest to wake Archer. And I take it you're perpetuating this delusion?"

"It's not a delusion."

"And you know this how?"

"Oliver, you've already clarified that you want nothing to do with this. The less you know, the better." I turn to leave.

"Wait!"

I stop. "Yes?"

Oliver checks over his shoulder, making sure nobody is within listening range. "Promise me I can trust you with Dominic. Promise me you'll never use herbal magic again."

I could never promise such a thing, but I'll say anything to keep him quiet. "If that's what you wish."

Oliver's anger has faded into deep concern, but I'm not stupid. He's only willing to help in order to keep Dominic safe from me. But because Oliver knows the depths of herbal magic better than anyone in this time, he also knows better than to go toe-to-toe with me.

In fact, I don't doubt that Oliver will be willing to help me with anything I need from this point on. Anything to protect his friend.

Anything to protect himself.

The air grows humid on my stroll to the dessert shop to meet Cadence.

Now that the jolt of Oliver's attack on me has lessened, I'm consumed with regret. It was stupid to reveal my intentions with Dominic. Or to expose my herbal magic. At least he doesn't know about Desimir or atavistic magic yet.

I'll keep a close eye on him. If I get any sign that he'll report me, I'll get rid of him. Though reporting me means endangering Dominic, which I doubt Oliver would ever risk.

The shops on this street are pastel. During the springtime, this stretch of the city must look magnificent, especially with the flower boxes on the windows.

As I near my destination, a small body pops out of nowhere. "Atticus!"

A woman with dark hair stands ten feet in front of me, waving. Who is this woman? A friend from school?

Might as well roll with it. "Ah yes! Nice to see you—"

The woman rolls her eyes. "I thought you'd recognize me, even with the enchantment." She looks around, making sure no eyes are on her, then claps her hands, instantly morphing into a face and figure I recognize.

"Oh...Cadence! Lovely to see you. Do excuse me, I thought you would have transformed back into yourself before I arrived." How annoying. She made me look like a loggerhead.

"Yes. But I wanted to surprise you." Cadence's smile is extra wide. I can see almost every one of her teeth. Her tan day dress flows in the wind and the green bow tied around her neck compliments her ivory skin. A small hat sits upon her head, her hair pinned up. Her hands squeeze around a small, beaded purse.

I kiss her cheek. "You look absolutely stunning."

She bounces a little, like every paltry word I say melts her heart, no matter how generic. "Shall we go inside?"

"After you." Being a gentleman, I hold the door open for her.

Cadence and I enter the small tea and dessert shop and sit at a table by the window. A girl brings us a teapot and a selection of loose herbs to choose from. Cadence chooses oolong tea. I select black tea.

"How are your studies at Roche? I hope it isn't terribly difficult." Cadence pours hot water over the strainer of oolong.

"They're fine." I need to ask her more about herself. Eventually, she'll notice that she's giving and I'm taking. "How's your family?"

She shrugs. "Father's been busy with new legislation. Mother fills her days with endless social events."

"Sounds dreadful."

"They seem to enjoy it." Cadence rubs the back of her neck. "You know, I was thinking. Perhaps you should meet my father."

I go still. Meeting the prime minister? That would be a horrible idea. But if I met him, I could gain his trust. Or, if the gathering is at her residence, I could scope the home out for the artifact. That way, I wouldn't have to sneak in. But meeting her parents means they'll see me as a suitor, and *that* is not preferable. But if I can hold on longer, this could work. "At your home?"

She places a hand on my forearm. "Of course."

Yes. This will do nicely. "I would *love* to meet your father, Cadence."

Giddiness takes over her entire body. Thoughts of wedding bells and children are swarming through her mind. I just know it. I can practically hear the deplorable toddlers screaming and running around our future home.

"Will you give me a tour of your home while I'm there?" I ask. "It's not everyday someone gets to step inside the famed 10 Downing Street."

She laughs. "A tour? If that's what you'd like. My father won't love the idea, but he can put up with it for one day if it means finding me a suitor I actually like." Cadence quickly covers her mouth. "Oh dear, did I say that out loud?"

I ignore her last comment. *No Cadence, I am definitely not your suitor. You'll do well to learn that quickly.* "Your home is your castle, and I want its princess to tell me all about it."

Cadence blushes. "I'm no princess."

I reach forward and stroke her jaw. "You are, if I say you are."

CHAPTER 25

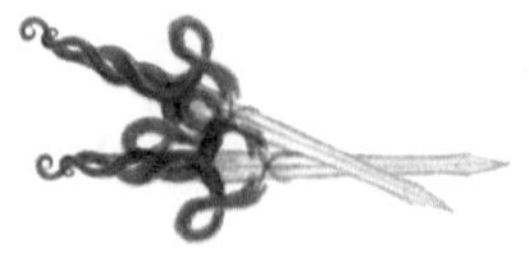

ATTICUS

I curse under my breath as I knock on Dominic's door. I know he doesn't want to see me, but what I'm going to tell him affects him, too. That's relevant enough to disturb him. Right?

There is shuffling behind the door, and my chest goes tight. The door opens, and I stand face to face with Dominic. Oliver is nowhere to be seen, thankfully. Right now would be the worst time possible to get him involved with Dominic and me. And when Dominic learns I told Oliver, he'll have another reason to be angry.

"Before you say anything—whatever I did. Using herbal magic, killing goons—" *Sleeping with Priscilla mere minutes after you did. Though I'll keep that one my little secret.* "Please, just—"

"No, don't apologize." Dominic rubs the back of his neck and stares at the ground. "I'm sorry for what I said."

I scratch my head. He's apologizing—to me? Well, well, isn't this a turn of events? Already I feel a couple pounds lighter.

"I've just been dealing with shit, and I took it out on you." Dominic's brown eyes appear bloodshot when he finally looks at me. Whatever is plaguing him must be something significant.

"Is it your brother? Your father?" I ask.

"It doesn't matter." He breaks eye contact, instead looking at an insignificant part of the door frame. "I want to make amends."

"Say no more." I move my hand down through the air, pretending as if I just cast some sort of spell of forgiveness. Not being friends with Dominic, even for that short amount of time, made me feel as though I couldn't take a full breath. Which makes my future with him all the more sour when I imagine it.

Dominic invites me into his room. "Is the apology the only reason you're here?"

I don't take a seat, even as he sits. "No. I spent more time with Cadence. And luckily for us, she's invited me to meet her family. And her father."

Dominic smiles. "Oh Atticus, that's brilliant!" He places a hand on his forehead, lost in thoughts of hope, no doubt.

I take in the sight of his dorm room. Until now, I have never really studied the deep contrast between Oliver and Dominic. Oliver's side is neat as can be, which is to be expected. There's barely any decor or trinkets. Just the bare necessities of life.

Dominic's side is like looking directly into his mental state. His bed is half made, and he has laundry hanging over the edge of his mattress. Papers, supplies, and journals cover his desk. Broken pocket watches sit off to the side along with tools, as if repairing them is a hobby of his.

"She's invited me over this weekend," I say. "And I've even convinced her to give me a house tour."

"But if she's inviting you over to meet her parents, you know what that means, don't you?"

"Of course I do!" My tone grows annoyed.

Dominic smiles and folds his arms. "And I take it you're still sticking to your guns about never marrying? You know, if we're able to put the artifact back without detection, you could wed her. She comes from a respectable, wealthy family. What's not to love?"

"Trying to pawn me off on her? I would rather eat cotton than become her husband."

He takes an audible sigh of relief. *Wait—relief? Perhaps I misheard.*

"Let me come with you. I'll watch from a distance inside the carriage in case anything goes haywire," Dominic says.

I think about it. Yes, it would be handy to have a backup plan in case anything goes array. "Yes. That sounds splendid."

Dominic and I iron out the details for the next hour until we eventually say our goodbyes for the night, and I head back to my dorm. The entire way, I can't stop replaying his relief-stricken response to my refusal to marry Cadence. Is he... No, he can't be. Dominic doesn't even like men. Or I suppose he never said he didn't. He's vilely in love with Haylow.

I grunt at the thought of Miss Solace. Last night, I dreamed of a world where she didn't exist. A world where I made that happen. And I enjoyed every second of it.

Dominic is my friend. It's as simple as that.

And he's nothing more.

As I look in the mirror in one of Vec's guest rooms, I smooth my hand over the red velvet jacket I had made by my favorite seamstress. The black collared shirt underneath compliments the dark red. Swirling designs emboss the pants.

See Vec, you don't need to dress like a seal to look dashing. I suppose getting this made in the first place was succumbing to Vec's will. But he's right. I can't exactly risk looking out of place in front of the prime minister.

Of course, I'll still be wearing my circular frames. Without their tint, I can hardly carry on a conversation indoors. I smooth back my dark curls just as I hear a buggy pull up. I rush downstairs and out the door, my boots clicking against the cobblestone.

I slide inside the buggy beside Dominic and shut the door. "I can't thank you enough for coming with me."

"Anything for Archer." Dominic adjusts his jacket as he finds a comfortable position in the seat.

I was hoping he'd say *anything for a friend*, but I suppose his brother is a good cause, too.

As we ride to 10 Downing Street, I replay Vec's instructions in my head. We practiced for hours last night on how I should present myself, and I actually took him seriously for once. Especially after he informed me of the strict security policies of the English government. It's also rumored that the prime minister is a big neurotic. Getting on the wrong page with him could have detrimental consequences. My theory is that Vec instilled fear in me, purely to keep me respectable. In high society, I am his nephew. My actions affect him more than they do me.

"Once you're dropped off, I'll wait in the buggy," Dominic says. On the seat across from us is a stack of textbooks for him to keep busy with. "If anything happens, find a window and cast magic, so I'll notice you." He hands me amber. "Preferably fire."

"Yes, I hope you're not too busy with your studies to notice my impending doom."

"If I don't see, the driver will."

"Smashing."

The carriage pulls in front of the yellow brick home. As we slow, the front door opens and Cadence emerges with an enormous smile on her face. Her mother follows behind.

The driver opens the door for me.

"Wish me luck, Dom."

"Good luck."

With a deep breath, I step out of the buggy and onto the pavement. Just as I do, the prime minister, Cecil Graystone, walks out the front door, his posture and expression awfully intimidating.

You're a gentleman. A sought-after suitor. A respectful lover of women. Act like it.

"Atticus!" Cadence squeals, her olive dress twirling with her movements. Her hair is carefully pinned into the shape of a rose. I can tell she wants to lunge and hug me, but it would be highly inappropriate in front of her parents.

"You're ravishing, Cadence." I smile down at her.

I step over to her mother and take her hand. "Lovely to meet you, Mrs. Graystone." I bend over and kiss the back of her hand.

"Mr. Desimir. It is a pleasure." Mrs. Graystone's approving smile brings me great relief.

Until I see the stern expression on her husband's face.

I stand up straighter as I move in front of him, positioning myself to shake his hand. "Prime Minister. It's an honor."

"Please, call me Mr. Graystone. If I remember correctly, you entertained my daughter at the Tulip Ball."

"Yes, I was graciously offered an invitation from a friend of mine. A wondrous twist of fate, since that is where your daughter and I met. The night was lovely, and she, an even better dance partner."

The prime minister still hasn't smiled. "She says you've written letters ever since, and that you're quite the poet."

Cadence bites the inside of her cheek. Clever liar. A way to explain our closeness without admitting to sneaking out to spend time alone. Oh, the scandal.

"With her, I can hardly contain the words that I express. You've raised a good one." Sometimes I surprise myself with how easy it is to lie.

Mr. Graystone's beard bounces with his chuckle.

Oh, sweet relief. He likes me.

The four of us enter the large home and step into the foyer. The floor is painted in a checkerboard pattern, covered only by a long red carpet down the center. A crystal chandelier sparkles from the ceiling. Gold textured wallpaper covers the walls.

In contrast, wood covers the walls of the dining room, as it does the floor. But the ceiling is a vibrant white. White curtains drape over the windows. Beneath the table is a hideous green and red rug.

The prime minister takes a seat at the head of the table. Cadence sits on her father's right, and her mother sits on his left. I take the seat next to Cadence on one of the red upholstered chairs, which will clash horribly with my suit.

A small boy, with a head full of brown curls, no older than twelve, walks into the room, his nose stuck in a botany book. He doesn't look up from it as he walks up to me.

Then he peers over the book, his stare full of scorn. My eyebrow arches in response.

"You're in my seat." His voice drips with apathy. He reminds me of myself at his age, knowing what he wants and not caring what others think.

"Forgive me, I will move." It's not like I had my sights set on sitting next to Cadence, anyway. I move to stand.

"No." Cadence grabs my arm and pulls me down. "Ronald. Go sit by Mother."

Her brother whines. "It's my seat, Caddie!"

Mr. Graystone clears his throat. "Mr. Desimir is our guest, Ronny. Sit by your mother, just for today."

Ronald groans, his shoulders slumped, while he drags his feet around the table and climbs into the seat across from me. Then he gives me a long death stare, his hand gripping his soup spoon. Between his fury, and his interest in botany, he'd make a brilliant dark venitor one day, skilled in the arts of herbal magic.

The seven-course meal begins. The servants bring out raw oysters. I don't like oysters, but I remind myself why I'm here and the price I must pay for vengeance.

"So, Atticus," Mrs. Graystone says, "Cadence tells me you are attending Roche. Quite a prodigious school. I'm impressed."

I insert the knife into the oyster and separate the shells. "Yes. As a second year."

Ronald obnoxiously slurps his oyster across the table. I try my best to ignore it, as does everyone else. For how the prime minister treats Cadence, even in her adult years, I'm surprised he puts up with such disobedience from his son.

"And what are you planning on doing when you graduate?" Mr. Graystone asks.

"I haven't decided yet. Maybe I'll work in venitor consulting. Or continue my studies and join the Venitor Brigade." Vec told me to give two options. One to show my brains. The other to show my strength.

The prime minister seems satisfied.

But Cadence doesn't, her face full of worry. "But you wouldn't do something like that! The brigade is dangerous."

"If it means serving my country, then I will risk my life if necessary." I nod at the prime minister.

He dabs his mouth with his handkerchief. "Cadence, joining the brigade is an honorable thing. That's something worth admiring."

Cadence gives a half-hearted smile. "I suppose you're right, Father."

The maids bring out brown Windsor soup for the second course. Cadence still looks anxious at the prospect of me going to battle. Lucky for her, I have no plans to. But her father is more than ecstatic at my career prospects, and that's all that matters.

"May I ask...why the tinted lenses?" Mrs. Graystone asks.

I suppose that is a fair question. "Let's just say Edison and I don't get along."

Mrs. Graystone laughs. "Whatever do you mean?"

"The bulbs give him headaches," Cadence chimes in as if she knows me after the few times we've spent together.

"How peculiar," the prime minister says.

The next few courses are so filling, I don't think I'll even be able to stomach dessert as they bring out a delicious, marbled jelly.

"Father," Cadence says. "May I give Atticus a tour?"

That's my good, obedient girl. I don't have to say a word for you to remember exactly what I want. But you'll do anything to keep me happy, won't you?

The prime minister frowns and doesn't answer for an entire minute. It's odd. I almost think he's ignoring her request completely until he finally speaks. "Yes, but bring Ronald with you. I won't have you dallying about without a chaperone. Meet us in the drawing room when you're finished."

She stands and gives him a kiss on the cheek. "Thank you, Father. Come Atticus."

I follow her out of the dining room, Ronny following close behind.

"Your parents are lovely," I say as we ascend the stairs. On the yellow walls are pictures of previous prime ministers. It's strange to think that I'm technically older than these wrinkled men.

"Father means well. I just wish he weren't so set in his ways. But he seems to like you," Cadence says as we reach the second floor.

"I don't like you," Ronny says.

"Ronny!" Cadence nudges his shoulder with her hip. "That's incredibly rude."

I laugh. "It's fine, Cadence. I was a man of strong opinions at his age, too." I bend down in front of Ronny. "The rest of them don't understand, but we're men at heart, aren't we Ronald?"

He crosses his arms and turns away from me. I can't help but chuckle.

Cadence shows me bedrooms, offices, bathrooms, and a conference room. Ronald refuses to let us view his room. There's no sign of the artifact yet.

A pair of double doors catches my eye. "What's that room?"

"Oh, that's the cabinet room. Nobody is allowed in there." Cadence sighs.

"Why not?"

"He only uses that room for meetings with other officials as there are *things* locked up in there."

"But it's not locked?"

"No, but—"

"I go in there all the time," Ronny says, puffing out his chest.

"Do you now?" I ask with a smile.

Ronny nods. "Father is too busy to notice most days. He caught me once, but he didn't punish me."

Cadence scoffs. "If it were me, I'd be locked in my room for weeks."

"How neat it would be to see such a secret room. But like you said, it's off limits." I feign a disappointed expression.

I know she wants to show me. She knows how happy it would make me. *And don't you want to see me happy, my sweet?*

I give her a half-smile, and I practically watch her heart melt. "I'll show you. But we can't be more than a few minutes."

"Deal." I rub my thumb across her chin. "I'll never forget this."

Ronny goes before us and opens the white double doors. There's a large meeting table in the middle with two pillars surrounding it. Above the fireplace is a portrait of a man with a plaque beneath him. Prime Minister Robert Walpole. Bookshelves completely cover one wall.

Directly across the room, between two large windows, is a large, translucent jade cabinet secured with an elaborate lock.

"What's that?" I ask, even though I already know. Its energy radiates throughout the room, teasing my atavistic blood. Taunting it with its immense power. Do Cadence and Ronny feel it too?

Cadence approaches it with folded arms. "The artifact."

I bite the inside of my lip. So much hard work has paid off and I'm one step closer to the end. I pretend to be uninterested and instead step in front of one window, staring out of the vast sheet of glass. From here, I can see Dominic's buggy and part of the gardens.

In the corner of my eye, the oval crimson artifact glows beneath its jade enclosure. Even beneath the hue of green from the case, I can see the hard, golden lace that covers the red stone. It's the size of my hand. A large padlock keeps it secure. The lock is cylindrical and spins in ten different directions. Even with its complexity, the zeledian root should have no problem unlocking it.

After a few minutes, Cadence anxiously directs us out of the room. But, unknown to her, minutes were all I needed. We make our way into the drawing room, where we eat chocolates and assorted nuts and sip coffee. I have a wonderful conversation with Mrs. Graystone about her hobby, where she likes to crochet blankets. She even offers to make me one.

Later, we say our goodbyes. Ronny refuses to wish me well and instead runs back upstairs with his book in tow. I'm absolutely relieved Mr. Graystone didn't ask about my intentions with his daughter. But is that a bad thing? No matter. I've already taken what I need from him. Knowing the location of the artifact, combined with his daughter's obsession, I have everything I need.

CHAPTER 26

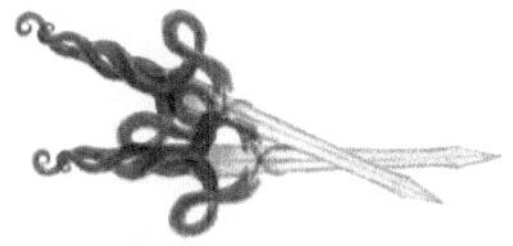

DOMINIC

It's been nearly three hours and my hips are sore from sitting so long. I adjust in my seat and continue my reading on secondary magic, but I have trouble concentrating.

I imagine what Atticus must be up to with Cadence and her family. What if the prime minister insists on Atticus marrying her? He'll be stuck with her for life, all because of me. Not that I should care. Atticus is a man, and he can deal with such propositions on his own. But a strange feeling rushes through me at the thought of him married off.

I flinch out of the trance as the buggy door whips open. Atticus stands there, his expression overly full from the feast.

I shut my book. "I take it everything went well?"

Atticus grins like an idiot as he settles into the buggy next to me. "More than well."

"And? Tell me!" I can't help my excitement. I really didn't know if Atticus had it in him. The thought of him trying to act like a gentleman during dinner with a figure of such importance almost makes me chuckle.

The driver takes off and I wait in dreaded anticipation for Atticus to respond.

"The artifact is in the prime minister's cabinet room, secured behind jade and a lock that spins ten different ways. The zeledian will unlock it," Atticus says.

"Even with the jade?"

"Jade?"

Did he forget? It's a stone taught about in grade school. "Yes. Jade has enhanced locking properties in the event someone tries to use other means to gain access to restricted goods."

Atticus's accomplished expression fades. "Can the zeledian override that too?"

I shrug. "I know almost nothing about herbal magic. Especially how it relates to stone."

Atticus swallows. "Would Oliver know?"

It's true. Oliver may know. In his obsession to bar the world further from herbal magic, he's learned almost everything about it, even securing banned books. He believes that if one wants to end evil, they must know its full weight. "Yes. It's very possible he knows. But do you really want to risk asking him? He's a loyal enough friend to not rat us out, but he hates herbs more than anything."

"If it means getting the artifact, then we should take our chances."

Outside the buggy, a woman shouts. I peek out the window, watching a mother chase a young girl on the sidewalk.

"Maryanne, get back here!" The mother almost trips on her skirts, running after the girl.

The buggy comes to a halt. Atticus and I both look out the window.

The young girl has a wide smile on her face as she steps off the sidewalk, running into the middle of the street. Cyclists and buggy drivers shout at her as she nearly collides with a bike.

I suck in a breath as she maneuvers around the horses. A few horses become agitated as she runs between their legs. "She's going to get crushed!"

I look at Atticus.

But he is long gone.

"Atticus?" I rush out of the buggy. *Where did he go?* "Atticus!"

Across the way, I catch sight of him running straight for the girl. As she walks in front of a white horse, it rears up. Her smile fades, eyes filled with fear.

Her mother yells out.

The girl screams and falls onto her back below the horse.

I want to close my eyes, but I can't look away.

Atticus sprints, diving at the girl. My breath hitches as everything plays out, seemingly in slow motion. He wraps her in his arms, rolling them both out of the way as the horse comes down.

I release a stuck breath. If Atticus were even a second slower, they would have been trampled to death.

I'm careful as I run across the street and down the sidewalk to Atticus.

I go still as I behold the sight. Atticus is kneeling as he holds the sniffling child in his arms, one of his hands cradling the back of her head, almost like a panicked father.

"Juni—you're safe, Juni." His voice cracks as he soothes the girl.

Juni? Where have I heard that name before?

"Atticus?" I place a hand on his shoulder, but he doesn't notice. It's as if he's lost in a deep trance. A deep, incompressible fear dusts his expression.

The mother rushes toward us. "Maryanne! Thank the heavens!"

But Atticus is still lost somewhere in the dark depths of his mind. Even the sound of the mother's voice doesn't take him out of the trance.

People are looking. The mother grows confused. I have to snap him out of this, and fast.

I kneel next to Atticus and whisper in his ear. "Come back. Wherever you are isn't real."

He doesn't respond. A few people are starting to crowd around.

Think, Dominic.

I allow myself to dive into his illusion. "Atticus—Juni is safe. Let go of her."

His eyes flicker beneath his glasses, reality colliding with him. I pull his shoulder back, and he finally lets go.

The young girl gives Atticus one last squeeze before running off to her mother. She places her thumb in her mouth as she stands by the woman.

"Thank you, sir," the mother says to Atticus. "She owes you her life."

All he does is nod at the woman.

Even freed from the trance, I have to guide Atticus to his feet and hold his arm all the way back to the buggy. He sits in the seat across from me, arms resting on his thighs. He still hasn't spoken.

"Juni...was she your sister?" I ask.

Atticus nods.

I remember Konstantin speaking of his family's tragedy, but I didn't realize he had a sibling who'd passed too. It's tempting to ask him what happened, but now doesn't seem like the right time. Not when he can barely speak.

So instead I ask him a simple question. "Would you like to meet Archer?"

I pay the driver extra to take us to the stasis ward. When Archer was first stricken, he was bound in a hospital for months. Once his life-threatening wounds healed, doctors transferred him here to live out the rest of his days. But with the hope Atticus has brought me, I believe Archer will get the chance to live a full life.

It's strange to have Atticus walking next to me up the steps of the stasis ward. But after everything he's done for me, and how he lets me see his demons, it's the least I can do. He lost a sibling. And now I get to show him what he's helping me fight for.

When we step inside Archer's room, a nurse is tucking him in with a new set of white linens. She nods to Atticus and me, then leaves once she finishes up.

Archer looks peaceful, as he always does. Another benefit of the red beryl stone is that it keeps the mind tranquil, even in those who should be dead.

Atticus stares at Archer and then at me. "He looks just like you."

I smooth my auburn hair back. The same color Archer shares, except his is brighter. "Red runs in our family."

Atticus pulls a chair over to Archer's bedside and takes hold of his hand, the same way I do when I visit. I sit on a chair near the end of the bed.

Atticus bows his head. His mouth opens slightly, but he hesitates, as if he was about to say something. His bottom lip trembles.

"Atticus?"

"I was twelve when it happened."

My jaw relaxes. Finally, he's going to tell me about it. His secrets. The core of his vulnerabilities.

"They had already slaughtered my parents when Juni entered the room. The men who broke into our home were going to spare her life."

Atticus's throat bobs. "But she tried to fight them." His shoulders shake and he goes pale. "One of the men threw her into the wall. She shattered like a porcelain doll."

My heart breaks in two. "Atticus...I'm sorry. I had no idea."

I never saw Archer's accident. He's not even dead. But my fear of losing him runs deep enough to bleed into my dreams. I may turn to dust if Archer ever passed. Atticus has already experienced that feeling. He knows my fears and my pains even better than I do. "How old was she?"

"She was ten. If I had been stronger, I could have saved her. I only survived because of a protective charm I was wearing." So young. And to witness such an atrocity—no wonder Atticus is the way he is. The drinking. The shameless sex.

"Atticus, you were twelve. When I was twelve, I couldn't even beat my father in a friendly wrestling match, let alone a group of home intruders. Don't be so hard on yourself. The people we love who have passed to the other side look down upon us with warm smiles. And your family knows how much you love them and the lengths you would have gone to save them. Trust me on this one."

Even his glasses can't hide the redness growing around his eyes. He looks at Archer instead of me just to mask it. Though he doesn't let a single tear fall, as if he's absorbing the sadness he should simply let go.

"Once, when my family and I were at our summer home, Archer, Ivy, and I discovered wild onions not far from the back door. We picked them all and threw them at trees for fun, not realizing they were our mother's poor attempt at gardening."

Atticus chuckles, his voice breaking slightly.

"Needless to say, she was peeved at us." I smile. "But I'll never forget her face. Or the way my father laughed with us when we told him the story."

The sunset glows through the window. We should get going, but I'm afraid if I let Atticus go back to his uncle's home or the dorms, he'll drink himself to death. Or go find someone to sleep with and numb his pain. I can't let him do that to himself. Not again.

"Atticus, my family owns a few townhouses in London. There's one just a few streets from here and it's empty tonight. Why don't we sleep there? Besides, it's a long way back to the dorms, even by buggy."

"Your father won't mind?"

I shake my head. "No. The home is there specifically for visiting Archer."

Atticus gently places Archer's hand to the side and stands. "Then yes. Let's stay there."

CHAPTER 27

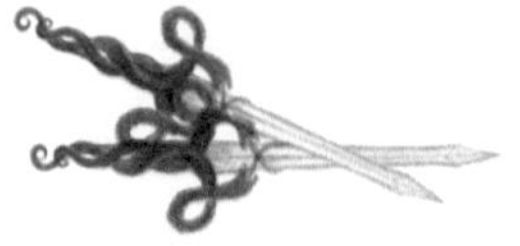

ATTICUS

So many emotions fill me, I'm not even sure which one to latch onto.

I didn't want to stay with Dominic when he suggested the townhouse. I wanted to stumble into a local bar and drink until I couldn't remember my name. But something stopped me from saying no. Maybe it was seeing Archer. Or maybe it was the comfort Dominic's words brought me.

The townhouse is small compared to Vec's. Granted, it's only used for the family's visits to Archer. Still, it has all the bells and whistles of wealth and power from wide hallways to glittering chandeliers.

"Have a seat in the drawing room. I'll grab us water." Dominic disappears down the hall.

I sit on the French-style couch. I'd prefer something a lot stronger than water. But something tells me Dominic won't offer me such a thing. As soon as he's asleep, I'll creep into the kitchen and find something to lessen the heaviness in my chest.

Dominic comes back minutes later with two glasses of water and sets one on the small table next to me. He builds a fire in the fireplace and turns out the lights, as if he's being mindful of my distaste for the lightbulb's illumination.

He sits on the couch next to me. For once, I take off my tinted frames and set them on the side table.

"How many homes does your family own?" I sip the water.

"Ten in total. It used to be eleven, but we sold our holiday home to fund Archer's life support."

"The same home from the onion story?"

"Yes, unfortunately."

"I'm sorry." It was a lovely story. One that made me laugh but also grow bitter. It reminded me of the silly stories I once had with my family. Though I can't think of those happy times anymore without feeling the tendrils of darker, tainted emotions. I place my hand on his shoulder.

Dominic visibly shudders from my touch.

How odd. Though he's been acting rather peculiar for quite some time. "You know, Dominic. Even after we rectified our little quarrel, you still act strange around me."

"I—" Dom looks away from me. "Maybe it's because you can just be a little intimidating sometimes."

He's lying, I can feel it. A red hue lines Dominic's sharp porcelain face. It could be from the heat of the fireplace, but I've been with enough men and women to know the difference between warmth and coyness.

He's attracted to me.

How could I not see this until now? Maybe it's because I thought he preferred women. But now that I think of it, he started acting strange once my mouth was on his neck after the debacle at Mr. Bates's home. It's a lot to assume. I could use Desimir magic to confirm my suspicions of his wavering thoughts, but that would be incredibly harsh for a confession my hands alone could bring.

Instead, I scoot closer to him.

He keeps his head turned away from me. "What are you doing?"

I place a gloved hand on the top button of his dress shirt. "Let me check your wound."

He grabs my hand to stop me. "Don't."

"Just trust me." I tilt my head.

His fingers run against the back of my hand as he drops it. As I undo the first few buttons, his breathing grows heavier and his eyes dart around the room, searching for anything to look at but me. I slide his suit coat off, then move the shirt's fabric away from his neck. There's still a faint imprint of my teeth.

I take off my gloves and run my fingers over the wound. Goosebumps line his collarbone as I do.

"Atticus," Dom whispers.

"Is this what's plaguing you?" I whisper back. "My mouth on your skin?"

Dominic bites his bottom lip. "It's not what you think. The bite left me confused, is all. But—"

I hold the back of his neck and press my lips into his. A groan leaves his throat.

So that's it. Dominic's been lusting after me? Pure and sweet Dominic, who only has a heart for, oh, what's her name?

He's scared to kiss me back fully, but he doesn't break away or try to turn his head. I don't push him further into it. If I make him uncomfortable now, everything may fall apart. He'll deny his feelings for me to the point where I'll never see an ounce of his magic.

I lace my fingers through the back of his hair as our lips tangle together. I break away from the kiss to look at him. The glow against his cheeks. His breathlessness. The bead of sweat running from his neck down onto his exposed chest.

My own feelings all make sense now. Hating Haylow. Fucking Priscilla minutes after he did, just to have a taste of him. I've been with countless men and women, but none of them have made me feel like this.

Dominic leans forward and captures my lips. It's not what I expected him to do. I thought the moment I broke away, he'd know this is a mistake.

I grow hungrier, grabbing at his shirt and holding him close. My tongue enters his mouth and dances around with his. He's my friend, yet all I want to do is touch him. I guide him onto his back and move my lips to his neck.

Dominic breathes out "Atticus. What the hell are we doing?" He shudders as I lick up the column of his neck and find his lips again.

"What we're meant to do." I roll my hard length over his and he whimpers out. Such a sweet sound. I want to hear it again.

I move my lips down his rising chest and kiss above his beltline, just to tease him. I kiss up his body and tangle my tongue with his once again. We roll off the couch onto the floor near the fireplace. He's grown just as desperate as me, working at removing the dark red suit and dress shirt from my skin. I don't want to push him too far, no matter how badly I crave to. Even though I've had more encounters with men than I care to count, I know he hasn't.

I move to lie behind him, sucking on the back of his neck. My fingers undo his trousers, making their way down the front of his pants. My hand grips his hard length and Dominic moans out.

I stroke his cock, taking things slow. But he grows greedy, moving his hips to thrust deeper into my hand. I can't help but roll my hips against his backside to get any sort of friction. Everything is perfect and right. I tighten my hand and work him faster.

Dominic bows up and cries out. "I hate you, Atticus."

"I'm sure you do." I smile into his scalp, slowing my pace as he comes.

He groans as I prolong his pleasure for as long as his body lets me. I wish I could see his expression right now.

I roll him over to face me. His eyes are filled with euphoria and confusion. I can't stop staring. I can't believe we're here like this. Dominic is the last person I ever expected to bed, yet here I am.

He doesn't break eye contact as he undoes my trousers. I try to keep my face calm as he lowers his hand down my beltline. My body trembles when his warm hand grabs my cock. Waves of electricity course through my veins as he works me. My forehead presses against his, and I can't help but groan against his mouth.

There's pleasure mixed with guilt in every breath I take while he strokes me. I never thought I would feel this way about anyone, especially not him, but my feelings for him run deeper than mere desire. Something softer. Something—

At that thought, I shatter. "Dominic...Oh."

He sucks in a deep breath as I break. My thoughts are in a very different place than my normal encounters. It's a pleasure like no other and I don't hate it. It's a feeling I never thought I was capable of.

We lay there in silence, the air between us thick with the realization that we've gone beyond the point of no return. Dominic rolls onto his back, the only sound in the room coming from the hiss and crackle of the fire.

He places his wrist against his forehead. "I don't understand—what enchantment did you use?"

"I didn't use any enchantments." My eyes grow heavy from the orgasm. An orgasm that Dominic Blythesea brought me to. I find his hand next to mine and hold it.

He's hesitant, but then finally curls his fingers around mine. "I thought I only felt like this around Solace."

"Oh, so you love me now?" I bite my bottom lip as I smile.

"No! I didn't say that." He tightens his jaw.

"Then I suppose you don't want me to touch you more?"

A blush crawls down his neck toward his hip line. His silence tells me everything.

I move, kissing down his body, pulling down his pants completely while I'm at it. I lick and suck his hip bones.

And once I've stirred him up enough again, I show him what my mouth can do.

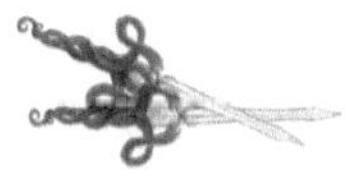

When I awaken, my legs are tangled with Dominic's beneath an array of sheets. He's still asleep. It's only been four hours since we stumbled up the staircase together, our lips barely breaking from one another the entire way. We continued our rendezvous until we both collapsed in exhaustion. At one point, I even had his wrists strapped to the headboard. The belt still lies centimeters from my head.

I don't know what this means for us. I'm not sure what I *want* it to mean. But all I know is whatever *this* is cannot affect my plans for him. His magic is mine and so is the life of the immortals.

Without waking him, I leave the room and descend the creaking stairs. Every remnant of our clothing lies scattered across the drawing room floor. I pick up what's mine and get dressed. The sight of Dominic's clothes crumpled across the ground makes me flush with pleasure, knowing he's stripped of them because of me.

After helping myself to some tea, there's an unexpected knock at the door. I stare up the staircase, waiting for Dominic to awaken to the sound. But when no sound of creaking hardwood follows, I straighten my clothes and glasses to answer it. Who could be here at this hour? Then again, it's late morning.

When I open the door, I almost dissolve as I stare at the girl on the other side of the threshold.

"Cadence? What are you doing here?" I never knew Dominic had a home here, so how could she?

"I placed a tracking enchantment on you yesterday. I'd only learned of it the day before. Now I'll always know where to find you!" Her expression grows giddy, as if she's waiting for me to be just as happy as she is at the prospect of an invisible collar being tightened around my neck.

I force a smile. "I'm so happy you're here, my sweet."

A tracking enchantment? Did she do it as my back was turned? Or did she stay up late into the night summoning enchantments from the depths of hell, and pinning it on me from across the streets of London?

I see it now. Her willingness to see me outside her house, even with the strict repercussions. How she has no qualms with disguising herself to sneak out. I was blinded by how easy it was to manipulate her, but now I understand.

She's absolutely nuts.

Dominic and Vec were right. Choosing the prime minister's daughter has consequences. Especially when she's lethally obsessed.

Cadence rocks her shoulders. "Well, aren't you going to invite me in?"

I seize up. If I let her in, she'll see Dominic's clothing across the drawing room. And if that happens, everything will shatter.

"One moment, dearest." I practically slam the door in her face and rush into the drawing room, scooping up Dominic's clothes. I sprint up the stairs into the bedroom.

"Get up!" I yell.

Dominic shoots up out of sleep. He has a smile on his face until I chuck the clothing straight into his face.

"What the hell, Atticus!" He throws the clothing off his head.

"Cadence. Is. Here."

"What—shit!" He stumbles off the bed and starts pulling his clothing on. "Why? How?"

"A tracking enchantment."

His eyes bulge. "You sure know how to pick them."

I glare at him. "We'll let her in for a few minutes, then send her on her way. Get dressed quickly."

"Stop bossing me around."

I move to leave, but then I veer back to Dominic and press my lips against his. He kisses me back, that familiar glow running up his neck.

I force myself to break away. "Meet me downstairs."

All Dominic does is nod. I run down the stairs and back to the front door.

When I whip it open, Cadence stands there with a confused expression.

"Sorry, Cadence. Just had a few things to straighten up. We—I mean—I wasn't expecting company. This isn't my place. A friend let me stay here last night."

Cadence crosses the threshold. "I should have sent word first. But I couldn't help it. After yesterday, I missed you more than ever."

"That's quite all right." Someone needs to lock her up and throw away the key. "He'll be down in a minute. You may remember him from the ball."

I seat her in the drawing room on the same couch where I consumed Dominic mere hours ago.

Right on cue, Dominic walks down the stairs. "Good morning."

Cadence stands. "I'm so sorry for my intrusion, Mr.—"

"Ashworth." Dominic steps forward and kisses the back of her hand. "And it's no problem. Atticus has told me a lot about you."

"Has he now?" She laces her hand with mine and pulls me close to her side. "All good things I hope?"

Dominic nods and forces a smile. "He does nothing but rave of your beauty and poise."

Cadence bounces a little. "Stop. You'll make me blush." She looks up at me.

"How about you have a seat, Cadence? Dominic and I will go prepare some tea and whatever else we can conjure up."

"That sounds splendid. May I use your powder room, Mr. Ashworth?"

"By all means. It's just upstairs to the right."

While Cadence ascends the stairs, Dominic and I rush into the kitchen and shut the door.

"That was close." I add water to the pot and start boiling it. Thankfully, it's still somewhat warm from my morning tea.

Dominic opens cabinets and digs out metal tins filled with desserts. "What are you going to do about her when this is all over? Tracking enchantments are hard to break. This girl won't stop until you're married."

"My uncle can break it, I hope." I spoon dried herbs into a strainer. Is immortal magic even capable of breaking something like this?

"And what if she tries to use investigators to find you? What then?"

I turn around and raise an eyebrow. "Jealous?"

His arms tense as he places cookies onto a serving plate and then onto a tray. "Of course not!"

I bite my tongue and place the china cups and teapot of brewing tea onto the same tray. The temptation to back Dominic into the kitchen wall comes over me. But I can't risk Cadence seeing us, no matter how badly I'd like to bend Dominic over the counter right now.

When we enter the drawing room, Cadence is already back on the couch, her hands folded elegantly across her lap.

"I hope you didn't wait too long." I set the tray on the small table.

"Not at all." There's something behind her eyes that I cannot decode. Her eyes are glassy and her smile looks forced.

When I sit next to her, I bring a cup and saucer to her hands. Dominic sits in one of the nearby chairs.

She takes a sip. "Mr. Ashworth, are you related to Thomas Ashworth, the iron mogul?"

Dominic nods. "Yes. That's my father. You know him?"

"How could I not? With his notoriety, I'm surprised you and I have not met before."

He takes a deep inhale. "We've been staying quiet since my brother's accident. And my father has never been one to attend many social events." Dom rubs the back of his neck.

"I'm so sorry to hear about your brother." She grabs a cookie.

"Thank you."

Cadence changes the topic. "Do you have any lady friends?"

Why is she so interested in him? Normally, when we're together, she has complete tunnel vision for anyone else than me. Unless she finds him handsome. But this feels like something else entirely.

Dominic goes still. "I—" He looks at me, then back at her. "I have one girl I'm interested in. Perhaps after university I will begin to court her."

Even I'm not sure if that is a lie or not. Can he lose all of his feelings for Haylow simply because we slept together once? Well, not once. Multiple times, in different positions, all throughout the house late into the night. But one night only counts as one encounter, I suppose.

Cadence reaches forward and places a hand on his knee. "Her heart will open when the time is right."

I bury my jealousy at the mention of Haylow as the three of us speak about current events. Events I only know because Vec updates me every time I visit him. I try to steer the conversation back to Cadence every time she asks Dominic more questions, but she's persistent, asking about how he and I met. His hobbies and interests.

I need to leave soon. Vec is expecting me today to give an update about the private investigator's findings on Konstantin. But Cadence doesn't seem to be anywhere near done speaking with Dominic. I'd almost be ecstatic at her interest in him—if I didn't want him all to myself.

I place my hand on hers. "My sweet, I have an appointment soon. Can I walk you out?"

Cadence kisses my cheek. "I hope you have a wonderful day, my love."

So, she's not leaving?

All right then.

Dominic's eyes widen.

Sorry, I mouth. "I'll let the two of you finish up your conversation. Good day, Dominic. I'll stop by your dorm later tonight to visit with Oliver."

CHAPTER 28

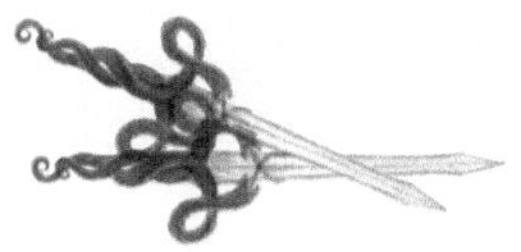

DOMINIC

Atticus leaves me alone in my home with Cadence Graystone, daughter of the prime minister himself.

Before Atticus had to leave, she asked me many questions. And if I can be honest, it was quite nice. Strange. But nice. Nobody has ever taken so much interest in me. Not even Atticus. I wanted to ask more about her, but she never gave me a single opportunity to interrupt her endless questions.

Once the door shuts, Cadence goes silent. Her elegant smile fades. It's a strange change, but maybe she feels more comfortable with Atticus around. After all, we are now an unchaperoned man and woman.

"You were in the carriage with Atticus yesterday."

"Yes. I offered to give him a ride with my family's buggy, since we were staying here last night. He had an engagement this morning, you see." I say the words slowly, so as not to expose the plot to obtain the artifact.

"And what business do you have with him? Besides just being friends?"

"I—I'm not sure I understand your question. Like I said before, we met at Roche and kindled a friendship from there."

And then it becomes increasingly obvious. She's jealous. Though I'm not sure what triggered it. This entire morning, Atticus and I didn't appear any more than simple friends. Unless simply being his friend is too much for her possessiveness to bear.

"On the way to your powder room, I saw your bedroom," she says.

"I apologize. I should have closed the door. There was no time to make the bed before your arrival."

"It was strange." She pauses and then stares straight at me. "Because none of the other bedrooms looked used, yet Atticus spent the night here."

Every bone in my body melds together at the bitterness that lines her voice. I know exactly what she's insinuating, but I can't admit it. It's not too late to fix this. "Atticus is tidier than me, so he made his bed." *Lies.* "His uncle taught him to always be a good houseguest. Especially because no maids live at this residence."

It's a good lie. A great one, even. Cadence's face softens. Then she smiles and stands, a small giggle in her throat.

I think she bought it.

Then she's in front of me, her hands on the armrest of my chair. She lowers her face to my level with a glare so vile and demonic I nearly piss myself.

"I'll tell you this once, and once only." Cadence's whisper is lined with spikes and talons. "Atticus Desimir is mine. Since the day we met, he's belonged to me alone. I was going to be his first upon our wedding night, and now you've ruined that for me. If I ever learn you touched him again, I will ruin you and your family. Do you understand who you're dealing with?"

If I wasn't so riddled with fear, I'd tell her I was *far* from being his first time, but that would only make the situation worse. She knows about

Atticus and me. It's not even been a few hours and we've already been found out. "Yes, Miss Graystone."

"Good." The venitrix smiles again and grabs her purse. "I'll see you around."

I stay glued to my seat until the front door slams. Only then does some of the tension release from my shoulders.

If I tell Atticus that Cadence threatened me, he may end things with her. And if that happens, I'll be far from the artifact. Far from saving my brother. Atticus must never find out. And I know Cadence won't tell him because even she knows he won't stay after such an accusation.

How did she even know we slept together? An unmade bed isn't enough to make any normal person suspicious.

I sprint up the stairs and into the bedroom. And then I see it.

The belt still looped through the headboard.

At lunchtime, I ride in a buggy to my family's primary estate. It's been a while since I've seen them because of all my studies. I'm still shaken, unable to erase the memory of the abominable look on Cadence's face.

After the taste I had of Atticus last night, I don't know if I'll be able to stop. A dark shiver crawls across the back of my neck at the memories. I see why women crawl back to him, fully knowing he's sleeping with others. His touch, his methods. His mouth. To him, sex is an advanced art form, and few have mastered it the way he has.

A hot, silky wave builds against my pelvis. I close my eyes and dip my head back, remembering what his lips felt like against my skin and around my cock. Alone in the buggy with the curtains drawn, I palm myself over my trousers at the memories.

Stop it, I tell myself. *You're minutes away from home.*

I stop touching myself and force my thoughts back to a more serious topic. Like, what if Atticus keeps bedding others while he sleeps with me? Can I handle that? We never spoke about it. Whatever happened between us could have been a onetime thing for him. My stomach drops when I think about being just another one of his conquests.

My family's primary estate is one that even the wealthy fantasize about owning. Vines and purple flowers cover the white exterior. It's too big for my parents to be the only ones living here, but one day I'm sure my father hopes to pass it to me and my future family.

I let myself in through the large double doors. Maids run across the foyer preparing for Sunday lunch. It's the first time all of us will be together in quite some time. Though we're never all truly together without Archer.

My mother descends the staircase in a flowing lavender dress. "Dominic, my dear!" She rushes up to me, placing her hands on my cheeks and smushing my face together. "It's been weeks! Why haven't you visited?" She kisses my forehead.

"Mother, please!" I keep my hands behind my back. If I try to pry her off, she'll smack me. "I've just been busy with my studies!"

"Oh, nonsense." She finally releases me. "There's never anything so pressing that you can't visit your own mother!"

"I visited father not too long ago."

"Yes, but he's not me."

I chuckle and follow her into the sitting room. My sister, Ivy, and her fiancé, William Peterson, lounge on a couch together. Over the summer, he proposed to her after a long courtship. It's been months since I've seen her.

"Oh, Dominic!" She stands and holds my hands.

I kiss her cheek. "Ivy, it's good to see you."

"Have you gotten taller?"

"Of course not! I'm too old to grow."

"Are you sure? I swear you've grown a few centimeters."

"It's probably the shoes." I laugh.

I shake her fiancé's hand and ask him about his business. It's the first time I'm meeting him. Apparently, he's well off, which I'm sure my parents are ecstatic about. Many of my sister's former suitors tried lying about their status to marry into our family. And though she's not one to marry for money, she doesn't tolerate greed or being lied to.

Mother walks up behind me. "Your father wants to see you in his office before lunch starts."

"What? Now?" I groan.

"Don't speak like that. He's your father. I thought you two were getting past this."

My meeting with him for the Tulip Ball was only because I needed something. I'm still upset with him. He's done nothing to help awaken Archer. Hell, Atticus has done significantly more to save him than father.

I approach the half-open door on the third story of the estate. When I enter, he's working at his desk.

"You wanted to see me?" I ask.

He stands, setting down his pen. "You never told me how the Tulip Ball went."

I relax. Of course, he wants to know how it fared. Why wouldn't he? "It was wonderful. Thank you again, Father."

"And the young lady who went with you? Did she enjoy it?"

I bite my inner lip. "She loved it."

"Well... when can we meet her?"

"We're taking things slow."

"Good. Though I hope you're keeping things appropriate with her. Long courtships lead to nothing but sin."

I almost chuckle. "We are always in the presence of a chaperone." And if I'm speaking of Haylow now, then it's not a lie.

"There was one other thing I wanted to speak to you about."

"Yes?"

"Have you been practicing the basic spells of Blythesea magic?"

"When I have a chance," I say, hoping the wavering of my tone doesn't betray me. If Father found out I almost used magic on *people,* he'd bury me out back. "It's hard. It gives me nightmares at times."

That, at least, was not a lie. Even basic casts involving the summoning of only one dead being at a time leave me weak. The voices of the dead are a tireless burden, even with only one whispering in your brain.

In theory, the more exposed to the dead you are, the more control you have. Though my father doesn't like me practicing any more than that without his supervision. That is a command I won't disobey again.

I know just how easy it is to lose sight of decency under the dead's whispers. How reckless my grandfather must've been. To be a master of the dead, but still lose control in such a way? The spell that destroyed the village in Scotland was an explosion filled with cursed souls. People didn't die instantly. Their minds and bodies were torn apart by the dead. Those who endured did so because of their preexisting allure toward the supernatural.

Father places a hand on my shoulder. "Having control over your power is important. And I need you to master it before I pass one day to avoid the mistakes of my father. And one day, you'll pass it on to your firstborn son."

"Yes, Father."

We make our way into the dining room, where everyone else is already seated for lunch. My sister speaks of her life as a fully graduated venitrix. She works as a researcher at the Viennese institute and lives in their women's compound while she waits to be married. They do studies on venitor magic and how to make it safer. Apparently, they're developing bracelets to help spies go undetected in non-magic circles.

Even though half the world can wield magic, it causes quite the divide in society. Many don't mind venitors and venitrixes. But humans without magic can use various stones to tell if a person is a venitor. With the bracelet, spying will be easier.

It's strange that my sister knows she's a Blythesea but is barred from using the magic. If I don't have a son, will the magic be lost with me? Even I must admit, Blythesea magic is dark and wicked.

Perhaps it's best if nobody ever uses it ever again.

It's late afternoon when I arrive back at campus. Instead of going straight to my dorm, I stroll around the outskirts of campus to stretch my legs after the long day of travel.

I still can't believe Archer may wake up soon. Though, I shouldn't get my hopes up. We still need to figure out how to override jade. Atticus will stop by later tonight to speak with Oliver. If zeledian cannot unlock it, we'll be back to square one.

"Dominic?"

I turn around. Haylow stands there dressed in a yellow Sunday dress, holding a wicker purse.

My chest tightens the way it always does when I see her. But this time it feels different. No longer do I get weak in the knees. "Haylow. How are you?"

"I'm well. I just arrived back from lunch with my family." She scans my suit. "As I assume you also have?"

"You'd be correct."

"Excellent." She smooths out her dress. "Would you like to walk together?"

The chill in the air grows colder. Of all the times for Haylow to seek me out, why now? Right when I consider the prospect of my future without her? Atticus knows I like her. Or liked her? I don't even know anymore. If he sees us together, he may get upset. Or would he? For all I know, he could be fucking some girl right now. Perhaps keeping my options open is wise in this instance.

"Yes. I'd love that," I say.

Haylow links her arm in mine, and we follow the flower-lined path between the buildings. She's never attempted to touch me before. If people see us walking like this, they may think we're courting. Word spreads fast around Roche, but I don't have the fortitude to tell her to stop.

I remember my conversation with her the other day, and with Atticus still on my mind, I can't help but ask. "Haylow, what did you mean when you said you felt something was off about Atticus?"

She shrugs. "It's just little things. Not just the way he dresses, but also his performance in class. Have you ever noticed that his command enchantments are always based in fear?"

It is strange. But darkness laces Atticus from his core. It's not only present in the way he acts but also in the way he beds. And now that I know what happened to his family, I can't blame him for being a bit messed up in the head. Not to mention, I've watched him bury men alive with his herbal magic. "That's just Atticus being Atticus."

Haylow sighs. "Maybe you're right. But isn't that a problem in and of itself?"

We pass the gardens, which aren't as vibrant with the imminence of fall. A couple of girls having a picnic on the grass giggle in our direction. I grit my teeth. Once the rumors start, I don't know how I'll explain this to Atticus.

Haylow stops us near an oak tree. "Dominic, can I be forward with you?"

"Yes?" I lean against the tree and put my hands in my pockets.

"Do you fancy me?"

I bite down on my tongue. If she had asked me that same question just days ago, my words of unrequited love would have spilled out immediately. But I don't know where Atticus and I stand.

Then I imagine him with some hypothetical girl in a hypothetical hotel. I shouldn't throw my life away for him, no matter how he's helped with Archer.

"I do, Haylow. I hope it wasn't too obvious."

She laughs. "Only with the blushing every time I'd see you. Though it's strange. This is the first time I've seen you without your face glowing red. I hope I didn't miss my chance."

"No, you didn't. I'd like to see you more." My words linger like a bittersweet lie on my tongue. But I must think about my future. Once Atticus gets bored with me, perhaps the feelings I once felt for Haylow will come crashing back.

"I'm surprised you haven't asked me out yet."

I'm honest with her. "I was at a loss whether you had the same feelings and didn't want to make matters uncomfortable. Especially since we must endure till our fourth year at Roche in the same circles."

"I suppose that makes sense." Haylow stands on her toes and kisses my cheek. "Let's talk soon. Perhaps we can take a boat ride in the evening one day."

As she strides away, I look over my shoulder, and the picnicking girls giggle even more.

There's no way Atticus won't hear about this now.

CHAPTER 29

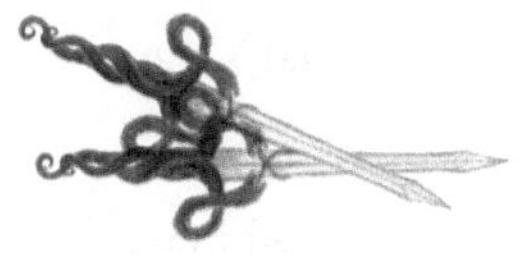

ATTICUS

Vec paces around the sitting room, sifting through a stack of documents from his private investigator, while I lie on his couch, absolutely stuffed from the lunch his staff prepared.

"Give it to me straight." My hand rests on my abdomen.

"Konstantin has lived in London for over two decades and grew his wealth through the shipping industry." Vec skips a few pages about trivial matters. "He lives in a very high-class district in a ten-bedroom mansion. I'm shocked I never bumped into him all these years."

"Nearly all the social events you attend are for artists. Not exactly the same circles."

The sunlight peeking in from the window glitters along the lace design embossed into Vec's neck. "Speaking of social events, how was your encounter with the prime minister yesterday?"

I sigh. "It went well. If things continue to go as they are, I'll be married in no time with his full approval."

He does not laugh, and I roll my eyes. "I found the artifact. It's encased with jade. I don't suppose you'd know how zeledian reacts to that?"

"I do not. My knowledge of stone magic is still novice."

"Figured as much." I sit up. "I'm meeting with Oliver Edevane later today. Perhaps he'll know."

"The Edevane family?" Vec says, and if he were testing the name on his tongue. "Edevane...as in the woman who nearly killed her son?"

I point my finger in the air. "That's the one."

Vec rubs his temples. "You need to be more careful. A guy like that must have a strong aversion to herbal magic."

"Oh, he does."

Vec's shoulders look tense. "And Dominic? What's happening with that?"

"Oh—we slept together."

He throws down the papers and storms in front of me. "Atticus!"

"What? You said to get close to him."

"Not like that! This is the worst possible thing you could have done. When will you learn there's no need to stick your cock in every living being!"

"You very well knew something was up and chose not to say anything."

"I'll admit, it's the first time I saw you so visibly jealous. But you're going to betray him, Atticus. And though I once thought you were incapable of love; it messes with people's heads more than lust. Even if your mind stays clear, we can't say the same for him. This may get a lot bloodier than you anticipate now that feelings are involved."

"Feelings? I never said I had feelings."

"I'm going to ignore that particular lie. Are you willing to abandon your quest to kill Konstantin to protect Dominic?"

"Never."

Vec claps once. "There. Now it's solidified. And because I know you're incapable of ending any opportunity for sex, I won't make you stop. At this point, it may backfire anyway. But from now on, your priority in life is to obtain his magic, no matter the costs or ramifications."

"Fine."

"Say it." Vec bites out.

"I'll steal his magic, no matter the costs." I repeat.

Vec picks the documents back up and sits in his chair. He flips through them one final time. At the last page, he frowns.

"That's strange," he says, reading it over a few times. "It says here Konstantin has a daughter that he adopted in 1870 as an infant."

"He doesn't seem like the fatherly type."

He flips over the document. "Her name is Haylow Solace."

It takes every ounce of strength not to shatter the mirror in Vec's powder room. My jaw and shoulders vibrate from the fury building under my skin. Haylow is Konstantin's daughter? As if I didn't already despise her enough.

The real question is, how much does she know about me? When she told me she didn't trust me, was it because Konstantin already informed her of our past? Or does she have a keen eye as a result of being raised by him? I splash my face with water.

It's impossible to banish her face from my mind as I head back to campus. Any daughter of Konstantin is an enemy of mine, even if she's completely innocent in all of this.

When I knock at Dominic's dorm door, Oliver answers.

"Atticus!" Oliver smiles. "Come in. What brings you by?"

I step into the room. Dom is nowhere to be found. "Dominic isn't here?"

"Oh, I just saw him from the window. He's a bit *delayed* by something. Or someone I should say." Oliver chuckles.

I step to the window and pull the curtains apart. My fists tighten at the sight before my eyes.

Haylow and Dominic stand by the tree together. He's smiling down at her. Then she stands on her toes and kisses his cheek.

My jaw hardens. I imagine popping her neck like a grape between my fingers. The thought of losing Dominic to her makes me murderous.

Oliver steps to my side. "Is everything all right, Atticus?"

"Yes. I'm perfectly fine. Why ask such an absurd question?" I watch as Haylow leaves. Dominic looks around before heading in the direction of the dorms.

Oliver scratches his head. "Well—you look upset."

"Well, maybe tell your *friend* to be on time to meet with me from now on instead of dallying with girls."

Oliver steps away from me, muttering something under his breath.

A few minutes later, Dominic opens the door. When he sees me, he smiles slightly.

Even in my anger, my chest flutters. It hasn't even been a whole day since we've seen each other and yet my body is already reacting to the sight of him.

Oliver approaches him and pats his shoulder. "There's the man of the hour. We should get drinks to celebrate."

"There's nothing to celebrate," Dominic says. The faint red mark of lip stain still resides on his cheek. The mark of Haylow. Lynch me now.

"Does this mean you're seeing each other now?" Oliver takes out his handkerchief and hands it to Dominic. "It seems she left a little present for you."

Dominic goes pale. He keeps his eyes trained on Oliver, refusing to look at me. Because if he does, he'll see what I really think of his little date with Haylow.

"She completely took the lead, asking if she could see me more." Dominic wipes his cheek with the handkerchief. "Some gentleman I am."

"I already hear wedding bells." Oliver firmly pats Dominic's back.

My muscles tighten, not just from jealousy, but from realization. If Haylow is Konstantin's daughter, and Konstantin knows who Dominic is, this could all be a ruse. She never showed a lick of interest in Dominic before. And now, as I get closer to him, she's suddenly all over him?

If that's the case, her daddy moved his first pawn. But that won't matter. Not if I capture any other pieces she tries to play.

"Oliver, I have a question for you." I interrupt. If I hear another word about Dominic and Haylow together, I might gag.

"Yes?"

"What do you know of zeledian and jade?"

Oliver's bubbly expression falls. "Not this about herbs again."

Dominic throws his arms out. "Again? What have you told him, Atticus?"

I realize I never told Dominic of my little duel with Oliver, nor the way I exposed myself. "Oliver discovered my use of herbs not too long ago."

Dominic's frown grows stern. "You really can't keep anything to yourself, can you?"

Oliver sits down. "I'm angrier that you're trying to awaken your brother again, and you had no sense to tell me."

"Because I knew you wouldn't approve!"

"Of course I wouldn't!" Oliver hisses, surprising me before he composes himself. "Even now I'm unsure. But you're my friend and I want to help."

I give Dominic a look of knowing. *Oliver doesn't know about the prime minister. Don't worry.*

Dominic gives me a small nod back.

Oliver relaxes his shoulders. "Back to your question. Jade protects locks from being unlocked by anyone whose blood is not encased within the primary lock. Even zeledian cannot override it."

Dammit to hell. Everything is falling through the cracks, and without the artifact, does Dominic even have any use for my presence?

All hope is lost. We must start back at square one. There are seven other artifacts in the world. Perhaps Vec still has contacts back at the Syndicate—if that even still exists—and we can steal it from the pope. Hell, he's a pope, perhaps he'll even find goodness in his heart to just let us borrow it.

Dominic's posture slumps; his face filled with defeat.

Oliver looks between us, soaking in our clear disappointment. "However, I suppose there is one exception."

I straighten my spine. Dominic's face lights up.

"It's near impossible to exact, but I've heard atavistic blood can bypass most stone magic safeguards. Something about old blood being strong enough to weaken things like jade. Of course, nobody in this time has it. But some black-market dealers carry the blood, preserved for centuries, in their stock. The cost is exorbitant, though."

Oh, thank the heavens and everything inside them. I have atavistic blood. But of course, I can't tell either of them that.

Dominic's eyes grow worried once again. "How much would we need?"

Oliver frowns. "I'm unsure of the exact price. All I know is that it's significant."

"I'll take out a loan. Anything." Dominic's voice shakes slightly.

"There's no need for that, Dominic," I say.

"But—"

"I said, I'll handle it."

Dominic folds his arms and gives a slight nod. But he still looks anxious, as he should be.

Oliver pulls his suit jacket off the coat rack "I am going to head to the dining hall. Whatever you two are up to, you better be careful. Got it?"

"Yes, Mother." I roll my eyes.

Oliver takes a prolonged breath and heads out.

Dominic and I stand there. I'm not sure who is more upset or pissed at whom right now.

"Just say it," I say.

"How could you tell Oliver and keep it a secret from me?"

"I have a lot of secrets." I walk to the door and turn the lock.

"What are you doing?" Dominic narrows his eyes.

I stand in front of him. "Reminding you who you belong to."

My lips are on his, and I harden instantly. If Cadence hadn't shown up out of the blue this morning, I may have had time for another round with him. Now I'll make up for that loss.

Dominic sucks in a breath when my hand palms over his clothed crotch. "Atticus...you can't just ignore my questions by—" He groans when my teeth tease his neck.

I speak into the sensitive skin just below his ear. "You still want Haylow? Even after everything I've done to you?"

"It's not like that." Dominic's fingers grip onto my coat. I apply more pressure with my hand and he moans out.

I kiss him again, backing him toward the bed until the back of his legs hit the side. "Climb on the mattress and get on your knees."

Dominic shivers as I run my fingers across his bottom lip. He obeys my instructions, facing away from me. I climb behind him and grab his hips, attacking his neck with my mouth. His head falls back to rest on my shoulder.

I lick up the side of his neck while I unbutton the front of his pants. When his length springs free, I grab his cock, pumping him toward bliss.

Dominic's hips move with my strokes. With my other hand, I hold the front of his neck. Then I slow a bit, just to taunt him.

"Faster. Please," he whimpers.

His little sounds urge me on more. I press my length into his backside. With Dominic, it feels like I could come right now, even without him touching me.

He can't come yet. I need more of him. I stop, to his dismay, to strip us both bare.

He lies beneath me as I press my length against his, thrusting along his cock. I peck and lick at his lips as we work each other to our climaxes.

I can't help but memorize every inch of his pleasured face. His closed eyes and furrowed eyebrows. His parted lips. All of it because of me. We both share in our releases, panting and sweating.

I kiss his forehead before collapsing next to him.

He kisses my shoulder. "Atticus, did you sleep with anyone else today?"

What? As if I had time after my meeting with Vec. "No."

"But you'll still sleep with others? Besides, just me, I mean."

I roll onto my side to face him. "What are you asking?"

"The reason I'm still open to courting Haylow is because I know you have your history. That you like to sleep with multiple people. That you said you never wanted to marry anyone. One day you'll get sick of me and—"

"You want me to only sleep with you?"

I can feel him swallow. "If you want this to continue, then yes. Otherwise, I need to think of my future."

A future with Haylow, is all I can think of. I could snap her neck. Then Dominic wouldn't have to worry about choosing between her and me. If only he knew her intentions may not be pure. "You know why I've always slept with multiple people? It's because nobody has ever asked me to stop before."

He moves back, his mouth agape. "Nobody at all?"

"Nobody."

"Then sleep only with me."

I smile. "Consider it done. Just know I have quite the appetite."

Dominic rubs his temples. "That I know."

We quickly get dressed. The last thing either of us want is Oliver coming back early to a deadbolted door. Explaining that one may be tricky, and Dominic isn't the only one who needs to think of his future. I still have a full life to live once I enact my revenge.

Once I betray Dominic, he could slander my name in high society. If that happens, making a new life for myself would be incredibly difficult. But after I kill Konstantin, maybe I'll stick with my secondary plan to sleep through the centuries again until Vec can find a more promising era.

It hurts to know that I can't share in this life with Dominic. That I must ruin him.

But that thought alone isn't enough for me to stop.

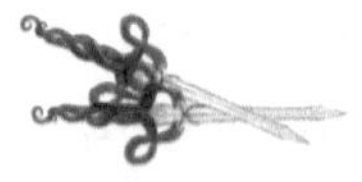

I exit a weapons shop after getting my knives sharpened. It's been a week since Dominic and I slept together. It's been only a few hours since I last touched him. It seems every time we get together to plan our next move, we cannot keep our hands to ourselves. There was even a time where we continued planning as we brought each other to completion.

"Atticus!" a shrill voice shrieks behind me.

I stop and close my eyes. *Deep breath in, Atticus. Deep breath out.*

On my exhalation, I put on my best smile, then turn around. "Cadence." *She's completely mad.* "Funny bumping into you here." I don't even want to know what would happen if she caught Dominic and me together.

She skips up to me. "I'm sorry I haven't gotten into contact. We had family in town and father wouldn't let me out of his sight."

I kiss her cheek. "It's no matter. I missed you." Lies. All lies. If I never saw her again, I'd be the happiest man in the world.

Cadence presses the back of her hand against her cheek. "Oh, I'm so glad to hear that. Sometimes I worry you'll grow bored with me."

"I wouldn't dream of getting bored with a charming woman such as yourself."

Her face grows uneasy for a second, until she covers it with a forced smile. Strange. She doesn't believe me?

"Walk with me?" I ask. If she's feeling unsure of my devotion, I need to change that. Quickly. If I lose her trust or interest, the artifact will fall through my fingertips.

"Yes. I'd like that." Cadence loops her arm with mine, and we head to a small, nearby park.

We sit on a bench by a pond in an area secluded from the rest and surrounded by trees. As we watch the ducks, I place my hand on the small of her back and circle my finger over the fabric of her dress.

Cadence shivers. "I have a question for you, Atticus."

"Yes?"

"My parents and brother are going out of town this weekend and my father is giving the staff time off. I have the entire place to myself, except for a guard or two who would never rat me out. So I was wondering—" Cadence's breath hitches as I place my hand on her upper thigh.

Isn't it perfect? Day after day, Dominic and I plan to figure out how to get back into the prime minister's residence, from climbing the walls, to enchanting Cadence to do our bidding. And then the perfect opportunity presents itself without me even trying.

I steady my breath. Her family is out of town for one weekend, and Cadence can't help but use the freedom for me to bed her. So much for being daddy's perfect little girl.

"You're asking me to spend the night, aren't you?" I ask, keeping my voice level and calm.

Cadence drags her bottom lip between her teeth and nods.

This is more than wonderful. I can't believe it. She's falling right into my trap without me even setting it. I'll do what she wishes and spend the night. Without her knowledge, I will steal the artifact and be done with her.

Though there is one issue. I can't sleep with Cadence. Even though Dominic gave me full permission to tease and kiss her when necessary, there's no way I can cross that line with her. Even if Dom and I weren't together, I don't think I could ever bed Cadence. Her fixation with me will turn to pure obsession. Sometimes I worry it already has. Especially after learning about the enchantment she cast on me, which neither Dominic nor Vec can seem to break.

I look around to make sure we're not in anybody's sight and press my lips to hers. She lets out a small sound. I hold the back of her neck and deepen the kiss, the entire time thinking of Dominic to get through it. Pretending she's him makes me run my hand up her ribs, stopping just below her breast.

I break the kiss. "I will spend the night tomorrow, but I don't want to take your innocence. You're too respectable of a woman to have that taken away from you before you're wed." I internally scoff, as if I have any right telling someone to wait till marriage.

She gives me an annoyed, yet seductive look, almost to say, *we'll see about that.* "But you'll still sleep in my bed?"

"If that's what you want, my sweet."

Cadence gives my lips a peck. "Arrive at five tomorrow."

CHAPTER 30

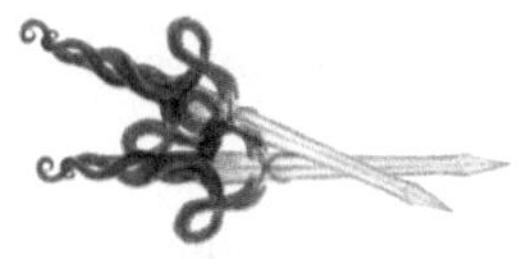

ATTICUS

I practically sprint back to the dorms after my unexpected outing with Cadence. Finally, an opening has presented itself on a silver platter, and soon, the artifact will be ours.

Dominic's door is unlocked. I whip the door open, panting. Oliver is gone, thank goodness.

Dominic turns from his desk and stares at me. "Did you run here?"

I don't answer him, instead I grin as I approach him, grabbing his collar and yanking him out of his seat and onto the desk. My mouth attacks his as I stand between his legs. I can't help it. We're so close to the end.

"Atticus," Dom says breathlessly between kisses. "What's going on?"

"Tomorrow—" I kiss down across his jaw. "We're getting the artifact."

"What?" He lets me kiss him a few more times before pushing me away. "You can't be serious? Already?"

I nod, my hands still grip his collar. "Cadence wants me to spend the night. Her family is out of town tomorrow evening. It's now or never, Dom."

"I can't believe this." Dominic looks lost in thought, his pupils unable to focus on anything. "We have to plan immediately."

"Right." I slide my hand up his thigh but he pushes it away.

"There's no time. Besides, Oliver could be back any second. You didn't even lock the door."

I turn and look at the doorknob. "Why must you always ruin the mood?" I tighten my grip one last time and peck his lips before finally stepping away.

"As if the *mood* ever leaves you." Dominic hops off the desk.

Before long, we're both sitting at his desk together, mapping out plans. I draw out the different levels of the floors from memory.

"The artifact is in this room." I place my fountain pen down on the drawing of the cabinet room. "Cadence's room is over here, which is where I will likely be most of the night."

A glare of jealousy coats Dominic's face.

"You're really going to get caught up on that? This is our chance. I have to entertain her. Besides, she's a virgin. I don't need to do more than kiss her to get her dripping and satisfied."

Dominic's frown stays put. "But she'll want to sleep with you."

"I've already made it very clear to her that I won't take her innocence."

"Does she believe you?"

"That's not important. I know how to give a girl a good time without sticking my cock in her. Besides, she's a human leech." Sometimes I fear I'll never be free of her.

His face contemplates, I cannot even decode what he's thinking. "Atticus, no matter how jealous I get, I need you to do whatever it takes."

He's changing his mind?

"Within reason, though." Am I being the level-headed one here? It feels good—I think.

Dominic's stare turns dark. "No. Whatever it takes. My jealousy will fade one day. But the pain of knowing Archer's cure was within my grasp, then lost—that's a pain that will never leave."

"She melts from my lips alone. I won't need to do more than that."

"Can I tell you something?" Dominic sets his elbows on the edge of the table. "When you left Cadence and I alone, she said something strange. Actually, it almost made me laugh."

"Well? Spit it out."

"She said she was determined to be your first."

"My first?"

Then both of us are laughing. I even grab my abdomen a little. I can't even count on all my fingers, toes, and teeth how many escapades I've had over the years. "What a strange topic to come up between the two of you."

Dominic presses his lips together, like he's holding something back. "She's going to press you for it. I know it."

"I will not sleep with her!"

"Want to make a bet of it?"

"You have so little trust in my faithfulness."

"I'm not questioning my trust in you." Dominic looks to the ceiling. "It's her persistence I'm worried about." He sighs and moves on. "So where do I play a part in all this?"

"You're going to sneak into the cabinet room and help me steal the artifact. Once she's asleep, I'll leave her room and help you. I won't be able to hide it on my person without garnering suspicion."

"Me?" Dom's eyes widen. "And what should I do about the jade case? You said you had it handled."

"I do."

"And where will you get the blood from?"

"It's not important."

"I won't have you draining any of your inheritance on the black market for this."

"Dom, I won't. Just trust me."

When I get back to my dorm for the night, I stretch my arms, a smile on my face in the mirror's reflection.

You've done it, Atty.

I cannot contain my joy. It's like I'm riding on a cloud in the heavens where nothing can stop me.

Before I can take my coat off, Arlo whips open the door with a letter in his hand. His brows are stuck in a deep furrow. "I was told to give this to you."

"Oh?" I swipe the letter from him.

Arlo places his fists on his hips. "You know, I try to keep to myself with your dubious matters, but passing love notes with your best friend's lover is crossing a line."

What is he talking about? I unfold the letter, my mouth on the floor as I read the cruel words.

Atticus,

Meet me at the docks by the campus pond immediately. If you do not, I will tell Dominic your true age.

-H.S.

I crumble the paper in my fists.

"Shit," I say under my breath.

So Konstantin really told her? Ever since I learned she was his daughter, I've kept a close eye on her. Even on Dominic's obligatory outing with her, I watched from the shadows of the forest as they took a boat ride across the campus pond. Nothing was amiss. I'm not even sure she knows that her own adoptive father is an immortal. It's too risky to tell people in this day and age.

"What is it?" Arlo folds his arms.

"It's none of your business." And I still don't forgive him for assuming she was my lover. I stand and sock him in the gut. "And never accuse me of betraying Dominic again."

Arlo folds to the ground, his voice strained. "I'm sorry."

"If I hear any rumors of Haylow and me floating around campus, I will hold you personally responsible." I leave and rush down the stairs into the courtyard.

How lovely this all is. Right when everything I've ever wanted is right in my grasp, some vile woman tries to rip it away from me? Well, I won't let that happen. Not today, Haylow. Not ever.

Roche University has its own man-made pond with docks and boats for students to use at their leisure. And it's hidden well enough that nobody will see if I choose to snap Haylow's neck.

I run to the docks. Maybe I can even bury her deep underground where I never have to worry about her with Dominic ever again.

At the edge of the dock, Haylow stands in a hideous dress. On Cadence, it might look cute, but everything looks horrid on Miss Solace.

I stomp down the dock toward her and hold up the crumbled note. "What is this?"

"Good, you got my letter."

I don't stop walking until I'm looking down at her with fury. "Dominic won't believe your slanderous lies."

"Lies?" Haylow folds her arms. She doesn't break eye contact with me. "And don't pretend like you don't know who I am. Vec's private investigator wasn't as discreet as I'm sure you hoped."

I could drown Konstantin's spawn right now. Nobody would know. I could cover it up quickly. "Then I won't pretend. What do you want from me?"

Haylow smiles, and as she does, shows every true color of her soul. "Get in the boat, Atticus."

I see. This way, neither of us can run, though I suppose if I don't get in, she'll deliver more threats. "After you." I smirk.

We climb into the rowboat, and I paddle us through the pond. The sun is setting over the water filled with lily pads. Everything looks like a dark painting, one I'm sure Vec would love to create. Maybe he can paint the part where Haylow's bloodied body floats lifeless across the current as swans pick out her eyes.

"My father knows what you're trying to do."

"And what would that be?"

"Don't play coy, Atticus. It's Dominic. He's the key, isn't he?"

My body tenses. So I was right. Her newfound interest in him is all a ruse to keep him close. She knows all about his Blythesea magic. "And that's why you're playing with his heart?"

"I am capable of loving him if I must," Haylow answers. "If only to keep my father and uncle safe."

Her words send murderous fire through my veins. I stop paddling and rest my elbows on my knees, leaning forward. "I will never leave Dom's side from this moment on. You won't ensnare him. And at the end of the day, I will have his magic and murder your godforsaken—"

Haylow is quick as she lurches forward, snapping a pair of cuffs onto my wrists.

"What the—" Then I laugh. Does she really think restraining me is going to help? *Darling, lovers will tell you I'm at my best when I'm subdued.*

"They're concealment cuffs. And they'll suppress all your magic enough for me to place a command enchantment on you. I'm going to take you to my father, and once you're there, he'll ensure you never see Dominic again."

I reach for Desimir magic but come up empty. Blasted venitrix.

I still have the zeledian root tucked safely in my pocket, but when I try to excrete its powers, it doesn't work. I'll never break free.

Unless...

If jade can be overpowered by just a drop of my own blood, then surely these cuffs aren't any different. I scowl at Haylow, and thrash in my seat, disguising my movements as I search the bench for any protruding splinters.

"Miss Solace, nothing you do will stop me. I'll rip Konstantin from you the way he ripped my sister from me."

Haylow scoffs. "Father and Uncle Austrie will end you, and when they're finished, I'll steal Dominic's heart. It's only a matter of time before he's so enthralled that he'll teach me Blythesea magic, and after that, we're killing Vec."

I know Vec can take care of himself, but her words make me tremble. I've never considered a reality where I could lose Vec. "Your father killed a child in cold blood."

"My father's employer gave him orders. He was a hired immortal, as many were during that time, including Vec. It wasn't personal."

An all-consuming storm takes over every fiber of my being. And all I have now is something worse than blood lust. I'm not thinking straight, but I don't care. "You weren't there!"

I press my finger into a sliver of wood on my seat, drawing blood across my fingertip. One swipe along the metal cuffs, and I feel a slight surge of magic. I direct the power of the zeledian root into the cuffs, unlocking it, then lunging forward in the same instance, nearly tipping the boat.

The previously calm expression on Haylow's face vanishes. She screams and charges up a spell upon her fingertip.

I grab her wrists to stop her magic. "Perhaps your father should have tutored you better on atavistic blood." I trip her to the bottom of the boat, sitting on her torso, keeping her pinned beneath me. "His orders were to keep the girl alive, and he ignored them, then threw my sister into a wall!"

I squeeze her wrists so tightly that she yelps. "Stop it, Atticus!"

I ignore her pleas. "Have you ever heard the sound of a spine shattering? From a child, no less!" She doesn't answer. "Well—have you!" I set all my body weight on her so that she can barely breathe.

"Please…"

"Say it!"

"No! No I haven't! Please, I can't breathe!"

Her chest tries to expand under me but cannot do so. I take my body weight off for her for a second to allow her to breathe. "And you're still able to defend your father? After killing a ten-year-old!"

"He's an honorable man. If he did so, there was probably a good reason!"

I snap and sit on her chest again. She doesn't deserve air. "You should have chosen wiser words, darling." My eyes darken as Desimir magic fills my body. I will drag her through every nightmare imaginable.

The magic that fills her mind mutes her screams. I bring to life her worst fears and tangle them with her deepest desires. It was her choice to come out onto the pond all alone with me, and for that I'll make her suffer.

As I project faux sensations of pain, hunger, thirst, and sleep deprivation into her mind, I make it feel like hours for her. I stop myself from killing her more than once. Dominic wouldn't forgive me.

Then, as most stricken by Desimir magic do, she goes unconscious. I could still torment her into her dreams. Losing consciousness isn't enough to stop my shadows. But someone could come to the lake any minute.

While I still have time, I must hide my sins.

I wait until dusk, and drag her through town, holding her against my side with her arm around my neck to make it look like she's simply drunk. I find a buggy and head to Vec's.

Once I'm in front of Vec's house, and the buggy is far away, I throw her over my shoulder and enter the townhouse.

The home is dark, and the servants are gone for the night. I tiptoe up the stairs with Haylow's body, cursing under my breath every time a stair creaks. Thankfully, Vec doesn't hear, and I lock the door once I'm inside my room.

I throw her unconscious body onto my bed and pull the cuffs she used on me from my overcoat. If Vec finds her he'll be livid. But he'll understand once I tell him what she said.

Maybe.

Once she's bound to the headboard, I step back into the center of the room and take a deep breath. Even on her unconscious face, I can tell she's still in agony.

If she hadn't said anything about Juni, perhaps even a glimmer of regret would wash over me, but it doesn't. It will take months, if not years, for her to return to normal after what I did to her. Even then, nobody ever fully recovers.

Before I first wielded my family magic, my father emphasized only using the full extent of Desimir magic when absolutely necessary. He found it dishonorable to use it out of anger or as revenge. It's one promise I've never been able to keep.

If he were alive, my father would be disappointed. But I did this for him. For Juni. And for my mother.

I slide to the floor and rest my head against the side of the mattress, my eyes growing heavy while the memories of my father's disappointed voice haunt my dreams.

CHAPTER 31

ATTICUS

When I awaken on the floor, Haylow is still out cold on my bed. It must be dawn, and today is the day I'm meant to steal the artifact from the prime minister.

Her unconscious face is clammy. Though her thoughts should be completely empty after a run in with my magic, her mind still remembers my imprint from somewhere deep within. The woman Dominic once loved is broken.

And the worst part is, I don't care.

All I know is she was the new wall between me and her father's life. And I had to remove the threat she caused, no matter the costs.

I can feel my father looking down at me, trying to increase my guilt, but I squash it. Within my mind, I scream at the sky. *Don't you know I did it for you?*

I grip the armrest of my carriage as it rolls through the evening streets of London. The sun is setting, sweat forming on my neck. It's rare that I get nervous. But tonight's the night we rob the prime minister blind.

The buggy slows as we pull up to the prime minister's residence. In the back of my mind, I say a prayer that nobody discovers Haylow while I'm away. Thankfully, if Cadence asks, I can play off my nerves and tell her it's because I'm just so incredibly in love with her.

Definitely not because Konstantin's daughter is chained to my headboard.

Dominic curses from inside the seat across from me as the buggy hits a bump on its way in. Thankfully, we found a buggy with hidden compartments under the seats to hide him from any guards who try to peer inside.

"Stop swearing, we're almost there," I say, adjusting my collar.

"Easy for you to say." His voice is slightly muffled from inside the seat.

"It will all be worth it, love."

The buggy stops in front of the house and I pull back the curtain. Cadence is waving with a huge smile on her face.

I replace the curtain and take a final deep breath. "The curtains are secured. Once the buggy parks, you're free to leave the compartment."

"Thank the heavens. I'm at my wits' end already. You didn't have to make me ride in here the entire way, you know."

"Sacrifices, Dominic, sacrifices." I lean forward and tap the seat with my fist. "Wish me luck."

"Be safe," Dominic grumbles. I suppose I should feel bad for him. He'll be stuck for hours between four buggy walls.

When I step outside, Cadence runs forward, attacking me. I give her an obligatory spin and kiss her head, thankful Dom can't see.

"I was worried you wouldn't come!" She beams.

I force a chuckle. "I'm only a few minutes late."

"All that matters is that you're here now." She grabs my hand and pulls me into her home. "Come on. I made dinner."

Cadence locks the door and walks in front of me. Still facing forward, I take a few steps back and unlock the deadbolt.

Instead of taking me into the dining room, she brings me into her bedroom where two plates of food are set on the small table. A vase of fragrant wildflowers sits in the center, as if she picked them herself.

I don't know why she's bothering showing me her homemaking skills. It's not as if women of nobility cook for themselves.

"I figured I'd change things up a little." Cadence gives a nervous shrug and bounces up onto her toes, waiting for my reaction.

All that's on my mind is the artifact, and how I can get her distracted enough throughout the night to steal it with Dom. He can't do it on his own. He still needs my blood to override the jade.

I kiss her forehead. "It's lovely, Cadence."

She smiles widely. "Please, sit."

We take a seat at the table and begin dining together. For a girl from nobility, she is an amazing cook. And since Cadence loves to talk, it gives me time to savor every bite of the chicken à la king.

I interrupt her tangent on how Ronny isn't subject to the same rules she is. "Where did you learn to cook like this?"

"The cook taught me. Father doesn't let me out often, so I made it my mission to learn. It's become quite a hobby of mine."

I take another bite of the chicken. If this were my last meal, I'd die a happy man. "A girl of your talent should open a restaurant."

She rests her love-struck face on the back of her hands. "And what would I call it?"

"Creations by Cadence the Beautiful."

"Stop flattering me." She laughs and fiddles with the neck of her wineglass.

I reach across the table and hold her delicate hand. "I mean it. You're talented." And this time, I'm not lying. Though it may be my only truthful sentence this entire night.

After we eat cake, she tells me stories of her childhood. Then we play a game of chess, and I'm taken aback when she nearly checkmates me.

As the hours pass and night encapsulates the evening further, all I can think about is Dominic and if he successfully snuck in.

Cadence yawns and stretches her arm. "Excuse me, I'm going to get changed."

"Yes, it is getting rather late." I force a yawn.

She disappears into her walk-in closet. I remove my coat, top, and gloves, leaving only my pants on. There's no need to get comfortable as I don't plan on sleeping much tonight, if at all.

After I turn off the chandelier, I set my glasses on the end table. Now, only the light of the fireplace remains.

When Cadence returns, she's dressed in a long sleeveless undergarment, meant to arouse and captivate me. Her curly blonde hair is free of the pins from before, golden locks flowing down her back.

Considering she's covered from shoulder to kneecap, I feel nothing. Not when I've seen every nook and cranny of womankind.

Still, I need to make her feel like she's a goddess, so I bite my lower lip. "I have no words to describe what you're doing to me."

Her eyes dip to my bare chest. She steps forward and runs the tips of her fingers down my torso and across my pecs.

I grab her waist, pulling her into me, capturing her lips in mine, kissing her slowly. I drag her lips between my teeth as I pull away. "Let's get to bed."

She nods shyly. Little does she know, I mean it. Not only will I not bed her, but I need her to fall asleep as quickly as possible. Dominic may already be waiting in the cabinet room for me.

And my promise remains—I will not take her innocence.

We climb onto her king-size bed and slip under the fluffy covers together. Before I can even get settled, her lips are on my chest.

"Cadence—"

She shushes me and runs her hands down my sides. I'll let her have her fun for a minute. If I shove her off, it will only cause me trouble.

Her lips climb to my neck. "Touch me, Atticus."

I hold her wandering wrist. "Your body is sacred, Cadence. I won't take that from you."

Lies. If I weren't loyal to Dominic, I'd have my fingers between her legs, showing her what a man of my skill could do. The things I could do to her would never leave her mind as long as she lives.

"But—I want you." Cadence's other hand trails down to my waistband.

But I catch that wrist too. "In time, you'll have me."

She breathes a breath of disappointment. "Will you at least kiss me?"

Dominic said I could go as far as I needed, and kissing is as casual to me as a handshake after the escapades I've been through over the years.

I pull her against me and lock our lips together. She moans as I move my mouth to her neck, painting her skin with my tongue. I circle my thumbs against her hips.

Her hand dips between her legs, stirring her pleasure along. Her moans deepen as I kiss her. *Not exactly what I expected her to do.*

She breaks away. "Is this all right?"

With a desire like that, if she doesn't climax, she may never fall asleep. But if she can bring herself to orgasm without me doing it for her? I'd say luck is in my favor tonight.

"Yes. Touch yourself for me, Cadence."

My words make her breath unsteady. I often forget their power. With simple words, I've been able to make ladies climax with nothing but light touches. Women are stunning. Complex. And once you figure them out, they're bound to you, no matter how hard they beg the gods to erase the memory of your time together.

I kiss and suck across her collarbone and neck while she rubs herself. "One day, when you're fully mine, my fingers will take the place of yours. You'll drag your nails down my back as I bring you more pleasure than you can bear."

Cadence's bottom lip trembles. She's close, but I want her to make herself come faster. Harder.

"Rub yourself against my thigh. Do it now," I command.

Cadence wastes no time spreading her legs. Once my thigh is between hers, she rolls her hips against me. I hold her as close as I can, sucking on her earlobe and whispering tales of our future life together. Tales where my hands are on her shivering skin and where her body obeys my every command. Every word I speak and action I take tastes like a different kind of betrayal, and I hope Dominic doesn't overhear.

I move her hips faster against my thigh. When I lick up her neck, her body stiffens. She cries out my name with watering eyes and a glowing face.

"That's a good girl." I kiss her once more, then pull her into my chest. Everything about this feels wrong, no matter how necessary it is.

It doesn't take long before her eyes close and her breathing slows. All I can imagine, while I hold her in my arms, is how I wish Dominic were in her place.

Once her muscles finally lose their tone to the whims of the sandman, I inch away from her and out of the bed.

I grab a few items from my coat. Herbs and a vial of blood. Pigs blood. Vec said he didn't have a proper ampule to contain and preserve my blood, so I'd have to pierce my finger on the spot. But this will make unlocking the jade believable to Dom.

When I open the door to the cabinet room, the chandelier light is on. I hiss, remembering I forgot my glasses back in Cadence's room.

When my eyes adjust, I see the top of Dominic's head from the other side of the long table. "Relax, it's me."

Dominic stands and looks around. "This home is magnificent."

"It's nothing to write home about." I meet him on the other side of the room, with the elements in hand.

The light sparkles off the jade case. There it is, the artifact left all alone in its enclosure, waiting for its new owner.

Dominic pulls a replica of the artifact from his pocket, one he bought from some scummy street vendor who claimed it was the real thing. His throat bobs. "I'm ready."

I nod, taking the vial of blood and smearing the pig's blood across the jade. Then I wave a small glass bottle of ground zeledian over the lock, imagining the contraption unlocking as I do. The lock tries to disobey me. With my body angled away from Dom, I prick my thumb with a sewing needle hidden in my pocket and place my blood against the side of the enclosure, pretending to steady myself.

The lock falls to the ground.

When we open the translucent jade doors, Dom and I stand there in awe of the famed scarlet artifact. It lies there looking like nothing but an heirloom. It must have been decades or even centuries since someone has touched one.

When I grab it, its energy whispers tempting words. The power tries crawling through my veins, but I resist. One could take over the world with even one of these. Imagine if it got into the wrong hands.

Dominic places the faux artifact in the case and replaces the lock. "How does it feel?"

"See for yourself."

He takes it from me, scanning the gold lace. "It's strange, as if it wants me to use it for evil." Dom places it in the satchel around his waist.

I nod. "It's a wicked thing."

Dominic and I both freeze as we hear creaking foot boards coming down the hallway.

"Shit," Dom whispers harshly.

"Hide." I point to the table. Great, of course she couldn't even give me fifteen minutes before seeking me out.

Dom dives under the table and lies flat on his stomach between the chairs.

"Atticus?" Cadence calls out.

There's nowhere to run. Nowhere to hide. The lights spilling into the hall from the cabinet room are evidence enough. I need to distract Cadence and get Dominic out of here. I quickly sit on the table and stare up at the portrait above the fireplace.

Cadence enters the cabinet room, rubbing her eyes. "What are you doing?"

"I couldn't sleep. Just admiring the history." *Stay still, Dominic. I'll get us out of this.*

"You shouldn't be in here." To my relief, she doesn't look at me with a single ounce of suspicion. Instead, she yawns.

"I'm sorry. Couldn't help myself. I hope you understand." As she nears, I hop off the table and place my hand on her lower back. "Let's go back to bed."

She raises her eyebrows and takes my hand into her, studying the blood dripping down my thumb.

Shit. I can't let her speak about the blood. Dominic will hear everything.

"Atticus, your thumb is—"

Then my mouth is on hers, our tongues tangling together. She melts into my touch as I grab her waist and raise her to sit on the table. I'd rather kiss her in front of Dominic than have her add weight to any suspicions he may already hold toward me.

I wave my hand under the table, signaling Dominic to crawl out. A pair of fingers pinches my ankle and I flinch. I'll take it he got the memo—and that he's pissed at me.

This is what I get. I should have accepted one of Dominic's cruel suggestions and drugged her the moment I got here, then I wouldn't be stuck in this mess. Now, the only choice I have is to distract her.

In the corner of my eye, Dominic is halfway out the door on his belly. Cadence tries to follow my eyeline.

I reach for the fabric at her chest and rip her gown apart, then kiss across her breasts. I'll give her less than she wants and more than I prefer.

"Atticus, I thought—" She stares down at me as my warm breath and lips trail down her chest and stomach.

"And you'd be correct. I won't steal your honor completely."

I keep my promise to both Dominic and Cadence through it all, but a man doesn't need to stick his cock in a woman to truly defile her.

CHAPTER 32

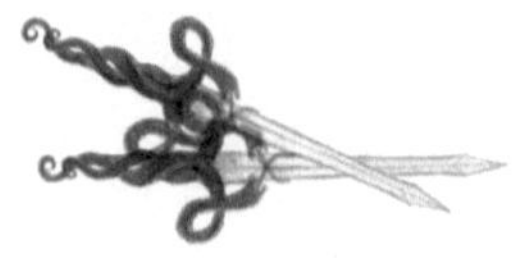

ATTICUS

After kissing Cadence goodbye in the morning, I almost fall on my knees and praise the gods. Not just because Dominic successfully smuggled out the artifact, but because I'm finally free from the snares of Cadence Graystone.

I'm sure Dominic's pissed, but once Archer wakes up later today, it will be nothing but a distant memory. If it weren't for the stringent visiting hours of the stasis ward, Dom and I would rush straight there. Instead, he'll meet me later this morning at a nearby bakery and we'll travel there together.

Then his magic will be mine.

It's bittersweet, though anytime the bitterness tries to take over I replace it with thoughts and fantasies of my plans for later tonight.

How I'll break Konstantin.

When I arrive back at Vec's home, I'm surprised maids aren't running around as usual. In fact, as I check the rooms on the first floor, I can't find a single one.

Where did everyone go?

As I ascend the stairs, I catch a view of my bedroom door cracked open and nearly tumble down the stairs.

Oh no.

I sprint up the stairs and throw the door open.

Vec stands at the end of my bed staring at Haylow. His arms are folded as he taps his foot. Nobody ever enters my room without my express permission, not even Vec. Why now of all times?

I hold my palms out, trying to tame him like some animal. "Vec, I can explain."

He turns to me. "Oh, can you now? Then do so, Atticus. Explain why there is an unconscious girl tied to your bed. Justify for me why I had to send my entire staff home before they too discovered her."

"She—she threatened to tell Dominic my origins. I didn't know what to do!"

"She's Konstantin's daughter! Do you think he won't come looking for her soon? That *you* won't be his primary suspect?"

"Dominic has the artifact and Konstantin will be dead soon enough." I scan Vec's furious face. "When did you find her?"

"An hour ago," he says quickly. "Now tell me what you used to knock her out. Perhaps I can reverse it quicker."

He can't. He's not a Desimir. Time must play its course. I step back like a guilty child.

Vec's eyes widen and he rushes around the bed and opens one of her eyelids, peering through her pupil and assessing the core of her being with immortal magic.

Vec grabs his hair and takes a step back. "You ruined her!"

"I—" *I have no adequate excuse, but I'll try.* "She belittled Juni's death, then all control left me."

Vec turns and sits on the edge of the bed. "This is sick, Atticus!"

"What do you want me to say? That I'm sorry? In time, she'll come around."

"You know the remnants always remain. She'll never be the same."

"You know what? Maybe she *deserved* it. Ever think of that?"

Vec throws his hands up. "Konstantin and Austrie raised her. They have lied to her for her entire life, twisting the truth in their favor. Of course she would side with them, they poisoned her mind. And now, it's been envenomed because of *you*."

I clench my jaw. "I did what I had to."

"Have you no remorse?"

I push down any semblance of pity for Haylow, no matter how hard Vec tries to pin it on me. "Ask me again once her father is dead."

"I've spent half my life focused on your goal of killing Konstantin. Immortals can handle a lot, but my heavens, I'm exhausted! You have a way of making things more difficult than they have to be." Vec's hands curl "You know I hate Desimir magic, yet you used it to its greatest extent on an innocent girl. You didn't even use it on Sir Raveen that way!"

"I know I fucked up!" I rip my gloves off and throw them to the ground.

Vec walks toward the door, stopping when his shoulder brushes mine. "May Konstantin die soon, for all our sakes."

He roughly shuts the door behind him. Then I hear his footsteps trudge down the stairs, the front door slamming shut shortly after.

My shoulders slump. Vec has forgiven me a thousand and one times, but this feels different. Soon, this five-century nightmare will finally be over.

I stalk over to Haylow and stare down at her. I may not be able to stop the permanent effects, but perhaps I can awaken her sooner.

The problem is I don't want to. She doesn't deserve any help or pity from me, but I'll do it for Vec and Dominic.

Gritting my teeth, I reluctantly place my hand upon her head and close my eyes, searching within her for where she's stuck. Trudging through her mind is like swimming through thick, suffocating, ink. A place filled with pain and misery.

Suddenly she jolts up, and when her eyes lock onto me she turns her body and rams her foot into my hip.

"Ouch, shit!" I take a step back. I should have restrained her ankles too.

"Fuck you!" Haylow shouts.

I keep my distance. "Good. You're finally awake."

She almost seems like herself, though there is something more sinister behind her eyes. It runs deep. It's incurable. And worst of all, it's of my creation.

"What did you do to me?" Her voice trembles now.

I motion to her cuffs. "Is it not obvious?"

"That's not what I'm talking about."

I take a step toward the bed and she flinches. There will always be a lasting wound upon her mind, and I will always be the monster in her nightmares. Good thing I never planned on keeping her part of my life. Or Dominic's for that matter.

"It's my family magic." My hip still throbs from when she kicked me. "You would have been out longer, but I managed to reattach a few strings."

Haylow scoffs. "Well, thank you Atticus! How brave! Wow, you're such a gentleman, and I'm so grateful for you. In fact, I could kiss you." She spits in my direction, then her eyes fill with tears. "Do you even realize what it feels like to experience your torment? Magic like that should be forbidden!"

"I don't have to listen to this." I get closer to the bed, ignoring her flinching, and pick up the bell off my bedside table, placing it in her hand. "If you need to eat, piss, or shit, ring this. When Vec gets back, he will assist you." I stomp to the door.

"I'll destroy you, Atticus! Mark my—"

I slam the door shut before she can finish.

CHAPTER 33

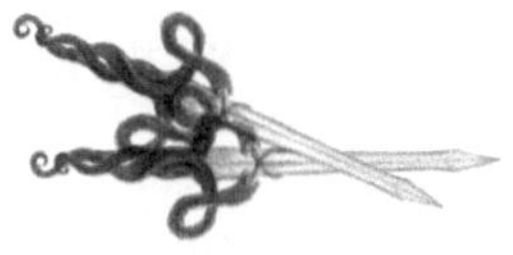

DOMINIC

I shouldn't have come to Vec's house. I should have listened to Atticus and met him at the bakery like he directed, but I couldn't help it. Atticus may not be in a rush to fix Archer, but I am. And if we leave now, perhaps the facility will make an exception and let me see Archer before visiting hours. I know they have never made exceptions before. But even if they say no, I know Atticus is good at sneaking around.

Nobody answers when I knock at Vec's door, but I can tell by the chimney that someone's home.

I fiddle with the lock. *Why is it that every time I'm here, I'm breaking and entering?*

I can't get the lock to give, so I walk around back, testing every door to the inside. To my surprise, the servants' door is unlocked. If a servant accidentally left a door unlocked like this at any of my father's estates, he'd fire them on the spot. But today, I'm thankful for the poor servant who overlooked it.

The wooden floor creaks as I step through the house. It's quiet. Lit candles sit on top of the fireplace mantle. The scent of mint and rosemary wafts throughout the house. It's pleasant. But somewhat unnerving.

I trek up the stairs toward Atticus's room. If he's anywhere, it's here. I take a deep breath as my hand grips the handle.

I open the door. My muscles seize up.

A person lies in the bed, bound at the wrists to the headboard. She looks exhausted and weary, like someone drugged her through hell, then spit her out.

"Haylow?" I whisper, covering my mouth. My knees buckle. *What is this?*

Her eyes flutter open. When she sees me, her face lights up, though no smile is present. "Dominic? Dominic! Oh, please, get me out of here!" Tears fall down her face. To my relief, her body doesn't look injured, but her eyes scream pain.

My steps are as heavy as a lead weight as I approach her. I can't accept this. Atticus couldn't have done this to her. There is no reason for him to. I know he has a tendency to get jealous, but not like this.

"Hurry," she babbles.

"I'm getting you out of here." I fiddle with the cuffs, my hands completely numb, unable to break free of the denial I'm in. "How did this happen?"

"There's no time! He'll be back any—"

The door slams behind me and I flinch. When I turn, Atticus stands there with furrowed eyebrows. His face is different. Unremorseful.

"Why are you here?" Atticus bites out, his fists curling. "I told you to meet me at the bakery!"

I can't look him in the eye. My voice shakes as I approach him. "What have you done, Atticus?"

"I had no choice, Dominic. She threatened me, and in doing so, she threatened Archer."

"I don't understand!" I search his face, trying to find any sense of reason. But his charm has disappeared, replaced by something vindictive and sinister. "Explain. Now!"

"It's of no concern to you. We have the artifact. Let's not waste any more time. It's time to save Archer." Atticus grabs my hand and tries to pull me to the door.

I tear myself from him and step backward toward Haylow. "I'm letting her go. And after I do, you'll explain!"

"Dominic, do not touch her."

I don't listen as I yank drawers open, searching for the keys to the handcuffs.

Haylow straightens her back. "If you won't tell him, Atticus, I will! Atticus is not who he says he is. He's—"

Atticus lurches across the room and slams his palm against her mouth, seething at her. I go numb as red-hot anger blazes through his face.

"Let her speak!" I tighten my fists. "You owe me an explanation!"

"That will never happen." Atticus's eyes stay locked on Haylow, threatening her without even saying a word.

I don't want to say this, but I have no choice. "If you do not let her talk, then this is over. All of it. The mission—us."

All he can do is stare daggers into Haylow's soul. His hand shakes in rage against her mouth, but then he slowly removes it.

Haylow looks from him to me. "Atticus is from another time. He's five-hundred years old. Not only that, but he uses atavistic magic. And he cannot wield all six tenets of core magic, only three, as well as the vile hell of his family magic. And Dominic, he's trying to steal—"

Atticus moves quickly, covering her mouth again. "That's quite enough, Haylow."

My mind feels as though it's filled with cotton. Steal what? The artifact? She'll be disappointed to know it's in my pocket. But what did she mean by another time? If Haylow wasn't bound to his bed, I would immediately discount it. "It's not possible you have atavistic blood. Atticus, tell me it's not true!"

But he doesn't say a word, only staring at the floor.

"No—you're both lying," I step back. "That defies the laws of nature. Humans cannot live that long to begin with, even venitors."

"Vec is an immortal," Atticus admits. "And he's not my uncle."

"But immortals are myths." I lean against a nearby wall. I'm not even sure what I'm angry about. The kidnapping? Or maybe it's because I thought I finally knew Atticus beneath his harsh exterior, but even that was a lie. I don't even know how to accept the possibility of immortals being real. "Then your family—what year did they die?"

Atticus swallows. "In 1402. It's why Vec preserved my body until a solution came along so I could kill the immortals. The ones who ripped away my happiness." Atticus signals to Haylow. "Her father was one of them. Konstantin was the one that killed Juni."

So many emotions swirl within me, I don't even know which one to focus on. I remember the day we bumped into Konstantin at the Tulip Ball. No wonder Atticus drank himself half to death after that interaction. And the words Konstantin said to him—well, knowing the whole story makes them so much more cruel. "Why have you been helping me? What do you truly get out of this?"

"With the artifact, our interests are paralleled. You'll see in time. If Archer gets his cure, then I get my revenge. It's that simple."

Haylow tugs against her restraints. I can't quite make out her words, though her expression alone tells me she's screaming at Atticus's plan to kill her father. Atticus pulls his hand away for a split second, then stuffs a handkerchief in her mouth.

Haylow's screams are muffled. I want to save her. I must.

But then Atticus nears and pulls me by my belt close to him, grabbing the artifact from my satchel as he does. Something about seeing it again flips a switch. It whispers to me. Now, all I can think of is my brother, and how I'll get to see his smile once more.

Atticus's lips curl as he stares at my entranced face. "This is what you want, right? Your brother's life."

I nod, the glowing red of the artifact hypnotizing me.

"And in order to do that, we'll need to leave Haylow bound for a little while longer. Do you understand?"

I nod again. I can't seem to take my attention off the artifact. Today is the day. I'll be able to hold Archer in my arms, and this time, he'll be able to hold me back. Not only that, but my family will be overjoyed, and I'll finally be able to prove to my father that Archer was a worthy cause.

Atticus puts it back in the satchel and pulls me into his chest, caressing the back of my head. I see Haylow's look of shock in the corner of my eye, but exposing my relationship with Atticus is the least of my concerns.

"Think about it." He kisses across my jaw. "We can leave right now and go see Archer. Wouldn't you like that?"

"Yes."

Then his mouth consumes me in a fury of passion. He drags his tongue over mine. Haylow turns her head away.

Atticus drags my earlobe between his teeth. "Archer will awaken." He captures my lips again. "I'll destroy her father." He speaks between kisses, my hair tangled between his fingers. "Then, when it's all done, it will be you and me. Together forever. Doesn't that sound nice?" His nips and sucks at my neck.

"Yes," I whisper, growing hard beneath my pants.

If Haylow weren't in the room, I know he'd do so much more to me. I want him to, but it will have to wait.

Atticus leaves one last kiss against my forehead. "Let's go."

"Yes," I say. "I'm ready."

Haylow pulls at her handcuffs, pleading with me through her eyes. Even I can't believe I'm letting this happen, but like Atticus said, this is only temporary.

"I'm sorry, Haylow," I say. "But I'll be back for you. Don't worry, just hang tight."

Tears spill down her face and onto the handkerchief stuffed in her mouth. It takes closing my eyes to make it to the door. To stomach leaving her like this. I still have a special place for her in my heart. But my heart is something Atticus owns now.

Atticus and I pay a driver to take us to the stasis ward. The entire ride, his hand rests on my thigh, softly caressing.

Archer, hang on.

We're almost there.

CHAPTER 34

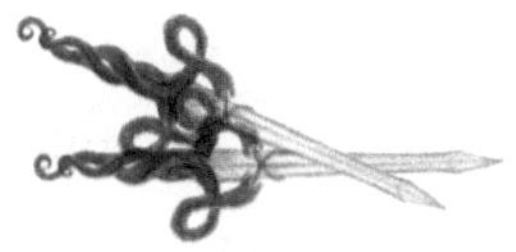

DOMINIC

Toward the end of the carriage ride, Atticus squeezes my hand a little tighter. My chest warms, though a prickle of guilt spreads through me knowing Haylow is still bound to his bed.

When we arrive, I'm a ball of nerves as we stride through the courtyard of the stasis ward. I keep asking Atticus if he remembered all the ingredients. Every time he says yes, even going as far as stopping in one hallway and pulling them from his pockets to show me.

When we enter Archer's room, everything feels so tranquil, like the feeling that overtakes me after a deep cry. I approach my brother, smoothing his hair off his forehead, as Atticus removes the ingredients from his pocket, setting them on the bedside table.

Blood flower, epazote, and tiger's eye.

"We'll need some of your blood," Atticus says.

"Yes, I almost forgot." I stand in front of him, pulling my sleeve up. A relative's blood is required for it to work. I wince as Atticus cuts into my palm. He moves my hand over Archer's face, letting the blood drip down onto his forehead.

I tend to my wound while Atticus places herbs in Archer's fist, then sets the tiger's eye stone in the middle of Archer's chest.

My chest tightens at how close we are to finally awakening him. Now all that's left is the artifact. I try to hand it to Atticus, but he doesn't take it from me. Instead, he pulls a piece of paper from his pocket. One I recognize as the recipe for Archer's treatment.

Atticus hands me the paper. "You remember our deal?"

With how busy we've been getting everything we needed for the artifact, it escaped my mind. "Yes. That I would hand over the final element to you, with no questions asked." I can't possibly think of what Atticus would need. I brought no stones with me, besides the one on my ring.

"And that I'll be the one to integrate it into the cure."

"Tell me quickly, what is it? A lock of my hair?" I will give him anything he needs. Archer is almost well, and I can't stand waiting another second. "Tell me, Atticus."

Atticus keeps his eyes locked on me as he reaches into his pocket and pulls out the ripped off piece of paper from the recipe.

I swipe it from him, piecing it together with the rest of the recipe. I raise it to my eye level.

My body starts to tremble as I read the words over and over again; my mind not accepting nor processing them.

No, no, no.

This can't—

Blythesea magic wielded by a user with atavistic blood.

"You're shaking, Dominic," Atticus says with near-amusement in his voice.

"Atticus," my voice trembles. "No."

"As Haylow already told you, I am the only one here with the correct blood."

He knew. This entire time Atticus knew *exactly* who I was. He's been targeting me and integrated himself into my life like an unknown parasite. Memories swirl through me, from the way he approached me the first day of class, to the way he found me at Haylow's party. Or even his seemingly selfless motivation to help Archer. Since day one, he's been a vulture, and I, his willing prey.

I crunch the paper up in my fist, throwing it across the room. I bury my face in my palms, barely able to catch my breath. My family's magic is in danger, all because I melted under Atticus's spell, just like everyone else.

I can't help myself as I grip the collar of his overcoat. "You knew about my family this entire time, didn't you? Didn't you!"

Atticus shrugs. "There's no point in denying it. Vec has been around for a long time. He learned your family's secrets and told me."

I step back, slamming my fists down on the bedside table. "I will never hand it over to you!"

Before I can say another word, Atticus captures my jaw in his grip, pulling me close to his face. "Don't be like this. Your brother is nearly alive. Not to mention, you don't have atavistic blood, my love. You'll end up killing him if you try. And we wouldn't want that now, would we?"

I move my eyes over to Archer, my jaw still subdued by Atticus.

If I don't give Atticus the magic, Archer will remain like this forever, trapped within his own mind. I'll never get to hear his voice or laughter again, but could I ever forgive myself if I give Atticus what he wants?

"Give it to me," Atticus whispers against my lips. "Then you and Archer can be together again."

I hold back the tears forming in my eyes, my throat drying out. "I—can't."

"You can. And you will."

My jaw trembles. I shouldn't do this, but I'll regret it for the rest of my life if I knew Archer could be healed, and I threw away my opportunity. I risked my life for this treatment. Watched Atticus kill for it. Committed treason for it.

I place my palm on Atticus's chest and close my eyes. Inside my mind, I form a replication of the magic, the way I was only meant to do for my firstborn.

The replica begins to transfer into Atticus's body. He shivers. If it's anything like the time my father gave me the magic, he's feeling a faint burning sensation in his veins and the whispers of the dead are speaking into his ears, already trying to tempt him.

I take a step back, watching Atticus as he looks around the room, trying to find the source of the voices.

He inspects his gloved hands, taking in this new power. My power.

"You just—" My voice is unsteady. "They are always at your command. In order to use it, you simply tell them what to do. But your mind must be clear and your emotions stabilized. Commanding them without keeping your thoughts in check caused my family to go into hiding. Now please, help Archer."

Atticus composes his awestruck expression. "Of course." He takes the artifact. And from his eyes alone, I can tell his thoughts are off in some far-off land, and if I'm not mistaken, he's holding back a smile.

Atticus holds the artifact over Archer's body.

I step back until I'm leaning against the wall, watching intently, unable to keep my knees straight for another second. As he holds the artifact, the blood and herbs detect its presence, glittering energy emitting off the elements, then toward the red stone.

Archer's body glows from the combined effects. It's working.

When will Atticus use Blythesea magic? *How* will he use it?

My heart leaps as Archer's eyes flutter open. I cover my mouth. It worked. I almost fall to the ground.

Archer turns his head to the side, staring straight at me. "Dom?" His voice is weak. Atticus helps him into a sitting position.

I rush to Archer and wrap my arms around him. "Thank the gods!" My eyes fill with tears.

Archer's arms are limp from underuse. "Dom, what's going on?"

"Rest now, brother, you've been asleep for a long time."

Archer inspects his arms and legs. "They're longer."

My eyes well with tears. No sorrow now, only joy. "Well, it has been two years."

The whites of his eyes turn to glass. He inspects the hands of the sixteen-year-old he is now. By his demeanor alone, he's still fourteen, but his body has changed, even with bedrest. Another perk of the red beryl. "I lost so much time."

"All that matters now is the time you have left. It's a miracle you're awake, I hope you know that." I lean forward and hug him again, but I can't shake the unease pressing in all around me. I try to push it away and focus on Archer, but it persists. I can feel Atticus standing above us, watching. Waiting.

A deep realization rips through me as I begin to reflect on Atticus's spell.

He never used Blythesea magic at any point to awaken Archer.

And if he didn't use my magic for the treatment then—

No.

He took it for himself, this entire situation a ploy for him to steal it outright. Archer was nothing but a pawn to get what he wanted.

Vindictive rage fills every part of me as I pull out of the embrace, glaring at Atticus.

Atticus's arms are folded, his lips curled up in a smile. "Dominic, what's the matter? Your brother is awake."

My teeth clench. "You—you lied to me!"

"About?"

Archer looks between us. "Brother, what's wrong? Who is this man?"

I help Archer lie back down. "Everything is all right, Archer. Please rest."

My brother looks scared, and all I want at this moment is to spend the rest of the day with him without a care in my heart about Atticus or anything else in existence, but I cannot.

"You didn't use Blythesea magic at all!" I shout.

Atticus doesn't even cower at my accusation. He leans back against the armrest of a chair. "That day your grandfather destroyed the village, he killed an immortal. It's the first time one has ever died, which means in order to kill Konstantin, I need your magic. And in exchange, I gave you exactly what you wanted."

I can't help myself, even in front of my terrified and confused brother. I rush off the bed toward Atticus, ready to sock him in the face, my mind too cluttered to even contemplate conjuring a spell.

Before it lands, Atticus knocks me backward with a gust of air manipulation, my back slamming into the wall. Pain explodes through me,

Archer reaches out. "Dominic!"

Atticus steps forward, looking down at me. "I'm sorry, Dominic. This was the only way."

I grab my abdomen, barely able to look up at those spectacles that bring an even greater darkness to his already sinister face. "You manipulated me. I thought you loved me!"

He bends down in front of me, tipping my jaw up with two gloved fingers. "Nothing will stop me from killing Konstantin. Not logic or reason. Not morals. And not my love for you."

I can't stop the tears dripping down my cheeks. "I loved—" With another jolt of pain ripping through me, I push his hand away, turning my head. I can't stand to look at him another second. "Go."

In the corner of my eye, I watch Atticus frown. "May you have a long and happy life with your brother. Perhaps we'll meet again one day."

Atticus stands and takes one last look at me before disappearing out the door, his boots echoing down the hall.

I rise and limp over to my brother.

Archer cries into my chest. "Dom... I don't understand—"

"I'm so sorry, Archer." I pull my handkerchief out of my pocket and wipe my blood from his forehead.

I want to kill Atticus. He betrayed my heart. My family. If he truly loved me, all of this could have happened without him stealing my family magic. But that's the thing—he never loved me. Atticus Desimir is not capable of love.

I bury my pain long enough to fully explain to Archer what happened to him during the train derailment. I need to be strong, if not for me, then for him.

"Was that man supposed to use father's magic to save me?" Archer asks.

I can't look Archer in the eye anymore. "He only wanted it for himself. He stole it."

"Dom," he says, pain in his voice, "It can only be given willingly."

I bite down on my tongue. His words rub salt into the wound of my stupidity. "I know. I am a fool, Archer."

I flinch at the shriek from the doorway. Archer's nurse walks in, completely speechless. Her face is pale, as if she's going to faint. Archer and I share a look of knowing that he cannot tell anyone how he awakened, nor what I gave Atticus for it.

Before long, the room is filled with flabbergasted nurses and doctors assessing Archer. I lie to them all, telling them I found him this way.

I send for my parents. When they arrive my mother weeps hysterically. My father falls to his knees and cries. It's not as satisfying as I had hoped. Not after caving to Atticus's desires and giving away my family's secret. The nurse says she'll send a telegram to my sister and let her know of Archer's miraculous recovery.

In all the hustle, I almost forgot about Haylow, who is likely still bound to Atticus's bed. I'm sure he went straight to Konstantin, and I won't partake in his murderous rage to stop him.

After the long family reunion, I say my goodbyes to my parents and to Archer.

Then I head to Vec's to free a girl who likely wants to murder me.

CHAPTER 35

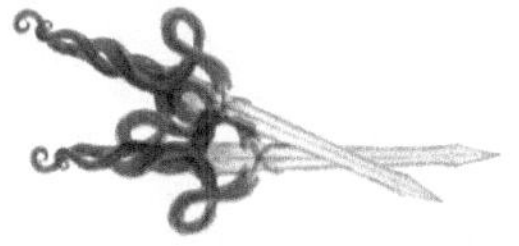

DOMINIC

I break into Vec's house again through the servant quarters. I know Atticus isn't here, but a part of me wishes he were. There's a false hope within me that he abandoned his quest to kill Konstantin.

I tiptoe through the house toward the stairwell.

"Do I know you?" a voice says. In the drawing room sits a man in his early thirties, flipping through a book, his face downcast and exhausted, his neck embossed with strange lace imprints. Imprints I recognize from books on tales of the immortals.

"Are you Vec?" I ask.

"I am. And I presume you're Dominic Ashworth?"

I nod. "I'm here to free Haylow. Don't try to stop me.

He returns to his book. "I wasn't planning on it."

I turn to the stairs, but I hesitate. "You're the one who told Atticus my family's secret?"

"You'd be correct."

"So I suppose you should be the one I'm angry at, not Atticus."

Vec shuts the book and sets it on the table. He looks at me with saddened eyes. Not a look I would have expected. "When his father died, he left Atticus in my care. Immortals take that seriously. The depths of

Atticus's desires—I have almost no choice but to make them happen. No matter how dark. Even if it takes me centuries."

"And you knew the immortal my grandfather killed?"

"His name was Alano, and he killed Atticus's father. His crimes extended centuries before that, but to list them all would be a disservice to your time. Just know he was a wicked fool, so I can see why your grandfather had enough incompressible rage to wipe out an entire town."

"If Atticus uses Blythesea magic incorrectly, he could destroy all of London. I hope you know that. Even after years of training, I can still barely control it."

"I'm aware that is a possibility," Vec says.

"And he has no training. My grandfather may have survived the events in Scotland before he was executed, but he was well-trained. Atticus could very well open his very soul to the dead, and his soul would be consumed."

At that, Vec stiffens.

I put my hands in my pockets. "But I suppose you never considered that when you helped him steal it from me."

Vec stands and walks up to me. "Your family is good at keeping secrets. How could I have known?"

"If only you had more *time*." I hope my words sting. I don't want Atticus to die, even after what he did. But there's nothing I can do to stop him. "I'll be taking Haylow now."

"Do what you must. I won't stop you."

"She'll probably report you," I say.

"If there's one thing I know how to do, it's relocating after adversity." Vec throws me a small set of keys.

I give him a small nod and ascend the stairs to Atticus's room. Inside, Haylow is trying to yank her hand from the handcuffs, her wrist completely reddened and chaffed. She doesn't look at all happy to see me.

"Let me help you." I approach her.

She looks like she wants to kill me, but still lets me unlock the cuffs. Haylow doesn't say thank you. Instead her hand lands across my face and I stumble back.

My skin stings from the slap. "I just saved you!"

She angrily slips off the bed. "You left me like this for hours. You're just as wicked as Atticus, I hope you know that."

I tense up. "Don't say that."

She takes a trinket off Atticus's dresser and throws it at me. I step out of the way just in time.

"I watched you practically melt in his hands. You'd throw yourself off a cliff for him if he asked you to!"

I take a step forward. "And what about you? Your father knew who I was this entire time, didn't he? You stated your feelings for me when it was convenient for you. Did you really have any romantic interest in me?"

"Fuck you." She huffs and stomps out of the room. I stay still until I hear the front door slam shut.

Then I fall to my knees on the bedroom floor. I have what I wanted, and I can't even enjoy it, not when this pain gnaws at my chest.

And then I'm thinking of Atticus again. The times we spent together. The way he made me feel strong. How his hands felt against my skin. How he opened up to me in ways I know he never did to anyone else. And now he's as good as dead.

Against all reason, I know I cannot let him die. There's not a doubt in my mind. If he uses Blythesea magic, Konstantin might perish, but so will he. And a good chunk of London for that matter. There's no way he can control his fury while killing for revenge.

Every time I have practiced Blythesea magic, I do so in a large open field. Half the time, I end up thinking of Archer for almost no reason and the dead destroy the grass the length of an acre.

I have to save him. Or die trying. Because at the end of the day, I could never force myself to stop loving him.

I sprint down the stairs and find Vec. "I'm going to save Atticus."

"Good luck."

"Aren't you worried about him? He will die."

Vec throws his book down. "Atticus is a man. He's capable of protecting himself." Vec is in denial. He took care of Atticus for years. Atticus is basically a son to him. There's no way he's going to just let this go.

"Not this time, and you know it. Our goals make us blind to many things."

"Perhaps he needs to learn the consequences of his own actions. I've protected him for far too long."

"Death is not something you can learn from, Vec," I say, reaching out my hand. "Come with me. My magic won't be enough, I may need yours too."

Vec contemplates for a moment before cursing under his breath and grabbing his hat. "Just know that trying to save him may cost you your own life."

CHAPTER 36

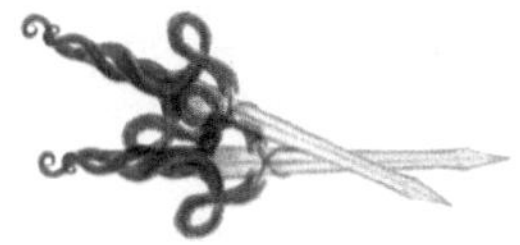

ATTICUS

The daggers inside my coat grow heavy as I walk all the way to Konstantin's home. I should have taken a buggy, but trudging all the way there gives me time to think and plan, and to stir up my anger. It gives me time to relive my family's death repeatedly, letting myself feel the full extent of pain in a way I never have before. I don't hold back any of the grimmer details this time as I reimagine the blood, the crack of Juni's spine, the gasps, the screams. The way my chest caved in as I watched their souls leave their bodies.

I become so lost in my grief that I flinch when I realize I'm in front of Konstantin's residence. The night is cold. A chilled breeze passes over the back of my neck, colliding with the goosebumps of violent anticipation. I use zeledian root to open the front door.

The home is just as quiet as the night. Not a single light bulb ignited, only the street lights from outside spilling into the hallways from the windows.

The home seems empty, but I know it's not. If there is one thing I've picked up on over the years of living with Vec, it's how to sense the presence of an immortal. The stagnant hour hands of time are heavy in the air.

Their hidden presence grows so thick I can practically feel Konstantin's breath on the back of my neck as I enter an empty ballroom.

Then I lose my patience. "I know you're here. Stop hiding!"

It's silent for a minute.

Then the chandeliers ignite. I raise my arm to shield my eyes from the glare.

Konstantin emerges from the upper balcony, leaning on his forearms upon the railing. "I never thought this day would come. A Desimir with Blythesea magic. It's unheard of."

Of course he'd go to great lengths to find out who killed Alano, even tracking down his grandson. Because Alano's death taught Konstantin one thing—he was now mortal. "If you knew Dominic was a Blythesea, why did you let him live? Why let me pursue him!"

Konstantin laughs. It echoes throughout the large ballroom. "You can't just kill a Blythesea. Do you think Ezekiel and Alano were in a simple bar fight? Alano tried to stab him in the streets, unsolicited. But the dead protect those they serve. Like a legion of impenetrable armor. The only thing that can kill a death-wielding Blythesea, besides sickness and old age, is their own magic. I tried to confirm that theory two years ago for myself."

All the pieces of the puzzle collide together. "You thought Archer was the heir to Blythesea magic. You and Austrie conducted that train attack!"

"Dominic was supposed to be on that train. It wasn't until the ball that I realized I injured the wrong person. They look so alike, you see, and I don't tend to follow up on my killings."

"And when you saw us together, you decided to sic Haylow on him, and have her threaten me. Dominic's loved her for years. He's been to your many homes! How could you not have known he was still alive?"

"Haylow is a bit of a rebel, only throwing parties when Austrie and I are away on business."

"Not even your own daughter can respect your wishes." I scoff.

"She's useful where I need her to be."

Then my entire body goes numb as a bolt of magic pierces into my lower back. I yell out and fall to my knees, tipping my head back enough to see my perpetrator.

Austrie.

Vec never taught me much about immortal magic over the years, much less used it on me. But my spine is frozen in some kind of glass encasement. My muscles turn to stone. I can't move from my kneeling position, my neck stuck pointed at the sky. It's hard to breathe. Every inhale is short and desperate.

Konstantin descends the stairs. In the corner of my eye, he is smiling and chuckling. Then he's standing above me and I have no choice but to stare up at his timeless face.

He smooths my curls back as if I'm a poor, weak child. "Like always, it's over before it begins. What a shame, I always wanted to fight a Desimir."

My jaw muscles seize up to the point where talking is physically painful. "Then let...me show you."

"And let you use Blythesea magic against me?"

"I won't." I grit between my teeth. "I'll play your game fair and square."

Konstantin looks to Austrie. Austrie shrugs.

"What an interesting proposition." Konstantin holds his chin. He nods to Austrie. My muscles relax and I can finally take full breaths. "I look forward to showing you that you're just as weak as your father."

"And I look forward to skinning you alive."

"Can't wait."

Austrie leans against a nearby pillar in amusement. I stand and step away from Konstantin, ready to duel with him. I shouldn't fall into his trap. If I were wise, I'd end it right now. But I'm not ready for him to die yet.

"You start." Konstantin says. "I want to see Desimir magic in action."

"This isn't chess." But how I do love a good game of chess. If he wants a show, I'll give him a show.

I place my fingertips together and close my eyes. Then I find the remaining shadows in the room and pull them across the floor to where Konstantin stands. He doesn't resist as I let them snake around his ankles, and up his torso until they're finally seeping into his mind.

The Blythesea demons are in my head now, begging me to let them kill. To let them compliment my Desimir shadows. But I ignore them all, because even without Dominic's magic, I'm strong.

Then I'm in Konstantin's head. He lets me explore his mind but blocks off his memories. *How does he know how to do that?*

I attack him, injecting horrid fantasies. I show him Haylow. I project an image into his head of her as a child dying the exact way Juni did—and by his own hands.

But then something shifts.

He has me, countering my shadows with my own magic. He's in my head. I scream as my shadows betray me and pierce into my mind. And if I had no training, I'd cower to his whims and become as broken as Haylow. But within seconds, I banish the shadows out of me.

I'm satisfied at the sight of Konstantin's heavy breaths. That something I did shook him. And in giving him pain, I showed him mine. The reality of what he did.

"That was clever," I say. "You almost had me."

Konstantin's eyebrows are furrowed, his frown deep. "What did you do to Haylow?"

"I ruined her enough that you'll no longer recognize her as your daughter." It's a white lie in some regards, but I won't pass up any opportunity to make Konstantin cower. "I only gave you a sip of my magic. Her? Well, I gave her the entire vineyard."

Austrie steps forward, fists curled and shaking. I'm sure he raised her just as much as Konstantin did.

But Konstantin shakes his head at him. "Now I won't make it quick."

"I never expected you to. But I also won't give you the chance." Directing my energy into the witch's tongue herb in my coat, I drop to the ground and slam my hands against the ground, controlling a small earthquake into a nearby pillar. Then the pillar falls, the balcony caving in and falling upon Austrie.

Konstantin doesn't react. Austrie is unconscious, but soon he'll be revived. But without Konstantin's help, he won't be able to uncover himself from beneath the rubble. And thankfully for me, his hands are contained. Now I don't have to worry about sneak attacks from Austrie as I destroy Konstantin.

And I'm angry enough to do what I need to.

"Father!" A scream comes from the doorway. Haylow runs inside the ballroom, panting as if she ran the entire way here.

"Get to your room, Haylow! Lock the door!" Konstantin yells through gritted teeth.

Haylow shakes her head and runs to Austrie.

Oh you sweet poor girl. You should really listen to your father.

I use snake stem to summon a tendril from the ground and grip her ankle. But she doesn't submit to me in screams or cries. And when I see a green stone glowing around her neck, I almost cower.

She slams a hand against the ground, vines growing across the floor. But not just any vine. Ones with spores. If one touches me, I'll immediately grow ill. I may even die.

One of her vines accelerates toward the tendril that encases her ankle, choking the life out of it to free her. Then it comes for me. I release her and back up. She's strong, but I should have already known that from classes. Haylow is unassuming when she wants to be, and I shouldn't have underestimated her.

I refuse to use Desimir magic on her again, but my rage is too great to spare her pain. I direct my energy into the tincture of winter's splinter in my pocket. Frost leaves my fingertips, rushing toward her like she's its prey.

"No!" She tries to rub the frost off her skin to melt it.

But I'm faster.

The frost encases her body, turning to ice. Konstantin doesn't step forward to save her because he knows how cruel winter's splinter is. And with the right intentions, the ice can easily turn to glass and pierce into someone like spears.

Soon, Haylow is no more than a frozen icicle. She's still conscious. She can still breathe. But if I keep her in the ice too long, she really will die.

My eyes grow darker. "Do you find me cruel, Konstantin?"

Konstantin ignores me as he seethes. He points at the sky with both hands. Then blood drips from the ceiling. It seeps up through the cracks in the tile and doesn't stop until the soles of my boots are covered. The room reeks of iron.

Drops of blood drip down my skin and soak into my hair. "What dark immortal magic is this?"

"Blood is warm. Haylow is cold. I'll melt her out while I slit your throat."

"It will take a lot more than blood to thaw her out before she dies." I smile. Then I yank the daggers out of my coat, flinging them across the room. Both land deep inside Konstantin's chest. They're child's play to an immortal, but it will give me an upper hand.

I sprint at Konstantin. He tries to throw his own dagger at me, but I use Boisclair magic, my inheritance from my mother, to quickly disappear and evade. He can't track me, my body glitching in different directions as I sprint toward him.

Then I'm on him, kicking the hilt of one of my daggers deeper into his chest and throwing him into a wall with a gust of air.

"You shouldn't have let me stew so long, Konstantin. And you shouldn't have expected me to play fair."

And then it's time. If I give him another second to react, I'll be the one buried in ice and rubble. Spirits of the dead whisper into my ear. They beg for a command. They remind me of my pain and what I'm meant to do. Then I fall into their temptations, allowing them to rise from beneath the floor.

The creatures are horrifying with their ghostly inhuman faces of gray and blue. I contain my fear, holding onto my anger.

"Hold him down," I tell them. "Don't let him go."

They cackle and swarm at him.

"You said no Blythesea magic!" Konstantin yells out, his hand restrained against the wall by the dead. "If you use them you're weak! You're nothing without them!"

I can admit to myself that his words sting. But that pain doesn't compare to the promises the dead whisper. How satisfied I'll feel when this is complete.

"Open his abdomen." I tell one of them softly, my face emotionless. "And do it slowly."

The dead go crazy, excited to do my bidding. Their nails claw at his stomach. Konstantin yells out in pure agony. His screams feel better than any climax I've ever had, and I can't help but laugh as shimmering blue blood and organs seep onto the ground, turning the red blood on the floor a stark shade of purple.

"Atticus! Stop!" a voice screams. The dead look to the person behind me, as if he's also their master.

"Pull out the immortal's fingernails." I tell the dead. I ignore Konstantin's screams as I turn around to where Dominic stands in the middle of the ballroom. He looks nauseated from the sight before him. Disemboweled Konstantin. Crushed Austrie. Frozen Haylow.

Dominic takes a step forward, blood dripping from the ceiling and onto his face. "If you command them to kill him, you won't be able to control it. You'll die!"

"I knew dying was a risk."

"No. It's a certainty."

I stride forward and grab his collar, bringing him close to me. "Not even you can stop me."

"I know." His voice breaks. "I know."

Austrie tries to shimmy out of the rubble, unsuccessfully.

"They are the ones who tried to kill your brother, you know. They knew your secret. It was you they were trying to murder all along," I say.

Dominic looks over to Austrie, then back to me. "You're lying again."

"Ask them yourself."

Dominic looks over to Austrie. All Austrie can do is stay silent, subdued under the rubble, with begging eyes. It's the first time in Austrie's millennium of life he's ever been scared for his life.

"Don't you want them to pay?" I ask.

Dominic's bottom lip trembles. "Of course—but I don't want to lose you! Please, I love you."

My heart thuds.

But the dead whisper Juni's name in my ears in an agonizingly seductive way. How does Dominic handle living this way? With beings craving death at every turn?

I keep my eyes locked on him as I raise my left hand toward Austrie. "I will avenge your pain. And I will show you I can control it."

"Atticus please don't!"

But it's too late. I spread my Desimir magic into Austrie's mind, making him weak with the fear of death so he cannot stop me from invading his brain. I torment him in the same way I tortured Haylow. And with him, I make it worse.

His cries of pain are so horrible, Dominic pinches his eyes shut.

My voice booms with commands. "Finish him."

The dead do my bidding rushing to Austrie. They are maniacal, ripping his skin off like it's grass. Dominic may have learned Blythesea magic, but he's never killed with it, or seen what his demons can really do.

Austrie's breathing ceases, his body now a pile of skin and organs.
Sweet relief.

I can't help myself; I pull Dominic into my chest and capture his lips in mine. The blood still drips from the ceiling as I consume him, his tongue only moving out of pure habit.

Then he shoves me away.

My lips curl. "See? I controlled it. I'm still here. No towns blew up. Perhaps your grandfather wasn't as strong as I am."

"Konstantin is the one you truly hate. When you kill him, you won't be able to control it!" Dominic yells. "I know you! Please." He presses his forehead against mine. His voice lowers to a pained whisper. "Please don't leave me."

I hold the back of his neck and pull his head away so I can look into his eyes. "When this is all over, we'll be together. Just you and me on an earth where immortals can no longer destroy both of our lives."

"No—"

I kiss him one more time, then turn my body toward Konstantin.

Dominic lunges forward and grabs the back of my coat. "I won't let you!"

"I'm sorry, Dom." I dredge up tendrils from the ground. They snake toward him and knock him to the ground into the blood, binding his ankles.

I approach Konstantin and tilt my head, his body more blood than skin. The sight deserves to be turned into statues and paintings and displayed in museums for all to see.

"Stop for a moment," I tell the dead.

They obey. Then I kneel in front of Konstantin. His body is slower to regenerate with the Blythesea magic, unlike the time he carved his own face in front of me. He's panting, arms limp by his side.

"Did you anticipate this, Konstantin? That today I'd bring you to your last breath?"

"It. Won't." Konstantin takes long gasping inhales between every word. "You will not win."

I grab the back of his hair, tightening my grip. Then I pull one of my daggers out of his chest and bring it to his neck. With a smile along my face, I slit his throat, then carve out his voice box. "I don't want to hear you speak ever again."

Konstantin makes choking sounds. The wound starts to heal, but I keep my knife close for when it does. "You deserve every bit of this. A man who can take the life of a child the way you did deserves no life at all!" As his wound closes, I reopen it, blood spilling down his chest again. "I hope you regret every moment that led you to this point. In the afterlife, I want my face to be your last memory. That is, if immortals even have souls."

I want to torture him more. I even want to thaw Haylow out of her ice cavern so she can watch her wicked father take his last breath the way I did with Jervany. Dominic uses every spell imaginable to free himself from the tendril. I have little time.

The dead are at my knees, bowing, begging to have him. I step back and point my palm at him. "Kill him. And make sure he suffers deeply. Let out all of your sadistic desires onto the being. Desires you've had for all eternity."

"Atticus, don't!" Dominic yells out.

"Do it now!" I command. There's such malice in my words that my muscles shake with a mixture of hate and blissful anticipation. I think of my parents, the fear in their eyes when the immortals forced them to take their last breaths. Sir Raveen. My mother's screams. Juni's final squeak. Malevolence encases me. I almost don't want to kill him just to continue his torment for decades. But I won't lose this chance.

The dead swarm him. Then more appear, some from out of the walls, others from the floor. Konstantin can't even scream as they carry out such vile acts of violence on him, even I have to turn my head.

When I do, Dominic has freed himself from the tendril, but he's not trying to stop me any longer. He's using an amber stone to thaw Haylow out of the ice. As she melts out of her encasement, he takes her unconscious body in his arms.

The room floods with the sounds of maniacal spirits of death and torment, but I block them all out to keep my eyes locked on Dominic.

He stops at the sight of me, a tear dripping down his face. Then he runs as fast as he can out of the ballroom with Haylow.

So many dead pile upon Konstantin, their blue-gray forms fill up the entire wall. He's not even visible anymore.

"I don't need all of you! Let me see him." But they aren't listening. "I command you to get off him!" This time they do listen to me, and when they do, his body is nothing but a few ribbons of skin.

It's done. I take a breath of relief and feel Juni smile down at me from the clouds. I have avenged her. She and my parents.

But the dead still look sadistic and unsatisfied. It's as if my rage summoned too many of them, and there wasn't enough food at the feast. Now they're looking at me like I'm their next meal.

I take a step back. And then I realize why Blythesea magic with emotions is so dangerous, and why Dominic warned me. Too many are here. My relief of vengeance turns to fear. I could become just like Austrie and Konstantin.

I sprint through the blood and rubble. The dead chase me, their screeches of desire on my heels. With no training in Blythesea magic, I have no way to defend myself. Then they're on me, slamming me to the ground. An undead fist wraps around my ankle.

I command my Desimir shadows from the ground but they're not even in the same dimension. Their efforts to protect me go completely unnoticed and they become no better than wind.

"Unhand me!" I raise my voice to almost a command. "That's an order!"

But they ignore me. More pile upon my limbs holding me down. Then claws slash across my chest, my skin broken. I scream out, my body arching in pain. Any deeper and I would be dead.

I'm brought to such misery through scratches and bites that my vision goes blurry.

Is this how I die? Achieving my vengeance, only to be extinguished in the same way my adversaries were?

To die like this... I should have listened to Dominic. This was a mistake. Even for Juni, I never wanted to go like this. I'm ashamed to die this way. With no honor and the regret of ever betraying Dominic.

And with the knowledge that I was wrong.

Then everything goes black.

CHAPTER 37

DOMINIC

Though still unconscious, I carry Haylow to where Vec is waiting outside. Because of the nature of Blythesea magic, I figured it wise in case the dead saw Vec's immortality status as a target.

His eyes widen at my skin and clothes dripping in blood, though he doesn't comment on it. Vec helps me lay Haylow in the grass.

She is still breathing, but her body is cold and pale. I place my blood-soaked coat over her, but it's not enough.

"Where's Atticus?" Vec asks.

I shake my head. "He's beyond reason."

Atticus went too far, and he's as good as dead. Even Haylow, Vec, and I are in danger still being on the property. He'll summon too many unforgiven souls in his rage, and then they'll maul us all. Nowhere in this part of London is safe.

I sit on the grass and pull Haylow into my chest, transferring my body heat into hers. But she's still an icicle. If she doesn't warm up soon, her heart will give out. I place my hand on her abdomen and use regeneration magic.

"Let me try." Vec sets his hat to the side. "My magic may work faster."

"If anything, the pain will awaken her."

Vec places his hands on her shoulder, a purple glow moving through her skin.

Then she gasps, her body trembling from the pain. "Stop!"

Vec brings both his hands back in surrender. "All done."

I hold her tighter, grateful there won't be another life lost to Atticus's actions. "You're freezing to death."

Haylow looks at me. "I will be fine. My father... Is he..."

I don't want to lie to her. "Almost certainly. I'm sorry." But in all honesty, I don't think I am. I may be sad for Haylow, that she is now left with no parents. But Konstantin harmed my brother and killed Atticus's sister. Atticus is right. Those immortals needed to die. I just wish there could have been another way. A way that doesn't end with all of us dead.

Haylow doesn't cry. I'm sure if she tried, her tears would turn to ice on her skin. She scoots out of my grasp. "I can manage."

A blue light emits from every window in the mansion. It's too late. Just as I suspected, Atticus went too far. I want to sob, knowing he's probably gone.

"You're the expert on your magic," Vec says. "What now?"

In the end, I know Atticus isn't a bad person. Life dealt him a horrible card at such a tender age. If Atticus were a bad person, he would have tricked me *and* not healed Archer. He could have made up a lie about healing my brother, and the bonehead in me would have believed it. Instead, he dove through hoops to get the artifact to awaken Archer, risking life in prison or execution. He didn't just sacrifice for me. He *killed* for me. *Tricked* for me.

Maybe there's still time. I can still stop this. And if I don't try, I'll probably die too. What choice do I have?

"I'll be back." I scoot away from Haylow, leaving my coat on her.

"Wait!" Haylow reaches out. "It's too dangerous!"

Her words fall on deaf ears as I sprint inside.

Every light bulb shatters as I run through the halls. The dead know I'm coming to stop them, and now they'll do anything to scare me off. The mansion rumbles like an earthquake is beginning, making me stumble and crash into the walls.

When I run into the ballroom, the sight is like hell on earth. The blood is no longer dripping from the ceiling, but the ground is still covered in it. So many dead infest the ballroom I can hardly see the floor or walls. More spawn from the ceiling. Atticus lost control, and now they're coming in droves.

Then I see him in the center of the ballroom, being held down by a large group of the dead.

"Atticus!" My heart nearly gives out as a group of them scratch and bite at Atticus's half-conscious body, his blood mixing with the blood on the floor. They tear his clothing to shreds as he writhes in pain. The only reason they haven't killed him yet is because of his other commands still having weight. They still know that he is their master. But through pain, they are trying to torture him into their will. To force him to give up his life and the lives of everyone in London.

But I am also their master.

I couldn't bring myself to stop them before out of fear. Even with my training, trepidation still took over, a dangerous feeling to have while using Blythesea magic. And of course, with Atticus's powerful will, his commands would have outweighed mine. But now I'm left with no choice. The consequences of not using commands are too great. Atticus can't stop them, and because of it, more will continue to spawn.

"Dom—" Atticus wails. He's completely out of it. I don't even know if he'll remember any of this if he survives. "Help me."

"Hold on!" I press the tips of my fingers together, forming my hands into a triangle. The last time I practiced with my father, he taught me how to combine stone and Blythesea magic. The only stone I have on me is chalcedony in the form of a ring on my finger. It will have to do.

I use the stone to extend a field of protection around me. "I command you to take this magic and place it around your other master."

The dead grow angry from my words. So much so they shake. The field projects them back when they lunge at me. Normally this wouldn't hold them, but with my command, it makes the field exist in their reality.

They are left with no choice. They borrow my chalcedony's magic and pull a duplication of it over to Atticus, protecting him from themselves.

His screams of pain stop as the dead can no longer touch him. But then he grows too quiet, his cries ceasing.

I shake. "Don't you dare die on me!"

My high emotions make more dead appear. I grit my teeth and bury my fear. I build more energy within me, a fortitude to withstand their claws.

And once I know my mind and heart are as clear as they can be, I release it all. "All of you—go back to Hades!" Then I throw my arms back, turning the field of protection around me into a weapon of destruction. The dead know their fate and try to scurry away, but my field is faster, melting their souls into the cracks of the floor, back to their true home.

My arms shake as I work to contain it all. My legs almost give out, but I stay strong. The field around Atticus is the only thing keeping his soul from melting.

I don't stop until every one of them ceases to exist in this dimension. When the final one is captured, I fall to my knees. Blood drips down my chin from where I bit down on my lip from the weight of it all.

Atticus is completely still. His chest isn't rising. I rush over to him and hold his head in my hands. "Atticus, wake up. Please, it's all over. Get up right now!"

He's completely unresponsive. This can't be happening. "Damn you, wake up!"

I inject regeneration magic into him. "You can still make it!" I take his glasses off so I can see any glimmer of life in his eyes.

But the regeneration doesn't work. He doesn't stir. There's no breath. No heartbeat. No life.

I bring his body to my chest and sob. Atticus didn't deserve any of this. How is this fair?

"Dominic!" Vec hurries forward and slides to the ground on the other side of Atticus's body.

"He's gone." Tears fall down my face.

Vec prods at Atticus's face, forcing one eyelid open. "No, perhaps not. I won't let him."

"Vec, don't deny it." My lungs burn. "He's already dead."

Vec doesn't listen and takes him from my arms, pulling Atticus's head into his lap. "There is...one way to save him." Vec's face is solemn. Almost fatherly. He places his hands on Atticus's temples and a glowing magic seeps into Atticus's skin. "Immortal life is a simple thing. It's all just boundless, unceasing magic."

Warmth envelops the room as a pulsing light shifts through Atticus's body from head to toe.

"This energy can be cultivated and passed on to another. It is the miracle of birth in the immortal world, when given to another perfect vessel." Vec gasps but does not waver in his concentration. "But when given to a mortal..."

I look at Vec. His youthful features start to fade.

"Wait—what are you doing?" I ask. Whatever immortal magic he is using must take something from him to give, just like regeneration magic. But this—this is permanent.

"I'm doing anything a guardian would. Giving my life for the child I raised."

He's giving up his life? If it works, Atticus will be devastated. And if it doesn't work, I will be.

Vec's features turn from thirty to fifty in a matter of minutes. Atticus flinches.

I cover my mouth, more tears spilling out, this time in relief. "Oh, my gods."

Atticus is still unconscious, but now he's alive. I scoot closer, grabbing his hand, squeezing it tightly in mine.

Then his hand squeezes mine back. My bicep tenses. Then he gasps for air. *Yes, that's it.*

"Atticus. Come on. Keep breathing!" I yell.

"Dom?" He struggles to keep his breath steady. Then he looks up at the man above him. The man who now looks like he's in his sixties. "Vec. You didn't—"

Vec smiles down at him. "It's for your own good." He doesn't stop his magic. If he did, Atticus would surely die again, his wounds still layers deep.

Atticus's voice cracks. "No, stop it! You're dying!"

"I've lived a long, fulfilling life. Now it's your turn."

My throat dries up watching Vec and Atticus. Today, I watched one immortal fight until his last breath to keep his long life. And another willingly give it up for his son.

"Vec, wait, stop! You know I don't deserve it!" Atticus tries to force Vec's hand off his temple, but Vec doesn't concede.

"Perhaps not. But now you have a life ahead of you to make up for it." Vec begins to slump. "You're a real bastard, you know that? But in the end, I always had enough love to see through it. Do well, my boy."

As the last wound heals, Atticus gains enough energy to push out of Vec's hold and sits up, grabbing Vec's old shoulders. "Don't even think about it! Vec!"

Vec's face becomes translucent. "Goodbye, Atticus. Live out the rest of your days a respectable man. Make me proud."

"No! Vec, don't leave me, dammit!"

Vec's papery skin turns to ash. His immortal body falls like sand. Sand that seeps between Atticus's fingers and onto the bloodied floor.

Atticus weeps on his hands and knees. I reach forward, touching his shoulder. The last person he knew from his childhood is gone. Vec was the one person Atticus thought he'd never lose.

"I'm sorry, Atticus," I whisper.

"I should have listened to you, Dominic." Atticus's back shakes with his cries.

"Don't think about that now." I pull him away from Vec's ashes and into my chest. I hold him as he grieves, cradling his head.

It feels like we sit for hours in the middle of the ballroom. A ballroom covered in blood, ash, and rubble as Atticus cries five-hundred years' worth of tears.

Eventually I move back to look at him. His eyes are reddened but also pooling with a deep darkness. One that no amount of vengeance will ever rectify.

I help him to his feet, and we leave the mansion. I say prayers that nobody will trace this back to us, or that Haylow won't report us.

But from the throes of immortals, we are safe.

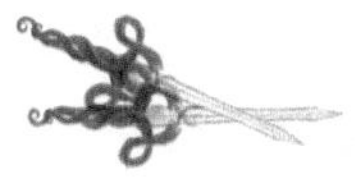

Atticus and I travel back to Vec's townhouse. The sights of intact buildings and businesses give me a great deal of relief. Little do the people of London know they almost visited their deathbeds this evening.

When we arrive at Vec's house, Atticus immediately heads into the cellar.

I sigh and follow him, catching his wrist as he reaches for a bottle of whiskey. "Atticus, no."

His arm shakes. "Who are you to tell me what I can and cannot drink?"

"I don't care what happened tonight or how awful it was, I won't let you."

Atticus glares at me. "And you really think you can stop me?"

"Vec wouldn't want this."

A wave of hurt and regret passes over his face. Atticus's shoulder hits mine as he storms out. I stand there with clenched fists until I hear his bedroom door slam shut.

I sigh. Eventually, he's going to have to learn how to deal with his pain without seeking the bottom of the bottle. I'll be patient with him and help him to the best of my ability. But I will never let him hurt himself again.

The next day, I sit at Vec's desk to close out his affairs. Atticus certainly isn't in any shape to do it. Besides, working helps me keep my mind off everything that happened. The horrors I witnessed from the hands of the man I love.

When I find Vec's will, I stare down at it in shock. Vec was far wealthier than even my own father. I expected his estate to be large with how many years he's been alive, but not this. Vec made millions off his painting, and that was only one of his many ventures. He's built up so much wealth that the size of this home feels laughable. It's a shack compared to what he could afford.

And, of course, he left every cent of his fortune to Atticus.

I lean back in Vec's chair. With this money, Atticus can be anyone he wants to be. He could travel the world, never having to work a day in his life. This inheritance covers multiple lavish lifetimes.

When Atticus recovers, he will need to decide his next steps. Though he'll have to perk up sooner than either of us wishes. The artifact still needs to be returned. If the prime minister notices, and then Cadence connects the dots, things will not bode well for either of us. Especially with the tracking enchantment.

The maids are still on holiday, so I do my best to prepare food in the kitchen. I make potato soup, spiced the way my mother likes. Atticus has yet to eat a single morsel since yesterday. and it's already dinnertime. I place the bowls on a tray and head upstairs.

"Atticus." I speak through the door.

"It's unlocked."

I keep the tray steady and head inside. Atticus lies on his stomach diagonally on the bed, completely undressed.

I set the tray down on his desk. "You need to eat."

"I'm not hungry." Atticus closes his eyes.

"Listen, I know this is hard. Horrible even. But you need sustenance or you'll wither away."

"I'm bigger than you."

I roll my eyes and bring one bowl over to the bed. "Sit up. Come on."

Atticus groans but actually listens and sits up against the headboard. He doesn't take the bowl from me so I sigh and bring a spoonful of the soup to his lips.

"I'm not a child." He grabs the bowl from me.

"Then stop acting like one." I set a pillow on his lap to cover him. With a huff, I leave the bed, sitting at his desk to eat.

"This is good," Atticus admits.

"My mother's recipe."

"A wealthy woman like your mother cooks?"

"Once in a while. She enjoys it and doesn't like when the servants do everything for her."

"My mother was the same." Atticus smiles softly. "The night she died, she cooked dinner for the four of us. Anytime my father was arriving home from his long trips, she would send the servants away just to surprise him with her creations."

"She sounds wonderful." I keep my words short. Atticus rarely speaks of his family like this. And when he does, it's always laced with tragedy and sadness. But now, he's speaking of the good times. Without alcohol, he has no choice but to cope with his words, and I'm a vessel willing to listen.

"Yes, she was. Her name was Marguerite Boisclair."

"French?"

Atticus nods and takes another spoonful of soup into his mouth. "Her marriage to my father was arranged. But he always told me it was love at first sight. Everyone in our village loved her. Even in her nobility, she never failed to help every soul she crossed. Nobody was too broken or too dirty in her eyes."

"You were blessed to have such a magnificent mother, Atticus."

We finish our food in silence, but my mind races. I think of what we must do to return the artifact. The thought of it gives me a complete headache after last time.

Atticus lets me sleep in his bed. I don't expect him to touch me, but before long, our mouths are on each other and he has me pinned beneath him. If I have any inkling that he is using my body to cope with his pain, I'll shove him off. But he doesn't use my body as an instrument of lust. Instead, he makes real love to me, our souls connecting, our pleasures uniting. Everything is slow and thoughtful, but of course he taunts my release, stringing my pleasure along until he releases me when I least expect it.

And as I fall asleep in his arms, I know I'm exactly where I need to be.

CHAPTER 38

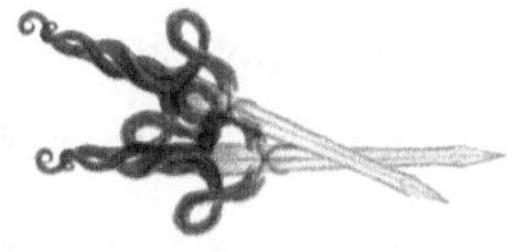

ATTICUS

Two Weeks Later

"Control it Atticus," Dominic whispers from where I sit cross-legged on the forest floor.

The dead whisper harsh words, begging me to kill. It's been like this for weeks. They speak to me every second of the day and deep into my dreams. Between the loss of Vec and the constant mental assault of the dead, I don't know which is worse.

"If they don't shut up for just one second!" I grit the words through my teeth.

"You're not the only person who had to learn to control them. I was in the same position as you just four years ago."

"And they just disappeared?"

Dominic shrugs from where he leans against an oak tree. "I don't usually hear a peep from them, for the most part, unless I'm trying to summon them. Now close your eyes and try again."

I grumble and do as I'm told. The dead whisper louder, as if they know I'm trying to get rid of them. I try to clear my mind, but as always, it drifts to the pain of loss and of recent events.

After a week filled with pain, my mind cleared enough to return the artifact. If it weren't for Dominic, I would still be trapped within the web of mind-altering activities. Not to mention, the English would be hot on my heels for the disappearance of the artifact.

It took some keen planning on my part to avoid seeing Cadence in order to return it. While the family was gone at Mass one Sunday, a guard recognized me. I told him I forgot something from my overnight stay with Cadence and he let me walk straight in. How ensnared in her grasp are these guards? What does she do to keep them so submissive?

Regardless, the artifact is safe again back at 10 Downing Street. Returning it meant I could breathe again. Though that relief was short-lived when I remembered Haylow is still alive and knows my secrets. Though the authorities never found Konstantin and Austrie's bodies, there's still a substantial reward for anyone who can find their killer.

I expected Haylow to report us. I even withdrew large sums of money in preparation to go on the run. But it never happened. Though her silence makes sense. Konstantin was an immortal. There's no way she could have explained the entire situation without outing his status, and in the eyes of 1890s London, immortals don't exist. And neither do humans preserved for nearly five centuries. If she tries to tell the authorities that, they'll throw her in an asylum. According to Dominic, Haylow stopped attending classes at Roche. I find myself looking over my shoulder more often than not. Any moment she could strike. I killed both her father figures. In her eyes, I did to her what Konstantin did to my family.

My only regret is that it all led to Vec's demise.

Her pain is none of my concern.

There's a deer just by the creek. Let us have it.

Give us the life of every plant on the forest floor.

Kill Dominic.

My eyes shoot open and I pound my first into the layer of autumn leaves. "Dammit, they won't stop."

"You're not even trying, Atticus."

I huff. "This is damn near impossible!"

"You asked for this. Stealing magic comes with consequences."

I ignore his jab. "You don't think it's because I'm not a Blythesea, do you?"

"No—at least I don't think so." Dominic looks up at the cloudy sky. "I'll look more into it, but you need to at least try to last more than five minutes in meditation. The more you let dark thoughts coat your mind, the more free rein you give the magic."

Dominic and I sit at my dining room table eating a lunch the cooks prepared. Except for classes, he seldom leaves my side since Vec died, unless it's to visit Archer.

I dropped out of Roche University. There was no need for me to stay. To my surprise, Dominic told me Arlo was upset. But apparently he was assigned a roommate worse than me. I'll take it as a compliment. As much as I pushed him around, I consider Arlo a friend. As I do Oliver.

Oliver still doesn't know the full extent of everything that happened, only that Archer is awake. He keeps asking about me, but I know for his safety, I need to keep my distance. Dominic lied and told him he's been living at home temporarily to take care of Archer, which was somewhat true. Though neither of us are ready to tell Oliver the true nature of our relationship.

Every day, I replay the moment that Vec sacrificed himself. The worst part is, I will still die one day. He sacrificed immortality for a human who can only live ninety years at best. I never expected Vec to give himself up for me. And when I look back, I know I took him for granted. I was selfish up until his last breath.

Everything I do, for the rest of my life, will be to honor him and his wishes, even the unspoken ones. And what he really wanted was for me to finally live in peace.

Toward the end of our meal, there's a knock at the door.

"The mailman?" Dominic sets his napkin on the table.

"I'm not expecting anyone." I stand. "Stay here, I'll go check." As I make my way into the foyer, part of me worries Haylow finally gathered her wits and convinced the authorities to arrest me. If it's them, I'm done for.

When I open the door, I almost collapse at the sight of the visitor.

"Atticus," Cadence says coyly at my doorstep. There's sadness in her face.

Did she find out about the artifact? Did the guard tell her about my impromptu visit when she wasn't home? I told him not to mention it. Dammit! First thing tomorrow, I'm getting this tracking enchantment broken, even if I have to travel to the ends of the earth. "Cadence. What are you doing here?"

"You brought me to heaven and back, then went completely silent. After what we did, I thought—I thought you'd want to see me more."

It's not like I made love to her. I only—it doesn't matter. "I know, Cadence. It's just—"

As if on cue, Dominic comes around the corner. "Atticus, who is here?"

Cadence's face scrunches up when she sees Dominic. She rounds her fists. "Tell me the truth! Is Dominic your lover?"

I take a step back. How did she find out? Has she been looking through my windows? I don't want to say *no*. It feels like a betrayal to Dominic, even though it's for both of our protection. "Listen, let's talk about this."

"I knew it!" She throws her purse down. "You'll bed him, but not me! I could strangle you!"

My last chance to play dumb. "Bed him?"

"Yes! And don't even try lying to me. I saw the unmade bed. The restraints." Cadence looks like she wants to kill me. But when she turns her gaze to Dominic, I know something sinister shifts within her.

Cadence tries to lunge past me and claw at him.

But I block her by catching her waist and restraining her. "I won't tolerate that, Cadence. You're a civilized lady. Act like one."

She steps back, snatching her purse back up. "Mark my words, Atticus Desimir, you will regret this! Once I find a husband and perfect my craft, you'll be the first target on my list!"

So I'm not the only one she is planning on murdering. "Do your worst." I slam the door.

"Shouldn't we walk her to her buggy?" Dominic asks. He still wants to help her after she tried to maul his face? Of course, at his core, he's still a gentleman.

"Absolutely not. In fact—" I remember the maids are gone for the next few hours. With a smirk, I grab his shoulders and slam him into the front door.

"Atticus, what—"

My mouth is on his, our tongues tangling together. I press my body into his, delighted to feel that Dominic is already hard.

I unbutton his trousers, grabbing his length. If Cadence had any nerve to stick around on my front porch, I hope she hears every part of this. I wish I could fuck him in front of her just to see the horrified look on her face. Dominic groans as I work him vigorously. He thrusts his hips at every stroke.

I unbutton his dress shirt and expose his shoulder. And just like that day he fell for me, I bite down into his shoulder, his warm skin between my teeth.

"Please—" Dominic whimpers.

"Are we begging now, love?" I nibble and lick at the new mark I created. A mark that signifies him as mine. Not Cadence.

I slow the thrusts of my hand every time I can tell he's about to transcend. Dominic doesn't stop mumbling and begging, and every time he moans, it only makes me harder.

Then I let him come. He writhes, whispering my name, pleasure in his words. His entire body shivers.

"You're mad," Dominic pants.

"Am I?" I smirk. Then I hear a horse and buggy pulling away.

Dominic goes pale, readjusting his pants, and moving to the window. He peeks out the curtains. "Dammit. There's no way she didn't hear all of that. She'll surely murder you now."

I lean against the wall. "I'd expect nothing less."

The voices of the dead don't stop. They never do, no matter how much I meditate. The meditations Dominic taught me may help me resist their taunts and temptations to kill, as I no longer have any desire to. But their words grow craftier the more time goes on. How much time will pass before I start to believe their words? How much time before I listen?

And what's worse is I'm lying to Dominic. I told him they have gone quiet, but that's not true at all. They never stop, and not even the sting of alcohol can quiet them.

Blythesea magic is far from my only concern. It takes an entire month to find a venitor capable of removing Cadence's curse. I had to travel all the way to my mother's home country just to see him. The French venitor seemed concerned when he used a stone to scan my body. I told him to give it to me straight, to which he said the tracking enchantment she used was a highly forbidden one. And that someone who went to such lengths is truly obsessed.

But when the venitor warned me further and told me the origins and lengths someone has to go to place it, I finally fear Cadence. She's not the sweet innocent daughter of the prime minister that I thought. The venitor told me to be wary of her, and that for her to use something so forbidden means she has no intention of letting me go. Ever.

After that, and with the enchantment broken, I sell Vec's home and move into the countryside. It's far from any population centers in case my mind does snap one day. The house is bigger than I need, but it was also my way of proving to Dominic that I'm not going anywhere.

He asked if I'd move back to Italy. Or take up my mother's roots in France. But I said no. I am happy enough here in London. Truth be told, without him, and without Konstantin, I don't know who I am anymore.

And until I figure that out...

I'm simply his.

ACKNOWLEDGEMENTS

I am grateful to have so many wonderful people in my life who have supported me through the writing process and made this book possible.

First, I want to thank my husband for his unwavering support and encouragement. He always believed in me, even when I didn't believe in myself. Thank you for content editing all of my books and giving me feedback that improves my craft immensely.

I also want to thank my sister, who has supported me through the highs and lows of my author career. Thank you for all the things you have helped me with, from audiobooks to marketing assistance. I truly wouldn't have been able to publish this book without you.

To my readers, I am forever grateful for your support and enthusiasm toward my stories and characters. Your encouragement has kept me motivated and inspired me to keep writing.

Finally, I would like to thank my beta readers, who gave their time and feedback to help me improve this book. Your input and suggestions were golden, and I couldn't have done it without you.

To everyone who loved Atticus from the beginning, thank you all for your love, support, and encouragement. This book is as much yours as it is mine.

ABOUT THE AUTHOR

Abelia Sumpter holds a Bachelor of Science in Nursing and discovered her love of writing while preparing for her national licensure exam. Her passion for storytelling began much earlier. As a child, she wrote screenplays and created short films with her friends. She currently lives in Ohio with her husband and owns a vision board the size of a novel.

9 798985 765656